SOMEWHERE OVER
LORAIN ROAD

Advance Praise for
Somewhere over Lorain Road

Can you go home again? Should you go home again? What if you have to go whether you want to or not? This is the dilemma of Don, the protagonist in this very readable, fractured rainbow novel by Emmy-winning author Bud Gundy.

It's a mystery and a love story for today's world, but the book never lets the reader forget the "acidic underground lake" of America's Midwest, which neither nostalgia nor forgetfulness can completely obliterate, making the book darker and more powerful than its outlines might suggest. Well done!

—Daniel Curzon, author of *Something You Do in the Dark*

The author pulls all the stops out in this gripping story of love, tragedy, and redemption, set against a backdrop of a murder investigation. An emotional roller coaster that will keep the reader guessing until the last, fully satisfying page.

There is beauty here as well, and wisdom. You come away from this book understanding yourself and humankind a little better, and a writer can't do any better than that.

In the end, the author scores a five-star win with the best mystery novel I have read in years, because ultimately, I realized that the mystery the author is sharing is not the murders of a small town, but the mysteries of Life.

—Alan Chin, author of *First Exposure*, *The Plain of Bitter Honey*, and *Buddha's Bad Boys*

By the Author

Elf Gift

Butterfly Dream (cowritten with Dave Lara)

Somewhere over Lorain Road

Visit us at www.boldstrokesbooks.com

SOMEWHERE OVER
LORAIN ROAD

by
Bud Gundy

2018

This Trade Paperback Original Is Published By
Bold Strokes Books, Inc.
P.O. Box 249
Valley Falls, NY 12185

First Edition: February 2018

CREDITS
Editor: Jerry L. Wheeler
Production Design: Stacia Seaman
Cover Design by Tammy Seidick

Acknowledgments

Thanks to the members of my writing groups, who keep me busy with revisions that force me to improve: Scott Boswell, James Warren Boyd, Barbara Brunetti, Christopher Calix, Jake Eastman, Pat Elmore, Cleo Jones, Dennis Holahan, Gabriel Lampert, Martin Magee, and Dennis Stradford. Thanks also to the editor with the golden scalpel, Jerry Wheeler, and the Bold Strokes Books team that decided my story was worth publishing. And to my family and friends—you know who you are and I love you.

For Chris

CHAPTER ONE

Don Esker looked over his boyhood neighborhood and wondered where the skeleton lay, the lonely bones hidden so long they would likely never be found. Maybe an archeologist would dig them up in a future century and scientists would scratch, pick, and peer at them, trying to divine mysterious burial rites from 1975. Why was this boy buried so differently from the customs of the age? Why all alone? Would murder cross their minds?

Maybe shoppers walked over the boy's remains in the mall, which was an undulating, thick field of crab grasses, toothwort, bloodroot, and spotted wintergreen back then. Maybe the bones rested in the backyard of a large home in a fancy housing development up the road, delicately landscaped with tasteful hills and ornamental ponds, in place of the flat, husky cornfield of Don's youth.

Don walked to the mailbox at the end of his parents' driveway as dusk descended. Wood and brick houses lined the road, with neat trim painted in bright contrasting colors. Small flourishes individualized the yards. He sometimes spotted a pink flamingo or a pointy-hatted gnome left over from his youth, bleached from years of service.

The musty, distinctive smell of autumn filled the air. The trees bristled with anticipation, edged with the first traces of their annual, exuberant transformation, a party of such riotous abandon they dropped their leaves in exhaustion and needed months to recover. He'd been there and understood.

At some point after Don moved away from North Homestead, Ohio, his dad had replaced the old aluminum mailbox with a heavy plastic version. Almost everyone else had, too, thwarting teens with baseball bats who sped down the streets leaving a trail of leaning, dented carnage.

Don waited for a car to pass before retrieving a small stack of letters and colorful store circulars. He flipped through the envelopes as he returned to the brick house where his parents had raised four sons born roughly two years apart. Tim was the oldest at fifty-nine and Randy came next at fifty-five. Don was fifty-three. Rich floated in the four-year gap between Tim and Randy, always sixteen.

He entered through the kitchen door. Panels of tan wood brightened the room, and cream linoleum covered the floor. His mom, wearing a soft pink sweatshirt, her short hair curled, turned from fussing at the sink. He tossed the mail on the table.

"Anything good?" she asked, meaning a personal letter or a card, something with a handwritten address.

"Just bills and junk mail."

She looked through the envelopes and ads, tossing them aside while shaking her head. "Does anyone ever buy this stuff they advertise in the mail?"

He turned on his laptop to check the new Wi-Fi he'd installed that afternoon and got a powerful connection right away, a big improvement on the older system he'd set up two years before.

His mom watched as he tapped and clicked. "Did you really have to go to all the trouble? Your brothers said the old one was perfectly good."

"If I'm going to stay here a while, I need to have good Wi-Fi. I have to be able to share docs and Skype with my clients."

She shook her head. "I don't even know what you just said. Here, I need you to do something." She opened the refrigerator and removed two plastic containers with blue lids. Inside, red sauce mottled with pasta and vegetables, the remains of dinner. She cleared her throat and gave a quick flick of her head, as if steeling herself. "Can you take these across the street for Chief Tedesco and Billy? I should have asked you before you got the mail so you'd only have to make one trip." She set them on the table.

"Mom, are you kidding me? You feed them?"

She flicked a washcloth and wiped a counter that was already clean. "Since Patty died, I make sure they have a home-cooked meal at least two or three times a week. The food they deliver from that home meal service…I'm sure they do the best they can, but I wouldn't feed it to a dog."

"Dog food is too good for them. Let them starve."

She clucked her tongue. "That's very unkind. You're better than that, Donnie."

"I was here just a few months ago. You didn't ask me then."

"You were only here for a few days, and you didn't notice when I took it over myself. But I'm not going to hide it from you while you're helping with daily chores for the foreseeable future. I'm also not going to stop. In spite of everything that happened, they're our neighbors and they're in need."

"How does Dad feel about that?" Don gestured in the general direction of the room down the hallway.

She looked at the floor, and Don regretted his question. It wasn't fair to involve Dad.

"Forgiveness isn't just a virtue, Don. It's the only way to heal yourself. It's in your own self-interest to forgive. You should have learned that by now."

"I have, Mom. But some things are unforgivable."

"Maybe. But if I can do it in this case, you can, too."

He'd never told her everything about that time, so he couldn't argue.

She went on. "Now, please. Just humor me. I don't want to fight about this. I'm not going to let a neighbor go without nutritional meals."

He sighed. "I'll never fight with you, Mom. If you want me to take them over, I will. But I'm doing it for your sake, not theirs."

She looked relieved. "Thank you. And remind the chief to take his medicine. He's so cranky, but remind him anyway."

Don took the containers, and the spring-mounted storm door hurled closed behind him. Except for distant headlights, Stearns Road was clear. Don crossed, looking about.

The city had ruthlessly scrubbed away all traces of the neighborhood's distant past as a farm, as if to erase all reminders of the summer of 1975. Today's parents wouldn't let their kids anywhere near fields with rusty farm equipment hidden among the weeds, or a weathered chicken coop up on stilts, and especially not an old barn with an empty hayloft hung with chains you could swing over the ledge. As a boy, he'd thought they were permanent.

As he walked up the Tedesco driveway, neglect not apparent at first glance surprised him. The white trim bubbled and peeled, spouts held teetering gutters in place, and the porch railing looked as rickety as a Popsicle stick project.

Walking across the porch, he wondered how many times he'd raced across this very concrete slab to meet up with his best boyhood friend. Billy was his first love, his first kiss, his first sleeping companion.

Billy pissing in the weeds. "What are you looking at, faggot?" Billy's hair ablaze with white fire as he descended on Don with steel-toed boots.

Don took a deep breath and jammed the doorbell. The classic ding-dong rang inside. Excited feet stomped to the door. It opened with a yank, and Don braced for the visual jolt.

On the other side of the thin glass of the storm door, Billy's face broke with joy.

Before this moment, Don had only seen Billy's head injury from across the street, where it still had impact. A canyon fissured his skull from his forehead to his crown, like a spear wound from an ancient battlefield. Thick scar tissue, glossy and white, flowed into the hairless valley. Gray tufts covered the rest of his head in the random lengths of home haircuts. The location and size of the injury made brain damage obvious. Billy was the poster boy for not staggering aboard a motorcycle while drunk.

"Don!" he cried, the name somehow half-formed, a man's voice with a boy's enthusiasm. Billy threw open the door, but it swung outward and Don jumped back.

Billy wore a grungy white T-shirt that ended at the middle of his rounded, hairy belly. His jeans sagged, crumpled between his knees and ankles. His eyes filled with tears, and he slapped Don about the chest and shoulders as if to confirm that he was real.

"Who's there?" demanded a sour, suspicious voice.

Don clenched his teeth.

"It's Don!" Billy cried with wonder and happiness. "Don!"

Billy grabbed Don and pulled him inside. Don stumbled over the threshold, gripping the containers in surprise, but he quickly restored his unfriendly glare.

The whir of an electric wheelchair came as relentlessly as a buzz saw, and the metal contraption soon rolled into the archway of the dining room.

"Donnie Esker," the chief asked. "Is that you?"

"It's me," he replied in a gruff voice to North Homestead's former chief of police.

Don saw the Navy SEAL memorabilia still on the living room walls, the core of the chief's legend. For years, the people of North Homestead had reveled in his status as a member of the elite group of warriors trained for clandestine and rugged adventures in remote regions of the globe. Don remembered people gawking at these spit-polished mementos of gung-ho military glory. Mayors came and went, but Chief Tedesco held his job the way George Washington was always on the dollar bill.

In his wheelchair, the chief looked as insubstantial as chicken bones. His useless legs leaned to the side, and his arms slanted to his lap.

Don recalled when, many years ago, his mom told him about the chief's tumble down the stairs that paralyzed him from the waist down. Don had made a joke about the unfortunate timing, that a paralysis below his waist should have happened a year before Billy's birth. She hadn't laughed.

The chief looked him up and down. "Been spending time at the gym? You were a little wisp of a kid. You look like you could be on those wrestling shows on TV, except you're probably too old."

Don raised the plastic tubs, but the chief ignored them. "How's your old man doing? He still has a few months, right?"

"I think he'll make it through the holidays." Don's voice thickened with meaning. "But he's got a lot of unresolved things on his mind."

The chief chuckled and gave his wheelchair arm a light tap. "I understand that, stuck in this thing for so long."

Don drew in a breath at the chief's audacity, as if he'd meant that his dad felt wistful about never seeing the *Mona Lisa* or hiking the Andes. "I think he's more worried about being falsely accused of murder."

The chief paused before nodding. "I had a job to do."

"A job you didn't do. You let the killer get away."

The chief's face crinkled, but with a touch of understanding and admiration in his eyes. "I respect a guy who defends his family. That's partly what I was doing, too. I had a responsibility to those other families and the community, but you need to remember that it hit us hard in this very house. My wife was destroyed. None of us was ever the same."

Don dropped his voice. "Neither were we." He held out the tubs. "My mom wanted you to have these."

"Billy," he barked, and Billy jerked to life, took the containers, and disappeared into the kitchen.

"The kid's a godsend," the chief said. "For forty years, I couldn't get him to do a damn thing worth doing. Screwing off, drugs and girls and booze. A bunch of kids he never saw. Couldn't hold a job. The kind of low-life trash I used to enjoy locking up. Crashing a motorcycle isn't the best way to get your life on track, but in his case it was an improvement."

Don paused. "My mom says to remember to take your medicine." He pushed his way out and made it halfway across the porch before Billy cried, "Don!"

Don stopped. His old friend stepped outside and moved in his direction, eager and yet consumed by caution.

"Billy, get your ass in here!" his father shouted.

Billy's face fell. His eyes flicked, wrestling with his impulses.

"Billy!"

He hurried inside, shutting himself up with his father.

CHAPTER TWO

1975

As the summer of 1975 began, both Don and Billy were ten years old. Billy's little brother Eddie was six. Billy hated Eddie, and since Billy was his best friend, Don took his side, but he felt sorry for Eddie. Don's three older brothers treated him like an afterthought, a radio in the background, a teacher at the chalkboard, something easily ignored. Don wished Billy treated Eddie the same way.

Billy shared a bedroom with Eddie. One afternoon, Don and Billy sat Indian-style on Billy's bed, flipping through comic books. Across the room under the window, Eddie played with plastic soldiers on his blue cowboy bedspread, making musical sounds and twirling them by the heads, dancing instead of making war.

"Come on," Billy said, ripping the comic book from Don's hands. "Let's go play in the chicken coop."

Eddie sat up, thinking he was invited. Billy set him straight with, "You are not coming with us. I hate the way you always follow me around." His brother's face flushed with disappointment, tears flooded his eyes, and his lips quivered. Don felt a stab of sorrow.

Comic books in hand, Billy knelt in front of his dresser. Quietly, he removed the bottom drawer and set it aside. He threw the magazines into his secret compartment, a shallow dip in the dresser bottom.

A minute later, the two friends raced outside. As they doubled back in front of the porch, Don saw Eddie peering from behind the summer screen of the storm door.

They crossed to Don's side of the street, heading for a field of tall weeds that grew above their heads. This area of North Homestead was a farm in the nineteenth century. Stamped down with no regard for the farm's structure, suburban lots held scattered remnants of that past. An old chicken coop towered on stilts near the tree line of the field. The farmhouse itself stood a few doors down from Billy's house, now just another home lining the road.

It looked haunted beneath huge trees, and the old-fashioned, massive windows rattled loudly enough to hear down the street. A very poor family by the name of Hartner lived there, headed by a gregarious, gangly man with thick glasses who always wore white shirts and black slacks and who loved Jesus. His wife always smiled tenderly. The Hartners had three girls and a severely retarded son.

On Don's side of the street, large fields concealed rusting farm equipment sinking into the earth. Storage sheds poked up from the weeds, melting into bristling cones of weathered planks, spiky with nails. The chicken coop stood tall and straight.

The farm had grown corn, but someone had planted a strawberry garden near the chicken coop. Over the years, the plants went wild, and the berries shrank to the size of pebbles. All the kids spent hours crawling through the weeds looking for the jagged, dark green leaves. Pushing them aside and finding a red, sweet strawberry or two felt like winning a prize.

The field held many other unwanted things like old chairs with missing legs, soggy rolls of carpets hosting swarms of bugs, mangled tires, busted lamps, and even an old green refrigerator.

A storm had blown through the other night, and Don and Billy balanced against falling when their sneakers slipped in mud. The first mugginess of summer thickened the warm air.

The chicken coop looked like a tiny house, thin and pointy. Don and Billy clambered up a narrow staircase, so steep it was more like a ladder. The door was long gone, and they jumped inside where sunlight streamed through the uneven cracks of poorly fitted slats. Three wooden tiers lined both sides. A rusty chain hung in the center. The uneven texture made it easy to grip, and they took turns pushing off the back wall and swinging through the doorframe.

"Let's play in the refrigerator," Billy suggested. They wiped their rusty hands on their jeans before leaping into the weeds.

The old refrigerator lay on its back at a slight angle, its white interior cracked and dirty. A brackish puddle filled the bottom. Everyone knew kids could suffocate inside an abandoned refrigerator, so someone had removed the door and left it slumped on the ground alongside. They tipped the refrigerator until they'd drained away most of the water.

They settled in next to each other, dangling their feet over the side. It was fun to be inside a refrigerator, a place usually inaccessible. Don and Billy looked at each other and grinned.

Don knew boys were supposed to feel strongly about girls. You have to go steady with them, buy them presents, dance with them and eventually kiss them. Lots of boys and girls at school did these things, but Don felt an immense and powerful tug from Billy, and he knew Billy felt the same way.

If people can be in love, then I can love Billy. I don't have to love a girl.

They leaned in to kiss. They did it a lot when they were alone. Someone at Billy's school, Hollyhock Elementary, told him that kissing meant moving your lips around, not just planting your mouths together. Don went to St. Anne's, where nobody knew about such things. The revelation filled Don with happiness, and new feelings stirred somewhere inside, mysterious and somehow immense.

"What are you doing?" Eddie asked, giggling. He'd followed them and smiled nervously, a finger hooked in his mouth.

They scrambled from the refrigerator. "I told you not to follow me!" Billy yelled.

"I just wanted to play with you," he replied, his voice breaking.

"You want to play with us? Fine, get in the refrigerator."

Eddie didn't move, so Billy picked him up and slid him inside. "Play!" he ordered.

Confused, Eddie looked around. "What am I supposed to play with?"

"We're gonna play prison, and you're the prisoner, okay?"

Eddie's face popped with overwhelming joy to be included in such an exciting game.

To Don, Billy said, "Come on." He knelt to lift the top half of the refrigerator door. Don didn't like this game, but didn't say anything and lifted the bottom end.

As the door loomed down on him, Eddie shrank with fear. Billy said, "We're the prison guards, and you have to stay in there until we bring you some bread and water."

They wiggled the door until the latch, an old-fashioned long metal handle, snapped into place with a solid click. They stepped back, sharing a questioning and worried look.

Immediately, Eddie began pounding on his prison ceiling, his yells sounding impossibly distant.

No wonder kids suffocate in refrigerators, Don realized, listening to Eddie's muffled screams. Don always thought as long as you made enough noise, someone would rescue you in time and that only stupid, silent kids died this way.

Billy grabbed the handle and pulled.

The door wouldn't open.

Panic seized Billy's face, and he tried again, harder this time, using both hands.

The door wouldn't budge.

Don frantically examined the hinged side. It fit snugly against the unit, but he wriggled his fingers into the crack and lifted the door about half an inch, as far as the lock on the other side would allow, but it gave Eddie some fresh air.

Eddie's chubby little fingers swarmed frantically along the opening, his hands pushing up. It broke Don's heart. Eddie had no hope of lifting something it took two ten-year-old boys to move.

"Eddie, put your mouth against the crack and breathe!" Don shouted, but he knew Eddie couldn't hear him above his own screams.

White with fear, Billy held his hands at his mouth.

"Go get help!" Don shouted.

Instead, Billy leaped on the door, crushing both Don's and Eddie's fingers. Don cried out and stumbled back. He hopped about, his hands throbbing with pulses of pain and ease, pain and ease.

Billy crouched on top of the refrigerator. He grabbed the handle and lifted with all his might, his face red with effort. After a moment, a screech ripped out as the handle wrenched free, followed by two coils that looked like metal guts.

Billy stumbled to right himself and shot Don an inquisitive look. Were the coils a good or a bad sign? Had he destroyed the latch or broken it so that it would never open? In either case, there was no handle to pull.

"What are we going to do?" Billy screamed while his little brother pounded beneath him.

"Go get help!" Don yelled again, and Billy scrambled off and started to run.

Don suddenly realized his injured fingers would prevent him from lifting the hinged side any longer, trapping Eddie without air. He should have been the one to run for help, not Billy. They were doing everything wrong, and his mind whirled with how quickly things were spinning out of control.

He screamed, "Billy, come back!" as he tried to work his fingers into the crack, but his world went white with pain and he staggered back. Eddie screamed and pounded.

Desperate to do something, Don cried out and charged, slamming into the refrigerator. The door slid a few inches. Billy had destroyed the latch. He leaned in to push, keeping his throbbing fingers up, the way Mom held hers when waiting for her nail polish to dry.

Billy returned, saw that the door was moving and pushed as hard as he could. They sent the door tumbling away.

Eddie flew screaming from the refrigerator and raced off into the weeds.

"You stupid kid!" Billy yelled in his brother's wake. "I told you not to bother me!"

Don's three older brothers thought the black and blue bruise across the top joints of his fingers looked cool, like a racing stripe, and Don was proud that his injury impressed them.

Billy was nicer to Eddie, and sometimes even asked him to join in games or to watch TV. Eddie gleefully accepted these invitations, and Don hoped Billy wouldn't be so mean to Eddie from now on.

A week later, Eddie Tedesco vanished.

CHAPTER THREE

Linnette was the hospice nurse, roly-poly and middle-aged in that vague space between forty and sixty years. She parted her gray hair on the side, wore little makeup, and used the glasses that hung about her neck only to read, bringing them to her face with no-nonsense precision.

"How long are you going to be staying to help, Don?" she asked, seated next to Dad's bed. She closed her notebook and rose, adjusting the strap of her large purse across her shoulder.

"As long as I'm needed."

"He means he'll stay until I kick the bucket," his dad said, his voice fuzzy with morphine.

"Oh, now," Linnette said cheerfully, giving his arm a quick squeeze. "You'll have to do better than that if you're trying to shock me. I've seen and heard it all."

Dad smiled. He and Linnette had hit it off like a house afire.

She said to Don, "You have my cell number, so call anytime. Now, you're sure you understand all the medication?"

He held up the schedule. "Got it."

"Great." She drew him into a hug, which surprised and pleased him. "I know your mom's relieved to have you here." She winked. "And I'll bet some of the local ladies would like to make your acquaintance, too."

"He's got two older brothers who live nearby," Dad said, sailing the carefree skies of morphine, "but the gay one has to come all the way from his fancy condo in San Francisco to help out the old man."

Linnette's expression flashed with brief surprise, but after a beat she replied, "And he can give you fashion advice at the same time."

Don chuckled along with his dad and Linnette. The stereotype didn't apply to him at all, but her kindly motive neutralized any offense.

After Linnette left, his dad closed his eyes, breathing deeply.

Don was used to the emaciated frame of his formerly robust father, like sticks under the sheets and woven blue blanket. The papery skin on his face revealed the shape of his skull. All his hair had fallen out a while back, even his eyebrows and the bushy, gnarled growth in his ears and nose that afflict most men as they age.

"Oh, Don," his dad said, taking a deep breath, his voice suddenly serious. "I know I don't have long, and I appreciate you being here."

"Sure, Dad."

A portable commode sat at the foot of the bed. Medicine cluttered the nightstand, along with a plaster statue of Jesus carrying a lamb, draped with a rosary.

Dad said, "That Linnette is something else. She's so nice, isn't she?"

"Yes, she is. You're lucky to get such a cool hospice nurse."

"Lucky to get someone who doesn't recognize my name," he muttered.

"Nobody remembers any of that, Dad."

"I remember it. You remember. Your mom. Your brothers. Everyone in the neighborhood."

"You're wrong, Dad," Don said, firmly. "Most people around here don't have any idea."

A long silence filled the room.

"I wish to God for only one thing, Donnie. I wish I could clear my name before I go."

"Your name's been cleared, Dad."

He shook his head slightly. "No. They never caught the bastard."

"It doesn't matter. You had an alibi, and everyone knows you didn't do it."

His dad sighed. "I wish I could believe that, but it isn't true. There will always be suspicion."

"Your family knows."

"But justice means everyone knows, and I'm old enough now to know that the idea of justice is a joke, Donnie. A frigging joke. You're lucky if you get justice in just one part of life. Work, home, school. If you get justice in one, you should thank your lucky stars."

Don didn't know what to say. He agreed with his dad. Why try to improve his mood by arguing? Dying doesn't make you stupid.

"Ah, shit, Donnie, don't listen to me. I can't think straight on these drugs."

At that moment, when his dad rushed to deny his grim analysis of justice for his son's sake, Don realized how solid his dad's wisdom and kindness were, strong enough to bust through even morphine.

Chapter Four

1975

The night Eddie disappeared, Don and Billy had played in the woods before separating at bedtime. Don read the rest of the story in the newspaper: when Billy returned home, he didn't turn on the light, and assumed Eddie was already asleep.

When Billy woke in the morning, Eddie's bed was already made. Hollyhock Elementary hosted an arts and crafts class every weekday at ten o'clock to keep the kids busy during the summer. Eddie enjoyed the classes so much, he leaped out of bed first thing.

In the kitchen, Billy's mother served him breakfast and asked, "Why is your brother still sleeping?" Eddie's empty plate sat waiting, and Billy realized something was very wrong.

By noon, all the police in North Homestead were searching for the chief's son. Officers talked to all the kids in the neighborhood, and Don said he remembered seeing Eddie around seven the previous night.

Don and his brothers joined Billy in running through the fields and woods, calling out for Eddie. They knew the hidden places to search: the small cave in the creek bed running through the woods where older kids drank beer and smoked cigarettes, the secret tunnels made by fallen trees, the hidden structures they called "huts" fashioned from high weeds, bent to form a roof, the interior cleared. They couldn't find him anywhere.

As dusk fell, the adults called the kids back home. They looked stony and fearful.

Don's family piled into the station wagon and drove to St. Anne's, where an emergency vigil gathered for the son of the chief of police. The church was full, and people stood in back and around the sides.

It surprised Don that many families weren't even Catholic, like the Hartners.

Billy sat with his mom in the front pew, his dad undoubtedly still organizing police efforts, and Don was upset he couldn't sit beside his best friend. Instead, Mayor Shadowski occupied Don's rightful seat.

Father O'Shay talked of grace, prayers, and miracles. People sang. They prayed. They lighted candles, and they agreed faith was essential, prayers would work, and God would look after little Eddie. Don found it both thrilling and comforting. The nuns from the neighboring convent led the congregation in saying the rosary, and Don found their soft, sweet voices soothing and safe. The non-Catholics bowed their heads and said their own prayers.

Just before the vigil concluded, Father O'Shay announced the police were forming search committees for the following morning, and that nobody's employer would mind if they couldn't make it to work the next day. All the dads approached the altar to find the nearest meeting spot.

Everyone parted as Billy and his mom left. She was tall and thin with dark curly hair so tight against her scalp, it looked like a cap. She wore huge glasses with square frames, and she acknowledged the soft promises of prayers with slight, fearful nods. Don tried catching Billy's eye, but his best friend looked at the floor.

The next morning, Mom woke Don and his brothers early, having prepared an enormous Sunday breakfast of hearty foods even though it was only Wednesday. "You'll need your strength for the search."

Dad drove them to the nearest meeting spot, about two miles up the road, to the edge of a vast field of deep green, mid-length early summer corn. Cars leaned to and fro along the ditches and scores of people arrived, including packs of uniformed Boy Scouts and 4-H kids.

Fueled by pancakes and bacon and scrambled eggs, Don was raring to go, to run through the field calling out for Eddie at the top of his lungs, last night's words at the vigil filling him with eager dreams of being the hero to find the frightened boy.

The first line of searchers set off, walking close to each other at a measured pace, swatting the corn leaves about with sticks. It was an open admission that Eddie was almost certainly dead. They were looking for a body.

Suddenly, last night's service seemed a carnival of wizardry and spells and hocus-pocus, all designed to distract from the terrifying reality nobody wanted to say aloud.

Don felt like puking and turned away, but the urge vanished when he saw a crew from one of the local Cleveland television stations. The reporter held a microphone and faced a camera, nodding. All of a sudden, he began to speak: "That's right, Doreen. The residents of North Homestead are hopeful today as they continue the search for little Eddie Tedesco..."

Hopeful. The man actually used the word "hopeful," while behind him the cornfield filled with people looking for Eddie's body.

❖

The searches wound down after a few days and ended in a week. Thunderstorms blew through, and Don watched from his window, wondering if the rain was soaking Eddie's body.

The people of North Homestead refused to talk about the inevitable conclusion, but all the same they braced against the blow. When it didn't come, their panic stretched until it snapped back in stinging, tangled fits of anger when well-meaning but unwitting outsiders wondered if the case would ever be solved.

Billy and his parents retreated to their house, huddling together against the world. As chief of police, Billy's dad had to report to work daily, but otherwise stayed home. His distinctive black squad car with the dome atop and the "Chief of Police" medallions on the doors sat in the driveway every night and all weekend.

Don wanted to see Billy, but his parents told him the Tedescos needed time alone as a family. Secretly, Don was relieved. He didn't know what to say or how to ease Billy's pain. While Eddie's fate seemed certain, the circumstances were not, so parents cautioned their children to play only within sight of each other, to avoid all strangers, and to never walk alone, especially in the woods. With his best friend living a million miles away across the street, Don started playing with his brothers again.

Don's oldest brother, Tim, was sixteen, and Rich was next in line at fourteen. They resented the presence of twelve-year-old Randy and ten-year-old Don. Randy soon earned their acceptance by swearing as much as they did, but they scolded Don for his language when he tried the same method. Don shuffled behind as the youngest brother, unable to fill any role beyond a burdensome embarrassment.

When out of earshot of their parents, Tim said things like, "I can't believe we have to fucking babysit."

"Yeah. It fucking sucks," Randy always echoed.

Don said nothing as he followed along, doing whatever his older brothers wanted, because he obviously had no say. And every day they wanted to walk about twenty minutes to a weedy field where dirt bikes screeched along narrow paths, zoomed up and down hills, and careened along curves. Crowds of teenagers gathered to laugh and cheer, while hard rock music pumped.

The boys wore tank tops and shorts, their longish hair parted in the center. The way they looked and walked and the deepening timbre of their voices fascinated Don. The girls wore bikini tops beneath shirts connected with a single button at their midriff, the flaps tied into a knot above their navels.

Don sat with other younger siblings forced to keep close, but forbidden entry to the magic sphere. They played dispirited games in glum groups. Now and then, someone would screw up the courage to approach the teen festivities, only to be driven back with shouts and threats. The older kids smoked cigarettes and tipped back what looked like beer.

One Saturday morning, Don plodded behind his brothers, growing angrier with each step. The dirt bike field bored Don, and he suggested they see a movie instead.

"Shut the fuck up," Tim growled.

"Yeah, shut the fuck up," Randy echoed. "Don't be a shit."

"Don, we were all as young as you once," Rich said. "Just suck it up. You'll get older." Rich was usually nice, and Don was disappointed he didn't take his side.

When they reached the field, his brothers raced ahead, expecting Don to take his place with the other children. Still smarting from Rich's betrayal, he ran instead for the woods towering in the distance, to explore a new place. The trees went all the way to Cook Street, a rural stretch of road punctuated by isolated homes.

He scowled at the distant screech of a dirt bike that sounded like an animal being tortured. When he entered the woods, the whine faded to nothing, swallowed by deep shadows speckled with leaf-light.

A misplaced butternut tree drooped sickly in the gloom. Normally the deepest of greens, its sharp leaves looked jaundiced, and the tree sagged to the mossy ground like a giant, melting bush. Shagbark hickory, honeysuckles, and elms grew slender and stately, while the oaks commanded the sky. The damp woods smelled of rot and new life. An errant maple seed, cast off far too early from beyond the tree line, twirled high between the trunks.

Don wandered, seeing the evidence of the search for Eddie Tedesco everywhere. Tangles of dead limbs and bushes were busted apart, rotting trunks strewn about, and boot prints tamped down the spongy earth. Normally, the ground felt like you could bounce like an astronaut on the moon.

He kicked along until he saw a wide cushion of soft leaves reflecting the sun with neon green intensity, lacing the border of the woods with a backyard. He got closer and gasped with wonder.

Huge ferns grew in a sweep, like something out of a dinosaur book. The searchers had pushed and pulled, and hacked and trampled fronds lay everywhere, but most survived. The massive leaves danced in the delicate breeze, as if excited to see him. Amazed, Don spread his arms and entered the primeval forest. To make this amazing discovery in a place as ordinary and normal as North Homestead seemed impossibly thrilling.

I have to tell Billy about this! he thought with manic delight, before remembering that Billy and his grieving parents remained indoors.

The ferns grew above his head, and he let the fronds brush his face as if he could absorb their power to transcend time and flourish out of place. His fingers brushed the delicate leaves, and he felt grand and glorious. As he reached the edge, he closed his eyes and imagined emerging into a new world, a new life, a thrilling landscape of dinosaurs and volcanoes and giant insects. He raised his arms in triumph.

Across the plain back lawn of a plain brick house, a handsome man stood beside a telescope, watching him.

He darted back among the ferns, feeling impossibly foolish, and his face heated with a flush. It felt important to crouch, to be silent, and he found a spot to hide.

He trembled for a while and cried a bit. His dramatic exit from the fern jungle now seemed girlish and flouncy, the things people said of faggots and homos. He didn't know what faggots or homos were, but they were so contemptible, he knew he never wanted to be mistaken for one.

After a while, he reflected on the man in his backyard. Did he really have a telescope set up during the day? Before he dashed away, Don had also glimpsed a woven rattan chair, and a small table set with a big glass of iced tea and a notebook fluffing in the breeze.

He moved to the far edge of the fern jungle. With each step, he felt more confident and sure of himself, less worried about having looked so ridiculous. It surprised him to learn that by moving ahead with purpose, you can leave anxiety and shame behind.

A gathering of three scraggly trees and a stump provided the perfect perch to watch the man in secret. Don squinted. The man was studying a plate affixed to the eyepiece end of the telescope, scribbling in the notebook.

It was so strange.

He leaned to get a better look, and his sneakers slipped across something slick, which could be one of a million rotting or crawling things. He cried out.

Far faster than he could respond, Don flew back. His head banged into a tree trunk. As he went down, he thought, *this is how you can die by falling. You just have to slip and not have anything to hold on to, and down you go.* He always assumed he would be smart enough to find something to hold if he fell, that only dull-witted people didn't think quickly enough.

He landed in a pile of twigs softened by the mulch of last year's leaves. From now on, he'd have to give more credit to people who died in accidental falls.

His head hurt and as he sat up, someone crashed through the ferns and soon telescope man was above, looking worried. His shoulders and arms were rippled and rounded in all the perfect spots, and his hair grew bushy brown. His mustache bristled, shooting out over his lip. Don was rooted.

"Hey, kid," he said, with a deep voice that rested on a soft rumble, like rocks polished in a silk-padded drum.

"I'm okay," Don replied. He winced at his voice, so small and fearful when measured against the man's graveled texture.

"Let me take a look here." He lifted Don to a sitting position and examined the back of his head. "I saw your skull stop that tree. It was a pretty good whack. I heard it all the way across the lawn."

He smelled the man's sweat, saw the tight fit of his jeans, felt a rush at the brown hair, shot through with gray, carpeting his chest above the V-collar of his white T-shirt.

"Doesn't look too bad," the man said. "You'll have a bump, that's all." He removed his hands, and Don nearly protested. "Can you stand?"

Don nodded.

"Take a few steps."

Don tried but felt dizzy, and telescope man steadied him. "Let's get you some iced tea," he said, taking his hand and leading him to the house.

Halfway across the lawn, Don realized that with Eddie Tedesco still missing, he shouldn't go into a stranger's house. Telescope man didn't seem dangerous. Not at all. Not in the least. He was much too handsome to be dangerous. His fist wrapped Don's hand, his grip loose but reassuring.

All the same, Don felt a growing apprehension as they approached the wooden deck. Behind the stylish sliding glass doors, blackness loomed.

"Take a seat," he said, gesturing to the patio step. "I'll wrap some ice in a towel and get your iced tea. Only be a sec."

Relieved and delighted, Don watched as he slipped inside, closing the door behind him, which meant that telescope man had air-conditioning.

The telescope was a sleek, white tube with a scope on top. The eyepiece pointed down to a plate attached with a metal arm. Don approached and gasped when he beheld the sun burning with ferocious intensity on the white-coated surface of the plate. It rippled with heat, dotted with sunspots. The fiery corona crackled away in all directions. It looked like a fantastical painting from an astronomy book, but this was real. This was the sun.

"Pretty cool, huh?"

Don jumped.

Telescope man placed a bundled white towel to the back of his head, and Don held it in place. The ice invigorated him, and he finished the whole glass of tea in one long series of gulps.

The man introduced himself as Hank. "Why are you out alone? Aren't your parents worried about you, what with that missing kid?"

"I'm supposed to be with my older brothers at the dirt bike field, but I could be gone all day and they'd never notice."

"How late do they normally stay?"

"Around five. Everybody goes home to eat after that."

"Well, I don't want your brothers and your parents to worry, so at four I'll take you back through the woods to the field, okay?"

Oh, my God, that's hours away!

"Are you an astronomer?"

"Yep. Do you want to see what I'm studying?"

"Yes!"

The next day, Don ran ahead as he set off with his brothers for the dirt bike field. He jumped anxiously and shouted, "Come on!"

"Calm down, you little asshole," Tim barked, but he looked confused.

Randy sneered. "Did you find a *Playboy* magazine and you want to jerk off?" Tim laughed. Fueled by the approval of the eldest, Randy pumped his fist at his crotch, moaning in exaggerated ecstasy. Tim roared and did the same. Rich shook his head, gave Don a smile, and rolled his eyes.

They didn't notice that he'd sneaked away yesterday, so when they reached the field, Don ran off without a look back. He raced through the woods and across the grass to where Hank sat with the telescope. Hank seemed welcoming, but Don detected a hint of caution. Hank wore jeans and a T-shirt in the blistering Ohio heat.

"How's your head?"

"It's fine. Are we going to look at the sun again today?"

Hank nodded and lifted a book from the table. "This is the book I told you about yesterday. I had to look around for a bit, but I finally found it."

Don clawed the book from his hands, desperate to see what caused Hank to spend at least a part of his evening thinking about him. He was instantly mortified by his frantic eagerness, and he decided to balance it with nonchalance.

"Yeah, this looks good," he said, lazily flipping the pages.

After a few beats, Hank said, "You can borrow it while you're here, but I want to hang on to it, so you can't take it with you. Do you want some iced tea?"

"Yeah," he replied, disappointed that the book was not a gift.

"Okay. Why don't you come inside, and I'll show you where it is. It's gotten so hot I want to change into swim trunks."

Don no longer feared the blackness beyond the doors. It promised cool relief from the heat, and as soon as he stepped inside, it was like an oasis from the sweltering day.

"There's the fridge," Hank said, pointing to a black—*black!*—refrigerator. "Grab a glass from that cupboard. The iced tea is in the fridge. Get some ice from the dispenser. Be back in a sec."

Don ran his fingers along the undulating, off-white tiles of the counters, grouted by a deep contrasting shade, and he examined the abstract designs in stained glass on the cupboard doors before making his way to the refrigerator.

A hollow in the narrower, left-side panel held two dispensers, and Don read with amazement that they delivered water and ice. He pushed a glass against the tab. An engine roared to life, so unexpected and loud that he jumped back. A single cube, elegantly shaped like a quarter moon, fell from the dispenser and clinked to the floor.

Don tossed it into the sink and watched with alarm as the ice slipped into a baffling circle of black rubber flaps. Was it safe to let an ice cube melt in a sink with an arrangement of rubber pieces at the drain?

Frustrated at all the things he didn't know, he hopped on the counter and reached into the maw at the sink bottom. He felt sharp blades and pulled up with surprise before trying again. Things squished and slithered but he found and removed the ice cube, astonished at the sight of a strawberry stem stuck to one side, much larger than the wild kind that grew around the chicken coop.

Hank entered the kitchen shirtless, in a pair of shorts that hugged him tightly about the crotch. Don pretended not to notice and stared straight at Hank's face, holding the ice cube with the strawberry stem. Hank laughed and told him about food disposals and Don felt even more foolish.

"I have to check the telescope coordinates. Why don't you get our iced tea while I work that out?"

"Sure!" Don scooted off the counter, and Hank became a silhouette in the light streaming through the glass. A halo of curly hairs burst around his form, a corona more thrilling and beautiful than the sun's. The sight mesmerized Don, and he couldn't move until Hank was outside and had pulled the door closed.

His hands shaking, Don prepared the iced teas and returned to the telescope.

"I was wondering what was taking so long," Hank said, as Don trod carefully down the patio stairs.

Again that afternoon, Don returned to the dirt bike field before his brothers set off for home, and they hadn't noticed that he'd been gone.

Hank worked during the week, so Don played among the giant ferns and stared at his house with longing. He didn't understand the ache in his chest when he thought about Hank's shoulders, the quivers when he remembered the hairy silhouette, or why he absently rubbed his penis while thinking about these things. He only knew that Hank centered his life, and the feelings Billy caused in him now burned hot on his face and shortened his breath. It exhilarated and frightened him.

The next Saturday, Don raced ahead of his brothers, desperate to see Hank after five days of separation. He didn't even bother to pretend to head for the spot where the younger kids waited for their older siblings before he charged into the woods.

Hank seemed less welcoming, avoiding his eyes. Fear gripped Don until they set the coordinates and checked the positions of the sunspots against last week's sketches. Hank seemed to settle into their regular routine, and Don relaxed.

After Don returned with their second refill of iced tea, Hank asked him to sit. He had a strange look on his face.

"You have a crush on me, don't you?" Hank asked with a gentle smile.

After a beat, Don nodded.

Hank bobbed his head, looking off. "I thought so. I think we understand each other really well, don't you?"

Don didn't know what he meant, but nodded again.

"And since we're friends, I think we should be honest about things, okay? So I'm gonna tell you something that I hope you never forget."

Don stared with amazement. No one had ever talked to him like this.

"Do you know how long it takes for the light from the sun to reach earth?"

Don shook his head.

"Eight minutes. Now, if a photon of light takes eight minutes to fly from the sun to the earth, it passes Pluto and all the other planets in our solar system after several hours. Guess how long it has to travel through empty space to get to Alpha Centauri, the nearest star?"

Don shrugged.

"Four years. That should give you a pretty good idea of how big the universe is. In the grand scheme of the universe, the sun and Alpha Centauri are two tiny specks so close together you can't even tell them apart. And yet it takes a photon of light, which moves faster than anything else in the universe, four years just to go from one to the other."

Don's mind jumbled with emotions and facts.

"Don?"

Wide-eyed and feeling stupid, Don nodded.

"I don't want you to ever forget that about the universe, how huge it is, how vast and brilliant it is, and you are a part of it. So always remember that. When a petty little mind here on earth tries to make you feel shitty about yourself for any reason, you just remember that you are a part of this universe. Any time you like, you can look up to the sky and know that you have a place here nobody can ever take away from you. Do you understand?"

Don nodded, even though he didn't.

Hank looked sad. "I also want to say you can't come here anymore." Don rushed to protest, but Hank stopped him. "One day you'll understand why I have to do this. It has nothing to do with you. It's about protecting myself, okay? A little boy is missing, and I have to be very, very careful."

Don pleaded, but Hank was firm. After Don's protests faded, Hank gave him a quick hug. "I'm going to meet up with some friends, so I'm going to pack up the telescope, okay? It's time for you to go."

Don sulked in the grass, sitting cross-legged while Hank carried the telescope inside. He never knew he could feel so horrible and lonely, and his love for Hank battled with rage at his rejection.

Suddenly, a plan popped into his mind and he sat up. All of the terrible emotions drained away, and he grew excited. He looked around, spotted Hank's book, and quickly hid it beneath his legs, resuming his crouched, resentful pose.

Hank returned to retrieve the chair and table, saying, "Don, it's time for you to go." When he didn't move, Hank said, "I'm going back inside, and then you can leave. You could make big trouble for me if you don't get home in time and your parents start to worry. I want you to think about that."

When Hank left, he leaped to his feet, hugged the book to his chest, and took off. If he took the book Hank wanted to keep, he would have to return it the following day. By then, Hank might have changed his mind, or maybe Don could think up some new things to say to make the outcome different.

Among the ferns, he slowed when he realized Hank wouldn't change his mind, and nothing Don said would make him. He found a quiet spot beneath a fern, and lay down on the fronds, ripped apart like confetti.

Staring up, he noted the serrated edges of each individual leaf that combined with dozens of others to form the majestic ferns. They branched off from the center, and except for their sizes, they all looked identical, brilliant green in the sun. He closed his eyes.

When he woke, shadows covered the ferns. He sat up. The sun was across the sky.

He grabbed the book and tore through the forest. Terror seized him when he reached the empty dirt bike field. Frantic, he took off for home. Instead of taking the longer sidewalk route, he ran in the fields along the tree line, made treacherous by gopher holes, creeks and ponds and things hidden in the weeds.

He got tangled in branches once, forcing him to tunnel underneath, but he made good time. The chicken coop was ahead, and he soon spotted his parents and brothers in their backyard, their hands cupped over their mouths as they called for him.

Now that he knew what awaited, he felt calmer. He positioned himself directly behind the chicken coop, hunching, before scrambling and tossing the book inside.

His mother spotted him and came running, letting out a shriek filled with both joy and rage. The others followed.

Mom rushed up to him and grabbed him by the shoulders. "Where were you?" she screamed.

"Why did you leave the field?" Tim shouted.

"You stupid idiot!" Randy cried.

Rich just looked relieved to see him.

Dad squatted and pulled him close, holding him tightly across the back. "Thank God, son, thank God."

Mom pushed Dad aside and enfolded him in her arms.

"We were so worried." Her voice cracked. "We found out this morning another little boy disappeared last night." She smoothed back his hair. "They found his body in the woods behind McDonald's on Lorain Road today."

CHAPTER FIVE

In his rental car, Don drove down Lorain Road, a huge thoroughfare that started near downtown Cleveland and ran westward miles past North Homestead to the rural communities beyond.

Don passed McDonald's, still in the same spot, gussied up in gray paint. Decades ago, the woods behind had been cleared to make way for a shopping center anchored by a massive grocery store. Somewhere in the parking lot lay the spot where the naked body of a five-year-old boy named Danny Miller was found in the summer of 1975.

Danny Miller had changed everything.

Don shopped by consulting his mother's list. The echoing voices of the past came as they always did, unexpectedly and without warning: *"Your dad is a baby fucker!" "Your dad should be shot for having sex with little boys!" "Did your dad rape you before he raped those other boys?"*

Even as a kid, Don knew the other kids were only repeating the things they heard at home from their older siblings and parents.

As he pulled out of the parking lot onto Lorain Road, the North Homestead police station loomed in front, and a brilliant idea formed in his mind within seconds. *Why didn't I think of this years ago?* Traffic was light early on a Monday afternoon, so he drove straight across all four lanes to the police station, a boxy, gray building.

Just beyond the glass doors of the entrance, a long hallway tiled in gray linoleum stretched into the building. Portraits of the chiefs of police over the years lined the wall, identical white faces with short hair in identical black frames.

Behind a counter, two police officers chatted over facing desks strewn with papers and computer monitors. A young female officer asked, "What can we do for you?"

"I'm here about a case that happened about forty years ago."

"What case?" the male officer asked.

"It was three little boys who were murdered around town in the summer of 1975. They only found two of the bodies."

They looked at each other and squinted, searching their memories. This must seem like ancient history to them, those terrifying, surreal months happening twenty years or more before their births.

They directed him outside to the archive building, formerly the city's bus shed. Don remembered a time when the shed numbered among the biggest structures he'd ever seen. It looked the same except for the light maroon paint. He couldn't remember the original color, but this wasn't it.

He knocked. He waited and knocked again. He waited some more and pounded.

"Hold your horses," a woman called from inside.

Several moments later, someone unlocked and opened the door. The woman who squinted out looked every bit like someone who would say, "hold your horses." Her face seemed molded from grayish clay, and long, straggly blond hair draped across the shoulders of her uniform. She examined him behind thick glasses. Don guessed her age at around sixty years old, and she moved with the deliberation caused by aches and pains.

"What do you need?" she asked, not unpleasantly.

"I'm here about a case that happened forty years ago. Two little boys were raped and murdered. Another went missing."

Her eyes widened. "I remember that! God, that was unreal." She waved. "Come on in."

Don stepped into a small room with some chairs and a meshed window, with an office beyond.

She ticked her tongue in annoyance. "Oh, look at that," she said, walking to a closet door to the left that was hanging open. A large ring of keys rattled from a short chain on her belt. "Either a ghost is running around opening all the doors, or this old building is held together by chewing gum." She slammed the door.

Don said, "Officer, I'm here because…"

She flipped her hand. "Call me Dolores. I'm not an officer. They make me wear this uniform for work. I guess it makes me look official. Good thing they didn't give me a gun, or I'd have shot my husband years ago. But what the heck, the uniform gets me half off at McDonald's."

She led Don to the office desk, where she lowered herself behind a computer monitor. "Take a seat," she said, tapping the keyboard. She held out a hand. "Let me see the request form signed by the chief."

"They didn't tell me I needed one. They just told me to come here."

Dolores dropped her hand. "Oh, you gotta have a signed form."

"How long will that take?"

She shrugged. "It can be a pretty big rigmarole. Especially with files that are still officially open, like that case." She shook her head. "Whoever did it is probably long dead. I was twenty-two when that happened."

"I was ten."

"Then you remember what it was like. The last one, Jeffrey Talent, lived just down the street from us. He was a nice kid, as I remember. But I'm sorry, I can't help you if you don't have a form."

"I don't really need to see any evidence. I'm just here to find out if anything was preserved that can be tested for DNA. I'd be glad to pay for the tests."

She squinted again, breathing heavily. "Why?"

He hesitated, but he had an instinct that Dolores would be sympathetic. "My dad was considered a suspect for a while. He's dying and he wants to clear his name. If we can test some of the evidence and compare that to my dad's DNA, maybe he can finally put all of that behind him and die in peace. Again, I'll pay for everything."

"Are you talking about Rob Esker?"

Don nodded, surprised but resigned at the same time.

"His alibi held up, as I recall."

"I'm glad you remember, but it didn't matter. A lot of people never knew he had an alibi. They just remember the cops raiding our home and taking him away. He never shook the suspicion. If they'd arrested someone, that would have made a difference, but they didn't."

"But you know he didn't do it, right?" she said, instantly getting to the heart of the issue, as far as Don was concerned.

"Everyone in my family knows he's innocent. But now with DNA we can prove it as long as there's something left to test."

"We don't hold much in the way of perishables here. We don't have enough room in our refrigeration and freezing units. If there's still some DNA evidence left, it would be down at the county building, but I gotta tell you they can't hold on to that stuff forever. They probably ditched it all years ago."

"Where's the county building?"

"Downtown."

"Before I go all that way, can you at least check with the county to see if they have anything? You'd save me a trip."

Dolores nodded. "Yeah, I can do that. All of that information should be in the summary binder." Groaning, she pushed herself to her feet. "Come on. I think I know right where those files are, but I don't want to lug them all over this building, so if you promise you won't tell anybody or touch anything, you can come with me. Do you have a case number?"

"No."

She sighed. "Okay. There was a lot of stuff from that case, so there's probably a lot of boxes with the same number. They should be easy to find."

She unlocked the door behind the desk, and Don followed her into to a vast space filled with fenced-in cages. Shelves sagged with boxes and bags. The keys jangled and bounced against her thigh. She muttered as she walked, holding a hand to her back. "One of those kids was the son of old Chief Tedesco, you know," she said.

"I know. Eddie Tedesco. I was best friends with his brother Billy."

"Were you?" Her voice went high with surprise. "From what I heard, that Billy was a holy terror. His dad had no control of him. Funny thing, too, what with the old man being a Navy SEAL and all." She gestured dismissively. "Most of the officers worshiped the ground he walked on, but I never understood why. Although it is a shame about his kid."

She stopped at a gate and unlocked the door. It swung open with a rattling screech. The space was the size of a two-car garage, with a metal table with matching chairs in the center, bordered on three sides by shelves.

"They're in here somewhere," Dolores said. "As you can see, they're all marked by the case number, the first one followed by an 'A,' the second with a 'B,' and so on." She waved. "If you can find the 'A' box, there's a summary report in a binder listing all the evidence. We had to do them about thirty years ago, right around the time I got this job." She shook her head. "It was just busywork. It took us two years to go through everything, and nobody ever looks at them. There's cocaine and all kinds of stuff all over this building."

Don scanned the shelves, quickly spotting a row of old blue and white boxes with the same case number lettered to "K."

"This must be them," he said, pulling the "A" box from the shelf and placing it on the table. He removed the lid, and just as Dolores promised, a binder sat on top with a "Summary of Evidence" typed on a yellowing label in the italicized font of an electronic typewriter. It looked old-fashioned. He remembered when those typewriters were leading edge of technology.

He placed the binder on the table and flipped it open.

"Now hang on a sec," Dolores said. "I don't mind you moving things around, but you can't be examining the files of an open case." She sat, waving for him to do the same. "Let me just take a look."

Holding the frame of her glasses, she removed a black-and-white photo from a slot in the inside the cover, police officers standing in a stiff line.

"This is the team," she remarked. "Don't know why they posed for a photo when they never caught the guy." Her eyes suddenly lighted with delight. "Hey! There's Chief Ladmore!" She laughed. "Look at him in his rookie uniform. Must have been one of his first cases."

She showed him the photo, but the uniformed men in a stiff row with sober faces and clasped hands looked the same to Don.

"Eric Ladmore was deputy chief for a long time until Tedesco retired about ten or fifteen years back," Dolores said. "He himself just retired last year." She shook her head. "He was a looker back in the day. He could have talked me into a bit of trouble." She snorted.

She returned the photo to its slot and squinted at the first page. She shook her head and flipped, scanning the next sheet rapidly. Then the third. At the fourth, she stopped.

"Here we go," she muttered.

Don waited a long while, until she looked up and said, "Well, I can tell you one thing. You don't have to go all the way downtown."

"Did the county discard the evidence?" Perhaps it was understandable that the county had chucked the only solid evidence after so many years, but the case had been so sensational that it struck him as strange.

She looked unsure. "I don't know how much I'm supposed to say. Like I said, technically this case is still open."

"Come on, Dolores. Nobody has worked on this case in years. It's just a formality to say it's still open."

"Yeah, I know, but I'm violating all kinds of rules to even let you back here. I'm not sure I should say anything."

"How about if you just tell me if there's a chance the county still has the evidence?"

"The county never held any evidence. All the evidence is in this building." She pointed with her chin. "In those boxes."

"Are you saying the North Homestead police department didn't file the perishable evidence with the county when they ran out of room here?"

She leaned in. "Listen closely to what I'm saying to you. There never was any evidence that we can test for DNA. There was nothing to refrigerate or freeze in the first place."

"The police didn't collect physical evidence from the bodies of two boys who were raped and murdered?" That was not amateur. It was negligence of the first order.

She sighed. "You gonna make me spell it out for you?"

"I wish you would."

"There's nothing to test for DNA because neither of those boys was raped."

CHAPTER SIX

1975

Nobody understood how Danny Miller had vanished. Friday evening, the five-year-old boy was playing in his yard with his older sister and her friend. They lived far up on Porter Road, where thick woods and fields isolated the homes. The girls went inside for a few minutes, and when they returned, Danny was gone.

"He knew he wasn't supposed to go with a stranger," his mother tearfully said on the news.

Late Saturday morning, while Hank had been breaking Don's heart, a few teenagers got lunch at McDonald's and slipped away into the woods to eat. Moments later, they found the boy's naked body. They came screaming from the trees, and at that moment, life in North Homestead changed. All over town, parents set out the new rules of life for kids: remain indoors or in yards, always within sight and shouting distance of a trusted adult, no walking or riding bicycles anywhere.

Sunday morning, Don and his brothers put on mitts and threw a baseball around in the backyard. He liked the challenge of sight and coordination, but Tim started throwing the ball with more force. Soon, all three of his brothers were hurling the ball as hard as they could, and Don left for the front yard, angry that they'd spoiled the fun of skill and accuracy. Across the street, Billy was playing with a Hot Wheels set in front of his garage. Chief Tedesco's black squad car was gone.

Don reasoned that if he crossed the street, he would still be in full view of his mother if she decided to check on him from the living room window, so he set off running.

"Billy!" he called as he approached.

Billy's head snapped up, and he looked at Don like he didn't know who he was. Don stopped, and the two old friends locked eyes.

"I'm sorry about Eddie," Don said.

Billy looked surprised. In an instant, rage transformed his face and he hurled a little metal car at Don's feet. Don hopped out of the way as the car landed with a ping and skittered off.

"Get away from me!" Billy yelled, his face going red. "You don't know anything!" Billy pounded across the porch and inside the house, slamming the door.

Don looked down at the discarded Hot Wheels set; cars jumbled, orange tracks scattered, a loop-de-loop on its side. It looked like an amusement park, torn apart by giants.

Filled with regret and humiliation, Don ran first to the chicken coop to get the book, then all the way to Hank's house with tears down his face.

He knew he would get into trouble for leaving his yard, but he didn't care. He had to see Hank, and he crashed through the giant ferns into his backyard, disappointed that it was empty. He raced to the house, and when he reached the patio the sliding glass door started to open.

"I brought your book back…" he said, but stopped in shock when Chief Tedesco emerged from the house, trailed by two police officers.

Don couldn't move. Seeing the chief in Hank's house was as disorienting and mortifying as the time he saw Father O'Shay in the shower at the YMCA.

"What are you doing here, Donnie?" the chief asked, sharp disgust in his voice. "Did your parents let you go running around the neighborhood all by yourself on a day like today?"

When Don didn't answer, the chief muttered to one of the cops, who nodded and gave Don an angry glare.

"Officer Becker is going to take you home," Chief Tedesco said.

Don imagined pulling up to his house in a police car. Without a beat, Don said, "I'll go right home." He raced away, ignoring the chief's shouts. He looked back when he reached the safety of the ferns. Officer Becker hadn't followed. Don threw Hank's book into the woods and raced off.

Back home, his brothers surrounded him, enraged yet relieved.

Their quiet rage meant that, amazingly, their parents didn't know that he'd left.

Don spent the rest of the afternoon sulking under the huge pear tree in the backyard while his brothers huddled on the driveway lighting black snakes. Don hated the way the perfect little black pellets caught fire and spat with sparks and smoke as they oozed into a misshapen gray tube. His brothers hooted and hollered and Don thought that only the thunder of pagan drums would make the savagery complete. The result looked nothing like a snake. The ashy cylinder always broke after an inch or so, leaving a faint black residue on the cement.

Their mother called them into dinner. Dad was on the phone, his face filled with confusion and shame. Don watched with growing apprehension until his dad glanced at him and his eyes flashed with anger. Don felt a wrench of dread. It never once occurred to him Chief Tedesco would call his father.

Dad hung up. "Donnie!" he barked. Since their father rarely raised his voice, everyone jolted with alarm and amazement. His dad grabbed Don's arm, pulling him from his chair and outside. Don had to run to keep from falling.

Dusk shaded the sky in a purplish mass moving from the east. His dad led him to a spot beyond the pear tree where a group of aluminum lawn chairs with fraying plastic weaves surrounded a card table. Dad motioned for him to sit.

"What's this I hear from Chief Tedesco? Do you have an explanation?"

He couldn't think.

"Donald? I'm speaking to you. What were you doing at that man's house?"

Donald, not Donnie. He'd better come up with something quick.

"I was looking through his telescope," he muttered.

A beat. "You were looking through his telescope during the day?"

"There's a little plate you can attach so you can look at the sun. He was teaching me about sunspots. He's an astronomer."

Reverence for science was second only to reverence for religion in the Esker home, and his father paused. "He never invited you inside his house?"

The black refrigerator, ice cube with the strawberry stem, the way the golden curls of hair burst like a halo about Hank's masculine form.

Don shook his head.

Even here in the grassy expanse of their spacious backyard, Dad dropped his voice. "Did he ever touch you?"

Again, he shook his head.

"You're sure?"

He nodded.

His father blew out a breath. "Well, there's something wrong with a grown man who would invite strange little boys into his yard. His neighbors thought there was something queer about him, so they reported him to the police after they found that little boy yesterday."

"Where is he?"

"Who?"

"Hank."

"You're not to see him ever again, is that clear?"

He nodded.

After a sigh, his dad said, "Okay, we'll never mention this again. Now let's go inside."

He imagined the questioning faces from his mom and brothers, and he asked, "Can I just sit out here for a while?"

"Your mother spent a lot of time making dinner."

"I'm not hungry."

"Okay, Donnie. I'll let it slide this one time." After ruffling his hair gently, Dad left.

Don let the tears come, the kind that are silent because they're formed by shame and anger that demand concealment. The world went dark as the sun set. After a while, he heard soft footsteps heading in his direction. He recognized Mom's pace and length without looking.

"Donnie?" she asked softly.

He sniffed.

"Are you sure that man didn't do anything to you?"

He nodded.

"Do you want to talk about it?"

He shook his head.

She stood for a long while. "Please tell me what happened with that man."

"Nothing happened. He was my friend. I just want to be alone."

"I'll give you a bit more time by yourself, but I don't want you alone out here in the dark with a maniac running around. If you're not back in ten minutes, I'm sending your brothers to get you." She stood quietly for a moment before leaving.

He looked up at the sky, strewn now with the silver glitter of the universe. He didn't know how to find Alpha Centauri, the nearest to the sun, but he selected a particularly bright light directly above and decided it was that one. He imagined a glow beginning around his stomach, spreading out, consuming him. He reached up and shot brilliant rays of illumination from his fingers.

He rocketed from the chair and cleared the trees in seconds. North Homestead hurtled away beneath him, blending with electric grid of Cleveland, then the Midwest, then the entire North American continent. The earth sank away.

He was a photon of light, and it would take four years to get to the heavens from this hell.

CHAPTER SEVEN

Dad asked for more morphine and Don squeezed the eyedropper, drawing up the brownish liquid to the dosage line. He looked at his father, eyes clamped, mouth grimaced, and squeezed up a bit more.

Dad turned when he felt the dropper at his lips, slurping. In a moment, his face sagged with relief.

Linnette tapped Don's shoulder. Unnerved, he followed her to the hallway.

"The pain is getting worse," he whispered so that Mom, clattering around the kitchen, wouldn't hear.

"I think it's time to start talking about fentanyl."

"Fentanyl? Isn't that a fatal narcotic drug?"

"Only the illegal kind. It's perfectly safe when it's manufactured legally. It's very powerful, but the morphine isn't enough any longer. We can start him on the lowest dose. From then on, you'll just need to give him the morphine when he asks for it."

"Is it okay to do that every time he asks?"

"Of course. The idea is to keep him comfortable and out of pain. Let him have the morphine whenever he wants. Fentanyl absorbs through the skin and takes about twelve hours to kick in, so you'll have to give him the morphine to tide him over when you put on a new patch. I'll write it up and have the doctor look it over, but I'm sure he'll approve. Do you want to tell your mom?"

"Yeah, I can tell her." Instantly, he wished he'd said no. He didn't want the pattern of delivering bad news to devolve from the professionals to his shoulders.

Linnette smiled and gave him a hug. As they pulled apart, she said, "I hope you've been able to have a little bit of fun while you're here."

"Just working mostly, and helping my parents."

Linnette struggled with a thought. She turned pinkish. "I was just wondering…well, I know how silly this might sound…but if you're interested, I have a gay friend. He's sort of lonely, but I worked with him for a while at the hospital and he's a nice person. He did IT work, computers and stuff. Would you have any interest?"

"In dating him?"

"Just meeting him. You could get together for dinner or something. He lives over by the mall. There's plenty of places to meet there." She giggled with nervous embarrassment.

He had zero interest in meeting her friend, but it would probably never happen. He'd learned long ago it was usually easy to delay these situations until the other guy lost interest, so to ease her discomfort, he said, "Yeah, that might be nice to do some time."

"Great. His name is Bruce. I'll suggest it to him and let you know what he says."

Don knew she had probably already discussed it with her friend, but he didn't mind. Setting up her first gay couple was a big step for a person like Linnette, and he found her happiness touching, in spite of his instinct that the meeting would prove disastrous on the off chance it even happened.

Flustered and bubbly, Linnette bid his mom a cheerful good-bye.

"Well, she's in a good mood," she said after Linnette left, stirring chicken stew on the stove. It smelled delicious.

"She wants to set me up with a friend of hers." He looked into the pot. Mounds of dumplings would soon cover the stew, perfect for the gray skies and chilly weather outside.

His mom shot him a look. "Does she know…"

"She has a gay friend. Everybody does today, Mom."

"Well, that's fine. Linnette is a nice person, so I'm sure her friend is nice, too." She dropped her voice. "Although she's not always the most reliable person you'd ever meet."

"Really? Dad loves her, and she seems to know what she's doing."

"Of course she knows what she's doing, but sometimes she's a bit flakey, is all I'm saying." She raised her voice to change the subject.

"I asked your brother Randy to stop by for dinner. I'm glad he had the time. They're so busy."

Don had arrived a week ago, and he knew his brothers weren't coming because they needed a breather after rotating shifts for the past several months. He didn't blame them.

Randy pulled up a while later, his hair noticeably grayer, wearing jeans and a faded polo shirt with stretch holes at the seams of the front panel. They hugged, and Randy told him about his life at the salami factory where he ran shipping. He hated his new boss.

They ate in the kitchen while Dad slumbered. Don and Randy raved about the chicken stew and dumplings, every word sincere. They sat next to their father's bed for a while afterward, giving him morphine when he stirred himself conscious just long enough to ask.

Randy announced he had to get up early for work because his new boss would notice if he was five seconds late, and his mom handed him a plastic container with a blue lid, fogged with the savory steam of chicken and dumplings.

She held out two more, and after Don took them, he followed Randy outside. His brother nodded across the street. "Are you taking that food over there?"

"Yeah. It's strange seeing Billy up close. We haven't been friends since Before."

For the Eskers, Before required no date. Before was how they lived until that night cleaved their lives like an axe.

"Billy was a bonehead," Randy said with scorn. "He's got something like four kids from four different women." He shook his head. "Fucking moron. He was drunk when he crashed his bike, you know. Probably on drugs, too."

"I know. How's life treating you?"

In June, Randy's wife, Renee, announced that she wanted a divorce just after returning from their daughter's graduation at Case Western Reserve University.

"My apartment's just a shitty old place up in Fairview. It's not as bad as it could be. The mortgage still has ten years on it, so I'm paying that in addition to rent."

"How's Julie taking it?"

Randy lit up. "She's a great kid. I don't know how I managed to make such a great kid with a flaming bitch like Renee. You have no idea how lucky you are that you're gay. The woman gets everything she wants, but if you have a dick hanging between your legs, you're screwed."

Randy jumped in his car, placing the chicken stew on the passenger seat. Don worried it would fall and spill. "See you soon, Donnie," he called with the door open. "If you want to take a piss in old man Tedesco's chicken stew, I won't say anything."

Don laughed and waved as Randy slammed the door and drove off.

Billy took the food, his eyes filled with desperation. Chief Tedesco hovered wordless in the dark.

When Don returned home, he was startled to see a medical van in the driveway, and he hurried inside. A man in a blue paramedic uniform was talking to his bewildered mom. She held a small box.

"I was just explaining to her about the fentanyl," the man said.

Shit! He hadn't told her yet. Linnette didn't explain that it might happen so quickly.

When Mom learned that Dad's pain was escalating, she rushed to his side, fumbling with the box. Mercifully, Dad was asleep, and the paramedic gently took the box and calmly showed her how to apply a patch to his chest.

"Will that help with the pain?" she asked, her voice breathy.

The paramedic smiled. "He's feeling no pain at all right now, trust me. He'll sleep like a baby all night long."

The paramedic was wrong. At around three a.m., Don heard the scratchy sound of his dad waking up over a baby monitor Don set up the day he'd arrived. He'd turned up the volume full blast, and he awoke the moment his dad stirred.

Already dressed in pajama bottoms and a T-shirt, Don flew out of bed. "Dad?" he said, turning on the light.

His dad sat at the edge of the bed. As usual when he got up in the dark, he looked scared and confused, but he focused with relief when he saw Don. This unvarying reaction made Don wonder about the terror of elderly people in facilities who woke up without the comfort of a familiar face to ground them.

"Oh, damn, Donnie. What's your status?"

His father could not be asking about his HIV status, using the inside lingo of San Francisco gay guys. "What do you mean by my status?"

"Are you a POW?"

"Um, no, I'm not."

"Oh, good, I was worried about you because I saw those Nazis running around in the yard earlier."

"The Nazis are gone, Dad."

"Oh, good. Those Nazis are bastards. Can you help me with the commode?"

His face glowed, and his body shook with delicate tremors. He talked a soft, nonstop fentanyl patter.

"I got to think about a new roof in the next few years. I don't know how I'm going to pay for it. I think I saw that there was a cabin for sale out on Kelley's Island and I've always wanted to have a retirement home there. That damned Rita Johnson shakes her boobs at me every time she goes past my office. I've told her I'm married with four boys, but she said she didn't care. You believe that? She doesn't care!"

As Don lifted him back to the bed, he went on, "I never wanted to see Bob Dylan. The guy sings out of his nose. He should end every song with a sneeze."

Don chuckled, helped him sit and adjust. "Lie down on the pillow, Dad." When he reclined, Don gently lifted his legs and tucked them under the covers.

His dad looked ready to fall back asleep, but instead he gently thrashed.

Anguished, Dad said, "Oh, Jesus, Donnie. Jesus, Mary, and Joseph." He opened his eyes. They swam with tears, a few leaking. Don recognized those tears. They're the kind that can shoot you off into the heavens, a photon of light flying free.

"I just want everyone to know that I didn't kill those boys, Donnie. That's all I want. It's all I ever wanted. I'd have done anything. David Smith. David Smith and me…" He coughed and closed his eyes, his head settling for sleep.

His heart pumping, Don hurried to the kitchen where he flipped open his laptop and typed, but he knew what to expect when it blinked on the screen. Hits for David Smith neared one trillion. Limiting the search to North Homestead and nearby streets reduced the numbers, but not enough to make a difference.

Would his mom remember a man named David Smith? Possibly, but she wouldn't wake up for hours.

Another name came to him.

"Of course," he muttered.

Dolores from police archives told him that a man named Eric Ladmore recently retired as the chief of police, and that the murders were his rookie case in 1975. Maybe he knew who David Smith was, or maybe he knew something else that would prove useful.

He found the address instantly. Eric Ladmore lived a few miles away on Pinecone Ridge. Don returned to bed and slept fitfully until rising at around seven o'clock to shower. He checked on both parents, who were sound asleep. He ripped out a note to his mom and left it on the table, saying he went out to pick up a few things at the store.

With little traffic, he was at Pinecone Ridge in no time. He found an unobtrusive spot a few doors down from the standard square brick home. Giant trees towered above, autumn colors taking control. Don worked on some emails, waiting until eight thirty to knock on the door, a time that seemed reasonable.

A man approached down the sidewalk with a firm stride. An unleashed little brown and black mutt ran in front, occasionally jerking back on itself when it caught a whiff of something interesting. It paid close attention to the man, keeping a measured pace. Something about the man's bearing, his square shoulders and long, sure steps, made Don wonder if he was Chief Ladmore.

In front of the house, the dog stopped and shot a look at the man before racing up the driveway. Don leaped out and stepped into his path.

The man was startled and suspicious. "Who are you?"

"My name is Don Esker. Are you Chief Ladmore?"

He nodded, still wary. He wore a tan corduroy jacket lined with fleece, covering a barrel chest. His silver hair was trimmed close underneath a brown-plaid, flat walking cap that topped a square face.

"I have a few questions for you about the murders of those little boys back in 1975. I'm sure you remember. Will you talk with me for a few minutes?"

"Why? Who are you to care?"

"My dad is Rob Esker."

The chief's expression was blank.

"He was one of your suspects. We lived right across the street from Chief Tedesco."

Remembrance flooded his face. "Oh, yeah. I do remember that." Less guarded, he asked, "What do you want to know?"

"Anything you can tell me. My dad is dying, and he doesn't want to go his grave with people thinking he committed those murders. I'm trying to help him."

With the family drama revealed, Chief Ladmore visibly relaxed. "Well, nobody thought he was guilty, if that makes him feel better. I sure didn't."

"Do you mind if we sit down somewhere? I'd be glad to buy you breakfast."

Chief Ladmore gave a sturdy nod. "Let's go inside. I'll put on some coffee. I just got back from having a bite to eat, so I'm not hungry."

The dog gave Don a tentative sniff, watching the chief to make sure it was okay. Ladmore unlocked a side door and led Don up a step. The dog waited until they were inside before racing ahead.

Ladmore led him to a small breakfast table. The home was all flounces and lace, with everything trimmed in some sort of decorative flourish. It looked far too feminine for a man of such stern demeanor.

As if seeing his thoughts, the chief said, "My wife died some years back. I've been thinking about getting my own place. Sit down." Ladmore clattered and banged and slammed things around until he had a pot of coffee brewing. He sat across from Don.

"I'm not sure what I can remember about that case. I was just a rookie, but I'll give it my best shot."

"Did the name David Smith come up at all?"

"Where'd you get that name?"

"Does it mean something to you?"

"No. But why are you bringing it up? Do you know something?"

"No." He didn't want to repeat his father's words, so he lied. "David Smith lived down the street, and I always wondered about him. He seemed sort of strange."

"Yeah, that's the thing. When I started out, it was all about the oddballs, the eccentrics. You know what I learned over the years? It's the people you least suspect. The ones who nobody would ever dream would commit a crime. Now, that would describe your old man, if I remember correctly. Solid citizen, not a blemish to his name. But nobody thought he did it."

"Then why did you storm our house like the Gestapo? I know it wasn't your fault. You were only a rookie. But the way the police department handled it haunted my family for years."

"No, it wasn't my fault, but that was a deliberate strategy to let the community know we were working hard on the case. Your dad would understand if you explained that to him. Plus, we found one of those little flute things your dad made for the local kids at one of the crime scenes."

"They were recorders. My dad made those for most of the kids in the neighborhood."

"It was still evidence. Your dad would understand."

"I doubt it. My family lost most of our friends. People stopped talking to us. We had to sit in the back pew at church so we didn't have to watch people get up and leave us sitting by ourselves. I guess if you'd caught the guy, it would have been okay, but you never did. It haunts my dad to this day, on his deathbed."

Ladmore looked sympathetic. "Look, I understand it must have been hard on him and your family. If it makes your dad feel better, tell him I don't think Tedesco really thought he was guilty either, but we had to do something. Everyone was breathing down our necks. The mayor, the city council, the sheriff's department."

"The county sheriff? I thought they can't get involved unless local police want their help."

"They can't. But the sheriff was concerned about a child killer on the loose and put a lot of pressure on the safety director. They wanted to take over after the first one, Eddie Tedesco." He laughed, shaking his head. "Hoo boy, that was about as popular with the officers as a rectal exam. They backed Tedesco one hundred percent when he said he didn't want a bunch of downtown cops around."

"Why not just accept the help? You obviously needed it."

"It never works that way. They say they want to help, and before you know it, you're filling out a form to take a shit. They just get in the way. Nobody wanted them around. Tedesco was just doing what all the cops wanted."

"And then you never caught the killer."

Ladmore threw up his hand. "Well, yeah, but nobody could have caught him. It's not that he was a master criminal or anything. He just got lucky. We had to follow every lead because there was so little evidence. That's why that flute thing took us to your home, to your dad. We did that to several other guys, too."

"I remember. Two of them in our neighborhood. One nearly across the street from us, a family by the name of Hartner. The father must have weighed all of ninety pounds. He was so thin, he'd fly away in a stiff breeze. He obviously wasn't guilty, but the family moved all the same. The other one was a guy named Hank. He lived on Cook Road and he was an astronomer. He had to move, too. Do you remember him?"

"Yeah, I remember the astronomer. I remember him well because I thought he was our best suspect. I followed him for years. He's still alive. In Lakewood." He blew out a breath of disgust at mentioning the city with Cleveland's most concentrated population of gay men. "Hank Swoboda was his name. Never could nail him, but that guy was as queer as a three-dollar bill."

Hank Swoboda, Lakewood. Finally, something useful.

Ladmore went on. "I remember when we brought him in, some little boy came to the door looking for him. Don't tell me that's not suspicious."

"Holy shit," Don said. "That was me!"

Ladmore's mouth dropped. "That was you?" When Don nodded, he asked, "What the hell were you doing there?"

"I had a great big crush on him. He was the handsomest man I'd ever seen. I didn't know anything about sex or being gay. He never touched me or anything, and he even told me I had to leave him alone because he could get in trouble just for being around me. I didn't understand at the time. All I knew was that I was in love, and I've never forgotten him. One of the nicest and most honorable men I've ever known. Thanks for your time, Chief."

Don elicited as much shock as he'd hoped.

CHAPTER EIGHT

1975

Just days after the teenagers found Danny Miller's body, fists pounded the Eskers' front door as they sat down to dinner. Everyone jumped.

Dad leaped to his feet and headed to living room. Everyone hurried behind. Don flushed with fear when he turned the corner and saw a blazing river of flashing red, white, and blue lights in the driveway.

"Whoa!" Tim and Rich said in unison, stretching the word.

The door rattled and shook again just as Dad reached it. He cast a worried look at the driveway. "Hang on," he called, sliding aside the bolt and unlocking the knob.

Chief Tedesco, surrounded by stern officers, held his cap crisply under his arm and said, "Robert Esker."

Coming from a neighbor, the formal use of his full name startled the whole family.

"Yes, Chief, of course it's me."

"Come with us down to the station. We have some questions for you."

The chief pivoted and walked off, and his shadow passed in front of the surreal backdrop of emergency lights.

Dad froze until one of the officers held out his hand. "Come with us, sir."

"Let me get my wallet and keys," he said in a papery voice.

"No need for that, sir. Let's go."

Mom stepped forward. "Rob?"

He looked back, his face blank. "It's all right. Finish your dinner. Whatever it is, it won't take long."

He stepped out and cops escorted him across the porch. Just as they passed, a line of officers approached and entered the house. The lead cop handed Mom a sheet of paper.

"This is a search warrant. It gives us permission to search this residence for certain items."

Rattled, Mom scanned it, but couldn't focus on the words. "What are you looking for?"

"It's all spelled out there, ma'am." He called over his shoulder, "Officers, you have your orders."

As cops broke off in every direction, Mom said, "But just tell me what you're looking for and I can tell you right where it is."

"Is there any dirty laundry around?"

"No. Today was laundry day. The only soiled clothes in this house are the ones we're wearing."

"Then it's best that you and your children stay out of the way."

More officers poured inside, going about their work with grim determination. Don and his family stood rooted to their spots, mouths agape. Soon, loud hammering came from the basement, and they looked down.

Mom put a hand to her mouth. "I don't understand what's happening," she said, as if expecting one of her sons to explain. As more officers came inside, she pleaded, "Won't someone tell me what's going on?" The cops ignored her.

Tim took her elbow and guided her to the sofa. Soon, Rich, Randy, and Don took seats too, watching this amazing, unbelievable spectacle in silence.

From around the house, things clinked, furniture scraped, drawers and doors opened and closed. Bumps, screeches, scratching, and hollow sounds echoing in the walls and floors filled the house.

"I don't understand any of this," Mom said.

Don understood. Or at least he understood enough to know this was related to Eddie Tedesco's disappearance and the other boys' murder. It had to be. But how?

From the basement came a tremendous screeching and tearing noise so shocking they looked down with astonishment.

"Dad's sanding table," Rich said and the rest nodded mutely. From the sound of it, the police had ripped the table from its bolts instead of screwing it free. Again, Mom put a hand to her mouth.

Don closed his eyes, and the flashing lights from the driveway etched patterns in his eyelids. Red, white, and blue. The colors of Old Glory, of patriotism, washed across his field of vision, shot through with pencil-sketch patterns that vanished and reassembled as he moved his eyeballs.

Panic suddenly gripped Don. He thought of the stories he wrote and stashed in his private drawer of the desk he shared with Randy. He never showed them to anyone, certain they were stupid and worthy of mockery. Would the cops find them?

At remembering another secret, Don shot a look at Tim, who kept a stash of *Playboy* magazines hidden somewhere in his room. Don had never seen them, but Randy had, and he would describe the pictures with awed reverence. Randy said their parents would go apeshit if they ever found out about the dirty magazines, so he warned Don to keep his mouth shut.

Down the hall, a group of cops burst into laughter. Tim looked terrified, but Don worried that the cops just read the first lines of *The Real Secret of Saturn.*

Mom rose and headed for the hallway.

"Mom," Tim said, worried.

"This is my house," she said with terrified bravado.

Tim jumped up and followed, and in the living room they listened to the conversation down the hallway.

"Ma'am, I'm going to need you to return to the living room. You too, son."

"This is my house," she repeated. "I need to get something from my own purse in my own bedroom."

"Ma'am, I don't want to have to warn you again."

Mom didn't respond, but the man raised his voice. "Ma'am." Don pictured her brushing past.

After a beat, in a voice quavering with righteousness, Mom said, "There. I got it. Are you going to arrest me now?"

"Please wait in the living room."

She returned with a red face, Tim scuttling behind. She sat, holding a pack of Marlboros and a lighter. She extracted a cigarette and lighted it. The flame danced in her shaking hand.

Seeing their mother smoke shocked them almost as much as the police storming through the door. The faint wisps of cigarette smoke lingering in and around the house when Don returned from school made sense now.

She blew out a gray funnel and without looking at any of them said, "Your father and I agreed to never smoke when you boys are around. We didn't want you getting any ideas from us that it was okay, because it's not. So let's just pretend it isn't happening." She flicked the cigarette on the rim of an ashtray that she always kept clean, except if smoking guests visited.

Don and his brothers shared stunned looks.

The cops ransacked the house for another thirty minutes or so, ignoring their questions. Shouted instructions and grunts came from the basement stairs past the kitchen. By the sound of it, they were maneuvering the sanding table up the stairs. Dad used it to saw, shape, and glue balsa wood recorders for every kid who wanted one.

A cop emerged from the hallway carrying a bulging bag and left through the front door. The others followed, empty-handed.

The lead cop brought up the rear and approached Mom, who stubbed out her latest cigarette and stood to face him. Don and his brothers rose too.

"Well, ma'am, looks like we're done here. Sorry for the disturbance."

"What was in that bag?"

"Nothing outside of the warrant." He gestured to the table where she'd placed the paper, next to the ashtray now filled with cigarette butts.

He left and his mother gave the door a shove, just enough for it to slam, immensely displeased but not rude. She pushed the deadbolt into place and twisted the lock, putting her hands flat against the wood, her face down. She shook.

The police cruisers, their lights still blazing, backed down the driveway and drove off. A large unmarked van brought up the rear.

The emergency lights faded to faint pulses that dissolved into the hazy wash of streetlights, revealing a ghostly army of shadowy heads and shoulders. They faced the Esker house, broke apart slowly, and moved off. Don's brothers ran from room to room, exploding with outrage at the mess, but Don watched until the last of the shadows left. It seemed to take hours.

CHAPTER NINE

Don recalled a story about a man in the old Soviet Union who went to a Russian airport to pick up his daughter for a visit. The plane never arrived and nobody would talk to him. Her faraway phone rang and rang, unanswered. He returned to the airport and grew increasingly frantic and asked anyone with a uniform where his daughter was. After several days, someone pulled him aside and angrily whispered, *"Comrade, the plane crashed!"*

The story haunted Don, but not because of the father chewed to pieces by the supercilious Soviet refusal to admit that the country wasn't perfect after all, a worker's paradise where planes never went down. No, Don always wondered about the other families, the people who waited patiently at the airport before shuffling home silently, accepting the absence of a husband, wife or child, their fear eclipsing their loss. In such dank silences, paranoia grows like mold.

Don knew those silences. His family knew them. *Maybe*, he thought, *it's time to act like that father and be a nuisance until you get an answer.*

Despite a looming deadline for a marketing memo due on Monday morning, Don felt an overwhelming need to visit telescope man, Hank Swoboda, and he left late Saturday morning for the drive across town. It filled him with conflicting emotions that mixed like volatile chemicals, setting off bursts of excitement and fear. Since he could only find Hank's address but no phone number, he would have to arrive unannounced.

Hank lived close to Don's oldest brother, Tim, and his wife, Sally, and Don decided to drop in for a quick visit.

Don pulled into the short driveway of Tim's house. The abundance of trees hosting feathery flocks gave this area the nickname Birdtown. In high school, Don remembered kids using the name derisively, crinkling their noses at images of doddering grandparents living in two-story houses with chunky porches in small yards. Detached garages sat alongside, with hinged, padlocked doors that sagged to the center. The grandparents had died off, and new generations moved in, painting the houses in tasteful color palettes and sprucing up the yards.

He'd called ahead. Tim was working in the garage, assembling a hot pink girl's bicycle, both doors ajar in welcome. Wrench in hand, he smiled as Don approached.

"Hey," they grunted, and gave each other a brother's handshake, clasping hands and leaning in for a hug and a few pats on the back, wrench and all.

"You look good," Tim said. His hair dragged across his scalp like metallic wire. He looked bloated, as if inflated a bit too much by the bicycle pump on the floor. "You're still going to the gym?"

"Yeah. Where's Sally?"

"Inside. You should go in and say hi before you leave."

It was an odd thing to say. "We should all hang out for a few minutes."

Tim shook his head. "She's pissed off at me. We've been babysitting Jeanette and some of her little friends for the last few Friday nights, and I thought they'd enjoy watching *Grease*."

"What was the problem with *Grease*?"

"The girls made up dances for all the songs, and they put on a show for us last night." He blew out a defeated breath. "Did you know that Greased Lightning was a 'pussy wagon' that would make the chicks cream and the boys were gonna get a lot of tit? I didn't remember any of those lyrics. Jeannette's friend sang the pussy line while pretending to pet a cat. After they were done, Sally pulled me into the kitchen and sliced my nuts off."

Don snickered. His brother gave a tight smile in response, and they soon dissolved into the scarlet-faced, huffing, snot-snorting of overwhelming but contained laughter.

Don knew they weren't an unhappy couple, but they weren't happy either.

Red-hot passion sometimes leads to the deep, affectionate bonds of their parents, or it burns itself into the white-hot rage of Randy and Renee. For Tim and Sally, an unexpected pregnancy when they were both young Marines made for a perfectly amicable marriage in the beginning. It evolved to a truce monitored with precision and vigilance. As long as they both understood they didn't have to approve of each other just because they were married, and that hatred was acceptable now and then, dishes remained unbroken and cutting words unsaid. Don thought it was a sensible way to handle their situation.

"So how's the old man?"

"He's out of it. That fentanyl knocks him on his ass, and he's still just on the lowest dose. I don't know what he's going to be like when we have to go to a stronger patch."

"He's not in pain?"

"He's not in this dimension of existence."

"Well, good. He deserves to get high. He barely even drank when most men in his situation would have blotted out the world in booze."

Don wanted to raise the topic with Tim, and this seemed like as good an opening as any.

"I'm looking into it, Tim. The murders. I've already discovered some things we never knew."

Tim shifted, gesturing with the wrench. "Jesus, Donnie, just let it be. What good will it do to open up that can of worms?"

"Dad wants his name cleared before he dies. It'll be like fentanyl on steroids if I can do it."

"You can't. It was too long ago. Whoever did it is probably dead."

"A guilty man in a grave is still guilty."

Tim looked down. "What did you find out?"

"The two boys they found? They weren't raped."

Tim gave him an uncomprehending look. Don knew all the hurled, shouted, and whispered accusations about their father's sexual perversions were echoing in his memory. The injustice tipped the scales of unfairness to a cosmic degree.

"Fucking shit," Tim whispered in disbelief. "All this time we thought it was some sex maniac."

"It probably was a sex maniac," Don said. "I read about it online. Not all serial killers rape their victims. Sometimes, it's the murder itself that provides the thrill."

"Yeah, but even still…"

"Tim, did you ever hear Dad mention a man by the name of David Smith?"

"That's a pretty common name. Who is he?"

"I don't know. Dad was high as a kite when he mentioned him. He said something like 'me and David Smith.' I have no idea what he was talking about."

"Did you ask Mom?"

"Not yet. You know how Mom is. You have to be careful with the topic. She even has me take food over to old man Tedesco and Billy."

"She's had me do that a few times, too. I thought about taking a piss in those plastic containers. I'm pretty sure Randy did a few times." He looked Don in the eyes. "How was it for you to see Billy again? I know you guys were tight Before."

"It's weird seeing him. He acts like he wants to be my friend again. I feel sorry for him, cooped up with that asshole all day long, but I can barely bring myself to look at him."

"He was a major-league fuckup for a really long time," Tim said, then went on about how the accident changed him and shouldn't Don focus on the present and accept Billy as he exists. Don barely heard a word of it, remembering that night in the field behind the recreation center.

Don realized that Tim had stopped speaking and was waiting for a response.

"He attacked me," Don said. "Remember that time when I was in high school and I said I fell down the basement stairs in that house they were building up the street? It was Billy. He called me a faggot and a queer the whole time. A bunch of his trashy, burnout friends were there, cheering him on. It happened behind the recreation center, and I had to walk home for something like what, three miles? I'd get so dizzy I had to sit down, and I'm pretty sure I passed out a few times."

Tim put a hand on his shoulder. "Holy fuck. Why would he do that?"

"We played around a little when we were boys, kissing and things like that."

"You mean Billy is gay?"

Don shook his head. "No. It was just playing around, like boys do. Billy must have remembered and decided beating me up was the only way to get rid of those memories."

"Why didn't you say anything at the time?"

"I thought everyone would know that I was gay if I said he attacked me for that. And don't pretend a lot of people wouldn't have thought he did the right thing back then."

Tim opened his mouth, objection on his face, but stopped. "You're right. We were all pretty ignorant. Including me."

"Including you," Don agreed, without accusation.

Tim smiled sadly. "What about you? Do you have a man in your life? What happened to that guy who sold that fancy jewelry?"

"Andrew was a cocaine addict. He was on a pretty serious downward spiral, and I didn't feel like being there for the crash."

"Oh, fuck no. No way. You did the only thing you could by getting out."

Suddenly, Sally called out, "Don? I thought that was you!" She approached, smiling broadly, and they shared an affectionate hug. When she'd married Tim, she'd boasted long, lithe legs and a stunning head of raven locks. Her transformation was gradual, but relentless. Her face looked twice the size, and gray powdered her gorgeous hair. Her waist was well-rounded, and if she wore a babushka and a house frock while carrying a sack of groceries, she'd look every bit like one of the old grandmothers of Birdtown.

They'd always got along, and Tim never seemed to resent that his wife was nicer to Don than to him.

They chatted for a bit, settled on dinner tomorrow night with Randy at their parents' house, and as Don left he heard Sally say, "Wow, you're farther along on that bike than I thought you'd be." Tim happily agreed. And so their lives flowed, "pussy wagon" now forgiven with a civil and sparse compliment. *There are worse ways to live*, he thought.

Hank Swoboda lived just a mile or so away.

The GPS led him to a fancy high-rise condo rising over the shoreline of Lake Erie, one of the better-known buildings in this part of town for many decades. Balconies with black iron railings curved along the upscale terra-cotta exterior. At the entrance, Don looked up Hank's name on the electronic door pad and pressed the call button.

At the first ring, he broke into a sweat. On the third ring, a friendly man answered and when Don asked for Hank he said, "He's not home right now. Who's this?"

"My name is Don. I'm an old friend. I live in San Francisco."

"Hank didn't say he was expecting anyone."

"I just happened to be in town."

The man hesitated before saying, "Come on up. Twelfth floor."

The interior looked fresh and modern, with crisp gray walls and carpeting. He found the unit and knocked.

A smiling older man opened the door, dressed in a buttoned-up polo shirt and tan slacks, his skin and hair paper-white. He held out his hand. "I'm Curtis. Hank's husband of thirty-five years, although it's only been legal for the past four." He gave Don a warm, welcoming smile as he stepped inside.

"You say you're from San Francisco? Did you meet Hank at the NASA conventions?"

"No, no, nothing like that. I didn't even know he ever came to San Francisco."

"Oh." Curtis looked confused, but politely asked if he'd like some tea. Don declined.

Curtis led him to a tastefully decorated front room with a white baby grand piano, plush chairs, and finely crafted wooden tables. A massive bookcase filled a wall, and doors trimmed in mother-of-pearl covered the central television console. Expensive art hung on the walls and balanced on tables.

As they sat, Curtis asked, "If you didn't meet in San Francisco, how do you know Hank?"

"From North Homestead."

Curtis changed instantaneously. His friendliness melted away, replaced by uncertainty. "You're from North Homestead?"

"I grew up there. I moved when I was eighteen."

Curtis shifted and looked at his watch. "Hank should be home any minute, but I have to tell you he's very bitter about what happened to him in North Homestead. He's never been back. Never. He even refuses to drive through it, so if we have to go somewhere in that part of town, we take routes to avoid it completely."

"I don't blame him. Believe me, I understand more than you know."

Curtis squinted. "Are you here about those boys?"

"Yes. I remember Hank from when he lived on Cook Road."

Curtis sighed deeply and stood, shaking his head. "You need to leave. You seem like a nice man, but Hank has never gotten over what the police did to him back then. You'll just upset him, and he has a heart condition as it is. I'm sorry to be rude, but I shouldn't have let you inside."

Don remained seated. "I know Hank is innocent. He was my friend. I'm gay, and he was the first grown man I had a crush on. I need him to know I've never forgotten him."

"Oh, no!" Curtis cried. His face filled with disbelief and he raised his hands to his head. "You're *that* boy? The boy who was helping him track sunspots?"

Don felt a long-forgotten thrill. Hank remembered him. Hank told his husband of thirty-five years about him. The handsome telescope man thought of him over the years.

Curtis gestured for him to get up. "You need to leave before he gets home. I'm serious, Don, this could kill him. Do you know that the police accused him of molesting you?"

"He never touched me! I never made any accusation like that!"

"Yes, I know, but they accused him all the same. You have no idea what trouble that caused for him. Years of it. You have to go." Curtis became frantic, almost angry. "Now!"

The door opened. Curtis snapped up, his eyes filled with fear. "Stay here!" he whispered angrily and disappeared down the short hall to the entrance.

Don heard the men talking, with Curtis angrily explaining that he'd been sandbagged and was sorry for letting Don inside. Don couldn't hear Hank's replies beyond a low rumble, but Curtis asked, "Do you want to wait in the bedroom until he's gone?"

For the first time, he clearly heard Hank's response. "No."

Don stood. Hank walked into the room.

Don would have recognized him anywhere. He had the same handsome features, though softened, and the same masculine cut of face and form. He even wore the same mustache, now solid gray. He wore jeans and a button-down shirt.

"I knew you'd grow up to be a handsome guy," Hank said, with a trace of a smile. "With some kids you can just tell, even when they're that young."

"You knew I was gay, before even I was really aware of it."

"I remember your name is Don, but I could never remember your last name."

"Esker. Don Esker."

Hank walked over slowly and shook Don's hand.

"Sit down, Don," he said. Curtis, who looked relieved at the calm, came up behind. "Tell me why you came."

Don talked while Curtis served tea. "Believe me," Don said, finishing his story, "After what my family went through, I appreciate the disruption to your life at being falsely accused. I understand it better than most."

Hank nodded. "But your parents still live in North Homestead? They never considered moving?"

"No. My dad said nobody was going to drive him out of his home when he was innocent. Truth be told, I think my mom wouldn't have minded leaving, and I know me and my brothers wanted desperately to leave, but my dad wouldn't budge."

"It was different for me. I had no roots there. I rented that house because it was close to the research center, and I'd only be living there for a year. The neighbors, they were so nosy. They were obviously suspicious of a thirty-year-old man with no female companions. Two times, a neighboring wife came over to make small talk, and when I looked away for a moment, they were stark naked." He snorted out a laugh. "They were embarrassed and ashamed when I turned them down. I think they started the rumors about me, but they would have started anyway. And I'm certain one of them tipped off the police that they had a genuine faggot living on Cook Road. After the police brought me in for questioning, I moved out within a day. I paid movers to pack everything up. I never set foot in North Homestead again."

"Did you know a man named David Smith?"

Hank looked bemused. "I've probably known several in my life."

"But does that name mean anything to you in connection to the murders?"

Hank shook his head. "I wish I knew anything about those murders. They fucked with my head for a long time. But I'm sorry about what happened to your family, too." His eyes filled with compassion and curiosity. "Explain to me again why they suspected your dad."

"My dad made recorders for all the kids in the neighborhood. They were just these little balsa wood things. He made them by the thousands over the years. He'd give them to all the classes graduating into middle school. He made them for Cub Scouts and Girl Scouts and church groups. It was just a thing he did. A hobby. The police found one of his recorders by the body of that second boy, Danny Miller." Don scoffed with derision. "They found him behind McDonald's, with wrappers and other trash around. They could have just as easily accused anyone who worked or ate there. It would have made as much sense."

"They accused someone else in the neighborhood, too, didn't they?"

Don nodded. "After the third boy, Jeffrey Talent, was found, the police replayed the whole circus at a house across the street from us. The Hartners. They paraded Mr. Hartner out, made a big show of searching that old farmhouse. He was about as threatening as a starving kitten. They were born-again Christians, but that was before born-again Christians became so angry. He was a very sweet man, as I recall."

"You can never tell about people. Ted Bundy volunteered as a suicide counselor and people say he actually saved some lives."

"Yeah, I know, but Mr. Hartner didn't kill those boys."

Hank stood and walked to the bookcase where he retrieved a cardboard box. He set it on the table and removed stapled stacks of paper, notebooks, a set of jangly keys, and a plain, yellowing white envelope stuffed with what looked like old Polaroid instant photos.

"Here it is," Hank said, leaning back with a spiral-bound report with a plastic cover. "About ten years ago, I decided to see if all of that talk about criminal profiling could help. I know a psychologist who's done a lot of work with the forensic psychologists from the FBI out of Quantico, Virginia. They agreed to look at the case of those three boys. It was nothing official. I paid for it myself. This is the report they came up with. I mailed a copy to the North Homestead Police Department and, of course, never heard a word in reply."

"What does it say?"

Hank shrugged. "A lot of it is common sense. They didn't have access to the police report. It was a private investigation, so Chief Ladmore refused to open the files. They said the killer was someone from the general neighborhood, someone the boys knew. Those last two boys especially felt safe with whoever killed them, because everyone already knew a killer was at work. They recognized and trusted him, but kids trust anyone older than they are if they're used to seeing them around. They narrowed it down to two profiles. The first was an adult, probably from school, since they all went to Hollyhock Elementary.

The killings stopped when the man was arrested for something else, or he died. But they thought the second profile was more likely."

"What was it?"

"A teenager. Someone those kids saw around the neighborhood. A car wasn't necessary, because both kids could have been carried through the woods from their homes. They found the one kid behind McDonald's and the other in the woods next to that miniature golf course, the Golden Tee, which was also a popular ice cream stand. A teenager would know both places pretty well. They think he moved away and started killing kids somewhere else. They don't think he went to a university, so it's also possible that he joined the military."

Don felt a beat of surprise and fear.

CHAPTER TEN

1975

Three nights after the police stormed their house, the Eskers had just sat down to dinner when they heard a polite rap on the front door.

His brothers groaned, but Don thought the knock sounded cordial.

They stood and followed their father, who shouted, "Who is it?" The driveway was dark and empty.

"It's Elmer Hartner, and I'm here with my wife, Evie, and our children. We've come to bring you a present."

Dad opened the door. The parents smiled warmly, the three girls looked bored, and the wriggling, retarded Johnny, who was about four or five years old, thrashed in his mother's arm delirious with joy. His head was huge, his body thin, and he had no coordination. His eyes fixed on Don, the youngest, and he grinned madly and moaned happily, flailing his arms. His mother responded to his movements with the ease of an expert, her free hand darting about, keeping him balanced.

Mr. Hartner held a pie, swirled blue and yellow. "This here is Evie's famous blueberry custard pie. It won a second-place ribbon in the pie contest at the Ashtabula County fair three years running, and that's a mighty big pie contest, let me tell you. At least two hundred entries."

"Oh, Elmer," Evie objected with bashful delight. "There's no more than fifty entries and you know it."

Don's mother stuttered before getting out, "We were just sitting down to eat."

Mr. Hartner stepped into the room and his family shuffled in behind. "Pay us no mind, then. You finish your meal, and we'll sit here quietly. Our oldest daughter Agnes here has some stories to share with us from today's Bible study. So after you're finished with your meal, we can all have a little slice of blueberry custard heaven!"

"Oh, no," Mom said. "I made a huge roast. There's plenty for everyone. Come on in and join us. I absolutely insist."

Everyone knew Mom made huge roasts for the leftovers, but nobody said anything. She rushed about, setting new places, and Don and his brothers retrieved chairs from around the house to squeeze in at the table. It was crowded, but there was just enough room, and in short order everything was ready. Don's mother put the pie in a place of honor at the center of the table. His family picked up their knives and forks.

Mr. Hartner said, "We appreciate the hospitality and your delicious food, Mrs. Esker, but it's our family custom to thank the Lord before we partake of his bounty."

She blushed as they put down their utensils. "Of course. Go right ahead."

The Hartners closed their eyes and raised their hands while Mr. Hartner poured out a torrent of gratitude to Jesus that struck Don as ridiculously overblown. He shared a look and a silent snicker with his normally restrained brother Rich that earned him a whap on the shoulder from his dad. Through it all, Johnny wriggled and moaned happily.

"And, Lord, we ask you to remember your children, the Esker family of North Homestead, Ohio, who have been cruelly subjected to slanders, and we ask that you send them your peace at this time of trial and tribulation. Help them to know your love and the love of those who reject such wicked falsehoods and evil suspicions." The room went still. Mr. Hartner went on about fields of vindication and walking with the Lord, and ended with, "Amen."

The Hartners shouted their amens. The Eskers muttered.

After all of that, dinner might have been awkward if not for Mr. Hartner's relentlessly cheerful monologue on the glories of heaven and the peace of Christ. "I know you all are Catholic," he said at one point, "but I don't believe for one moment that the pope is a messenger of the devil, and the church the whore of Babylon. No, sirree. All the Catholics I've ever known have been good people, Godly people, kind to a fault and loyal Americans to boot. I don't go in for all that incense myself, but it's just another way of praising his holy name."

Don's mother said to Mrs. Hartner, "Would it help Johnny to eat if I cut up the meat into smaller pieces?" The boy never stopped contorting.

Mrs. Hartner said, "Oh, no, thank you, Mrs. Esker. He can only swallow soft foods."

"That's right!" Mr. Hartner replied. "He's had his mashed peas and potatoes already. He's just restless because he knows his mother's famous blueberry custard pie is coming up next! Isn't that right, son?" His eyes shining with love, he tickled Johnny with two fingers and the boy erupted with guttural sounds that horrified Don until he recognized the noise as unrestrained laughter.

"Can I hold Johnny?" Don asked.

His family was astonished, and the Hartner girls amazed, but Mrs. Hartner smiled with gratitude and delight. "You sure you can handle him? As you can see, he's quite a handful."

"Yes, I think I can. Can I try?"

"Don, maybe that's not such a good idea," his mother said.

"Oh, it's perfectly all right," Mr. Hartner said. "Evie, let the boy hold him."

She plunked Johnny into Don's lap and the boy screamed with joy, reaching up to tug at Don's hair.

Don remembered being afraid of Johnny, but now he wondered why. The boy radiated happiness, bright with the thrill of life. Johnny recognized Don's smile as friendly, and he squealed and gnashed his mouth with bliss.

As soon as Mom started to slice the pie, Johnny forgot all about Don and reached for his mother. He held still just long enough for Mrs. Hartner to put small pieces into his mouth.

The pie was delicious, tart and sweet and creamy, and everyone said they loved it. The Hartner girls rarely spoke, casting resentful looks at their brother.

At around eight o'clock, the Hartners insisted they'd overstayed their welcome, and although Don's mom offered polite resistance, they made their way to the front door. Effusive thanks from both families filled the living room, and the Hartners left, trailing the blessings of Jesus.

A stunned silence descended, and when the Hartners' shadows moved across the street, Tim said, "What a freak!"

Rich and Randy and even Dad broke up laughing, but Mom scolded them. "They were very kind to come here and offer support. And that pie truly was exceptional."

But Tim didn't let up, mocking Mr. Hartner's prayers and effusions about everything. "Remember when he said he loved our table salt?" he asked, and everyone broke up laughing again.

Mom said, "You just wait and see. That may be the last show of support we get for a while."

Even though Don suspected she was right, he couldn't help but laugh along to Tim's perfect impressions of Mr. Hartner. Mom finally gave up.

The next morning, Jeffrey Talent's frantic parents, who lived just up the street and around the corner, reported he wasn't in his bedroom. Rain had been predicted overnight, so at about nine o'clock he'd gone outside to get his Cleveland Browns cap and they assumed he'd returned, but his bed hadn't been slept in.

Don's family was glued to the six o'clock news. Jeffrey's parents stood in the front yard of a house Don recognized immediately since he'd ridden his bike past it a thousand times.

"He wouldn't have gone off with a stranger," his mother said tearfully, and the father said, "He must have known whoever it was. And we don't care who it was. We just want our boy back safely."

Earlier that day, the police informed Dad his alibi cleared him of suspicion in Danny Miller's murder, and Dad was home when Jeffrey Talent vanished. Don felt a desperate hope life would return to normal.

In the following days, Don learned logic and reason are pitiful weaklings against rage and fear. Everyone in the family talked of the sharp looks of hatred they encountered, the deliberate turns of the head, the phone calls where people whispered the most hateful things. The ringing phone became such a source of dread that Mom unplugged it, despite Tim's promise to be the only one to answer.

On the second morning after Jeffrey's disappearance, the groundskeeper at the Golden Tee Miniature Golf and Ice Cream stand noted some trash along with a fleshy bunch of something at the edge of a wood between the course and the neighboring Assemblies of God church. He walked over with a trash pail to collect it, and the smell hit him at the same moment he noticed it was a small hand.

Late that afternoon, with Dad and his brothers off fishing, Don and his mother sat alone inside the house. He hated fishing and had curled up with the book *When Worlds Collide*, a science fiction story that he found mesmerizing, even though it was written in the 1930s and the science was sometimes laughably outdated. It was an end-of-the-world epic, a thrilling depiction of society spinning out of control as doom approached from space.

He was on the sofa in the living room when he heard a frantic pattering of feet cross the porch. In seconds, someone banged on the door, screaming: "Mrs. Esker! Mrs. Esker!" He recognized Mrs. Hartner's voice and Johnny's terrified howls.

Mom was in the kitchen drinking coffee and reading the afternoon newspaper. She cried out and raced for the door. Don stood with his hands to his mouth, and the book dropped with a thud.

Mrs. Hartner looked frantic, and Johnny wriggled and wormed, tears streaming down his face. "Mrs. Esker, I need you to come right away! Please. It's urgent!"

"What is it?" she asked, breathless from her dash, a hand to her chest.

"It's the police. They've taken Mr. Hartner to the station for questioning, and now they're searching our house." She started to cry and forced out the next words between gulps of air, spit flying. "I told them we were here the night that boy disappeared. You saw us."

Mom's face hardened with resolve. "Yes, of course I'll come. You were here until eight o'clock."

"No! No!" Mrs. Hartner screamed, grabbing Mom's arm for a second before returning to deal with her son. "You have to say we were here until after nine. That's when that boy disappeared."

Mom's mouth moved silently, like a fish in a tank.

"Mr. Hartner wouldn't hurt a soul, not a soul." She pulled her son's fist from her face. "He once spent an hour chasing a rat around the house until he got it outside. He could have killed it with one whack from a baseball bat, but he loves all of God's creatures. Please come with me. Now!"

Her face uncertain, Mom ordered Don to stay indoors and followed the hysterical woman.

Don couldn't stay inside. He stood on the porch and watched the scene unfolding at the old farmhouse. The driveway was no more than a dirt patch, so the police cruisers, their lights flashing, piled up in the road. Officers directed traffic away to side streets.

He could easily imagine the scene inside that house: the girls crying on a sofa, the mother whirling while holding her son, pleading with stony-faced officers to tell her something, anything, and his own mother adding her voice to Mrs. Hartner's, her face conflicted with worry because she'd been asked to lie.

Soon the ghoulish, hateful gossips who lived up and down the road started to gather. Some spotted him but quickly looked away. A small crowd assembled, and Don hated them for their need to watch the destruction of another family. He felt he had a right to watch, that he knew the truth about police searches, that it didn't have to mean anything other than the police were under pressure to stop the killings of little boys. That's all this was. Mr. Hartner was not a killer.

"This is bullshit!" he screamed, but he was too far away and nobody heard.

He stormed back inside and sat up against the couch, shoving the book out of the way. He cradled his knees in his arms and waited for Mom to return. He thought of Johnny's tearstained, frightened face and wept. Now he knew what it meant to weep bitter tears, the kind that burn your cheeks because they are hot with the rage of injustice.

It seemed to take hours for Mom to return, but it probably wasn't that long. They shared a silent look. With a sigh, she sat in the chair across from the sofa. After a while, she said, "I told the police I wasn't sure what time they left. It could have been nine o'clock, but I wasn't sure."

He didn't reply.

"Then I told them that I was remembering more clearly, and that it was nine, that they had been here up until around nine."

She gave him a strange look, and with a start Don realized his mother was seeking his opinion. She wanted her ten-year-old son to validate her decision to lie.

"He didn't do it, Mom. Neither did Dad. It doesn't matter if you lied."

She nodded. "I think you're right."

CHAPTER ELEVEN

Don woke early on Sunday to work on the marketing memo, but his mind drifted away on choppy thoughts about criminal profiles and pointless memory searches for nights long forgotten. By dinnertime, he was only half as far on the memo as he'd planned. He'd have time later tonight and tomorrow morning to finish up.

His dad was adjusting to the fentanyl patch, and his mind was clearer, so when Tim and Sally and Randy arrived for dinner, they all gathered in his room to talk. They skipped from topic to topic until Dad said he was tired and was instantly asleep. They left the room as he started to snore.

Don couldn't help but give Tim a few wondering looks. His brother had joined the Marine Corps days before his eighteenth birthday, dropping out of school. But that was long after the murders ended, which didn't fit Hank Swoboda's profile of a killer teen who had joined the military to continue murdering in faraway places.

They ate their mom's delicious meatloaf and mashed potatoes. Don scolded himself for wondering if Tim, booming with laughter at Randy's description of his skeevy new boss, was capable of such brutal crimes. What the hell was wrong with him? The paranoia ended years ago, he'd thought, but he realized it was much closer to the surface than he ever suspected. It was unsettling.

After dinner, Mom left to wash her hair.

Randy suggested, "Hey, why don't we go see Rich?"

"I'm pretty tired," Sally replied, plainly not liking the idea.

Randy said, "I'll drive Tim home afterward." Tim nodded with a downturned mouth. Fine with him.

"Will the gates be open at this hour?" Don asked.

"They don't lock them anymore. They have surveillance cameras everywhere, so nobody's going to fuck with anything. Come on, how long has it been since the three of us went to see him at the same time?"

Don wanted to object that he had work to do, but how could he? They piled into Randy's car and set off. It was only a ten-minute drive.

A low, curving river-stone wall enclosed Memorial Park Cemetery. Randy drove slowly through the deserted, narrow lanes. High lamps spotted the ground with light, illuminating the nearby polished gravestones like small, precise rectangular ponds.

Randy stopped when they reached a circular shelter lined with benches where visitors could wait out rain, seek relief from the sun, or contemplate in silence. Many such structures sat about, each shaped differently, but Don never saw anybody inside one. Most people used them the way his family did, and what was probably their real function, as an easily recognizable landmark in identical rolling hills scattered with maples and firs and pines.

The weather was chilly, their breaths just visible as the most fleeting of ghosts. Nobody brought gloves, so they shoved their fists into their jacket pockets. The leaves on the ground were the first of the season, velvety and tender, and they made a silken rustle for the silent brotherly procession.

Even though Rich was buried away from the lights, they knew exactly where he was and Tim reached him first. He brushed the leaves from the gravestone and used his phone to reveal the words in a burst of light: *Richard T. Esker, 1960–1976. Beloved Son and Brother*. In smaller cursive script beneath, it read *Always with us*.

More and more, the year 1976 jolted Don. Rich had missed so much. Even the light from the small phone would have astounded him, let alone that the device allowed instant communication with the world.

They looked down in silence, and Don knew Tim and Randy were also remembering the Niagara Falls weekend, and the day they first gathered here, events so shocking and life shattering none of them would ever fully recover.

The cemetery workers had ruined this spot for Don, but he never told anyone the story. His brothers also didn't know about Don's last conversation with Rich.

"I always wonder what he'd be like today," Tim said. "I think about it a lot." Don and Randy muttered their agreement.

After a few moments, Randy said, "I don't care what the police reports say. He was the last victim of that man." Don and Tim nodded.

❖

Don stayed up late into the night after visiting Rich and rose after only a few hours to help his dad, but he finished the memo and sent it off. It wasn't his best work by far, but it was on time, and he figured he was entitled to one subpar performance.

Just as he sent the email, his mom walked into the kitchen, already dressed for the day. "Have you eaten?"

"I had some coffee and bananas."

"Oh, that's not enough. Let me fix you a real breakfast."

"It's okay, Mom. I have some errands."

"Errands?" She looked at him like he was crazy. "What errands? We have enough groceries in this house to feed an army."

He thought up a quick, innocent lie. "I want to get some records from St. Anne's. My school records."

Her confusion deepened. "Why?"

"One of my clients wants a full biographic profile. I don't know why." He smiled and held up his hands in a helpless gesture.

"Well, okay, but that seems silly. You've already proven yourself in your field. And nobody should be interested in your grade school records except your high school."

It was almost nine, so he jumped in the shower, threw on some clothes, and was out the door inside of twenty minutes.

Hollyhock Elementary, a brick building low to the ground with a roof and eaves shaped like a secure square cap, looked identical to his recollection. Even the paint was the same deep brown. Each step forward took him farther back in time. When he reached the entrance, which matched his memory down to the smoked glass, Don would not have been surprised to hear a passing car blasting the Strawberry Alarm Clock or the Carpenters.

Like his brothers, he attended kindergarten here before moving on to St. Anne's, but as he stepped inside, his memories ended. The layout and the noise confused him.

The hallways were empty, but a racket burst all around, with singing, laughing, recitations and the raised voices of teachers. It had an almost comforting smell of crayons, markers, and glue, along with a faint undercurrent of generic boiled vegetables and some sort of meat-flavored tomato sauce that was probably the combined odor of thousands of different cafeteria meals.

Behind a counter in the office sat a nicely dressed young woman tapping at a computer. As he entered, her eyes widened slightly with apprehension, and she pulled her hands up from the keyboard. Don suddenly realized that in modern America, where any mentally disturbed person can get as many firearms as they want, a stranger in the school was cause for alarm. He smiled pleasantly and moved no closer. The back-in-time feeling vanished utterly. This was the new America. *Thank you, NRA, you twisted bastards*, he thought.

"I'm really sorry to disturb you." He clasped his hands to show he wasn't holding anything. "I was a kindergarten student back here in 1971. I was hoping you could help me find someone."

Her alarm faded, replaced by impatience. "We can't release any information about former students. We don't really have very much information anyway."

"It's a teacher I'm trying to locate. Or at least I think he was a teacher. He might have been a janitor or something else." It sounded suspicious even to him. "His name was David Smith."

"That's a pretty common name." Her voice was flat and unhelpful.

"I know, but he would have worked here in the early to mid seventies." He thought up a quick lie: "He was a friend of my dad's, who's dying of cancer, and he said he'd like to get in touch with him before the end." Using his father's condition to gain her sympathy felt a bit sleazy, but he was only trying to help.

"Former employees don't usually keep their contact information current." Her voice had the barest hint of sarcasm. He imagined her retelling this story to friends with a full-on tone of exasperated disbelief: "So I told him, 'Duh! How many former employees tell their old employers where they live?'" Her friends would be amused at how stupid people could be.

This had seemed like such a good idea, but it was utterly pointless. Even if an adult at Hollyhock Elementary committed the murders, what were the odds his name was David Smith and his dad knew he was the killer? Wouldn't he have said so long ago? It was just a shot in the dark, and he realized it was useless.

"I'm sorry," he said, turning to leave.

"Just a minute," she replied, typing. "Let me just see if that name comes up." She typed and clicked, and typed and clicked some more, but in the end shook her head. "I'm sorry. I can't find any record of an employee of Hollyhock Elementary by that name."

"Thanks for checking. Sorry to disturb you." He left, keeping himself in her line of sight so she could see he was headed for the doors. Halfway there, an electronic chime sounded, and the school exploded with thousands of stomping feet, shouted conversations and doors slamming open. He broke into a trot and managed to exit just as swarms of students filled the hall.

As the grade school din faded, he berated himself for such a brain-dead plan. He didn't know what he was doing. He had no clue how to investigate any crime, let alone one unsolved for more than forty years. There was no DNA, and the criminal profilers from the FBI couldn't even settle on one suspect, for fuck's sake. He was so desperate for some answers, he'd entertained, if only briefly, an insane thought about his brother. It was hopeless.

Don wanted to give his dad justice, but life is unjust and you have to learn to live with it, just like Dad said.

When he returned home, he was hungry and his mother berated him for skipping breakfast. She made sandwiches. He bit into the soft white bread, the mayonnaise and mustard and deli meat, the kind of sandwich that even supermarkets didn't sell any longer without the phony fig leaf of wheat bread. It was simple, classic, and delicious.

"Thanks, Mom," he said, chewing. "This is really good. You don't have to always feed me, you know."

She smiled happily. "I like feeding people. You know that. Did you get your errands done?"

He nodded, and suddenly thought, *if I'm going to give up, I shouldn't do so before I explore every last possibility.* He didn't want to upset her, but it was his last shot.

He swallowed, took a drink of water and asked, "Mom, Dad mentioned a man named David Smith to me the other night. Do you know who he meant?"

Her face froze and she said, "That's a very common name." She lifted her sandwich.

Gently, he placed a hand on her arm. "I saw it in your face. You do know who he is. You have to tell me, Mom."

She lowered the sandwich. "Why?"

"Because I haven't told you, but I've been trying to investigate who killed those boys. Dad wants his name cleared before he dies, and I keep hitting brick walls. So if you know who David Smith is, you have to tell me."

She pinched her lips. "What makes you think you can solve those murders?"

"I'm not saying I can. I'm pretty sure I can't. But I have some free time, so I might as well do something useful. I'm not incompetent, you know." He thought of his ill-considered trip to the school, but pushed it aside.

She breathed deeply. "I know you're not incompetent, Don. You're a very able man, a good man. I'll be honest and say I wish you'd been content with finding a good woman, but I know we can't change that. And that's what you have to accept. You can't change what happened. Even if you did find out who did it, it would never erase those terrible things."

"I know, but that's not the point. And in the end, it's not just for Dad, it's for all of us." Until he said it, he didn't even realize it. He was doing it for his dad, his mom, his brothers, their kids and grandkids and future generations and himself. The whole family. It was for all of them.

"I can't get past David Smith," he said. "Dad's too looped most of the time to have a coherent conversation, and I don't want to tell him what I'm doing because I don't want to get his hopes up. So as unpleasant as it is, I need you tell me about David Smith."

"It won't help you solve anything."

"I won't know that until you tell me."

She thought for a moment, sighed, and pushed herself up. "Wait here." He heard her sneak into Dad's room, open a drawer, and in a few moments, she returned with three hard cover, well-worn books. She set them on the table and Don picked up two, looking down at the third.

The Moors Murders. Killer Couples. Death on the Moors.

Alarmed by the gruesome titles, he asked, "What's this all about?"

"The Moors murders in England. There was a couple, a man and his girlfriend, that started killing children." She clucked and shook her head at such unspeakable things. "They buried them on the moors. I think they killed five, but they never could find one of them. This all happened in the early sixties."

"Was the man named David Smith?"

She shook her head. "David Smith was the woman's brother-in-law. He was married to her sister." She took a deep breath. "This couple, well, they decided David would enjoy being part of their murder spree and they came up with a plan. They brought home a seventeen-year-old boy one night and," her voice dropped, "they killed him with an axe in front of David." She swiped tears from her eyes. "Well, he was beyond terrified, but he was afraid they would kill him, so he helped clean up the mess and wrap that poor boy up. Then David went home and told his wife what happened, and they went straight to the police. They found that dead boy still in the house."

"Why would Dad talk about David Smith?"

She started crying, softly. "Well, it was just awful what happened next. Here this poor man and his wife turned in the murderers—her own *sister*, for heaven's sake—but nobody believed he wasn't involved." She was weeping now. "They were hounded for years. They were attacked in their own home." She pulled a paper napkin from the holder and dabbed her eyes and nose. "On the street. At restaurants. They didn't want to be driven from their community for something he didn't do, and they held out for years. But in the end, they had no choice and they moved. They suffered years of the most horrible, hateful abuse." Her voice rose. "Their lives were destroyed. They got a divorce." She sobbed once, and it sliced his heart. "And all they did was the right thing."

David Smith. A man falsely accused. Robert Esker. Also falsely accused. Hank Swoboda. Elmer Hartner. It was a roster of injustice, of mob rule, the rotting and filthy and rank underside of civic pride.

"Your father wrote to him, to David Smith. I don't know how he found his address. He'd moved to Ireland and remarried. He just wanted to let him know other people had gone through the same thing. David wrote back. I don't know what he said, but it cheered up your father. I was so grateful to him for responding. I wanted to write him a letter myself, but I didn't know what to say."

"Wow." He knew his father was injured in unfathomable ways but didn't know he'd resorted to reaching out to a man across the ocean, someone he didn't know, for commiseration and support. Don felt guilty at his inability to comfort his dad in this way. What could he have done differently?

In a little while, Linnette arrived, cheerful as always and this time armed with her friend Bruce's phone number. "He's looking forward to hearing from you," she said, excited. The novelty of witnessing and being near a gay romance had a narcotic effect on some straight people. A few of his friends in San Francisco resented it, but Don thought it was sweet. Such people are excited to demonstrate their acceptance in a concrete way, and nothing but goodwill was behind it.

With his dad's condition largely the same, Linnette's visit was brief. At the door, she asked, "Would it be okay if I gave Bruce your number, too?"

Don wasn't sure, but Linnette was too good-hearted to deny, and they pulled out their phones. He didn't have a good feeling about Bruce, but for Linnette's sake, he would call in the next day or two.

After she left, Mom took a nap, and with his dad sleeping, Don was alone at the kitchen table. In the distance, a train sounded as lonely and forlorn as the foghorns in San Francisco Bay.

He opened his laptop to check Facebook, scanning the familiar posts about pets that died, shows people saw, fabulous vacation photos, friends at the weddings of people he'd never met. Someone he couldn't place announced his aunt was very sick, and someone else he remembered meeting for one night at a bar in London posted a photo of his arm in a cast.

He made appropriate comments when he felt like it. He offered sympathy for deaths of every kind, because whoever posted it was in pain and shock and crying out for someone, anyone, even somebody they met a single night years before to acknowledge their loss.

He was just about to close his laptop when a new post silently appeared at the top of the screen. It was from a man he went to high school with, one of the straight guys he barely knew during his four years at St. Peter's but who had, for some reason, sent him a friend request. At first, these requests troubled him, but now he thought, *Fine. If you want to take a peek at the life of a gay man in San Francisco, have at it.*

He froze. A lot of people from his school years used Facebook. Old neighbors likely did, too.

Elmer Hartner was the final unfairly accused man on the list. He thought it unlikely Elmer had a Facebook account, even if he was still alive, but he typed in the name all the same. Nothing.

He searched his memories, digging deep into that night of the blueberry custard pie, resisting the temptation to wake his mother to ask if she remembered the Hartner daughters.

Then a name came to him: Agnes, the oldest daughter who had Bible study that day. He typed the name and found her. She lived in North Homestead.

"Holy shit," he said. The woman in the photo was haggard, but wore a bright smile. Bleached blond hair tinted with three blending shades of purple at the tips surrounded a thin face. She didn't look remotely familiar. Her profile was public, and he scanned her posts. She posted a lot. Already that day she'd shared four different comic strips featuring a grouchy old lady complaining about life and getting old. He scrolled down and found what he was looking for. Yesterday, she had written, *If you're looking for me at Loonie's I'm workin nites the next few weeks. Come on by after six for a drink or five!* Two people had liked the post, and Don was tempted to add a third but restrained himself.

Don looked up the address for Loonie's. It was down Lorain Road near the Pinecrest border, the working-class neighborhood of his youth where factory workers fixed cars in driveways, fought with their wives inside, and drank beer the whole time. Almost all the factories had closed, and these perfectly respectable neighborhoods were falling apart. Carports sagged, paint peeled, and lawns grew unkempt. America's working class was dissolving away into the muck of poverty for two generations, and they still voted for the politicians who let it happen. He gave up trying to understand why years go.

Maybe a conversation with Agnes would shake loose some new information. If his dad went to the trouble of writing to a stranger in Ireland to find some peace, he could at least talk to Agnes up the street.

His phone rang, and he automatically picked it up without looking at the number.

"Is this Don Esker?" He didn't recognize the man's voice.

"Yes."

"My friend Linnette gave me your number."

Linnette left thirty minutes ago. The guy was calling already?

"Right," Don said, and if he heard the hesitation in his own voice, the other guy—Bruce?—almost certainly did, too.

"Yeah, so I'm Bruce. How would you like to get together soon? I'm free tonight."

He sounded solid, assured, but Don wasn't sure. Bruce might be desperate. But what the hell. Don was horny, so even a bad date might turn out okay. "Do you know Loonie's on Lorain Road?"

"Loonie's," Bruce repeated, sounding surprised by such an unlikely suggestion. "Yeah. I've seen it but I've never been there. It's kind of a straight biker bar. Rough customers. I guess it's okay, but are you sure you want to meet there?"

"Yeah. I need to connect with an old friend at around six, and maybe we can meet up after that. Say, seven?"

"See you then."

Bruce hung up and only then did Don realize he had no idea what he looked like.

Don announced he wouldn't be eating at home, flustering his mom, but when he explained he was meeting Linnette's friend, she nodded and said, "I hope you have a good time." As he drove off, it occurred to him he'd never left his parents' house for a date with another man. This was a new experience for his mom. *She handled it well*, he thought.

Don passed the wide entrances and exits of the Ohio Turnpike, which looped over the street. Gigantic gas stations lined Lorain Road with massive parking lots filled with big rigs, along with motels from the decent to the fleabag, a huge restaurant his brothers loved that served nothing but shitty fried foods, and bars and convenience stores.

Even here, Loonie's looked downscale, a wooden claptrap honky-tonk with an asphalt parking lot sloppily shaped by hand and a painted message on the door that read, "Where the Elite don't drink!"

Inside, a three-sided bar nearly cut the large room in two. The scattered stools, chairs, and tables made it seem that a boisterous crowd had just left, and Indians and Browns banners hung on the walls, along with posters of beautiful women in varying stages of undress. An empty plywood stage filled a corner, and from the speakers Bob Seger sang his aching ballad about his knockabout youth down on Mainstreet.

Close to twenty people drank beer from bottles or mugs. They looked like regulars, comfortable with themselves and each other, sharing an occasional comment.

A burly, bearded guy worked one side of the bar, while Agnes, instantly recognizable by her purple-tipped hair, tended the other. She held a rag as she talked to a customer, a young greasy guy with long hair and a black leather jacket, softened from constant wear. She laughed at something he said and flicked the towel at him. He didn't flinch and beamed a dirty grin.

Don knew he had to ease into the topic. He took a stool near the corner of the bar. Agnes saw him and made her way over, and the guy in the leather jacket gave her ass an eye-fuck.

"What'll you have?" she asked. She had a good figure, bosomy and curved inside a pink top and jeans. Maturity lined her face, not dinginess. She looked better than her Facebook photo and she spoke in a friendly and raspy voice, totally at ease. He ordered a bottle of beer and as she set it down, he said, "You seem really familiar to me."

She squinted but shook her head. "Sorry, mister, but your face isn't registering. That's three fifty."

Don handed her a five and left the change on the bar. "No, I'm serious. I know you from somewhere." He leaned back, a finger at his lips, and she posed like Betty Grable, hands on hips and a saucy tilt of the head. "I think I knew you a long time ago," he said, making a show of scrunching his forehead, trying to tease a memory free. "What's your name, darling?" It was the first time he called someone darling, but it rolled off his tongue, seeming to fit the place, and her.

"Name's Agnes," she replied, and they shook hands as she went on, "and I've heard this line before. Not that I don't appreciate the effort." She winked.

"Nice to meet you, Agnes, and this isn't a pickup. I just have this uncanny sense I know you from somewhere. I'm Don Esker."

She had no reaction other than to say, "Nice to meet you, Don. You from around here?"

Perfect! "Yeah. Just up the way on Stearns Road."

Her face lighted. "I grew up on Stearns Road. But there's no way you could remember me from that. We moved when I was eight years old."

Don snapped his fingers and pointed. "But I do remember. You had two sisters, right? You lived in that old farmhouse. You had a brother, too. I remember his name was Johnny."

"Well, don't that beat all. That sure as hell was me. But I can't remember you, not even a little bit. What did you say your name was again?"

"Don. I was Donnie then. Donnie Esker."

"Oh, my Lord." She put a hand to her mouth and her eyes filled with uncertainty. "I do remember you, but I wouldn't have known you from Adam. You had three brothers, isn't that right?" He nodded, and she formed a nonchalant but tight smile and in a forced casual tone, she asked. "And how's the family?"

"My brother Rich died when he was sixteen, but my other two brothers are still around town. I live in San Francisco now, but I'm here to help my mom because my dad's really sick. He doesn't have much longer."

Her face melted in sympathy. "I'm sorry to hear that about your dad. And your brother. Johnny died way back when, too. Poor thing didn't have a chance, his health was so bad. Kids were afraid of him, but he loved everyone the minute he laid eyes on them. He taught me so much about happiness and living for the moment. I resented him because he needed so much attention from my folks, but after he was gone, well, it's still the biggest hurt I ever felt." She went silent.

"Remember that night you guys came over with the pie, and I played with Johnny? I was one of those kids who were afraid of him, but as soon as I held him, I realized he was the happiest person I'd ever met. Probably still is."

Her eyes moistened as she squeezed his arm. "Thank you for saying that, Don. It's a real joy to know someone else remembers him outside of my family. Not that there's many of us left. My folks are both dead, and my two little sisters moved away years ago. And that's awful about your brother. Sixteen is so young. What happened to him?"

"Heroin." She ticked her tongue and he went on. "Rich was quiet, not like the rest of us. After everything that happened, what with the police and all, well, we just didn't know how deeply it affected him. He was an addict before any of us realized he was even taking drugs."

Agnes formed a steeple with her hands, pressed to her forehead. She squeezed her eyes, forcing a single tear down her cheek. "God, those were rough times. My folks prayed and prayed and prayed some more, but nothing helped. Dad went to his grave looking over his shoulder. My mom said we should bury him standing up on one of those rotating Christmas tree stands so he could always see behind him." She barked out a laugh but grabbed a towel to soak up the tears before another fell.

"They were rough days," Don agreed. "It was so stupid, too. They had no evidence tying my dad to the crimes, but they made that big hoopla about taking him in for questioning and searching our house. I don't need to tell you how that felt."

"You sure don't," she said angrily. "That police chief who lived right there, what was his name?"

"Tedesco."

"That's it. That man ruined my dad's life and my mom's, too. Do you know why they searched our house?"

He shook his head.

"Because my dad was always trying to save souls, you know, and he'd been out there passing out pamphlets at that Assemblies of God church. He wrote his name and phone number on them so people could call and talk to him if they wanted to. They found one of those pamphlets next to that boy's body, the one they found at the Golden Tee. Most likely it just blew over there, it was so close to the church and all. But the police took every belt and tie that was about one inch thick."

"They took all of our thin belts and ties, too," Don said. "After they decided my dad wasn't guilty, we only got about half of it back. They said they didn't know where the rest of it was."

She threw the towel on the bar. "Same thing here." She stabbed the air with a rigid finger. "They took our Polaroid instant camera, too. My folks didn't have two nickels to rub together, and it was the most expensive camera they owned and the police said they didn't know where it was."

A Polaroid camera? His mind flashed to the yellowing envelope on Hank Swoboda's table, stuffed with what looked like instant Polaroid pictures.

"Something wrong, Agnes?" The horny greaseball had appeared from nowhere, his legs wide, his fists clenched and a stony warning on his face.

"Oh, just holster it, Nigel. This here is an old friend, and we're discussing some things, but he's not causing me any trouble."

"You sure?"

"I'm sure. When I need your help, I'll holler loud enough for you to know it."

"I could use another beer."

"Sure thing." She smiled at Don. "It was nice seeing you again, Don, but I gotta get back to work. This bar don't run itself. And good luck with your dad. Stop by again some time." She was sniffling away the tears, regaining her composure.

"I'm waiting for a friend, so I'll be here for a while."

"That's fine, then. Just let me know when you need a refill."

Don took his beer and headed for an empty table next to another where a single man sat, working his phone. He was dressed in jeans and a pullover shirt tight enough to show some muscle. With salt-and-pepper hair and a handsome face, he looked up at Don. They shared a nod and Don noted that they were wearing similar gray shirts.

"Are you Don?"

Don hadn't even hit the chair. "Bruce?"

Bruce nodded and stood, extending his hand. They shook as he took the next seat.

"You're really early," Don said, wary but intrigued. This hot guy didn't look desperate, but it was only six twenty.

"I finished my workout and had nothing to do, so I thought I'd swing on by." He hooked a thumb at the bar. "Did you catch up with your friend already?"

"Yeah." In addition to being good-looking, Bruce was direct, relaxed, and confident. Don felt a powerful tug of desire, and Bruce looked equally intrigued.

Bruce took a swig from his beer and said, "So Linnette tells me you're helping to take care of your dad."

"Yeah. My schedule's pretty flexible, so it was easy for me to come from San Francisco."

"Gotta be a lot of work, though."

"It's not too bad. Linnette is a huge help, and there are other hospice workers. My mom handles a lot, but I'm doing my share."

Bruce popped his eyebrows, his expression now lustful and hungry. "I guess you could use a break. Wanna come back to my place and blow your load?"

He felt a hot rush. "You don't believe in small talk, do you?"

"I'm horny as fuck. Aren't you?"

They left their unfinished beers on the table.

CHAPTER TWELVE

1975

Weeks after the groundskeeper found Jeffrey Talent's body, Don's mother marched over to the Tedesco home against Dad's protests. She handed the chief of police the name and number of the president of Aerospace Engineers, where his dad worked as Vice President and Head of Staff. Mom demanded the chief call and set the man straight. Robert Esker was not a suspect in the murder of anyone, let alone little boys. He had a solid alibi the police verified days after he was taken in for questioning.

The call from the chief, when buttressed by a personal visit from Father O'Shay, saved his father's job, but he stopped sharing funny stories from work.

School resumed with Eddie Tedesco still missing, but Don's mother could not march into every classroom where he and his brothers sat in mortification all day, hearing whispers and seeing angry glares. Don's mother could not talk to all the teachers, who weren't unkind but seemed embarrassed and unsure about how to deal with the situation. Don's mother could not visit the home of every friend to explain her husband's innocence.

One time his mother returned from the beauty shop, her hair damp and half done, the metal curlers still clipped close to her scalp. Faint chemicals scented the air. She'd been crying and didn't respond when Tim asked what was wrong. She rinsed her head and closed herself in her bedroom. For weeks, her hair looked scraggly and unkempt.

Deep into October, when the sun moved south on the horizon and cast long shadows in the evening, a faint knock on the door interrupted their dinner.

Dad tried to stop Tim as he rose angrily.

"I'm answering this time," Tim insisted, his voice low. Don thought his brother suddenly sounded like a man.

The family gathered behind as Tim opened the door. A man and a woman stood on the porch, shadows holding each other close. Don couldn't see their faces, but they somehow seemed familiar.

"We live up the street," the man said. His voice was defiant and fearful. "We're the parents of Jeffrey Talent."

Everyone went still until at last his mother stepped forward, saying, "Mr. and Mrs. Talent, we are so distressed about what happened to your little boy. You must be going through hell." She nudged Tim aside and took their arms, pulling them inside. They looked young and stylish but moved like robots.

Mrs. Talent lowered her head, weeping, her long dark hair falling like curtains to hide her face. Mr. Talent, however, looked directly at Dad.

"We'd like to speak to you," he said, emotionless.

"Yes, of course," Mom replied. "Why don't the four of us go into the family room? I'll send our boys to their rooms."

"No," Mr. Talent said firmly. "Just him."

"Why?" Rich asked sarcastically, and everyone turned to their normally silent brother.

"That's our business," Mr. Talent replied, a touch of anger in his voice.

Rich snorted with derisive laughter, devoid of all humor. "Gee, let me think. You want to accuse our dad of raping and killing your son."

"Rich!" Mom cried in horror.

"I don't care!" Rich shouted, shocking everyone, and Mrs. Talent winced. "He didn't kill your son. Why don't you leave us alone?"

Dad put his hand on Rich's shoulder, but Mom stepped forward and gave her second son a sharp slap across his cheek. The sound cracked as neatly as pond ice, and Rich stepped back in disbelief as he rubbed the spot.

"How dare you be so rude?" Mom said, guttural and raging. "These people have lost their son."

"Fuck their son!" Rich screamed, his face inflamed with fury. He spun on the Talents. Dad tried to hold him back, but he wrenched free and screamed into their faces, "It's your own fault! Why did you let him go outside when you knew there was a killer? I wish your shitty, stupid son had never been born!"

Knowing such volcanic anger had been churning inside mild-mannered Rich all this time reduced the Eskers to open-mouthed stares. Even Mom could only look on, wide-eyed with bewilderment. Rich spun around and started to run but slipped and crashed to his knees. The impact shook the room. He pushed himself up, skidding for a few seconds until he got traction, and he thundered through house and out the kitchen door.

"I'm so sorry," Mom whispered to the Talents.

Tim roared and pushed past everyone, running down the hallway where he slammed the door of his room, sending a tremor through the walls. Randy repeated Tim's exit, down to the slamming door. Unaccountably, all the adults looked at Don, as if to see what he would do.

Don leveled a gaze at the visitors and said evenly, "Our dad didn't kill your son. The Hartners were here for dinner that night, and we all remember exactly where we were. We were all home, including our dad."

In an instant, Mrs. Talent turned lunatic. Her pretty features seemed to come to a point in the center of her face, a transformation so swift it was almost comical. She screamed, "You're all lying!"

"Honey," Mr. Talent said, but as her husband reached for her, she rained a hail of slaps around his face and shoulders. He crouched against them. "Don't tell me what to do, you bastard!" she screamed. "Jeff hated you, and I hate you too!" She got in one final slap across the top of his head and whirled to the door. "Don't come home!" On the porch, she broke into sobs and Don measured the rapid speed of her departure by the way they faded.

Mr. Talent stared at the floor, a hand at the spot of the final slap. He looked slender and tiny now, as if his body had collapsed in half.

Mom wept, holding one hand to her mouth while the other gripped the corner of the hallway. "Mr. Talent," she said, forcing the words out between gasps. "I'm so sorry."

He nodded absently. His face had the smooth, symmetrical beauty of an A-bomb's mushroom cloud viewed from above. "Were you really all here that night?"

"Yes!" Mom rushed to say. "We wouldn't lie."

"The Hartners were here, too," Dad said softly. "They were with us up until around eight."

Don and his mother shared a glance.

Mr. Talent nodded. The room went silent, save for the sharp clicks of the starburst clock on the wall.

"Do you have some whiskey?" Mr. Talent asked, and Mom made a sharp sound of grief.

"How about a beer?" Dad suggested, taking his arm gently and leading him to the kitchen. He shuffled like a dutiful child.

With all the tumult of the past few minutes, the house took on an eerie calm. Mom closed her eyes, put a hand to her chest and rested her forehead against the wall.

A few weeks later on a Saturday afternoon, when a swift wind and chilly rain tore most of the remaining leaves from the trees, Don and his dad and brothers watched a black-and-white movie in the family room while Mom balanced the family checkbook at the kitchen table.

Rich had gone off somewhere, but Tim and Randy lounged on the floor, mocking the movie about a giant octopus attacking San Francisco. They sneered at every shot of the monster, declaring it "fakey" and stupid. Dad chuckled at their scorn, but Don wished they would shut up. The octopus wasn't so bad, as long as you didn't look too closely.

Don used to watch the Saturday afternoon monster movies with Billy, but since Eddie's disappearance, he watched them alone or with his brothers, except for Rich, who never answered anyone's questions about his whereabouts, stopping all inquiries with a snarl of warning. He'd changed since that night of rage with the Talents, and he sometimes didn't even make it home in time for dinner. Their dad said they had to give him some space.

Mom appeared at the top of the stairs above the family room, holding her open purse. "I had eight dollars in my wallet," she said. "Does anybody know what happened to it?"

Suddenly, a figure loomed at the window next to the door, followed by a hearty knock. It was the intimate door around the back of the house, used only by family and close friends. It was Chief Tedesco, dressed in civilian clothes.

Dad leaped to his feet and opened the door. His brothers stood and Mom descended the stairs with apprehension. As giant tentacles attacked San Francisco to jarring music, Chief Tedesco stepped inside from the rain. He shot a look of disapproval at the television, and Dad reached over and turned it off. The crackling of static electricity filled the air as the movie shrank to a dot.

"I'm glad to find you all here," the chief said. "I wanted to handle this quietly."

"We're not all here," Mom replied, primly. "Our son Rich is out with friends." Her voice rose, just a touch. "He still has some friends. We're all thankful for that."

"I'm here because there are discrepancies between some of your statements about the night of Jeffrey Talent's disappearance."

Don looked at his mother, but she kept her eyes on the chief. "Mrs. Esker, you told our officers the day we searched the Hartner home they'd been having dinner with you that night, and they left at around nine. Four officers all agree that you gave that time. Is that correct?"

After a beat, she replied, "I don't remember what I told them. It was a very upsetting experience."

Don felt proud of his mom. Her reply changed the facts from altered testimonies to murky memories, a universal human failing nobody could be faulted for and was certainly no grounds for suspicion. She probably hated the dishonesty, but Mr. Hartner was innocent, so there was no point in muddying the investigative waters with something so irrelevant.

The chief glared, and the Esker men bristled at this threat to the only woman in the house. "Think very carefully, Mrs. Esker," he replied, rich with warning. "Did the Hartners leave at nine, or an hour earlier?"

"They left at nine," Don said.

"Stay out of this, son," Chief Tedesco snapped. He turned to Dad. "Did you tell Larry Talent that the Hartner family left at eight?"

"If my wife and son say they left at nine, I'm perfectly willing to admit that I was mistaken."

"That's not what I asked."

Don raised his voice. "They left at nine."

"Mrs. Esker, you need to explain yourself in this matter."

Dad took a protective step in front of her. Tim and Randy did the same, forming a barrier. They broadened their shoulders and stuck out their chests.

The chief curled his lip and made a dismissive sound. "Mrs. Esker,

I need you to come down to the station with me." His eyes dared them all to challenge him. "If you don't come willingly, I'll call for a squad car and officers to escort you."

The chief's attempt to humiliate a husband and sons in front of their wife and mother infuriated Don. "You need an arrest warrant before you can force somebody to come with you. We can sue if you don't have one."

He wasn't sure it was true until the chief shot him a look of hatred.

"Leave my house this instant," Dad ordered.

Looking unsure, the chief didn't move. Dad said, "On Monday I'll phone you with a number for a lawyer, and any further communication will have to go through him. Now get out and never return." Tim and Randy shuffled, their fists pink and white with compressed fury.

Thrumming with anger so electric his shoulder twitched, the chief turned, giving Don a private look of screwed-up rage that shocked and amazed him. Why would a grown man direct that sort of energy at a ten-year-old boy, unless he had no one left to terrify?

The chief left, and the Esker men panted through their noses like dragon fire. Dad led Mom up the stairs and held her as she went limp with fear and relief. Tim and Randy, radiating the pride of warriors after smiting the enemy, actually shared a growl, testosterone come to life as sound.

Over the next few months, Don kept expecting one or more of them to ask why he and Mom had lied about the time the Hartners left, but they never did.

CHAPTER THIRTEEN

Pain contorted his dad's face, and Don cut a fentanyl patch in two and applied half next to the full patch on his chest. Linnette warned him specifically against cutting the patches, but she didn't explain why he shouldn't. He didn't care. He wasn't going to let his dad suffer.

After a dose of morphine, his dad nodded off. Don went to the kitchen where he made a cup of coffee with cream. It was only six in the morning, and another memo was due at the end of the week. His mom would sleep for another few hours, so it was a good time to get started. He opened his laptop and stared at the screen for a few minutes before closing it again and walking down to the family room.

He carried his coffee, sipping, looking around. The room echoed with memories. Don stood in the spot where his dad had ordered Chief Tedesco from the house, a pivotal moment for the Eskers when they'd transitioned from pitying the Tedescos for the unexplained loss of Eddie to despising them without reservation.

He glanced out the windows and drew in a breath of wonder.

Seemingly overnight, the full glory of fall foliage had burst out. The morning sun shone onto the woods out back, and the three windows framed the view like impressionist masterpieces. Stands of mid-length nannyberries and buttonbush backed by towering elms and beech and ironwoods all glowed with brilliant yellows, while a maple to the left fluffed with bright orange clouds. To the right, an oak's limbs sagged under deep purple capes herringboned with rust.

He felt something stir inside, and he realized that he'd forgotten even the memory of the long-dormant feeling now reawakening. In San Francisco, the occasional tree changed pigment to a waxy shade of autumn, a timid move amidst the spiky eternal greens of California natives, but nothing like this vast panorama of rippling colors that filled him with desperate longing sweetened with hope. A tingle bubbled back into effervescence in his chest, the fizz of possibilities for his life, and they popped and sizzled by the thousands.

Without warning, he thought, *Could I live here again?*

Flashes of Bruce's body from the previous night flipped through his mind, his chest and legs carpeted with silver-streaked dark hair, which feathered onto his back and tapered to a thick but fine moss on his ass. The rough wool of his pubic hair tangled at the base of his meaty dick, pulsating with veins. Muscled shoulders and arms flowed in rounded forms beneath a handsome face textured with late-night stubble.

Bruce was not only hot as hell, but he knew how to have sex with another man, and Don let out a grunt remembering their kisses and tugs and slaps and grips. It was unashamed and forceful, two bulls fighting for dominance, giving way before asserting control once more. The contest went on for hours, leaving them panting, exhausted and ripe. The room had smelled like a locker room.

A movement outside caught his attention, a woman setting something down next to the family room door. She looked unhappy and tired.

Careful not to spill the coffee, he opened the door. She turned at the noise, and he asked, "Can I help you?" She wore a heavy parka and tight jeans. Her brownish, curly hair was slightly damp. She looked both middle-aged and exhausted.

She gestured to a plastic bag on the ground. "Those are the food containers your mom sends across the street. I like to make sure she gets them back before she runs out. Those things can get expensive. They need to be washed, though. You must be Don."

"Yeah." He stepped outside, the cold from the cement soaking through his socks. "And you are?"

She approached and they shook hands. "Roxanne. I'm Billy's wife." He couldn't hide his surprise. "I was married to him when he had his accident, and we're still married. I live over in Greenhill."

Don had gone to Greenhill once in high school, and remembered a strange place that appeared after a long stretch of woods. Down a short but steep slope, the neighborhood rested on a large, flat clearing.

It looked as if it had been transported from the inner city, complete with liquor stores and bars. Tiny houses separated by chain link fences lined streets arranged in a tight grid. Broken-down appliances and cars on cinder blocks littered many of the small yards, where dogs prowled and barked.

Roxanne looked at his cup. "Is that coffee?"

"Would you like a cup?"

"Love it. My machine broke, and the coffee at work sucks."

"Come on in." He grabbed the plastic bag, which was stuffed like a hamster's cheeks, and led her to the kitchen. Her hard, weary expression never lightened. "Cream and sugar?"

"Lots of both."

He set them out and took a seat as she poured and stirred. "How long were you guys married before Billy's accident?"

"Five months. Just long enough to get pregnant and to have all the responsibility of making sure someone is taking care of him. I had two other boys from my first marriage, and with another on the way, I couldn't even think about having Billy in my house as an invalid. Besides, his dad wanted him back at home."

"He's probably better off with his father."

She shrugged. "Maybe, maybe not. Don't matter. I just couldn't do it, and I don't feel bad about it." She met his eyes. "You're the guy he used to be friends with? The gay one?"

He nodded with a faint smile. "What did Billy say?"

"Billy never said much of anything. But his old man told me everything about this neighborhood and all the people in it. He learned a lot being chief of police all those years." She took another sip, shaking her head. "I thought he was nice when Billy first took me to meet him, but he's as mean as a one-eyed pit bull. I learned too late that Billy took after him. Our son is afraid of Billy because of that crack on his skull, but his other kids and ex-wives were afraid of him for different reasons, and they hate his guts. I'm the only person that comes over, and I only stay long enough to pick up and drop off laundry. Two grown men and not a friend between them. What does that tell you?"

"Why did you stay married to him?"

"The state gives me disability payments as a wife and mother. Billy left me without a red cent to take care of our kid. Old man Tedesco said he had his pension, and I could have all the disability money. 'Bout the only nice thing that family ever did for me." Her face focused with a thought. "How's your dad doing?"

"It's always up and down, but I think he has a few months left. Thanks for asking."

Roxanne blinked, as if unused to gratitude. She held the cup to her mouth and closed her eyes. "This is the best coffee I've had in a while. It's nice to sit in a house drinking coffee and just have a chat. No music or Xbox or TV or boys fighting." She took another sip and drank until she drained it.

"Do you want another?"

She hesitated, but put the cup down. "I'd love it, but I gotta get to work. Maybe we should exchange phone numbers, just in case we need to get in touch for something or other. You're right across the street, but I live thirty minutes out. Snow's coming, and they don't always plow our roads right away, so I might need to get ahold of you. I've been wanting to have the number from someone in the neighborhood."

Don saw no reason to refuse, so they exchanged numbers. "Let's have coffee again sometime."

"I'd actually like that," she said. She waved above her head as she left.

Back in the kitchen, his mom was filling the sink with soapy water, wearing a flannel nightgown and slippers, her hair in curlers beneath a net. She slipped the crusty plastic containers under the bubbles.

"What are you doing up so early, Mom?"

"I heard talking and came out to see who it was." She held up a blue lid. "I'm guessing it was Roxanne."

"Why didn't you tell me Billy is still married?"

She clucked her tongue. "It's not like I was keeping it a secret. I just never thought to mention it. Do you want breakfast?"

"Not yet. Here, let me do that." He took over the washing.

"How did your date with Linnette's friend go last night?" she asked as she fixed a cup of coffee.

"It was pretty good, actually. I was sort of surprised at how well we got along."

"Why were you surprised?"

"I don't know. It's been a while since I've met a guy like him."

"What does he do for work?"

"He's developing an app for mobile devices."

"He's what?"

"Something for computers."

"Oh. Are you going to see him again?"

Fuck yes. "Yeah."

"Well, that's nice. I'm glad it worked out for you. You sure you aren't hungry? I can make some eggs and toast."

"I'm positive." The food crusted the plastic like cement, so he sank the rest beneath the soapy cloud and got more coffee. It was the perfect time to ask about the other issue on his mind. "Mom, did we ever have a Polaroid instant camera?"

She frowned. "I don't remember. I don't think so, but I suppose it's possible. I never liked the way those photos looked. They had a flatness to them, like you were taking a photo of a picture. And all those distortions. Why are you asking?"

He shrugged. "It could be pretty valuable. They're collector's items these days." He wondered if he should feel concerned how easy these little diversionary lies were getting.

"I can't remember if we ever had one," she said. "You could look. It would be in one of the bottom cupboards in the family room. I can't believe you're not hungry. When was the last time you ate?"

"I'm fine for now."

"Oh, wait," she said suddenly. "Your brother Tim had a Polaroid. That's why I remember those bad photos."

He felt a pulse of unease. "Are you sure it was Tim?"

She nodded firmly. "Yep. I remember because he sent those photos from Camp Pendleton, but he had that camera long before he enlisted. He took pictures at the football games and homecoming." She waved her hand. "All the people looked like a steamroller just ran over them. There was no depth to any of those photos." She slapped her thighs and stood. "Here, I'm going to make you some breakfast."

Don noodled with the marketing memo until early afternoon, when Bruce texted to invite him to his place for dinner that night. He laughed to himself when just sending off his acceptance prompted a swelling in his crotch.

Linnette didn't arrive for her two o'clock appointment. His mom said, "She's done this a few times. Just between the two of us, I think she's somewhat disorganized. But she is very sweet, and your dad loves her." At two fifteen, Linnette called, apologizing profusely because another client took longer than usual and she was rushing to make her next appointment.

"Okay," Don said, mildly irritated because he wanted to discuss increasing the fentanyl dosage, but it was difficult to be angry with Linnette.

At four o'clock, Don replaced the fentanyl. He gingerly pulled the transparent, sticky patches away, gritting his teeth in fear of ripping up the flesh that clung to the patch like cellophane to tape. He wondered what happens to skin when you get old, why it becomes so thin and translucent. He still recalled the shock about ten years ago when he noticed that the back of his hands looked like plastic, shiny and crinkled.

As he applied another patch and a half, his dad said, "So how's it going, Donnie? Are you able to get your work done?"

"It's been challenging, Dad. I keep getting distracted."

After a dose of morphine, Dad's eyes went soft as the fresh opiates flooded his brain. "Those fall colors sure are beautiful, aren't they?" he mumbled, looking out the window.

He followed his gaze, smiling. "Yeah, they are."

Don left in the dark. Except for those few moments with Roxanne, he hadn't been outside all day, and the crisp air felt invigorating. The number of Halloween decorations surprised him. The holiday was a week away, and giant inflatable pumpkins, witches, and ghosts, all lighted from within, swayed on lawns up and down the streets. Some yards featured elaborate scenes stalked by skeletons and ghouls, illuminated by floodlights. When Don was a kid, only pumpkins or scarecrows decorated the occasional porch, and Halloween in North Homestead was a two-day event, Charlie Brown's special followed by a rush of costumes and candy before it was driven off by the looming arrival of the serious holidays.

Bruce's wooden house, a tidy white with black trim, perched in a neat yard landscaped with tight edges and clean lines. Out back, a row of high evergreens blocked the lights and noise of the gigantic mall.

Bruce met him at the door, and they didn't make it four steps before they were in each other's arms, kissing and clutching. Don grabbed Bruce's ass and pulled him close, grinding their crotches together. They moaned and growled, sharing dirty smiles. It went on for a few minutes and threatened to last for the next several hours. Bruce pulled away and said, "Come on. Dinner will get cold."

The house looked small from the exterior, but inside had the roomy feel of a whole building for only one person. It was a minimalist home for a single man who didn't need much, with a bit of furniture in the living room that looked hardly used. An archway led to the dining room with a table piled with papers and books and sorted mail. Don also noted several neatly bundled electronics cords.

Bruce led him to a small table in the kitchen, set with salt and pepper, two plates without utensils, a couple of empty glasses, a roll of paper towels and a large bottle of sparkling water. He served lasagna and salad side by side, and handed Don a knife and fork. "Dig in," he said, pulling his chair forward from between his legs.

Don had dated lots of men unconcerned with careful displays of style and manners, and he always hoped it was a good sign of focusing on more important matters. But he knew from experience it was more likely to mean the guy was thoughtless and didn't see any reason to bother with niceties. The neat piles and bundled cords on the table suggested Bruce was a serious guy, but it was a mistake to read such details like tarot cards.

Bruce asked about his dad, and he told him about adding the extra half of a fentanyl patch. "I guess we're going to have to up the dosage. I wanted to discuss it with Linnette today, but she was running behind and had to cancel. How did you guys become friends?"

"I knew her from the hospital. I ran the IT department and Linnette's department was full of old-school nurses who hated the computer stuff. I don't blame them. They used to keep track of things with a pencil and charts. All the online forms and logins and wiki pages take a lot more time. It's more efficient on the back end with things like billing, but it's mostly just a hassle for nurses. I was down there almost every day, and we hit it off. She's a nice lady."

"I know. I liked her right away, too."

Bruce grinned. "She had sort of a crush on me. I had to tell her the facts of life, but she took it well. There's lots of single women our age who live around here, and I'm telling you if I were straight, I could have a different woman in my bed every night of the week if I wanted."

He stabbed at his salad. "I don't know why straight guys complain about finding women."

"Tell me about it," Don agreed. "And why do straight women complain about finding a man when a ton of guys are out there playing computer games by themselves night after night?"

"Maybe deep down they don't want to find each other." Bruce rubbed his chin and said, "I'm a little worried Linnette missed her appointment today. Has it happened before?"

"Not since I've been here, but my mom said it happened a few times in the past." Bruce looked very worried, and Don assured him with, "It's not a big deal. I can always speak to her tomorrow."

Bruce sighed. "I was afraid something like this might happen. I don't want you to think I'm talking behind her back, but I care about Linnette and don't want to see her get hurt again. But she spaces out and forgets things and gets in trouble with her bosses. Everybody loves her so she doesn't get fired, but they ask her to quit. It's happened a lot."

"Really? She's always been great. My dad loves her."

"Yeah, she can manage for a while, but she needs some extra TLC, and I just want you to know in case something else happens. I mean, your dad has to have good care, I'm not disputing that. But I'm asking you to cut her some slack if you can."

"Yeah, I guess so," he replied, unsure.

"You don't seem like the kind of guy to run your mouth, so I'd appreciate your discretion. Linnette asked me not to tell anyone. But I'm looking out for her, and at the same time, I feel I owe you an explanation."

"Sure," he replied, his unease growing by the moment.

"I grew up down by Akron so I didn't know anything about it, but you grew up here so you probably do. About forty years ago, there were three little boys in North Homestead that were raped and murdered. Do you remember?"

Don went rigid and held his breath. He managed a slight nod.

"The second boy, Danny Miller? The one they found behind McDonald's on Lorain Road?"

The one they found with a recorder nearby. The one whose death led to the police storming the Esker home and taking Dad away. The one whose murder also led to Rich being lowered into the ground at Memorial Park Cemetery; to Tim fleeing to the other side of the country as a Marine; to Randy's passionate embrace of evangelical Christianity. Don's heart pounded, filling his ears. He nodded again, squeezing his eyes and bracing against whatever was coming next.

"That was Linnette's little brother. She was supposed to be watching him that day. She's never gotten over the guilt."

CHAPTER FOURTEEN

1976

The Esker boys' birthdays came four months in a row. In December of 1975, Rich turned fifteen. In January of 1976, Tim turned seventeen, and in February, Randy ticked up to thirteen. Don turned eleven in March.

Don blew out his birthday candles and opened his presents early because their parents had tickets to a show downtown. It was a good sign they were going out again. Rich also left to meet up with friends.

Don, Tim, and Randy got another slice of cake and watched TV. During a "Bicentennial Moment" featuring an actress talking about the Constitution, the phone rang. Tim answered, and by his look of disgust, Don knew the caller was one of the persistent few that still harassed the family by phone. Everyone else hung up on them, but Tim was too stubborn.

After months of shouting, Tim had developed a much more effective routine. In a faux-innocent voice he said, "What's that? You want to lick the sweat off my balls? Gee, that sounds swell. What did you say? You want me and my brothers to take turns with your ass? Golly, that would be crackerjack. Oh, no, I don't think I can let you smell my farts, but I'll be glad to piss on you." Don and Randy laughed and egged him on. The callers usually gave up quickly, but Tim could go on for quite a while.

By April, rehearsals for a massive Bicentennial celebration consumed all the elementary school students in North Homestead. The city scheduled it for the last Saturday of the school year in the main park. The chief of police, a genuine American military hero, would lead the festivities at the mayor's side.

"It's stupid," Don said, sulking in the passenger seat with his arms folded while his mother drove to Sears to buy the boys' outfit of a red vest, white shirt, and blue slacks. "The only reason they're having it a month early is because school will be out on the Fourth of July."

In a surprised voice, she replied, "They just want to make sure that everyone has a chance to participate."

"People should participate because they want to, not because their school is forcing them."

"Nobody's being forced. You should be proud. You'll always remember when you helped celebrate our country's two-hundredth birthday."

"Why should I remember doing something a month early? They should have it on the Fourth of July. *I'd* come to rehearsals over the summer. If other people are too lazy to show up, that's their fault."

She exhaled loudly. "You're a very intelligent boy, Donnie. You're far more advanced than most boys your age, but you think about things too much. You risk coming across as ridiculous when you do that."

He basked in the glow of the unexpected compliment but smarted at the caution. How did she know that his greatest fear was to have people think he was ridiculous?

Flags flew from most homes. With less than three months to go, the colors of the flag were seemingly on every available surface inside and out. Don worried that all of this enthusiasm would feel stale after the Fourth of July, like the day after Christmas when the tree and decorations instantly morphed from sparkling promises of joy to droopy reminders that the festivities were over. The aftermath of the Bicentennial was bound to be worse, because people box holiday decorations for the following year. He wondered what people would do with red, white, and blue drapes, clothing, dinner plates, and shutters.

Sears had set up a whole department to make it easier for parents to buy the patriotic outfits in one place, along with rows of flags and banners and a huge array of red, white, and blue items for the home. Fife and drum played over the speakers, and banners and bunting ruffled on the walls and pillars.

At the counter, Mom's face melted with confusion when she unsnapped her wallet. "Wait a minute," she said. The sales girl, wearing a white wig and a tri-corner hat, looked annoyed as Mom rummaged through her purse.

"I'm sorry," Mom said, smiling with apology to both the girl and the people in line. "I guess I'll have to write a check."

In the parking lot, she said, "I've been coming up short on cash here and there. I just put it down to being forgetful, but I withdrew fifty dollars from the bank on Thursday, and there's only ten dollars left. I ran to the grocery store and Woolworth's and a few other places, but I couldn't have spent forty dollars in just three days."

"Maybe Dad took it."

She shook her head. "I gave your father his pin money last week. If he needed more, he wouldn't take it without telling me." She sighed. "I'll have to go over my receipts again. I've been so distracted."

Back home, Don raced to the family room. *The Wizard of Oz* was on in thirty minutes. Splayed across a chair and the sofa, Tim and Randy watched a war movie. Worried, Don asked, "What time is your movie over?"

"It's over when it ends," Tim barked, and Randy snorted.

"*The Wizard of Oz* is on at six."

Tim said, "That's a kiddie movie." With their parents in the nearby kitchen, Randy whispered, "Maybe he wants Dorothy to curtsy on his face." They laughed and slapped out a high five.

"They only show it once a year," Don argued. "You can watch war movies all the time."

Tim raised a hand, flipped it down at the wrist, and in a high-pitched lisp repeated, "They only show it once a year." Randy doubled up in snickers.

Don sat, stormy with fury, wishing they were gone. Only Rich still had friends.

The minutes crawled while his brothers kicked their legs and stared into space. By five fifty, the Americans were still in dire trouble, and they clearly wouldn't win the war by six o'clock. With five minutes to go, Tim and Randy hadn't watched for minutes, and Don flipped the dial.

His brothers sat up, outraged. Don was sickened. "You weren't even watching. You don't care about that movie, so let me watch mine."

Tim said, "Okay, watch your stupid movie." They settled in, and Don realized that they'd wanted to watch *The Wizard of Oz* all along. *What was the point of putting on such a big act just to make someone else feel bad?*

Don always thought of the beginning of the film as the necessary, boring set-up for the magic, but this year he felt an unexpected kinship with Dorothy and her life on the farm. Nobody spoke to her except to explain how she was doing something wrong, or to give her a lecture, or to tell her to get lost. When she wandered off hugging Toto, he understood the depths of her loneliness. He drew in a breath at the first notes of the song.

"Somewhere over Lorain Road…" he sang along, softly.

Randy shot up. "What did you say?"

Tim asked, "What?"

Randy bellowed, "He sang, 'somewhere over Lorain Road'!"

Tim's face filled with scornful delight. "What?"

"It's 'somewhere over *the rainbow*,' you dummy!" shouted Randy.

Don always wondered why Dorothy sang about Lorain Road, where flocks of bluebirds filled the sky. He'd decided that the street must be famous everywhere because it was so long.

His brothers got into positions to rain down mockery. Don bolted.

"What's all the shouting about?" Dad asked from the top of the stairs. Don darted past, holding back tears. Mom looked up from her checkbook and receipts at the kitchen table. "Donnie?" she asked, but he ran to his room where he slammed the door and sat on his bed, his knees drawn up and his face buried in his arms.

He cried and quivered, silent save for hollow gasps.

A little while later, a soft knock of warning came before the door opened. His brothers filed in regretfully, followed by their parents.

"Donnie, your brothers have something to say," Dad said.

"We're sorry," Tim said. "You can come back and watch your movie."

"Get out," he replied, the words broken by pumps of rage.

After some whispering and shuffling, the door closed, but someone was still in the room and sat on his bed.

"Don," his dad said, placing a hand on his shoulder. "You should always forgive someone when they ask for it. It's the classy thing to do."

"I hate them."

"You don't hate them. I can't have my children hating each other, not at a time like this." His voice tightened. "I know how hard this has been on you, everything that's happened this past year, but it's been hard on all of us. Your brothers are just lashing out because they're angry and hurt and lonely."

"They always make fun of me, even Before."

"Don, I'm counting on you to hold yourself together, even if your brothers fall apart a little bit. It would be a big help to me and your mother."

Don sniffled. The words intrigued him, numbing some of the pain.

"You're smarter than all three of your brothers put together, but you're not stronger than they are, not yet. You could be, because you have a powerful intellect. You're going to be the star of the family someday, but I need you to start acting like it right now. Sometimes we have to grow up faster than we want."

Astounded, Don wiped the snot from under his nose and smeared it on his jeans. "Do you really think I'm smart?"

His dad grinned sadly. "I know you are. You don't have any idea how much your mother and I know that."

Don felt better and returned just in time for the wicked witch's flaming exit from Munchkinland.

A few weeks later, their parents announced that they were taking a last-minute weekend getaway to Niagara Falls. They would go alone, an announcement that electrified his brothers.

"We're trusting you to be responsible while we're gone," Mom said. "Everybody has to listen to Tim. And Tim," she closed her eyes and shook her head, "you have to look after your brothers, or so help me God…"

"I promise, Mom," Tim said eagerly. "Nothing will go wrong."

They left on Friday morning. In the afternoon, the St. Anne's bus dropped off Don and Randy in front of the house. They heard Tim and Rich arguing from the driveway. Inside, they stood nose-to-nose, seething.

"You can skip seeing your friends for one weekend!" Tim shouted.

"Fuck you!" Rich shouted back. "You can't tell me what to do!"

"Yes, I can! Mom and Dad put me in charge!"

Rich reared back to mince and prance about the kitchen, flipping his hand like a lady waving her hanky. He repeated in falsetto, "Mom and Dad put me in charge! Mom and Dad put me in charge! Mom and Dad put…"

Tim charged and grabbed Rich by the torso, wrenching to take him down. Rich faltered, but braced himself with his legs wide, pummeling Tim's back. Their feet scuffed and squeaked on the linoleum, and they grunted with enraged faces.

Rich grabbed the edge of a decorative café table that Mom arranged with a frilly tablecloth and a vase of silk flowers. Tim yanked with all his might and as Rich went down, the table crashed to the floor. The vase shattered and the flowers skittered like BBs. Tim struggled to control Rich and accidentally kicked the table into a rapid spin, sending the delicate café chairs hurtling to the wall, where they bounced and tipped over.

Don and Randy watched, frozen.

On top, Tim landed a few good punches on Rich's shoulder. He pinned Rich down by a wrist and tried to flip him on his stomach, but Rich used his free arm to flail at him and managed a solid knock on Tim's head. With Tim disoriented, Rich twisted his arm free, drew back, and popped him in the eye.

Tim reared up, his hands to his face, roaring with pain. Rich kneed him in the nuts.

Tim jerked forward choking and gasping, his hands at his crotch. He looked ready to crash to his side, unconscious. Rich scrambled to his feet, but Tim rallied and grabbed the leg of a fragile café chair and smashed it against Rich's hip. It exploded, and the pieces scattered like bowling pins.

Rich winced in fury and descended on Tim, hammering his back. At the same time, he grabbed the other chair, and as he raised it over Tim's head, Don screamed, "No!"

Tim saw the chair coming for his skull. He turned away, raising both arms in defense, and it came down on his forearms. A sharp split cracked the air, and Don hoped it wasn't bone. Tim cried out.

Rich stood over Tim, swung his leg back, and landed a swift kick into their oldest brother's stomach. Tim instantly vomited a spray of bright yellow puke that skimmed past Rich's leg and splashed to the linoleum.

Rich vaulted over Tim's heaving, hunched body and slammed his way outside.

A purplish blotch shaded Tim's eye, growing worse by the minute. As they sorted the mess, Tim winced every so often and held a delicate hand against his crotch. The smooth linoleum made it easy, if disgusting, to clean the vomit. The shattered chairs and vase were beyond repair, and they bagged the pieces to throw away. They put the flowers on the table and set it in place, and Don thought it looked like a grave. Afterward, they sat at the kitchen table. Nobody wanted the meals Mom left in the refrigerator: chili and noodles, chicken stew, spaghetti and meatballs.

It was dark when Tim asked, "Where do you think Rich went?" The blotch around his eye had deepened to dark purple, sinking into black, crawling with wormy veins.

Randy said, "You know that friend of his? Dwayne? A couple of times I heard Dwayne tell Rich to meet him at the abandoned house."

"I promised Mom and Dad I would make sure you guys are safe," Tim said. "I should go get him."

"Rich won't do what you tell him," Don said. "Even if he's there, he won't come home with you."

"But I can make sure he's okay." He pushed himself to his feet with a grimace. "You guys stay here."

"Let us go with you," Don suggested. "So we can stay together." Randy agreed. Tim grabbed a flashlight, and they set off.

The abandoned house sat on the other side of the cornfield. In the moonlight, they picked across the earth, softened from plowing, taking giant steps to hit only furrows and not disturb the seedling corn. Don remembered the searches for Eddie Tedesco, and his excitement at the thought of being the champion to find him in this field. That was almost a year ago, yet it seemed like a million years had passed, or that it happened to somebody else.

The abandoned house materialized in the dark, a two-story hulk backed by a high black tree line that bristled with the herky-jerky darts of barn bats. Don hated the house and hadn't been inside in years. He remembered the windows were empty and crude graffiti covered the walls. Cigarette butts and empty bottles littered the floors around sooty fire spots. The stairs that led to the top floor yawned with a terrifying black gap of three steps that fell straight to the basement. His brothers had jumped over the hole with confidence, but it took Don ages to work up the courage. The reverse jump was even scarier.

As they approached, a lonely owl hooted out a rapid lyrical refrain that sounded like, "Who cooks for you all? Who cooks for you all?" Crickets sang and frogs belched.

When they neared a field of rubble that encircled the house, Tim stopped. "Listen," he whispered.

Inside, indistinct voices murmured. Lighters flicked on and burned steadily before blinking out.

"Walk quietly," Tim said. "Don't step on anything."

It was impossible to not step on anything. Debris crunched underfoot, the remains of glass and doorframes and plywood, thrown outside and trampled to bits over the years. They crept to the front, halting when the voices went silent, moving on when the droning conversations resumed.

They approached from the side, inched around the corner and ducked below the low line of the porch. The voices became clearer, and a man said, "Let me tell you something I learned the hard way. Don't mess with a girl like that unless you want your dick to shrivel up and fall off." Dirty chuckles followed.

He sounded far too old to be hanging out with his fifteen-year-old brother. *Rich can't be here*, Don thought, *not with that man.*

Two silhouettes emerged from the house and sat on the top step of the porch. He held his breath.

"Here, I'll do it." Don recognized the voice of Rich's friend Dwayne, who flipped open a silver lighter, scratched it to life, and held it with his teeth, squinting against the flame. He slapped the other guy's arm before lifting and flicking a glass tube. Dwayne bent down with intense concentration. After a moment, the other guy sighed and slumped, while Dwayne unwrapped a cord from his bicep.

"Who cooks for you all? Who cooks for you all?"

Dwayne plucked the lighter from his mouth and snapped it shut. "That's some excellent shit," he said in a sultry voice.

"I only get the best," the older man said, emerging from the doorway. His dark form seemed heavy with malevolence, and Don despised him.

Tim stood and turned on the flashlight. The beam caught the man fully in the face. He was at least twenty-five years old, and his forehead and chin protruded, scrunching his features. Light, scraggly hair surrounded his face. He smiled with dark approval at Dwayne and the other guy. Oddly, it took him a moment to react to the light, and he went frantic.

"What the…" Dwayne said, and Tim aimed the flashlight at him.

Don knew the other guy was Rich before he turned. His brother rose unsteadily. He wrapped his arms about the rotting support beam, weaving, and blinked rapidly into the light. He looked different, his face droopy and expressionless.

The flashlight set off a flurry of half shouts inside the house, followed by a stumbling stampede. Uncoordinated bodies fell into walls as they tumbled out the back door. The older man disappeared inside and Dwayne tried to follow, but he tripped and scrambled across the porch like he was trying to swim, kicking back bits of debris.

Tim marched up and pulled Rich away. Don caught a flash of Rich's arm in the beam, and a jagged line of blood startled him. "Come on," Tim said. He sounded more sorrowful than angry. Rich offered feeble resistance, slipping and stumbling from the post.

Tim turned off the flashlight and they stalked away. Voices babbled in the darkness beyond the house. When they were a good distance into the cornfield, defiant shouts echoed across the expanse. Far off, the owl still asked, "Who cooks for you all? Who cooks for you all?"

Rich flopped about, but they kept him upright and pulled him along. Don and Randy took turns following, to reset the seedlings that Rich kicked and stomped.

Back home, Tim sat Rich in the kitchen and he wilted until his cheek lay flat against the table. He drooled and stared vacantly. Don shared a terrified look with Randy.

Tim, his bruised eye still a shocking sight, filled a glass with water and set it next to Rich. "Drink something," he ordered, but Rich didn't move.

Tim dampened a paper towel and lifted Rich's arm to clean the blood, smeared from the efforts to keep him upright. Tim froze. Two faint but distinct brown lines entered blue veins, in contrast to the fresh red mark. Tim cleaned the arm and plopped down.

"Goddamn it, Rich," he said.

"Is it dope?" Randy asked fearfully. Tim nodded.

"Dope is for dopes." Don had assumed the posters about town warned of drugs, but he wasn't sure. "What's dope?"

"Heroin." Randy's voice shook.

Don was stunned. He knew that local kids smoked pot and drank beer, but heroin was something from distant slums, as alien to life in

North Homestead as riots and hookers and desolate brick alleys strewn with filth.

Hours later, Tim woke Don and Randy in the dark.

"Those guys from the abandoned house are creeping around in the backyard," Tim whispered. Randy squeaked in terror, and Don felt a chill. Tim went on, "We need to make sure they don't try to break in. All the doors are locked."

They crouched at the window until a movement drew their attention. In a few minutes, the moonlight illuminated Dwayne and the creepy older guy along with a third person. They approached slowly, stooping. Randy made a strangled sound of fear.

Don felt searing hatred for a man who spent his nights taking drugs and talking dirty with teenagers ten years younger. He was ridiculous and stupid, and coming here was proof. The air was cool and the windows shut. How could they hope to wake only Rich, and for what purpose?

His fear vanished, and he thought up a plan that he shared with his brothers. Randy objected, but Don said, "They're just boneheads. They don't know what they're doing or why they're doing it. It makes no sense to come here. It's not like we kidnapped Rich. *He lives here!*"

His scornful tone persuaded Randy, and they gathered five flashlights and crept out the front door, Tim and Don carrying two each. In their bare feet, they raced lightly to the side of the house.

At the corner, Tim whispered, "Ready? One, two, three."

They flicked on the flashlights, waved them about and tore around the corner roaring as loudly as they could.

The intruders bumped in an aimless huddle beneath the window, looking up stupidly as if trying to figure out what to do next. As the brothers charged, they yelped and drew back in fear, turning tail and racing off unsteadily. After the boneheads vanished into the dark, Don and his brothers returned to the house with pride and elation, laughing as they shared their impressions of the shock on their faces.

Mom called in the morning, and Tim said, "Yeah, everything's fine, Mom. I swear." He caught Don's eyes and looked away.

An hour later, Rich stumbled into the kitchen. Randy left the room in silent fury. Rich seemed unfocused until he got a look at Tim. "Holy shit. Did I do that to your face?"

"Fuck you, junkie."

Rich ran his fingers through his hair, tottering like a tree in the chaotic wind before a thunderstorm. "Man, what the hell happened last night?"

"We found you at the abandoned house. Your friend Dwayne was shooting dope in your arm. We brought you home, but they followed us and we had to run them off at three o'clock in the morning."

"Holy shit," Rich said, giggling.

"It's not funny," Don snapped.

"We're going to have to tell Mom and Dad. I wouldn't be surprised if one of them drops dead. It's not like they haven't been through enough already."

In placating tones, Rich said, "You don't have to tell them. I smoked a couple of times in the past, but it was my first time shooting up, and I didn't like it." He was trying too hard to sound convincing, and Don didn't believe him. "I swear I'm not going to do it again. I only did it once."

"You have three needle marks!" Tim yelled.

Rich hid the underside of his arm at his belly. He spluttered until he managed, "We shot up three times last night, but it was still the first time I used a needle." Again, Don knew he was lying. "I'm not a junkie. I can give it up it whenever I want. I already decided to stop, but you made me so mad I went out and did it one last time."

At hearing "one last time," Tim looked somewhat placated. "What are we going to tell them about my eye and the café chairs?"

"I'll say I accidentally tripped you and that you fell into the table. You broke the chairs and busted your eye at the same time, but it was all my fault."

Don thought the story preposterous, but Tim nodded, apparently satisfied Rich would take the blame.

"Have you been stealing money from Mom's purse?" Don asked.

Tim went still. Rich stared blankly until he smiled and asked, "Why would I do that?" The breakfast stuff was on the table, and Rich pulled a bowl into place and poured cereal.

Don went cold when he spotted a fourth, fresh needle mark spearing his brother's arm, with a smear of blood at the puncture wound.

CHAPTER FIFTEEN

Linnette looked at Don the moment she stepped inside the kitchen. "I heard you and Bruce hit it off!"

He smiled instead of shrugging because he didn't want to let her down so quickly. "Yeah, he's a great guy."

"Are you going to see each other again?"

"We haven't made any plans yet, but yeah, probably."

Linnette chatted happily about the way Bruce was so patient and considerate when they worked together at the hospital. "All the nurses thought he was a stud, and nobody could figure out why he wasn't interested in any of them. Some of those gals were shameless. They threw themselves at him like teenagers at a drive-in. When we started hanging out, they couldn't believe it." She laughed. "I had them going for a while. You could tell they were thinking that Bruce was nuts to choose dumpy old me."

Don wondered if he should intercept such a harsh self-description, but Linnette went on with a rapid monologue about Bruce, building him up as a model of manly virtues.

He pretended to listen while he studied her face for a clue that she knew that his dad was briefly a suspect in her brother's murder. How could she not recognize his name? Maybe she was too young at the time and nobody ever told her.

She stopped. "You look like you want to say something. Is it about your dad?"

He told her about adding the extra half of the fentanyl patch. "I know you told me not to cut them, but I didn't know what to do. One patch wasn't enough anymore."

She looked concerned. "We tell people not to cut them because we have to keep track of every one. It's the law. People cut them up and suck on them. The drug users call them chiclets. But if you still have the pieces, I can report that everything is accounted for, and we can discuss a higher dose."

Don found all the scraps in the trash, and Linnette seemed relieved as she took notes next to the bed. "Okay," she said, turning to his dad, reaching out to pat and rub his arm, "and how are you feeling?"

Dad's mood was not good. His impending death angered him at some times and depressed him at others. "How do you think I'm feeling? I have cancer and I'm dying."

"I know, I know." Linnette was more distinct, less bubbly, dialing it down to balance his mood at his level. She was a natural. "But in the meantime, we want to keep you comfortable. Your son thinks you need a higher dosage for your patches. What do you think?"

"I haven't been feeling any more pain."

"Dad, I've been putting on the extra half patch, remember?"

His dad turned away.

"Well, since Don has been increasing the dosage on his own, let's ask the doctor if we can jump ahead and double it. It'll take a few days to get used to, just like the last time."

"I didn't like it those first few days. I felt like I was in a coma."

"But this way, you'll adjust before you need so much medicine, and you'll have a longer stretch without pain before we have to increase it again. Does that sound okay?" When he didn't respond, she stood and said, "Well, Rob, I'm going to take off now. I'll need to get the doctor's approval, but I don't think it will be a problem. I'll send the medical van with the new patches tonight. And I'll check in with Don tomorrow to see how you're doing."

His dad remained silent. "Dad, Linnette is leaving. Aren't you going to say good-bye?"

Dad huffed. "I need my big-shot son to tell me how to behave?"

"You taught me my manners, Dad."

"Good-bye, Linnette," he muttered.

In the hallway, she said, "Don't be upset for my sake. I'm used to it, believe me. There's no telling when a mood like this might hit. He'll get over it soon. He's got a naturally good disposition."

Again, Don searched her face for any hint she knew about Rob Esker's past, but he saw nothing beyond concern and understanding, and she soon left.

Don listened to her car pull away, and he realized the subject was too dangerous to ignore. He had to ask if she knew, for her sake as well as his dad's. What if she learned near the end and flipped? Don wouldn't let his dad go to his death with those old accusations from a new mouth ringing in his ears.

Don considered calling the hospice and asking for a new nurse, but how would he explain that to everyone, including Bruce, who was already worried that she might lose another job?

"Jesus," he said to himself. He wondered if he would ever shake off the summer of 1975.

He returned to his father, who was still moody.

"Dad, can I talk to you about something?"

"I'm not in the mood for a lecture."

"That's good, because I'm not in the mood to deliver one. I want to know if the police confiscated a Polaroid instant camera when they searched our house."

His head snapped around. "Why?"

"I don't want to get into that right now. You're just going to have to trust me."

"How can you have any interest in something like that without it having an impact on me?"

"Let me quote something you might recall: 'Sometimes the best thing you can do is keep a secret from someone.'"

"You've got to be kidding me. You were a teenager when I said that."

"If it's true for a teenager, it's true for a man in his eighties. That's why I remembered it. It took me a long time to understand what you meant, but now I do. This is your big-shot son speaking. The star of the family. I know what I'm doing."

His dad shook his head. "Why did you have to ask me this when I'm in such a bad mood already?"

"I didn't want to ruin a good mood. I've been waiting for you to be a sourpuss for days." Don grinned, and his dad responded with a reluctant smile. "Come on, Dad. Tell me."

After a few moments, he said, "Yeah, they asked me if I had a Polaroid instant. I told them the truth, that I'd never owned one in my life." He sighed. "But…"

"But what?"

"Well, my mind was spinning like a top during that interrogation. I didn't remember until afterward that Tim had one. Not that it mattered, of course. But after I remembered, I asked your brother if he still had it. He said he lost it months before, and he was afraid to tell me because I gave him the money. He said he was going to buy a new one with his own money."

"Do you know why they asked about a camera?"

"Yeah. I knew a couple of the fellas on the force. One guy, name of Chris O'Donnell, we were golf buddies until… Well, anyway, I saw him a few years later. He wasn't on the force any longer, and he sounded pretty bitter about it. He said he felt bad about how they treated me. I asked about the Polaroid camera, and he said they never released the information to the public, but they found some fresh contact papers alongside those boys, like the killer took pictures…"

Once again, the envelope stuffed with Polaroid photos on Hank Swoboda's table flashed in Don's mind, but his pulse raced for a different reason. A resentful ex-cop might be ready to reveal a trove of inside information. "Do you know where Chris O'Donnell is today?"

"I don't want you bugging people with this stuff, Don. I don't want you running all over town stirring it all up again."

"Just tell me where he is. You're going to have to trust me."

His dad gave a long sigh. "He ran security at the mall for years. I heard that he was living in that retirement home. The Villas. I don't even know if he's still alive."

A few hours later, the paramedic arrived with the stronger fentanyl patches. Don applied one and gave his dad a dose of morphine.

Bruce texted to ask about his plans for the evening. Don put the phone facedown on the table. He leaned forward, his fingers locked. All those years, all those men. He never hid his family's true story from any of them, any more than he kept it a secret from store clerks or waiters. Back when he worked in an office, his coworkers never knew. Good friends in San Francisco never asked anything that required full disclosure. Why would they? Gay friends especially understand privacy and are tactful about the past.

After decades of easy silence, he'd finally met a guy who filled his mind and raced in his imagination, and after two dates, he had to tell him everything. The connection with Linnette was too close, the stories too entwined and the need to find the killer before his dad died too urgent. The scale of the unfairness was so darkly comic he wanted to defy it on principle alone. Say nothing, delay the fallout and hope for the best. He thought of Rich and put a hand to his forehead with a frustrated groan.

Don had no experience with potential spouses' reactions to dead boys and horrific accusations. He assumed Tim and Randy told their wives and kids at some point, but nobody ever mentioned it, and his brothers had the luxury of time and preparation. Don had a text about tonight that needed a response.

He picked up his phone. After thinking a minute or two, he turned it off.

Randy stopped by for dinner, and after they ate and cleaned up, their mom filled two containers with beef and gravy and sealed them with blue lids, leaving them on the counter.

Don said, "I'm not sure I'm up to delivering food to Chief Tedesco tonight."

"Then throw them against his house."

Don snorted. "Don't tempt me."

"What's wrong? You've been acting like a zombie since I got here. Someone busting your balls?"

He kept it vague. "I met this guy that I'm interested in, but on our second date he blew it to smithereens. He didn't know he was doing it. But I'm worried that the only guy I've met in years I'm really attracted to screwed it up before we even had a chance."

"What happened?"

He couldn't tell Randy the truth about Linnette. His brother didn't need to know, at least not yet. "It's too complicated to explain, but it wasn't his fault. I just wish it hadn't happened. I really like this guy."

"Sorry, bro." Randy sounded sympathetic. "If it helps, it's way better for this stuff to happen before you invest too much time. Trust me."

Like all of them, Randy's life held wide blanks he never discussed except in the most general terms. Don decided to take a chance. "If you don't want to talk about it, I understand. But what happened with you and Renee?"

Randy sucked in his lips. "I don't like talking about it, but I'll tell you this one time. Maybe it will help you, I don't know. But do you remember how all that Jesus stuff brought me and Renee together? We went through that religious phase, and then we hung on to each other after we stopped believing. I thought we were in sync, but it turned out she never got over what happened in Colorado. By the time I found out, Julie was already five years old and I couldn't leave my daughter alone with a bitch like Renee. No way."

Don didn't understand. "By the time you found out what?"

"You know all that yoga and scent therapy and guided meditation Renee did to relax? She was popping Xanax and Ativan and Valium the whole time. She was numbing herself so she didn't have to think about Haywood Ministries, and how much she hated me for dragging her into that."

"Was the ministry that bad?"

Randy went grave. "When we got those jobs as prayer counselors, it was a dream come true, praying with callers and spreading the message of Jesus through the Reverend Jimmy Haywood. Renee was iffy because the pay was shit and she wanted to start a family, but I told her God arranged it and she had to be a submissive wife. We moved to Colorado so fast I left skid marks all the way to Kansas." He shook his head. "I was so naive."

"You guys always said you quit Haywood Ministries because it wasn't right for you."

Randy chuckled without humor. "It wasn't, in the same way that herpes isn't right for anybody. Prayer counselors, my ass. We spent almost a year being browbeaten into selling Haywood's shitty books and shitty tapes and shitty videos. Every morning they'd list the inventory they wanted to unload, and you had to steer the callers into buying that crap. These lonely people would call, pouring their hearts out, babies screaming in the background. They were desperate to talk to somebody about their problems, but there was this huge sign on the wall that said, 'You aren't a trained therapist.' You had to take their petitions and move right on to these scripted sales pitches." He made a sound of disgust.

"What's a petition?"

"Something the callers wanted Haywood to pray for. He said on TV he personally prayed over the petitions, but they would just throw them away, so you stopped writing them down. It made you as cold as ice. You'd get mad and hang up on little old ladies because they always wanted to send a check, and that didn't help your quotas. If someone had a heavy accent or was crying too hard to speak, you knew the sale would take too long so you'd hit the Next button. You had to protect your dollars-per-minute ratios." He crinkled his nose. "Haywood's wife was there almost every day pitching a fit about the numbers. The people that ran the prayer center were terrified of her. They were the meanest bunch of self-hating hypocrites you ever saw, and Renee and I were becoming just like them."

Don was floored, but he had some wisdom to share about shame of this sort, all-consuming but hidden so that nobody else will ever see, like an addict's stash. "You're not responsible for Haywood's dishonesty."

Randy raised his voice. "I uprooted our lives and moved us halfway across the country for a miserable telemarketing job you can get anywhere. It was like moving there to work at a McDonald's, except that would probably have paid better. I got shown up as a gullible fool. Want to guess how I felt, and how she looked at me after that?"

"I'm just saying that you were as much of a victim as the callers you hung up on."

"Except that I dragged Renee into it. She wasn't a fan of Jimmy Haywood when we met. I was so smug and told her I couldn't marry a girl who didn't believe he was God's messenger. She fell for him hook, line, and sinker. Our marriage was already broken beyond repair on our wedding day, but I didn't have a clue. When it all fell apart, she didn't have the experience our family had with clawing your way back from destruction."

Randy looked exhausted by the brutal memories, and although Don had a million questions about Haywood Ministries, he said, "All of that happened in the eighties. It can't be the reason you broke up with Renee only six months ago."

"Oh, yes, it can. It started the pattern of blaming and hating me for everything. After a while, all I could do was hate her back." Randy looked up. "I'm telling you all of this because if you meet someone, and a fundamental issue splits you apart, you are fucking lucky to spot it early on."

"It doesn't feel lucky."

"Let me tell you, little brother," Randy said, rising and stretching, "you see most of your lucky moments and your mistakes in the rearview mirror."

The next morning after cleaning the breakfast dishes, Don tried to start work on the memo that was due in a few days, but he couldn't concentrate.

Bruce sent a text saying he was sorry he hadn't heard from him last night but understood Don was busy. He asked if they could get together soon. Not wanting to accept or refuse, Don ignored it. He was anxious to feel forward momentum on something, so he made a call to Chris O'Donnell at the retirement center. The ex-cop agreed to meet with him.

The three-story buildings of the Villas Retirement Community scattered across the green field of an old golf course. At the base of each grew a solid line of burning bushes, so named because their standard, glossy green leaves burned fiery scarlet in the fall, like a thick streak of lipstick.

Inside the main building, Don spotted the administrative offices down a hall tiled in soft brown marble. He checked in at the counter and rode the elevator to the third floor. When the doors opened, a thin man waited against the far wall in a wheelchair with a curious and expectant look. An oxygen tank hung to the side, connected to a mask in his lap. His face sagged, his skin gray.

"Chris O'Donnell?"

"Are you Rob Esker's boy?" he asked, his voice hissy and strained by emphysema.

"Yes. Thanks for seeing me."

Chris twisted a knob at his fingertips, spinning the wheelchair about and waving for Don to follow. Don walked a step behind until they reached a door with his name in a removable slot and an oxygen warning sign.

The unit was roomy and comfortable, with a view out back where little cottages in the same color scheme lined landscaped walkways.

"Mr. O'Donnell—"

"Call me Chris." He lost his voice, lifted the mask, and took a deep breath.

"Okay, Chris, I'm here because my dad is dying."

"Aren't we all?" His chuckle set off a paralyzing spell of coughing. His face flamed bright red. He scrambled for the mask, holding it tight over his nose and mouth. Don forced himself not to cringe. He hated to watch helplessly while someone strained to breathe, and yet to keep speaking seemed even worse. Mercifully, the cough started to fade. Chris's eyes drooped with relief, but several moments passed before he could talk.

"Sorry about that," he whispered, saving the air in his tattered lungs. "I know it sounds scary, but I'm used to those fits by now. Just don't say anything to make me laugh." Up went the mask again.

"Well, again, I'm trying to give my dad some peace before he dies, and I'd appreciate anything you can tell me."

"I know what you mean. Those little boys. Your dad wasn't guilty and everyone knew it. I told Chief Tedesco. Lots of the guys did." Up went the mask.

Don saw his chance to forge an alliance with Chris. "My entire family hated Chief Tedesco. My dad said you quit the force..." He stopped, leaving the invitation to complain hanging wide open.

Chris charged right through. "I can't say I hated the chief, but I didn't respect him. I was a pretty good cop. I had my eye on being chief one day, and I made no bones about it." Mask again, with a finger to keep Don on hold so he could finish. "Out of the blue, Tedesco promoted a guy named Ladmore to deputy chief. Nobody could believe it. I never went in for worshiping Tedesco for being a Navy SEAL, but a lot of the guys did, and it was a shock."

Don remembered Ladmore sitting in his kitchen, and his shock at Don's admission that he'd had a crush on Hank. "Is that why you quit?"

He nodded. "Most of the guys couldn't stand Ladmore. He had no instinct for police work, and he wasn't good in the community. We had lots of calls from parents about his behavior toward their teenage daughters. Some pretty vile stuff." Mask. "But Ladmore was lucky because his uncle was a big shot in the Navy, a four-star admiral or something, and there was a lot of talk that Tedesco owed the admiral a favor from his SEAL days. That was the only reason anyone could think of." Mask. "That's why I quit. I knew I'd never be chief, so why stay?"

"Why didn't the chief listen to you when you told him my dad wasn't guilty?"

"He made a mess of that investigation because his own son was missing, and he was too close to the case. It would never fly today, but at the time, it seemed perfectly natural he should lead it. On top of that, the community was in a full-scale panic, and we were all feeling enormous pressure." Mask. "Your dad had a good alibi, because he was working late the night Danny Miller vanished, and the cleaning crew saw him. They couldn't remember the time, but it was still solid. The chief didn't even ask for an alibi until after he brought him in for questioning and executed the search warrant. In normal circumstances that would never happen, but nothing was normal about it." Mask. "Your dad should have sued, but those were different times."

"I've learned a couple of things I never knew," Don said. "The two boys they found weren't raped, and it looks like the murderer took Polaroid instant photos of the bodies. Can you confirm that?"

Chris looked surprised. "We never made that public, but yes, both are true."

The details seemed in conflict. The photos argued for a serial killer who kept mementos of his crimes to savor later, but the absence of sexual assault still bothered Don. "Doesn't the lack of rape suggest the motive wasn't sexual?"

"No," Chris said, clearly taken aback. "The killer was a classic predatory sexual psychopath. Those boys were naked and had no connection to each other. They went to the same school, but that was just a function of geography. They weren't in the same grade and they didn't know each other." Mask. "There was no other possible motive."

"I know that not all sexual psychopaths rape their victims, but the vast majority of them sexually assault them in some way."

"He did. You're getting confused because you're misreading the evidence. You have to remember that the violence combined with the power over the victim provide most of the sexual stimulation, not the act of sex itself. He didn't rape them almost certainly because he was a teenager or a young adult, and they were his first victims."

Fearing the answer, Don asked, "How do you know it means that?"

"He got too excited and climaxed spontaneously while he was killing them. That lack of control is the signature of an immature offender. It sometimes happens with young rapists, too. He took photos of the bodies and kept the clothing as souvenirs. It's a textbook case."

Don couldn't remember if he ever knew the clothes were missing. "Is there anything else you can tell me, any clues that weren't released?"

His eyes filled with understanding. "If you're trying to solve those murders, it's impossible. I spent a lot of time over the years thinking about everything that went wrong. It was chaos. Evidence was mishandled and lost. The crimes scenes weren't secured properly, even for the primitive forensics of the day." Mask. "We were overwhelmed, but the chief refused outside offers of help. The county sheriff was very eager to pitch in. They almost forced their way into it, if I remember correctly. Most of the guys on the force backed Tedesco to the hilt. I thought it was crazy. We needed all the help we could get." Mask. "Even then, I knew it was misguided machismo, and it let a very dangerous killer go free."

"Is there someone you personally suspected of being the killer?"

"No. We never got close. It was a teenager from the neighborhood, but any chance of identifying him was lost back in 1975. He must have moved and started killing little boys somewhere else. I'm willing to bet he's serving a life sentence right now, or he was executed. Whatever happened to him, he got away with it here."

"Is there more evidence I don't know about? Something from the crime scenes?"

"There may be a genuine clue somewhere in those evidence boxes that would've led straight to him, something modern forensics could uncover, but there's no way to connect it to one individual any longer." Mask. "But most of the stuff we collected was just the normal trash you find in the woods. Does any of it mean anything?" He raised his hands. "Who knows?"

"So you found nothing out of the ordinary?"

He shook his head, but a sudden memory stopped him. "Well, one thing surprised us, but it never led to anything. We found it near Jeffrey Talent's body, the boy in the woods between the Golden Tee and that church. It really jumped out because they were highly regulated at the time."

"What was it?"

"A hypodermic needle. You needed a prescription to get one, and illegal ones were expensive. It was an IV drug addict's most prized possession, just about the only thing they cared for and looked after. You'd never see them just lying around. It was interesting, but it went nowhere." Mask.

CHAPTER SIXTEEN

1976

Don started fifth grade in the fall of 1976, more than a year after the murders. The shock had faded. Parents let the strict rules slide, and sometimes Don spotted groups of younger teenagers wandering by themselves, but it was still rare to see anyone but an adult out alone.

The kids at St. Anne's had isolated him last year, and they didn't forget over the summer. He knew they never would. The stench would follow him, because wherever he went kids from St. Anne's would be there to tell everyone else. Comments were bad, but also infrequent. He managed the silence easily, knowing his classmates were ignorant.

Events in late October shattered this static unhappiness, when an eight-year-old boy disappeared from a bleak, windswept Cleveland neighborhood, and his mother and stepfather went on TV to plead for his return. Their pastor and neighbors gathered for a chilly candlelight prayer service outside the home, and reporters solemnly wondered if the disappearance was connected to the killings in North Homestead last summer. Don's family watched the news in sickened silence. Their dad was home the night the boy went missing. The Cleveland police never contacted him, but they knew it wouldn't matter, and it didn't. "Where was your dad?" kids whispered in the halls and cafeteria. He showed no emotion, but each comment felt like a slap.

For two days, the whereabouts of the boy dominated the local media, until police noticed the fireplace in the boy's home blazed constantly. They arrested the mother and stepfather after finding little charred bones among the ashes. The morning after the arrests, when Don took a seat on the bus, a girl angrily asked, "Did they ever check your fireplace?"

She was one of those girls often described as popular even though most kids hated her, and Don replied, "When you go missing, I'll make sure they check all the fireplaces in the neighborhood." She looked shocked someone of Don's lowly stature would stand up to her, but soon her eyes watered and she scrunched her face up, accusing him of cruelty. He marveled that she expected him to feel bad.

In November, the first quarter report cards arrived. Don's grades remained on top, but all three of his brothers' dropped. Rich's report card was the worst.

"You got four Fs and two Ds!" Mom shrieked. "How could that happen?"

Rich giggled, but stopped when nobody else found it funny. His eyes went wide and stupid. Don checked Rich's arms for needle marks at every opportunity, but to his relief he never saw any.

"I'll do better next time," Rich said. "I haven't been cutting classes or anything."

Mom said she was tired of his promises. "Your grades dropped last spring, and you said you'd do better, but it's clear that our trust was misplaced. You've been very irresponsible lately, losing so many of your belongings, like those new tennis shoes and your jacket. I've been patient, especially because you've been sick so often, but enough is enough." She swiped her hand low. "You're grounded. You are not going out with any of your friends until your grades improve on the next report card. And I'm going to meet with your teachers to find out what they have to say."

Rich seemed untroubled and compliant, but the next morning his bed was empty. Tim said he probably slipped out the window in the middle of the night.

"Is his book bag still in your room?" Mom asked.

"Yeah."

The Eskers sat dumbfounded in the kitchen, breakfast stuff strewn across the table.

"Should we call the police?" Don asked, and the silence thickened. He realized his parents had already run the awkward scenario through their minds. Call a department run by Chief Tedesco? To report a missing boy?

"If we haven't heard anything in an hour, we'll call," Mom said quietly. "But first let's see if we can guess where he might be. Does anyone know Dwayne's telephone number?"

Dwayne never came over anymore. Rich always left to meet him.

Tim and Randy didn't speak, and Don knew it was up to him. "He might be at the abandoned house," he suggested. Rich had made it impossible to keep the secrets of that weekend any longer.

Six months ago, before their parents returned from Niagara Falls, Tim extracted many elaborate promises from Rich that he was done with dope. Mom and Dad went ballistic at the broken café chairs and Tim's black eye, never believing the unlikely story that Rich accidentally tripped Tim. They sniffed out the battle but nothing else. Don decided to share his suspicions that Rich was stealing money from Mom's purse, but only if she mentioned the subject again, and she never did.

"Why would he be at the abandoned house?" Dad asked.

Don glanced at Tim, who squirmed nervously. Randy scrunched up.

"He sometimes goes there to take heroin," Don said.

The shock wave boomed across the room, and there it was again, this time on the faces of his parents: the untroubled serenity of the top of a mushroom cloud.

"He promised he would stop," Tim said.

"He told us he didn't like it anymore," Randy added.

Dad stood slack-jawed, while Mom looked at them in turn. "You all knew and didn't tell us?" she asked softly.

Don winced. He should have spoken up months ago. Why was it so clear only on the other side of the revelation?

Don braced for fury and pandemonium, but his parents reacted with bottomless fear, which was far worse. Mom sank to a chair, speechless. Dad, dressed in a business suit, grabbed his keys from the hook and said, "I can't remember exactly how to get to that abandoned house. Isn't it across the cornfield?"

"I'll go with you," Tim said. "If you park on Cook, you just have to walk through some woods, but it's not far." Dad gave him a strange look but nodded, and Tim followed him out the door.

The car pulled away, and Mom was eerily calm. "Do you know how much he takes?"

Don and Randy said, "No."

"How long has he been taking it?"

"We found out the weekend you guys went to Niagara Falls," Don said. "He was taking it before then, but I don't know for how long."

"He promised he would stop," Randy said desperately. "He swore over and over again he wasn't a junkie."

"Drug addicts always say that," she replied as if relaying an interesting fact in a regular conversation. "Kenny Dister down the street was a heroin addict when he came home from Vietnam, and he couldn't give it up and then…" She swallowed and her voice began, at last, to waver. "His mother became very outspoken about drugs and gave a talk at the Old Town Hall. I went just because I felt so sorry for her. It never crossed my mind…" She stood abruptly, heading for the phone. She shook as she flipped open the phonebook. The more precise task of searching through the thin pages defeated her. "Donnie, look her up for me."

He found the number and dialed, handing over the receiver. Don heard a thin, electronic "Hello?" on the other end and his mom straightened. "Yes, hello Mrs. Dister, this is Jenny Esker up the street. I'm sorry to disturb you so early, but you said that anyone could call you at any time about…" Heavy breaths followed by heaves swallowed her voice, and she withered to the chair.

Don took the phone. Alarmed, Mrs. Dister asked, "Jenny, is everything all right?" Don gave a brief account of the situation, and Mrs. Dister said she was on her way. She arrived minutes later, her eyes deep with concern, her gray hair disheveled, and her tracksuit askew as if pulled on distractedly. She went right to his mom, who couldn't look up or speak.

Don answered Mrs. Dister's questions: Rich would turn sixteen in a few weeks. Yes, he was injecting. For at least six months, but probably longer. Yes, he had a number of bad colds and flus the past few months. No, they never lasted long. They didn't know where he was, but their dad and brother were out looking for him.

Don heard the rumble of the St. Anne's bus as it slowed in front of the house before driving off.

"The first thing we need to do is get him into a treatment facility," Mrs. Dister said. She dialed a number by heart. "Hello Matt, this is Eileen. I have an emergency here, and I need a bed." She listened for a moment. "It can't wait that long. I need to call in a few favors here." Soon she was discussing details, and she thanked Matt and hung up. "Don't worry about the expense," she said softly, rubbing Mom's shoulders. "It's run by the state, and it doesn't cost anything."

Dad and Tim returned, holding Rich between them. Dad's shirttail hung loose, the rest of his suit rumpled and dirtied. Tim was similarly pulled apart. Rich shook and sniffled. Mom burst into tears.

Mrs. Dister asked Rich, "When did you last use?" Rich snarled it was none of her business. Unfazed, she asked, "How many hits of smack do you shoot a day?"

"Four. Sometimes five." She nodded and instructed them to put Rich to bed, but someone should stay with him.

When Dad returned to the kitchen, Mrs. Dister explained to him that she was here to help. "I reserved a bed for him in treatment. It will be free in a few hours. We're very fortunate that they have space." Don noted with admiration that she skipped the chance to boast about pulling strings. "I'll go with you to introduce you to the staff and help you through the intake."

"How long will he have to stay there?" Mom asked.

"They'll tell you when they admit him, but based on his age and how much he uses, I'd guess about a month."

Mom's mouth dropped. "That's impossible. He'll miss all that school. They'll have to hold him back a grade."

"He's a heroin addict. The only thing he has to do is get clean, because nothing else matters. I'm going to go home now to get freshened up and change, but I'll be back in and hour or so." She took a deep breath. "And one more thing. He's already in serious withdrawal. He's probably used to shooting up first thing in the morning. I know it seems counterintuitive, but you need to let him use. We won't be able to handle him otherwise, and we need to keep him calm for the next few hours."

"Let him use heroin in this house?" Mom asked with disbelief.

"Believe me, you aren't ready to deal with an IV drug addict in acute withdrawal. All those colds and flus he's been having were withdrawal episodes, but he was able to score smack before it became desperate. It's also very, very dangerous to transport a withdrawing heroin addict in a car without proper restraints. Things like handcuffs and leg irons and body straps." Mom and Dad drew back. "He's likely to attack the driver or jump into moving traffic. At this point, one more hit makes no difference."

Tim came running. "He's got a needle!"

Rich was on his heels. "I just want some cereal," he cried. His eyes watered, and his nose ran. He looked wild with fear. "I need a bowl and a spoon."

"Do you have a lighter?"

Rich nodded.

"Someone give him a spoon and a glass of warm water and stay with him to make sure everything is okay."

When nobody moved, Don said, "I'll do it." He expected somebody to object, but no one did, so he gathered the items, and Rich followed him to his bed, where he flopped down and reached for the spoon and glass.

Don grimaced with distaste as Rich gingerly lifted a hypodermic needle from the loving folds of a soft woolen scarf. As he flushed it with water, Don asked, "Why do you like taking heroin?" Rich pulled a tiny paper square from his pocket. He unfolded one end and poured a small pile of brownish powder into the spoon. "It's medicine now. I get dope sick without it."

He licked the residue from the paper, shot some water into the spoon, and held a lighter underneath. Soon, amber liquid bubbled, releasing a sweet chemical scent Don recognized as the wispy vapors he'd smelled the past few months.

"Be honest and tell me how long you've been injecting it," Don said. "I could tell you were lying the last time, so just tell the truth."

Rich sniffled and wiped his eyes. "Since January. It still makes me high, but it doesn't last long. It just makes me feel normal."

Carefully, Rich drew the brownish liquid into the tube through the needle. Sniffling some more, he raised a foot to the bed, ripped off the sock, and said, "After you guys busted me for track marks, I had to find new ways to shoot up." He aimed the needle between his toes at a spot already inflamed with angry red skin, and Don looked away.

Rich let out a grunt of pain that dissolved into a sigh of relief. "Oh, yeah," he whispered. Don watched in amazement as his brother went from frantic to calm in a matter of seconds. He wiped his eyes and nose, and nothing else leaked. His shakes ebbed and stopped. He seemed calm and reflective. Normal.

"Why take drugs to feel normal when you can feel normal anyway without them?"

"When you start, you didn't even know it was possible to feel so good, and you want to keep feeling that way, but it changes. It's like a ten-thousand-man orchestra is playing and before you know it, it's a kid with a kazoo. Don't ever take drugs, Donnie. You'll end up wishing with all your heart you'd never started. I wish I could go back to the day before I took my first hit."

"Why did you start?"

Rich shrugged. "Because I don't give a shit about this stupid town, and I hate everyone that lives here. And I hate their rules. I always have, even Before." He looked at Don. "You hate them, too. I can tell."

He didn't know what to say, and Rich went on. "Tim and Randy believed me when I said I was gonna quit. Only you knew it was bullshit. I see you checking my arms and giving me looks. It means a lot to me that you worry about me so much. Sometimes I wanted to stop using just to make your life easier. You never laughed when you were little, did you know that?"

Don stared.

"I mean it," Rich went on. "It used to kind of freak me out. I tried clowning around, and you'd just look at me like I was crazy, like you had too many things to worry about to waste your time on laughing. I'd think about that sometimes when I shot up. I felt bad about how scared you were for me. I wanted to stop more for you than for anybody else." He closed his eyes. "I really tried, Don. For your sake. I tried so hard, but smack feels so good at the beginning that it wants the rest of your life as payment."

Don thrashed his mind for an appropriate reply, but all he could think of was, "Mom and Dad are going to take you somewhere so you can stop."

Rich nodded. "I figured that's why that old biddy was here. I guess I'll go." He chuckled. "I'm flunking out of school anyway."

Mrs. Dister returned, and his parents bundled up Rich and they left. After they were gone, Tim relayed the scene at the abandoned house. They found Rich sleeping, slumped against the wall. Dwayne and the creepy older guy tried to help Rich as he resisted.

"They were so fucked up," Tim said, his face twisted with disgust. "They were like rag dolls. You should have seen Dad whale on that ferret-faced guy. I pounded on Dwayne, and we left them on the floor crying like babies. Dad told them if he ever saw either one of them at our house, he was gonna kill 'em.'"

Their parents returned with Mrs. Dister in the early evening. She said she had something to say, and they sat in the family room while she stood.

"Heroin is a very difficult drug to kick," she said. "Rich is willing to try treatment, and that's a good sign. He's in the best hands anywhere in Ohio, and your prayers will help even more. He's in for a very difficult time these next few days and won't be able to see any of you." She looked at the boys. "We already went over most of this with your parents, but you should know your brother is going to crave heroin for a long time. He's young, but he could be battling this for years."

"You mean the psychological withdrawal?" Tim asked.

"Well, yes, but there are many of us who don't like that term. Psychology is in the brain, and the brain is an organ, so it's a type of physical withdrawal as well. The point is that massive amounts of opiates like heroin can alter the brain over time. If he's only been shooting for six months, his odds of a complete recovery and a normal life are better than most." Don knew Rich had been injecting for almost a year, but said nothing. The people at the treatment facility would be able to work out the truth.

Mrs. Dister looked like any other sweet old lady in North Homestead, and it was strange she was so familiar with such a gritty topic. He felt a rush of gratitude that someone who was little more than a friendly stranger would drop everything to help his family.

"Relapses are very dangerous," she said. "After not using for a while, an addict's body isn't used to the drug, and if they take the same amount, it's often fatal. I don't want to scare you, but you deserve the truth."

She went on for a while longer about the importance of family support. "I don't want any of you to feel ashamed or embarrassed about this. My son was a heroin addict, and since his overdose, I've learned that it's much more common around here than any of us ever imagined.

You aren't alone, and I want you to feel free to call me whenever you like."

She gave them each a tender hug, and after their parents poured out their gratitude, she was gone. The family stood silently. Had all of that happened since only this morning?

Four days later, their parents visited Rich and returned sad and reflective. "He doesn't look the same," Mom said. "They say the worst is behind him, but they don't want any more visitors for three weeks."

"Then we won't get to see him on Thanksgiving," Don said.

"I didn't like that either, but they said it was best for him." She cleared her throat. "Someday, we're going to have a discussion about how this happened, and why certain things weren't said." Don and his brothers dropped their heads. "But Mrs. Dister explained to us that this isn't the time. We need to focus on helping Rich, so let's keep our minds on that one goal." Everyone nodded.

December fourth was Rich's birthday, and it fell on a Saturday. Mom baked a big birthday cake. As they set off, Randy asked, "How come we're not allowed to bring presents?"

"Some of the other patients aren't the nicest people. They warned us that anything we bring would only get stolen. But it's fine. They'll be waiting for him when he comes home."

"When will that be?" Don asked.

"It might be as soon as next week, but they're not sure. They'll let us know when the time is right."

The treatment facility was in the corner of a massive concrete hospital, with its own unmarked entrance around back. The interior was just as gloomy, with gray walls, floors and doors. Don didn't even see any windows.

Rich waited in a saggy blue jumpsuit and slippers, in a large room with rows of metal tables bolted to the floor. They sprouted rigid bars supporting seating pads that looked cold and uncomfortable. Hand-drawn posters covered the walls, proclaiming liberation from drugs. Their chirpy certitude made Don uneasy, reminding him of Rich's fulsome promises the Niagara Falls weekend.

Rich looked tired, but he was ecstatic to see them and gave them tight hugs. Because the facility forbade visitors to bring matches and lighters, Mom carefully placed sixteen candles topped with bits of cotton balls dyed with orange food coloring. After they sang "Happy

Birthday," Rich blew on the orange fluffs with all his might until the last of them sailed away. They laughed, cheered and ate cake, chattering. Tim and Randy joked about how much they didn't miss him. He took it in good humor and responded in kind. Everyone beamed, and Don felt better about the posters.

"Your father and I have to go see the head nurse," Mom said. She smiled broadly. "We'll only be a few minutes, so behave yourselves."

After they left, Tim grinned and said, "Remember what happened the last time they left us alone?" He nudged Rich, who laughed. He looked like his old self, and Don felt a warm glow of hope.

A swinging door to the side opened, and a skinny but pretty blond girl in a blue jumpsuit peeked in, waving at Rich. He sat up, blushed, and waved back. She nervously checked the corridor behind her, jumped with a squeal and blew him a kiss before laughing and hurrying away.

Rich's blush deepened as his brothers turned to him. "Holy shit!" Tim whispered. "Is that your girlfriend?"

"No," he said with a wide, bashful grin. "She just likes me."

"She's a knockout! What's her name?"

"Candy."

Tim and Randy made little throat noises of appreciation. "Are you kidding me?" Tim said. "Do you know how many guys would love to have a blond girlfriend named Candy?"

"It's not like that. She's nice, but I don't know."

"Your dick doesn't get hard for nice girls?" Tim asked with a grin, his voice low and dirty.

Rich chuckled. "I didn't mean it like that. I meant she's nice to me, but she's a little too…I don't know. She's too wild or something. She's fifteen, and she's been in treatment three times already. You can't believe some of the stories she tells in group."

Tim looked at the spot where Candy had appeared. "She's a wild blond girl named Candy." His eyes glinted with indecent thoughts.

"Knock it off," Rich said without rancor. "Don't turn it into that."

Tim tore his eyes from the door. "Okay, but you have to promise to give your brothers all the details if she sneaks into your room at night, right, guys?"

"Yeah, like that's gonna happen," Rich said, growing jittery. His legs pumped slightly under the table, and he fidgeted with his fingers.

"At night, all the guys are locked up in the dormitory in the south wing, and all the girls in the north. The only people who get their own rooms are the new patients, and they don't even know who they are or where they are. I didn't."

Don asked, "How bad was it?"

Rich blew out a breath, shaking his head, but it was too speedy and unnatural, and Don felt a nibble of fear. "It was bad," Rich said. "All I did for four days was puke up bile, shit gallons of water and sweat like a pig. I smelled like a sewer. I didn't know you could be in so much pain and survive. I wanted to die."

"But you feel better now, right?" Tim asked.

Rich nodded. Again, the movement was too fast and went on too long. "Yeah, but it's hard. All I can think about is scoring a fix."

"You're all through with that. We're gonna make sure you turn over a new leaf. We'll all turn over new leafs, right guys?"

Randy nodded earnestly, but Don asked, "Did you tell them that's all you think about?"

"They know," Rich said. "Everyone here is the same way. They released the guy in the bed next to mine yesterday, and he told me the first place he was gonna go was his dealer's." His eyes sharpened with envy. "I'll bet he's strung out right now. Candy's got big plans about trying a speedball. It's cocaine and heroin mixed together."

Don rushed to say, "Don't see her again!"

Tim leaned in. "Jesus, Rich, get a grip. You've been clean for almost a month. You'll just have to go through all of this again if you slip up."

Rich shook his head, and kept shaking as he said, "I'm never going through this again. Never."

Tim and Randy apparently took him to mean that he would stay clean, but the fear inside Don gnawed and thrashed.

Their parents returned, and Rich pulled himself together for another fifteen minutes of cake and conversation. The visiting hour ended, and they hugged Rich. Their parents told him they were proud of him, a sentiment Tim and Randy echoed. Don didn't express his pride, but they shared a brief look of fear and understanding.

As they left, Don turned back. Rich stood in the same spot in his blue jumpsuit, and they locked eyes again. His brother looked sorrowful and apologetic, and he lifted his hand in a dispirited good-bye gesture before turning away. Don wanted to race after him and grab hold, but Rich pushed his way out. The swinging door settled into place.

The terrorized screams of a new patient, a woman, echoed faintly in the hall, and Don wondered if she had a brother who let her addiction advance for months before saying anything, exponentially increasing her pain. The screams went silent only when the heavy outside door slammed behind them, entombing the anguish inside.

Don stopped. His family walked on. "No!" he shouted, startling them. He told his parents what Rich said. "They can't release him. You have to go back inside and tell them."

His mom bent and gave him a hug. "They know, honey, but thank you for telling us. They're going to keep him another two weeks because they don't think he's ready."

Don was relieved, and his mom put a hand on his shoulder and led him away.

The next morning, they returned from Sunday mass and settled in for breakfast. Around nine thirty, the phone rang and Mom answered. Concern filled her face. "Yes, I understand. You'll keep me informed?" The ominous words drew everyone's attention.

She hung up. "Rich seems to be missing from the treatment facility. They think he ran off with a girl. It's very difficult for patients to get past security, but somehow they managed."

"Candy," Tim breathed.

Her voice barreled to a shout. "Did you know this was going to happen?"

"No!"

"We didn't, Mom," Don said. "Tim's not lying. Rich never said anything about running away with her."

Dad stood. "What are they doing to find them?"

"They called the police and gave them a description. Apparently, all the cops in Cleveland know those blue jumpsuits and slippers. They said they usually catch escaped patients within a few hours."

A few hours later, Dad called the facility for an update. He hung up and said, "Nothing yet." Hours later, he called again. Still nothing. He tried again late afternoon, but it was the same.

"Should we go out and look for him?" Mom asked. "I'm going crazy just sitting here waiting for the phone to ring."

"Where are we going to look? Cleveland is a big city. We can't just choose random neighborhoods."

All day, Don felt like puking. Mrs. Dister said relapses are deadly. Rich said he could only think about scoring another fix, and he'd run off with a girl who wanted to try an even stronger mix of heroin and cocaine. They were hiding someplace, someplace they could take drugs.

At six thirty, the phone rang and Mom raced to answer. Don stood, biting his thumb. Mom's reaction would tell. "Hello? Oh, you did! Oh, just her? Did they leave together? Then she must know where he is. Well, where is he, then?"

She listened, and her eyes widened before they rolled back into her head while her legs collapsed. She dropped the receiver and crashed to her knees and her upper body levered to the floor, slamming face down. Her forehead hit the linoleum with a loud bang, and an arm flopped outstretched. It only took a second or two, and even through his terror, Don noted that a real faint is ugly and violent, nothing like the elegant descents on TV.

Dad struggled to turn her over, screaming "Jenny! Jenny!" His voice was thick with panic that words alone had the power to knock her unconscious, but Don saw that he knew why, too. They all did.

CHAPTER SEVENTEEN

Don woke to the scratchy, grumbling sighs coming from the baby monitor. He checked his phone in the dark. It was only four thirty.

He jumped up and flipped on Dad's light. His father sat on the edge of the bed, clenching the mattress. He looked confused, until he saw Don and his expression softened with relief.

"Do you need to use the commode, Dad?"

"Yeah." He held up his arm, and Don stooped to let him grab his shoulder. Don encircled his waist and nearly lifted him from the ground. He was losing weight.

After Don returned him to bed, his dad closed his eyes and asked weakly, "Donnie, do you think I have much longer?"

"I don't know, Dad. Everyone says cancer is up and down. You look down right now, but that doesn't mean you won't come back up for a while."

"I'd like to make it through the holidays. See another year come in. It'll be my last, but I'll take one more New Year's Eve."

"I'd like that, too."

His dad took a deep breath. "But it's a bitch getting to the holidays, Donnie. You know what I'm talking about?"

"Sure I do, Dad." December fifth dawned every year, and all he could do was make it through the day, get into bed that night and stare at the ceiling for a while.

Dad said, "We used to go to the cemetery every December fifth, remember?"

"Of course. We went just last week. Me and Tim and Randy. Obviously, it wasn't the anniversary. We just wanted to say hi."

"You did?" He sounded pleased. "You've never forgotten him?"

"No, Dad. I'll never forget Rich."

Dad opened his eyes. They were wet. "Rich was a good guy. He made some bad choices. Course, we all know why, poor kid." Despair froze his face and thawed gently. "He would have turned out to be a good man if he'd had the chance."

"I know."

Over the years, Don pondered his last private conversation with Rich, held in this very room the morning his brother left for treatment and never returned. Don wrapped the memory in the delicate silk of the most sacred remembrances, opened reverently at rare moments of reflection and solitude, too fragile to share with anyone, ever. The center of the memory in particular remained hushed, hidden, words that Rich spoke of such singular value he didn't appreciate their worth for many years.

"Dad, can I ask you a question?"

"Sure."

"Do you remember if I ever laughed when I was little? I mean, when I was really little?"

Dad scrunched his mouth, considering. "You were serious as hell. When you were five, you already acted like the oldest brother. Your mother and I talked about it. We figured it meant you had above-average intelligence, but we had no idea yet."

"But can you think of a time when I laughed?"

"What do you mean? What time?" Dad looked baffled.

"Any time. Just one time when I was a kid. A little kid. Can you remember me laughing? Even just once?" The rapidity of his questions clearly unnerved his dad. He regretted raising the topic. It was too close to the priceless words at the center.

"It's a weird question, Donnie. I'd have to think about it." He flicked his eyes searching his mind. "Like I said, you always looked exasperated by your brothers, like you couldn't believe how silly they acted." His face slowly lightened, and he laughed. "Remember the comet Kohoutek? How excited you were?"

Don hadn't thought about Kohoutek in years. He smiled to recall the excruciating thrill of waiting for the comet's ballyhooed appearance in 1973, and the crushingly disappointing smudge in the sky. "Yeah, I remember all right. They said it would be the comet of the century. Bright enough to cast shadows."

"Oh, my God, they hyped that comet like there was no tomorrow. Biggest flop since *Cleopatra*." He was more animated than he'd been in days. "You were about eight, which would make Tim about fourteen, I guess. Anyway, the media had everyone worked up, and Tim said that we should take down the television antenna in case the comet knocked it off the roof!"

They laughed hard, and Dad swiped his eyes, raising his voice, "And you were so appalled, you sat him down at the kitchen table and you made him read a magazine article about it. Tim never read a cereal box if he could avoid it, and you stood there and you made him finish." Dad slapped the bed, and Don felt good to see such a spontaneous gesture of happiness, weak as it was.

"Your mother and I were in the family room, just cracking up. We'd sneak a look every now and then, and you'd be standing right there at his shoulder, about half his size, to make sure he read every word." The strength of his father's old voice returned. "I wanted to take a picture but your mother wouldn't let me."

They laughed so hard Don wondered if they would wake her. After a bit, it slowed, tapered to chuckles and ended in shakes of the head, soft breaths. Dad gave a final sigh. "Oh, boy. Well, I gotta admit I'm a bit tired now, Donnie."

Smiling, Don patted his shoulder. "Okay, Dad. Go back to sleep, and I'll see you in a few hours."

Don turned off the light and pulled the door closed, but not all the way. He was about to return to his own bed when an impulse gripped him.

Dad was already snoring, and Mom was in her bed, facing away. She never closed her door, and if the laughter hadn't woken her, probably nothing would.

Don padded to the attic stairs and opened the door, setting off its distinctive creak. Every door in the house seemed to have one.

Softy, he climbed the steps, nudging aside the stuff Mom stored here, ducking as he reached the trapdoor. He flipped the latch and pushed up with his shoulder, reaching for the light chain. He gave it a yank and the old, bare bulb came to life with the yellow glow of a bygone age.

He hadn't been up here in years. The roof beams slanted over two-by-four supports, and a plywood path led into the deep shadows at the far end. Cardboard boxes of various sizes sat about, smashed and ripped at the corners, flaps hanging open. It was cold and smelled dusty.

He started down the path with a stoop, the way he remembered doing it. Alarmed, his back zapped him with a sharp twinge. He scowled and sank to all fours and scuffed past the brick chimney that speared through the bottom and punched through the roof, just passing through.

In the corner, the gentle light lingered softly about four unspoiled boxes. They sat in a neat square, untouched since their careful placement. The clear packing tape, deepened to amber, crinkled away from the cardboard.

He kneeled, looked them over, and placed a hand on the closest.

Rich's life in four boxes: his clothes, his shoes, his album, and the rest. Mom packed them by herself back then. "I'm his mother," she'd insisted through sobs, refusing help. "I saw him into this world, and it's my responsibility to see him out of it."

When Don was younger, the packing tape prevented his blinding desire to hold Rich's things, turn them over, remember. He was free to open the boxes now, but he no longer craved the sparks of recognition that come from physical things. He always possessed the only memory that mattered.

He smoothed an edge of ancient packing tape. It crumbled and the flakes fell away, glinting in the yellow light, sinking into shadows as silently as golden treasure into the sea.

He rested his forehead against the box, wrapped his arms about it and closed his eyes. Don felt closer to Rich here than at his grave. He brushed a kiss against the cardboard and took a few deep breaths.

He remembered getting the spoon and glass of warm water on Rich's last morning in this house, expecting someone to say he was too young to help a heroin addict shoot up. It almost frightened him to think about how easily Tim or Dad could have brushed him aside. Those last private moments with Rich wouldn't have happened, and Rich wouldn't have spoken the words that merely surprised him at the time, but grew infinitely more meaningful in the years since. Don burned for Rich to know the depths of his gratitude.

"Thanks for trying to stop for my sake," he whispered. "Nobody's tried to do anything as difficult as that for me ever since. I appreciate it, brother." He kissed the box again, patting it softly.

A slight bump in his chest, an intake of breath, and the grief slipped free.

CHAPTER EIGHTEEN

1976–1977

When 1977 arrived, the world was frozen, the sky covered by those unique, formless gray winter clouds, one solid mass, like pavement hanging above the earth.

Don desperately wished the freeze had settled in a month before.

Christmas passed in darkness, unwrapped gifts that nobody wanted piled on the table, bought before Rich died. Don watched his mom pull her stash of wrapping paper from the cluttered attic stairs a week before Christmas Day. She took one look at the colorful designs and threw them back, slamming the door. He heard the rolls tumble down the steps, and he stored them properly so she wouldn't see them when she opened the door for something else.

Don longed to return to school, although those days in the classroom between the funeral and the holiday break felt unreal. Every sound set off a muffled echo. The tap and slide of chalk filled the classroom with a cottony static. The other students, who cringed and turned away at his approach, let loose with excited holiday babble once they got a few feet beyond his dark bubble. Songs and Christmas carols banged away in hollow notes, as if in other rooms.

He thought the noises would make him crazy, but the silence at home during the holidays of 1976 was more oppressive, two weeks of shuffling, mumbling, sniffling, and sobs behind closed doors. Sometimes the TV droned, amazing him with how unnatural it sounded. The fakery of the laugh tracks was insulting.

A few days after school resumed in January, a month after Rich's death, Don sat in the cafeteria when an older boy in eighth grade, his mannerisms and voice a transparent copy of Fonzie from *Happy Days*, told a girl at the next table that he'd like to take her to a sock hop. She responded like a flirtatious, sassy character from the same television show, ignoring the obvious problem. To find a sock hop in North Homestead, you needed a time travel machine. Their need to play roles instead of live their own lives filled him with a bright sense of disgust. The potency of the feeling startled him. It happened again and again over the next few days, emotions that stung as sharp as prickle weeds. He didn't know he'd been so numb.

The second Wednesday in January of 1977, while the Eskers ate dinner, Tim stood. Formal, he lifted his chin and said he had an announcement.

"I've joined the Marine Corps. I haven't told you, but I've already taken my physical and the tests. There's still time to get into winter boot camp if I leave on Sunday morning."

Dad was silent, but Mom put a hand to her chest. "You're graduating from high school in five months," she said, breathy with worry. "You can't go out into the world without a diploma."

"I turn eighteen next week," he replied, eyes still fixed to the wall, as if addressing superior officers. "I need your permission to take the oath while I'm seventeen, but they can get me processed in San Diego first, and I can take the oath on my birthday. I'd like to do it in the proper order and get the right start, but I'm leaving whether you give me permission or not."

"What's the rush? Tim, you need to think about your future, and you won't have one without a high school diploma."

"My future is in the Marines. I can take an equivalency test later."

"Rob?" Mom said, trying to enlist Dad's help.

Dad and Tim shared a look before Tim said, "I'm not gonna change my mind. I want your permission, but I don't need it. I'm going."

Dad looked crestfallen. "Okay, Tim. Do what you think is best."

"What?" Mom shrieked, rising. "Don't help him throw his future away."

"He becomes an adult next week. We can't tell a grown man what to do, even if he's our son. If he has the spirit to go off and build a new life for himself, we shouldn't stand in his way.

Tim's eyes shone with gratitude and surprise.

"He's making a terrible mistake!"

"I'm not sure I agree, but even if he is, it's his life and his mistake."

"Tim," Mom said, dropping her voice to reason with him, "I will support whatever you want to do, but after graduation. Please. Be sensible. The Marine Corps isn't going anywhere. They prefer high school graduates anyway."

"I had to pass the math and English tests with higher grades because I don't have a diploma, but I aced them. It's not a problem."

The conversation went on for a while, and Don left, listening from his bedroom. Mom's voice veered from panic to pleading, from rational to raging, but she couldn't sway him. After two days, during which Tim methodically went about preparing to leave, including formally withdrawing from St. Peter's, Mom saw it was hopeless, and she agreed to let him take the oath four days before his birthday.

Saturday night, Mom made Tim's favorite meal of fried chicken and mashed potatoes, but dinner was unbearable. Nobody ate much. Mom mostly wept and Dad looked crushed.

After they cleaned the kitchen, Tim asked, "Can I use the car for a little while? I want to take Randy and Don for a ride on my final night."

"Of course," Mom said, nodding through her tears.

They bundled up against the cold. Tim whispered to Don and Randy, "Grab a bucket. We have to fill it from the basement because the outside pipes are frozen, but don't let Mom and Dad hear." It was the first hint that Tim had something specific in mind.

They worked as quietly as they could and slid the bucket of water on the floor against the backseat of the car. As Tim pulled out of the driveway, Randy asked, "Where are we going?"

"I found out where Dwayne lives," Tim said. "We're going to pay him a visit."

Don didn't like the sound of that. Tim drove a short distance to Cook Road, parking next to the woods in front of a small brick house. Several windows glowed with yellow light.

"We have to be quick," Tim said. "Once we start, we have to get it over with as soon as we can, but we need to teach that little faggot junkie a lesson."

"What are we doing?" Randy asked.

"Get the bucket."

Carefully, they crossed the deserted street, Randy carrying the bucket.

"This is gonna be cold as shit," Tim whispered as they crouched, "but make a bunch of snowballs. We're gonna dip them in the water to make ice balls. Then we're gonna pile them up and let loose on the house. We gotta hurry before the water freezes in the bucket."

"No," Randy objected, "Ice balls will break all the windows."

"Think, shithead," Tim said, military gusto already in his voice. "Aim for the roof and make sure you hit it. Don't cause any damage. We just want to scare him."

"But other people probably live here," Don said. "We're going to scare everybody."

"Good. Look at what Dwayne did to us."

It was hard to argue, and they set to work. Soon, Tim deemed the pile large enough.

"Okay," he said, "let me show you how to dip them in the water." In one rapid move, he picked up a snowball, dunked it in the bucket and tossed it into the snow, where it froze instantly. He repeated the dunk and throw with the same ice ball, explaining, "The more times we dip it, the harder it will hit."

On their first attempt, both Don and Randy ended up with a frozen ball of ice attached to their gloves. They shook them loose.

Don got better after a few tries, but the cold stiffened his fingers painfully. Once again, he couldn't help but wish the freeze had come sooner.

As Don worked, he thought about his mom's face at dinner, her sadness approaching despair. Don understood how barren she must feel, with one of her sons buried and another breaking off and reeling away, half her children gone inside of two months. Don knew these massive gravitational shifts began imperceptibly a year and a half ago when Eddie Tedesco vanished, and the police stormed the house. He felt foolish when he remembered how he hoped everything would go back to normal after Dad's alibi held up, as if a solar system could remain untouched by the fiery arrival of another sun. Of course not. It sent everything spinning into the void.

His hands grew numb from cold, and his fingers felt as frozen as the ground. Back in early December before the freeze, when he went with his parents to make the final arrangements at Memorial Park Cemetery, Don spotted a backhoe at work across a hill. He suspected it was preparing Rich's grave, and he slipped outside while his parents wept over paperwork.

He approached as the backhoe parked and the engine spluttered off. The driver dismounted, joining two other workers in attending to the new hole with shovels, probably to shape it properly. A massive pile of earth rested on a green tarp.

The hole swallowed the workers, and Don looked down on the knit caps of the men busy in the grave. They worked quickly, speaking roughly, and one said, "It's lucky this one died before the freeze. The junkie had good timing." They chuckled.

Don couldn't move. Eventually, one of the workers saw him. "Hey, kid. Go find another way to have fun." All three stared up from the grave.

"Fuck you!" he screamed. Their faces went bewildered before he ran off.

"Okay," Tim said softly when they had a big pile of ice balls. "Remember, quick. Bam bam bam. We hit the roof one after the other and get out. Ready?"

Don reached for an ice ball, wishing the cemetery workers were standing in the yard. He hoped a bunch of people died, and they had a whole winter of backbreaking work.

"Okay, here we go," Tim said. "One..."

Don rose and hurled the ice ball as hard as he could. It was too low, and he clenched his body as the white ball arched down, heading for a window. It crashed into the gutter at the last moment, and an aluminum clang shattered the still night. He wouldn't be surprised if it woke half of Ohio.

"What are you doing?" Tim said furiously. "Wait for the countdown!"

An outside light popped on next door, splashing a reflection across the snow that skimmed the yards on both sides, all the way to the street. They were visible.

"Now," Tim said, and they flew into the assault, throwing and stooping and rising and throwing again. The ice balls hit the roof with a cacophony that surprised Don, like a rain of billiard balls. They landed with booming thumps and bounced and rolled, knocking each other about. From the inside, it must sound like the end of the world.

The front door flew open, and a frantic man appeared. "Hey!" he yelled with throaty confusion and fear. "Get away from here!" A pudgy little girl behind him put her hands to her mouth and screamed.

Tim said, "Okay, that's enough." He cupped his mouth and yelled, "Tell that junkie Dwayne that we aren't through with him."

Don grabbed the bucket and they ran.

CHAPTER NINETEEN

Don drove down Cook Road slowly, certain he would recognize the house where Rich's friend Dwayne used to live. To his left, the woods slipped past, thicker than he remembered, awash in fall colors. The abandoned house used to be on the other side. The city tore it down years ago, after the gap in the staircase swallowed a little girl who broke her back when she landed in the basement. The world was harder on kids then.

Here and there, big new houses loomed above sweeping front lawns that looked as carefully landscaped as an English manor's park. The long driveways curved like streams, pooling into large parking areas in front of garages with at least two, sometimes three doors. Light-colored wood accented with upscale cream bricks clad the homes.

They lorded over their nearby poorer and much older relations, small red brick houses huddled up to the street with short, functional driveways poured when people shoveled snow by hand. Don looked at these humbler houses carefully, but none quite matched his memory.

He drove for a mile or so and turned around when he was certain he'd driven too far. It had been dark that night at Dwayne's house in 1977, but Don still saw it in his mind: a brick rectangle with a tiny addition in back on the left. There was no front porch, save for a concrete square with two steps. Many of the older homes on the street had the same look. Dwayne's house might be long gone, mowed over by a tasteful lawn.

Don knew almost nothing about Rich's heroin friend. Maybe Dwayne had lived with distant relatives, or with an unrelated family because his own no longer wanted him, arrangements not uncommon in the upheavals of semi-rural hardship. What were the odds that even if Don found the house, anyone would remember a heroin addict named Dwayne from more than forty years ago? Not very high, he figured.

Hollyhock Elementary, Part Two, he thought and decided to give up when he saw a detail on a small brick house. He hit the brakes, screeching to a halt.

"Holy shit!" he cried. His mouth hung open. It didn't seem possible, but it was just as he'd left it on that freezing night in 1977. He stared in disbelief.

At the polite tapping of a car horn behind him, Don waved his apology and pulled into the short driveway, parking behind two small cars.

"No fucking way," he muttered, looking up. It was unreal.

He got out and studied his childhood handiwork, a sharp dent on the brown aluminum gutter below the front roof, near the corner. It amazed him to see the rage of that night.

The front door opened, and a middle-aged, heavy-set woman behind the storm window peered at him with curiosity and suspicion. She opened the metal door a bit and called out, "Can I help you?"

"I'm sorry to disturb you," he replied, heading for her. She closed the door, obviously wary of the stranger staring at her roof. He didn't blame her, and he smiled and gave a friendly nod, standing well back on the walk. "I'm here about a guy named Dwayne who used to live here."

"Who?" she asked, her voice muffled. Don saw she recognized the name. His heart began to thump. Maybe this would work after all.

"Dwayne. He lived in this house back in the seventies."

She looked stupefied.

He heard another voice inside, and she exchanged a few unintelligible words. When she turned back, she looked only curious. He found the change in her expression comforting. In general, people look so much more appealing when rational. She opened the door wide and asked, "Who are you?"

"I knew Dwayne back then. My name is Don." Best to not give a last name, in case she knew about the attack of the Esker boys. She'd have been a very young girl back then.

Inside, a plump older woman in a shapeless dress clutched a walker. She squinted behind thick glasses. "Carol, who is that?"

"This is a friend of mine from work, Mom. He just needs to show me something in his car."

"Well, aren't you going to invite him inside?"

"I can't stay, ma'am," he called. "I'll visit again some other time."

"I'll be back in a sec, Mom." She stepped out and pulled the door closed, shutting off her mother's "Carol?" midway.

"Sorry I can't let you inside," she said, speaking in a voice now filled with self-assurance and intelligence. She wore a professional blouse and jacket, with a matching long skirt. She led him down the walk, but stopped when she spotted the silver BMW Grand Coupe. "Is that yours?"

"It's a rental."

She raised her eyebrows. "Pretty sweet ride."

"It better be for what I'm paying."

She faced him. "I'm sorry, but we can't discuss Dwayne in front of my mom. She still can't talk about it. I'm sure you understand. I'm his younger sister, Carol. I was just a little girl when everything happened, but I remember like it was yesterday."

Don had the feeling he would like Carol if he got to know her, and he felt sorry for her. He knew the excruciating pain a heroin addict inflicted on the family. "What happened to him?"

"You don't know?"

"I knew Dwayne from around the neighborhood. I grew up on Stearns. I haven't been to this house since, oh, I don't know, sometime in the mid-seventies."

"I see. You're just here to check up on a childhood friend?"

"That's right."

"Well, I'm sorry, Don, but I don't have anything good to tell you. Dwayne became a heroin addict and left home in February of 1977. We didn't know where he was for the longest time. He called us a few years later to tell us he'd been living in Cleveland. My parents went to see him. He was staying at a flophouse in the Flats." She shook her head, and Don knew why. Her brother had lived in a decaying house among the rusty, crumbling ruins of empty factories that skirted the Cuyahoga River next to downtown.

"Did he die of an overdose?"

"No. He was shot." She looked away. "He was dealing heroin by that time, and there was a dispute about something. Who knows what?

Just a few months after he contacted us, they found his body in the weeds next to one of those old factories. The Flats was a pretty desolate place back then. Nobody in their right mind went there, so he'd been dead for a few weeks." She grimaced and dropped her head.

"I'm really sorry, Carol."

"Yeah, so am I. I'm sorry to be the one to tell you all of this."

"I'm glad I know." He wondered if he was pushing too far, but this would probably be his only chance to learn anything more. "Do you remember a friend of his who was older? Blond guy, with long hair? His face was sort of scrunched up?"

She gasped. "Tom Malicheski!" she said in a high, surprised voice. "Yes, I remember him." Her voice dropped. "He was the dealer who got Dwayne hooked in the first place. After Dwayne ran away, my parents raised holy hell about Tom with the police, and he skipped town."

"Do you know where he went?"

She shook her head. "No idea. Did you know him, too?" She looked surprised. "I was under the impression that he only hung out with drug addicts."

"I knew him a little bit. I was just trying to remember his name recently, so thanks for reminding me. Do you know if his family lives around here somewhere?"

"Why?" Her tone was challenging.

"I'm just curious."

"You just have a mild curiosity about some low-life drug dealer from forty years ago? Were you an addict back then?"

"No, I was way too young. I was only about eleven years old."

She folded her arms. "Then you couldn't have been friends with Dwayne. Why don't you tell me who you really are and what you're doing here?"

Carol was good. She looked at him with suspicion and anger. Again, Don understood. She'd just revealed her painful family history to a dishonest stranger. Who wouldn't be cautious and resentful?

He nodded in defeat. "Okay, Carol, I wasn't friends with Dwayne. I barely knew him. My brother was his friend. I guess you could say they were heroin friends. He died of an overdose in 1976, the day after his sixteenth birthday."

She gave him a long look before saying, "Thank you for being truthful. Did you come here to accuse Dwayne of getting your brother hooked?"

"No. I mean, I used to think that way, but I learned a long time ago Rich made his own choices."

"Rich?" she asked, and Don realized his mistake. "Rich Esker?" *Oh, shit.* "Yes."

She looked up at the gutter. "So that's why you were so interested in the roof. You were looking at the damage you caused."

Don could scarcely believe how easily she unmasked him, but now that it was over, he felt relieved. "Jesus, Carol, if you're not a lawyer, you should be."

"I am. I'm an assistant DA for the county. I became passionate about law and order after what happened to my brother. And," she added angrily, "after a bunch of hooligans attacked our house one night and terrorized us."

"Come on, Carol. I was a kid. My brother just died of an overdose about a month before. We were crazy with grief and anger."

"I can understand that, but why did you come after us? My brother wasn't the dealer, at least not yet. He was just another addict."

"Me and my brothers saw Dwayne injecting heroin into Rich's arm. It was at the abandoned house." She focused, absorbing this new information, and Don saw that it made a difference. "We didn't know Dwayne wasn't the dealer. We didn't know that ultimately Rich was responsible for using drugs, that nobody tied him down. My family went through so much that year that we were just lashing out."

She nodded. "I know exactly what you're talking about. Those little boys and your dad. For what it's worth, my father always said your dad should have sued the city, and my parents felt terrible about how your family was treated. That's why they didn't call the police after you attacked our house. Why are you looking for Tom Malicheski?"

"I'm sorry, but I can't tell you that. It would take too long to explain, and it would probably sound crazy, but I promise that I'm not trying to cause any trouble for anyone. I just need to know."

The sky had noticeably darkened since his arrival, and Carol breathed heavily for a few moments before saying, "Well, it was all a long time ago. And you should know that the dent in the gutter is shaped perfectly to funnel the water through like river rapids and it cleared the leaves in front all by itself, so my parents never had it fixed." Her hard face went soft with a smile. "You saved my dad a lot of work over the years."

He chuckled with amazement.

"Tom Malicheski was from Greenhill," she said. "I heard he left the state. Good riddance. I'm sure he's been dead for a long time."

Don remembered Billy's wife, Roxanne, lived in Greenhill, and they'd exchanged phone numbers. His heart quickened and he asked, "Do you know if he still has family living there?"

"I don't know anything about him, other than that he caused my family our worst pain. And yours, too, sounds like. I don't mean to be rude, Don, but I have to get going. I need to get my mom settled, then I need to get home because I have court first thing in the morning."

"I'm sorry about that night. I wish I'd never done it."

She smiled. "How many times have we had to say that?"

Carol watched him back out of the driveway before turning away. As Don drove off, he plugged in a headset and ordered his phone to call Roxanne. In a moment, she answered and asked, "Is this Don?"

"Yes. Listen, I know this is last minute, but do you mind if I come over for a bit? I have a couple of questions for you. I can be there in thirty minutes or so."

In the brief silence, Don imagined her look of surprise.

"Yeah, I guess. I don't have dinner or anything. We just ate."

"That's cool. I just need a few minutes of your time."

She gave him the address while Don punched it into the GPS.

The longish drive gave him time to contemplate. It was crazy to think that he could link a hypodermic needle found at a crime scene more than four decades ago with a specific person. How many heroin addicts could have lost a needle in the woods near Jeffrey Talent's body? Or maybe it was the child of a doctor who took it to show friends. Or the child of a diabetic. Or anyone else with a legitimate reason to have one.

He should concentrate on that envelope on Hank Swoboda's table, but that was even more difficult. He couldn't just walk in and say, "Can I see those pictures to make sure you didn't photograph the bodies of little boys you murdered?" But why would Hank keep incriminating photos in a box like that, and casually lay the envelope on a table in front of Don? Wouldn't his husband Curtis have gotten a look at them over the years?

Hopelessness washed over him. Every day, his father came closer to death while Don blundered about uselessly. He'd learned the boys weren't raped. He knew the killer took Polaroid photos. He knew the clothes were missing. It was a lot to unearth for just muddling about, but the details did nothing to contradict the idea of an anonymous, crazed sexual killer, just as everyone always thought. It was information that made no difference.

In the past, Don would have been thrilled and satisfied to learn of Dwayne's murder, but he felt neither. He was sorry for Carol and her mom, but he was surprised to feel an untroubled, room temperature indifference for Dwayne. Were the old wounds healing at last?

He cleared the woods about half an hour later. The lights of Greenhill spread on the flat clearing below. The steep hill landed him in the thick of the neighborhood. It looked as shabby as his memories, except the residents no longer tolerated junky yards.

Don followed the GPS directions until he reached Roxanne's house. It was indistinguishable from the others, white and square and far smaller than the spacious new garages on Cook Road. He knocked.

Immediately, pounding steps raced inside, shaking the tiny house. The door flew open. Don looked down at a boy in jeans and a T-shirt and socks and a Cleveland Browns baseball cap, and drew in a deep breath.

Billy. The kid looked just like Billy when he was a kid.

The boy looked up at him, unsure, and Don knew Billy's son was struggling to react properly to opening the door and finding a stranger in the dark. Behind him, a huge television blared, and a hand-held device on the floor played electronic music.

Roxanne appeared, wearing jeans and a sweatshirt, her curly hair tied back. "Cody, turn off the TV and go to your room."

Cody whined, but Roxanne was firm. "You need to finish your homework, and I need to spend a few minutes talking with an old friend of your dad." Cody looked up at him curiously. "This man knew your daddy when he was your age."

Like most ten-year-olds, Cody looked amazed the old person in front of him was once a child in some misty, ancient world. His mother shooed him away again, and he turned off the TV and ran from the room.

Roxanne said, "Come on in, Don. It was a surprise hearing from you. My neighbor's here, but I can ask her to leave if you want to talk in private."

"No need for that," he replied, following her through the living room to the immediate right, into a kitchen with a small eating nook. A woman with sharp features and an intense, inquisitive look sat at a round table. She was probably in her fifties, with platinum blond hair styled like a cascade of wispy brushstrokes. She smoked a cigarette and seemed to be taking mental notes, in the way that gossips drink in such details. He introduced himself. She said her name was Linda and offered a delicately angled hand.

"Would you like a beer or soda?"

"Water's fine."

"One-a those health nuts?" Linda asked. She had a rural Ohio accent, a faint Southern twang blunted with sturdy Midwestern vowels. He never heard it anywhere but Ohio, and it was instantly recognizable.

"Not even close," Don said.

Roxanne filled a glass with water from the tap. He didn't realize how thirsty he was until the first drops hit his tongue, and he took a long gulp. Roxanne cracked two cans of beer and set one in front of Linda. She picked up a box of Marlboro Reds and offered it to Don. He paused, remembering Chris O'Donnell's struggles to breathe, but a single cigarette wouldn't kill him, so he pulled one from the box. Roxanne held the lighter for him. "So what can I do for you, Don?"

The first hit gave him a rush. He'd forgotten that wonderful, woozy, spaced-out bliss of a nicotine high. A cigarette is a cheap date, and within a minute or two, it lands you back to earth, done for the day.

"I have sort of a strange question," he said. "Have you ever heard of a guy named Tom Malicheski?"

The women shared a surprised look. "The serial killer who grew up here?"

Serial killer?

Suddenly alert, he said, "I didn't know he was a serial killer. I was asking about a heroin dealer."

"That's him," Linda declared, slapping the table for emphasis.

"Holy shit," Don said. "What can you tell me about him?"

"I didn't grow up in Greenhill, but Linda did, and she remembers him." She held up her hand, inviting her neighbor to speak.

Center stage, Linda extinguished her cigarette by carefully rolling off the cherry, and leisurely lit another. She took a drag, blew out the smoke, and finally said, "He was always bad news." She picked a speck of something, probably imaginary, from her tongue and rubbed it away. "I was just seven or eight years old when he left Greenhill, and I don't have many memories of that time, but I remember him." She shook her head and took another drag.

Don's heart pounded at what might be his first real breakthrough.

"Do you want to know why I remember him?" she asked, and theatrically waited for a reply.

"Of course."

She leaned in, and her voice went macabre. "Because when he looked at you, you'd swear he had no eyes. My sister said it best. She said, 'He only smiles at wicked things.'"

Don remembered Tom Malicheski watching the teenaged boys shooting heroin on the steps of the abandoned house, and how he smiled as if filled with sadistic comfort. He recalled his own instantaneous hatred for him.

Linda continued. "All the girls around here of a certain age have a story about Tom Malicheski. Perverted stuff. You'd be riding your bike and come around the corner and there he'd be, hiding behind a bush or whatever, doing things that little girls shouldn't see. He'd have that smile on his face. People would find cats and dogs in the woods, family pets, that looked like they were tortured, and someone would remember they saw Tom around. A coupla times, someone broke into the houses of old ladies that lived by themselves. They'd wake up to something wet splashing on them, and see someone jump out the window, then she'd realize what the liquid was. Disgusting things. Everyone knew that when something happened, it was Tom Malicheski that did it."

The stories transfixed Don, and his heart raced. Linda was describing the exact sort of psychopath who killed those boys, but not all the details fit.

"Why wasn't he arrested?"

"He was. A buncha times, but he'd be back home before you knew it. Arrest, conviction, juvie, prison, release. A revolving door. His dad split when he was a baby, and his poor mother was just the sweetest thing ever. She said she raised him right and didn't know why he turned out so bad. I believed her, but not everybody did. I personally think he was born bad, one of those creatures without a soul. She died fifteen, twenty years ago. She was a broken woman, the saddest thing ever. Especially after what happened in South Dakota."

"What happened there?"

She held up a hand. "I'll get to that. He was still living here when he started dealing heroin. Well, this neighborhood had never seen anything stronger than moonshine up until then. And a little bit of weed. Well, that did it. People had had enough. He got kicked around a lot. It finally sank in that he was gonna end up buried in the woods one day, so he took off. He drifted around for a while between Pinecrest and North Homestead, but things got too hot for him there, and he left for South Dakota. He got a job as a trucker." She shook her head. "His poor mother was so proud that he got a job, and she told everybody that would listen. She thought it made up for everything else, just the fact that he was working." She scoffed and flicked her cigarette.

"And that's when the real trouble started," Roxanne said pointedly.

"You got that right. One after another, these lot lizards all across his trucking routes started getting raped and killed."

"Lot lizards?" he asked.

"Truck stop hookers. Enda-the-line cases. Those girls are usually hooked on smack and spend all their money as soon as they make it." She took a long drag. "A few girls from around here ended up that way. Some folks looked down their noses at them, called 'em skanks, but I just couldn't be that mean. They were the sorriest things you'd ever seen. They were like skeletons and they reeked of perfume because otherwise they'd stink like yesterday's fish. Honest to God, I don't know how a man could pay…well, let's just say that there's nothing more desperate than a lonely man." She looked over her shoulder at Roxanne, and they shared a knowing nod.

"When did he start killing?"

"Sometime around 1979, but probably earlier. He got away with it for about four years before they caught him. His official body count is seven girls, but even the cops said there were more."

Don searched his memory. Tom Malicheski's crimes happened during a fever pitch of national paranoia and coverage of serial killers, but he couldn't recall any of this. "I've never heard of this case before," he noted.

"Not surprising," Linda said. "Kill a pretty college girl and the national news comes to your trial. Kill some lot lizard junkie, and you're lucky if the family shows up. There were a coupla stories in the local papers about the case because he grew up here, but if you weren't looking for them, they were easy to miss. Mrs. Malicheski would stay inside for days after one ran. God, I pitied that woman."

"And what happened to him?"

Linda went very still, before breaking into tiny shakes while making an electric buzzing noise, her face frozen by imaginary pain. She relaxed. "Or maybe they put a line in his arm, I don't know. But they executed him, and I won't lie and say we didn't all breathe a little easier, knowing he was back in hell where he came from. His poor mother couldn't look anyone in the eye ever again."

He thought about those few seconds of Tom Malicheski's face in the flashlight beam. Don always heard you can't see evil on a person's face, but he knew that wasn't exactly true. You can see into the depths of bottomless malice when you shine an unexpected light, like when a man looks on in the dark as boys enslave themselves to the deadliest drug of them all.

Linda went on with complaints about the laws and the way the police handled Tom Malicheski, and Roxanne added a comment here and there. Don listened out of politeness, but as soon as he could, he said he had to get back to check on his father.

As he drove, he thought about the new revelations. It made perfect sense Tom Malicheski killed the three boys. The needle in the woods was tenuous evidence, but the undeniable history of murder was compelling. Don tried to feel excited but couldn't manage it. He could make a strong case to anyone that Tom was the killer, but it was far from solid. Maybe that was the best he could hope for after all this time, but it felt like a letdown.

Back at his parents' house, he checked his phone in the driveway and clenched his teeth when he saw another text from Bruce. This one said: *let's connect soon.* He was pleased that Bruce wasn't giving up, and this text was so vague that he tapped out a quick reply: *Love to.*

Inside, his mom was at the kitchen table, two places set. She rose when he walked in. "I made some baked macaroni and cheese. I know you love it."

"Thanks," he replied, thinking about how tightly his pants had fit when he slipped them on this morning. He wanted to hit the gym but hadn't felt up to it, consumed as he was by so many other things. His workout routine was casual but fairly consistent, which was all he needed to feel comfortable, but after two weeks of his mom's cooking, he was starting to feel bloated.

"Now, remember," his mom said, sliding a huge piece on his plate, "tomorrow morning I'm going with some of the gals from the community center to that crochet fair downtown, so I'll be leaving early. They have it every year, and I just love it. People come up with the cleverest things. I always find a few good Christmas presents."

A crispy brown layer topped the mac and cheese. The square melted on every side, the half-moon pasta carried away in a luxurious golden sauce. He shouldn't eat it. "Mom, I don't think…"

"What?"

A buttery, rich scent of stirred sharp cheeses rose from the plate, softened by milk and flour, and lightly seasoned with a bit of onions, salt and pepper. "Nothing," he replied, picking up his fork.

His mom left first thing in the morning, and Don checked on his dad. The stronger fentanyl knocked him for a loop, and he was just alert enough for Don to help him at the portable commode, and to drink a small bottle of chocolate-flavored liquid that promised all the nutrients and vitamins he needed. It was all his dad could manage to get past the cancer in his throat, and Don wondered why the manufacturer didn't offer prime rib or corned beef flavors. They'd make a fortune. His dad fell into a comatose stare after Don positioned him in bed, propped up by pillows to look out the window.

It was long past time to get started on the marketing memo, and Don went online to a private file-sharing folder that stored all the social media stats. With the agility of a maestro, he downloaded data sets, sorting them on the desktop. He opened and positioned files side by side, his eyes running down the columns that measured clicks and opens and unsubscribed numbers. He latched onto the figures, spotting the posts that generated interest and those that didn't, but he didn't charge his clients for crunching numbers. He analyzed the language, the platform, the time of day, the open rate and even the day's weather and news events. The interplay swirled in his head, individual facts he plucked and assembled, trying various configurations until they told a cohesive story. He kept a Word document open, typing his impressions and making notes. Soon, he was deep into an analysis due the next morning.

A car door slammed in the driveway, breaking his concentration, and he checked the time. It was only ten thirty, and his mom wouldn't be back for hours. Linnette wasn't due until midafternoon. Someone knocked.

He growled as he stomped to the door. He couldn't afford to be interrupted. The analysis was going to take most of the day as it was, and it still wouldn't meet his usual standards. He took a deep breath to settle himself, but he couldn't help yanking the door with an impatient jerk.

Bruce looked up from the other side of the storm window. He wore a deep brown corduroy jacket lined with fleece, and he gave a crooked, restrained smile that made Don feel as smooth as molten cheese sauce.

Don opened the door, and Bruce stepped inside. They nodded, and Don noted a cautious but hungry gleam in his eyes, which was almost certainly mirroring his own. They stood a few feet apart, and Don felt twitchy, wanting to grab him in a tight embrace, complete with a sloppy, panting, wet kiss you only give in private.

Bruce said, "I thought maybe you'd be free for a while. We could grab lunch at this place I know. They have the best fried perch sandwich on the Great Lakes, but it's a drive, so I'd thought I'd come by early to see if you can get away."

"That sounds awesome, but my mom's out and I have to look after my dad."

Bruce nodded. "Okay. Then maybe I can hang out here for a bit."

Don felt short of breath because Bruce wanted to spend time with him, no matter the circumstances. He looked at his laptop, the screen covered with overlapping windows. Reluctantly, he said, "I would love that, but I have some work that's due. I've been putting it off for too long, and I'm up against the wall. I should have some time tomorrow."

"Yeah, tomorrow's good." Bruce locked eyes with his. "But maybe you have enough time to tell me why you've been avoiding me. I thought we hit it off pretty good."

"We did."

"So what's the problem? Why have you been ignoring most of my texts?"

"It's complicated. It's something you told me, but I don't have time to get into it right now."

"Was it what I said about Linnette and her little brother? I saw how much it bothered you."

He took his first step from the silence. "Yeah, that was it. But I don't know if I can really explain."

"Sure you can. Explain it to me right now."

Don rubbed his forehead. "The thing is, it will take a while, and I'm jammed with work."

"I have work, too," Bruce said, his disappointment edged by impatience. "But I gave up my time to come here. I need to know why the only guy I've met in twenty years that makes me feel like you do is treating me like some second-rate trick."

The words punched. He hadn't prepared for this conversation, but so what? He closed his laptop. "Sit down," he said.

He paid no attention to the time, but hours slipped past. Bruce asked a question now and then, but otherwise listened without reaction. Don looked for any sign that the sordid tale was damaging Bruce's feelings for him, but he seemed to take it in as easily as a lake accepts rain.

While Don told him about the speculation that the killer was a teen or young adult, he left out his insane suspicions about Tim. There was no point in telling Bruce. It was crazy.

"Do you think Linnette knows who my dad is?" Don asked.

"If she does, she never said anything to me."

"I hope she doesn't. It would be one less thing to worry about."

"And what can I do to help?"

Don paused briefly to consider how easily he could fall in love with Bruce.

"I think I may have solved it. I'm thinking that Tom Malicheski was the killer. There's no way to prove it, but it seems likely."

"But some of the details aren't right," Bruce said. "If he was committing sexual assaults before then, he wouldn't have climaxed too early when he was killing those boys. And all of his victims before and after were female. Why would he suddenly change?"

"Those things bothered me, too. But what are the odds a known serial killer wasn't responsible for another string of murders in a town where he lived at the same time they were happening?"

"I agree it's a strong argument. It might be the answer, but it feels wrong. There's something missing. We have to find a way to look at those Polaroid photos."

We. Don's chest filled with warmth. "How do we do that?"

Bruce leaned forward thoughtfully. "Let's think about it." He smiled. "You are so damned handsome, you know that?"

CHAPTER TWENTY

1980–1982

By 1980, North Homestead felt like a different place to Don, the events of the summer of 1975 as distant as mythology. Backhoes had cleared the old farm equipment from the fields, a crew demolished the farmhouse where the Hartners used to live, and the chicken coop made way for a new home with a big yard.

The last relic of the old farm, the barn in the suburban backyard, had burned down in 1978. The fire started in the dark of the early morning, and sirens drew the neighborhood to watch. The barn popped and crackled until it slumped, releasing a tornado of flames and sparks, a thrilling mix of neon orange and red against the dark blue shag of dawn.

At the start of Don's freshmen year at St. Peter's High School in 1980, he spotted a few of his classmates from St. Anne's in the hallways. Soon, boys he didn't know said crude, angry things about his dad. At St. Anne's, nobody resisted the intense glee of cruelty. But as everyone grew older and experienced it for themselves, they peeled off from the game. Only the jerks continued to play by the time he got to St. Peter's.

Except that everybody still participated in belittling and scorning faggots. He heard the comments everywhere: routine insults hurled in the school hallway, people in stores making small talk, politicians, priests, and pastors raging on television.

Don scarcely remembered living in the body of the boy who misheard Judy Garland's lyrics and had only a faint awareness of a dark, distant threat so shocking and unbelievable he banished it to the hazy lands beyond his consciousness. It was a massive shadow in the mist. Sometimes it spoke to him, whispering its name, daring him to repeat it.

St. Peter's required gym class for all freshmen and juniors. A study break just before gym allowed him to enter the sanctum of the locker room early, before the juniors left. It dripped with thick steam, coating everything with the heavy musk of sweat. He never gave much thought to boys his own age, but the juniors seemed to be men already. They shouted, slammed lockers, and tore off their clothes. Flipping towels over their shoulders, they strutted to and from the showers, hairy and swinging. He looked around casually, but his mind snapped images like a camera at the Oscars.

One pair of friends always lingered after junior gym class, standing atop a bench with their prodigious parts hanging out for all to see, like long and plump links of bockwurst. They displayed themselves as they dried off, buttoned shirts, tied ties, and put on socks. Only then did they slip on underwear, often after holding it for a while, pretending to be absorbed in conversation.

Night after night, Don called up the photographs, especially of the proud and brazen duo, his fist pumping, the images raging, the feeling perfect, the joy escalating, the release ecstasy, the aftermath a guilt that tightened him into a fetus. *Say my name*, the shadow hissed.

He made a couple of friends in his sophomore year at St. Peter's. They hung out in the cafeteria, collaborated on extra credit assignments, and sometimes went to each other's houses to study and watch television, but not often. The boys at St. Peter's came from twenty miles around and lived too far away to see each other outside of school without a car.

At the end of Don's sophomore year in 1982, he was sixteen and amazed to be older than Rich would ever be. In June, Randy graduated from St. Peter's.

The same month, Tim moved back to Ohio with his wife and baby son, just after his discharge from the Marines. Tim and his family set up in the room he'd shared with Rich, evicting Randy, so they could land on their feet and make plans. Tim's wife Sally was sweet and friendly, and she and Don took to each other, but she was often busy with the baby or deep in big projects like finding a house.

Instead of moving back into Don's room, Randy set up a cot in the basement, where he talked and prayed for hours with his new friend

Daniel, a fervent Christian who could shoehorn a reference about his devotion to Jesus into any topic. Randy soon adopted the same skill. They reminded Don of the two naked juniors on the bench showing off their oversized dicks, except that Randy and Daniel had nothing as impressive to display.

In late June, a thunderstorm ripped its way to Cleveland, North Homestead in its path. On television, panicky reporters went breathless with warning, reports of tornadoes and extensive damage pouring in from Indiana and western Ohio. "Batten down the hatches, Cleveland," one cried. "Stay inside and don't go anywhere unless it's absolutely necessary. It's going to be a big one."

Don went outside to watch the distinctive wind of an approaching thunderstorm at work in the treetops. It swished the limbs in circles and took sudden, random jerks. Approaching clouds grew dark as ash and deepened into smoke until the thunderclouds rolled in like a flood of oil, rumbling with warning.

Rain fell and stung like pellets. Don raced inside to his room, picking up *The World According to Garp*, a strange but compelling book that twisted gender like pipe cleaners.

The wind ripped and whistled, escalating to a teakettle screech. He jumped at unexpected bursts of lightning that filled his room with white light. The boom and crack of thunder vibrated in the walls and inside his chest. Inevitably, the electricity went out.

With nothing to do in the dark, he placed the open book on his stomach, closed his eyes, and listened to the storm. Linemen would need hours to restore the power.

Small, rocky pings of hail hit the roof, growing more insistent as their numbers increased to a million angry little hammers. In the next room, Tim and Sally's baby, named Robbie in honor of Dad, screamed in terror and confusion.

Suddenly, a new sound began, like the low moo of a cow. Don opened his eyes at the strange noise. It grew louder, pitched low and deep beneath the storm, in a steady and solid moan.

"Tornado!" Dad screamed from somewhere in the house.

Don sat up. The groaning sound was a tornado siren, deliberately tenor because storms shred higher notes. He'd never heard one before. Tornadoes tore across vast, flat plains, not at waterfronts, and Lake Erie was just seven or eight miles to the north.

Explosions cracked open a parallel dimension of fury, and lightning blasted his room with white pulses. The tornado siren moaned ceaselessly, as if despairing of the life trapped in this time, at this place.

Dad threw open Don's door. "In the basement!"

Don met his mom in the hall. They clasped hands and hurried downstairs carefully in the dark.

"In the corner," Mom yelled at Randy, who knelt next to his cot in front of a candle, his head bowed in prayer. The ever-present Daniel raised his eyes piteously, his hands high, palms up.

"The Lord is with us, Mrs. Esker," he called. "Have no fear of the elements, for he is our safety!"

"Randy!" Mom shrieked, sharp enough to pierce his prayers. "Over in the corner, now!"

Randy checked with Daniel, who nodded, and he huddled with his family. Daniel remained candle-side and began to rock, his prayers a rapid monologue.

Sally, her sunshine California eyes wide with fear, carried her thrashing son, followed by Tim and Dad. They grouped together, and the baby's screams mercifully overpowered Daniel's prayers. The surrounding earth softened the storm, but the siren slithered along the ground and sank inside, clear and loud.

Ten or fifteen minutes later, the full fury of the storm started to pass. In a little while, the tornado siren slowed to a grind before tapering off.

"It looks like the worst is over," Dad said.

Daniel rose, the candle behind him casting a cartoonish dancing shadow. "The Lord has spared us," he declared with studied satisfaction. "That is his promise to all who pray unto him for salvation."

Unto? Angrily, Don said, "I'll bet there are people right now who are dead who were praying like crazy. What good did it do them?"

Tim and Sally laughed softly in agreement, and Daniel's eyes went wide with surprise, verging on hatred. Don noted that piety can be a convenient mask for vanity.

The tornado tore through the cornfield, closer than anyone could remember. It destroyed three houses on the back end, way up on Sprague Road. Four people had died.

The next day, he wandered along the rows of deep green corn

stalks flattened by the tornado into giant pinwheels. A path sheared all the way to a distant, scattered pile of lumber where the four lives ended.

He kicked his way along, nowhere to be, nowhere to go, no one to see. He could go home and finish *Garp*, but the baby screamed incessantly and Randy's religious mania exhausted him. It grew worse by the day, and Randy had apparently pegged him as an obvious and easy convert. It baffled Don. His brother didn't know him at all if he thought he was interested in his happy-clappy and brimstone religion.

Yesterday's rain evaporated, thickening the hot June air. He set off for the air-conditioned peace of the library. Along the way, people worked in their yards, clearing broken limbs, straightening fences and rearranging flowerpots. The previous night, they cowered in fear of their lives, and today they tidied up. Such contrasts fascinated him.

Glass filled the corners of the cement library. It shone like a silvery, magical city at night, but the exterior was drab in the daylight. No matter. The thousands of books thrilled Don with their promise of escape, release, and knowledge, and he wanted to read them all. The librarians recognized him and smiled in welcome.

He pulled his favorite large photo books of ancient Greece from scattered spots on the shelves, crinkly plastic protecting their covers. He carried them to a deserted table where almost nobody ever sat. Pictures of ruined temples captivated him, places where men in tunics once wandered and intoned wise things. Chipped mosaics told tessellated stories he heard as impressions in his mind.

He flipped the pages to artist renderings of these ancient places in full, bustling glory. He'd studied some of the paintings a million times: gymnasiums full of smiling, naked athletes; laughing soldiers stripping to bathe in a stream; dozens of jovial, nude sailors setting up a seaside camp. He imagined the comments that prompted their easy smiles, the jokes that made them laugh, and he ached to live among them. They looked serene, content to exist with only men, no modesty because they never concealed anything from each other, nothing like the brassy, competitive nakedness of locker rooms that inspired only lust. The atmospheric perfection of the ancient scenes overwhelmed him, heightening mere sexual arousal to the hypnotic eroticism of desire. It pounded in his head. *Say my name.*

Late afternoon, he left the library to walk to the pond in the woods behind the recreation center, far down Lorain Road. He hadn't been to the pond in years, and he was curious to see it again. The woods smelled of wet nature, pungent with life but earthy with decay. He kicked through the bushes. Muddy piles from snake holes melted in tubes above the ground, like candle drippings.

He reached the pond at dusk, a placid oasis surrounded by thickets of bushes and trees. Tiny skate bugs skimmed the water, and their trails looked like invisible fingers raking the surface to test the temperature.

It was deserted, but the beer cans, liquor bottles, cigarette butts, and other trash warned of the summer night revelries soon to descend. Over the years, he'd heard about the boys and girls skinny-dipping, marijuana, and music, things going on in the trees. Nude frolicking in the knee-deep pond must show everything to everyone, boys and girls alike, a universal yet bewildering violation of the sublime natural order engraved in his mind. He knew the men in their ancient worlds agreed with him, even if nobody else in a hundred miles did, and sometimes that felt like enough.

He removed his sneakers and socks and rolled up his jeans. He stepped into the water and the bottom felt opulent, like velour. He sloshed to the center, looking up as the first stars sputtered to life. He sometimes still imagined himself as a photon of light, but favored more intense rescues these days.

Two girls arrived, snapping through the twigs like giggling nymphs, carrying bottles of liquor. They wore feather earrings, tight tops, and shorts that rode high on their thighs. If they knew him they would scowl, but they didn't and they laughed, offering sips from their bottles.

He splashed his way from the pond and took a swig from each, one clear, one brown. The fiery liquid blazed down his esophagus like gasoline, but when it reached his stomach, it filled him with serenity as smooth as the marble of a Greek statue. They asked if he had some weed and didn't seem to mind when he said, "No." They said he should stay because he was really cute and of a bunch of their friends would arrive soon. One of the girls was looking for a new boyfriend.

He blushed, and they loved it.

Others came, the girls friendly, the boys wary. One of the leading guys, wiry but muscled in a tank top, asked where he went to school and Don told him. He hooted and shouted, "We have a St. Peter's faggot here! Go back to boy's town, homo." *If only*. Don shot a look at the girls who'd invited him, but their faces said he should make it easy on all of them and leave. He did.

He didn't want to navigate the woods in the dark, so he headed for the recreation center, the lights of the complex guiding him through the branches. He emerged into a field robust with summer weeds as thick as wheat. They swayed for a good quarter mile until stopping at caged tennis courts. Even from this distance, he heard the hollow pop of tennis balls, a sound he always liked.

The field rolled with hills formed by plows when they'd flattened the massive pad for the athletic complex. It loomed in the distance, ablaze with lights, hosting year-round ice-skating and swimming, along with weight rooms, tracks, and racquetball and basketball courts. Don trod carefully through the unfamiliar terrain, some valleys so deep he couldn't see over the hills.

As he made his way across, he summoned his fantasy that he'd stumbled across a portal in time. The pulsating edge glowed and crackled, and it opened to a company of naked men in an ancient, radiant landscape, a blue sea glittering in the distance. They smiled and urged Don to join them, waving to hurry him because they knew things, many things, that he didn't. They gripped his arms to help him enter, and as he passed through, his body transfigured to equal their perfection and his clothes dissolved. As they crowded about in welcome, the portal popped out of existence behind him in a burst of sparks, gone forever.

Instead, about halfway across the field, he rounded a corner and came upon a shaggy boy pissing into the weeds.

Billy. Don would recognize him anywhere. Billy concentrated on his aim, his face down.

Over the years, Don had seen Billy infrequently, glimpses as his first love left or arrived across the street. He watched their lives diverge as Billy aged. In middle school, Billy grew his hair long and wore pants ragged at the hems, racing off on his bicycle with friends who dressed the same. In the past two years, Billy's hair grew past his shoulders, and he slouched in clumpy boots with untied laces flicking about. He wore black T-shirts with colorful but demonic rock group decals, and heavy jackets in all weather. When their eyes accidentally met, they looked away.

Billy shook his penis and pushed it back inside his jeans. As he zipped up, he raised his eyes and this time, Don didn't look away.

"Hi," Don said, his heart thumping. *Say my name*. Don remembered the way they'd kissed and clung to each other in sleep. He felt a hot rush, here in the darkness of the sheltering hills and weeds, out of sight of the rest of the world.

Billy looked indecisive. Don knew he was remembering everything, and he hoped Billy felt an impulse to pick up where they'd left off in the refrigerator when Eddie interrupted. The first touch would vaporize the years. He saw emotions battle in Billy's eyes, but something ugly won the fight, and his face went cold.

"What are you looking at, faggot?"

Don had somehow always known it would come to that word.

Billy's voice drew friends behind a hill, and they stood, the boys scruffy and instantly filled with fight, the girls glassy-eyed and curious, fingering their hair aside. Don smelled marijuana, cigarettes, and beer. "What's up, man?" one of the guys asked Billy, fastening his eyes on Don.

Don felt a clench of fear, and the surroundings now seemed like a wasteland, far from the safety of the recreation center lights and the bright pop of tennis balls.

"This fag was checking out my dick while I was taking a piss."

"I was just walking home," Don said. "I didn't know anybody was here."

Don saw they knew he was telling the truth, but the boys' faces went hard again in allegiance to Billy. One girl looked scared and said, "Just leave him alone." A boy scoffed and replied, "There's only one thing to do to faggots," as if everyone knew it was true, even the outsider rebels getting high and drunk, scornful of the recreation center's wholesomeness. They weren't as rebellious as they imagined. Not nearly.

The boys formed a half circle behind Billy. Don froze in hopeless fear. Billy said, "You guys stand back. Leave this one to me."

Attempted flight or resistance would bring on the wrath of the whole group, and they were itching to join the fun. He crouched, and just before he closed his eyes Billy trotted in his direction and leaped, his hair flying in clumps that caught the fluorescence of the distant lights like white fire, the hottest kind.

A kick to his head set off the St. Anne's school bell, shrill and relentless. His neck snapped back, and a beat later, the boot crashed into his cheek. He drew in a breath of shock at the force, and blood filled his throat. He reared up to cough it away, desperate to breathe. Billy hit him full in the chest, and something inside broke. He tried to scream, but his lungs were empty. Desperate, he tried gulping air, but every intake of breath prompted an involuntary retch of splattering blood.

Another blow on his shoulder sent him reeling back, and he twisted face down into the weeds. Billy kicked his legs and side, and Don's face tightened with the effort to breathe. He felt feverish, gasping and choking and gasping again, a honking rhythm that sounded like the bray of a donkey.

He heard shouts and laughter, and one voice above them all breaking through the ringing bell, "You faggot queer! Fucking homo! Do you like looking at my dick? Fudgepacker faggot fairy homo cocksucker ass licker pole smoker rump ranger bum fucker shit eater!" He heard, "Stop it!" in a crying, shrieking girl's voice. "You're hurting him!" It was almost funny.

One final kick in the side, and he puked up a thick, small clump of vomit that tasted weird, like aluminum. Then another, not so strong, on his thigh.

"Let's get out of here."

A spitting sound, high-fives slaps, a girl sobbing, all fading away except for the bell, still ear splitting.

He wasn't sure if he slept, but he was alone when he opened his eyes. The bell wasn't as sharp, although it rang on and on. He pushed up and intense pain blinded him in a world of spiraling sparks. His fuzzy reality ebbed into shaded focus. He was in the field behind the recreation center. He had to get home.

He couldn't seek help at the tennis courts, nor could he take to the sidewalks. Everyone would see he was broken and bloody because he was a faggot. He could only return through the woods. He found himself among the trees, and tried but failed to remember when he left the field. Then he saw a busy intersection through the trunks, St. Anne's on the corner. How he came this far, he couldn't recall, and he pushed on. He looked up at the McDonald's sign glowing through the leaves, the last thing Danny Miller saw, maybe from this very spot. He was close to home.

He reached a housing development that curved around to Stearns

Road, and he stumbled along the tree line of the backyards. He heard television and music, but nobody spotted him as he limped and dragged along.

He had to cross Lorain Road at some point, where somebody in the steady traffic would see him. He crouched behind bushes but tipped over, unable to balance. When he opened his eyes, the traffic was notably sparser, and he waited until a car sped past and only distant headlights twinkled.

He tried to run, but his knees sank with each step and halfway across the street, he doubled over, his hands flat to the pavement. Headlights from a speeding car raced closer, and he hobbled to the sidewalk just in time. It veered out of the way with a squeal of tires, a whiff of rubber, an angry blast of horn, and a shout of "Stupid fag!" on the wind.

He didn't care anymore if someone saw him, and he clopped and staggered down the sidewalk. He kept a steady pace, because if he walked too fast, the houses whirled like he was on a spinning ride. Cars passed. One or two slowed, but they drove on when he ignored them. Outside his house, he practiced standing and walking, but he could only move if bent over. It would have to do.

The bell still rang as he opened the door and propped against the frame. He planned to mutter excuses about not feeling well and make for his bed.

At the kitchen table, Sally held a spoon of mush to the baby's mouth. She cooed and sparkled, speaking in the honeyed voice of a mother. She looked up. Don smiled. Her face cracked with horror and she screamed. Don collapsed.

Tim and Dad sliding him into the backseat of the car. Mom, hands to her mouth, sobbing and urging everyone to hurry, hurry, hurry. Sally, her face running with tears, holding her baby tight to her shoulder in the driveway, saying, "Hang in there, Don!" The car drove, and he rocked, dimly aware Tim was squeezed in back to hold him steady. Don heard the mournful groan of the tornado siren and realized it was coming from his mouth.

Emergency room nurses, eyes going wide, leaping into action. "You should have called an ambulance." He was on a gurney. A doctor with a penlight asking his name and his school and who was President of the United States. "This will only pinch for a bit." The bell faded.

He woke to a blurry monochrome world that resolved into an unfamiliar view of light brick walls and a smokestack, trees beyond. He was propped up in a bed, wearing a bizarre orange gown. His dad slumped in a chair at his feet, sleeping. Don lifted a hand to his forehead and was shocked to see tubes feeding into his arm, attached to sacks of clear liquid hanging from a metal pole.

He had a dull headache, but it felt funny, the full onslaught of pain detectable, raring to break free of some sort of chemical dam. The bell rang full in his ears again before fading almost instantly to a distant high-pitched rattle. Suddenly, he remembered Billy's form as he leaped, and he cried out.

His dad jerked awake, his shirt rumpled and untucked. He gripped the arms of the chair. "Donnie? Donnie, what year is it?"

Why would he ask such a silly question? "1982." His voice came out as a babyish whisper, like he could only imitate speech.

"What's your name? Your full name?"

"Donald Christopher Esker." *Donel Crissofer Esser.*

"Do you recognize me?"

He blinked, wondering if his dad had gone insane. "Yeah, Dad." *Ya, da.*

His father dropped his head to Don's chest, and Don smelled that he was unwashed. Dad sobbed and grabbed Don's shoulders, careful to keep clear of the plastic tubes.

After his dad cried himself out, he pulled the chair to his side, shielded by a white curtain. He rubbed Don's free arm, splotched with bruises. "Don," he asked softly, "do you remember who did this to you?"

Billy zipping up as their eyes met. "Leave this one to me." His hair haloed with fluorescent hellfire.

Even in his haze, he knew he couldn't admit that Billy attacked him for being a fag. "I fell. Basement steps. New house up the street."

Dad stared. "You didn't get these injuries falling down a flight of stairs, Donnie."

He nodded. "In the dark."

His dad sighed. "I ordered Tim to take your mother home so she could get some rest. She was here until three o'clock this afternoon. It's nearly seven. We did not spend all night and all day with doctors coming in and out to hear some cockamamie story about falling down the stairs. Someone did this to you. Probably several people. Tell me who and why."

Say my name. "Fell," he said.

His dad leaned back. He looked out the window. "Donnie, I'm sorry for everything you've had to go through for being my son. I want you to know that if I could fix it, I would, but I can't." His face screwed up, but Don watched him fight the emotions away. He wished he knew how to do that. "If someone is giving you trouble because you're my son, I need to know."

Don had never realized his father harbored such fears for his sake, but the truth was worse. He shook his head. "Fell."

After a while, his dad nodded, but Don saw he didn't believe him. "The doctors say you have a concussion. Your mother had one, after... when she fell in the kitchen."

Fainted.

"She got over it just fine. You have a lot of other injuries but nothing critical. You'll need some dental work, and you're going to need the rest of the summer to recuperate, but you'll recover. It's your mind I'm worried about." His father looked into his eyes. "You're the most intelligent person I've ever known, Donnie. I can't tell you how proud I am that you're my son. I work with engineers and maybe they know more than you do, but you're still more intelligent than any of them. St. Anne's wanted to advance you a grade or two. They even said you might be able to skip three grades based on your skills test. St. Peter's wanted to discuss the possibility, too. It would kill me if something happened to your brain."

Even through his fog, Don registered the monumental implications. Where could he be right now, instead of this hospital?

"Why. Not. Let them?" He felt betrayed.

Dad shook his head sadly. "We couldn't do that to you, Donnie. We considered it very carefully, but we made the right decision. You're not strong enough yet to deal with older kids, especially the boys. It's nothing to be ashamed of, but you need to grow into the world at a slower pace. It's no big deal. Some boys do. There's time enough for you to shine."

He couldn't make sense of Dad's argument. He felt cheated. "You never said."

"If we'd told you, it would have eaten you up every time

something bad happened, every time you didn't like a teacher or a fellow student." He shook his head. "No, Donnie. We did what we had to do."

"Let me decide. Why not?" He wanted to cry.

"Secrets can be very bad things, Donnie. Like Rich's secret, which your mother and I bear full responsibility for, not you or your brothers."

Don had never considered the possibility his parents felt guilt for Rich's death. He thought everyone knew it was his fault for not saying anything all those months. His brothers couldn't be faulted for not knowing enough to speak up, but he could. He should explain it to his parents so they could stop blaming themselves.

His father went on. "But some secrets are good, Donnie, if you have a good reason to keep them. Sometimes the best thing you can do for a person is keep a secret."

Don closed his eyes and rested his head on the pillow. His dad meant his own secrets, not Don's, but the moral was the same. *Say my name.*

I'll never say it, he replied angrily. *Shut up.* It silenced the shadow for a long time afterward.

CHAPTER TWENTY-ONE

Don drove down Lorain Road, and the trick-or-treaters reminded him it was Halloween. The autumn dusk was light amber, and the older kids were apparently at home getting into their costumes. Parents herded crowds of toddlers dressed in elaborate get-ups, most of which he didn't recognize. The boys crunched along in plastic superhero armor, not a hobo or pirate in sight. The girls still favored princesses, but the new animated ones he couldn't name. Their costumes flashed with lights and bleeped with music and sounds. *Lucky kids.*

He stopped at the red light near the police station, and large groups came from both directions. Young parents greeted each other as they crossed paths. Don spotted a grandmother in costume wading through the children but realized it was Dolores from the police archives in her uniform, unencumbered by the large ring of keys that bounced and jangled incessantly at her thigh while inside the archive building.

The light changed, but stragglers peppered the crosswalk, and while he waited, he noticed Dolores heading for McDonald's. When the last of the parents hurried their children to the curb, Don drove on, charmed by the traditional parade teeming on the sidewalks of North Homestead. In San Francisco, Halloween was a riot of sparkly and sexy characters, ironic and satirical. His Facebook feed was probably filling with raunchy and exuberant photos, but it all started here, because every drag queen took her first costumed steps in a place like this.

Don turned onto a residential street leading to Bruce's house and drove into the hollow of a swaying canyon of colors. Sugar maples, the glorious stars of autumn, towered by the dozens. It looked like the clouds of sunset had descended and settled on the branches, each tree boasting pure reds, smooth yellows, and rich oranges. They threw their limbs wide, as if eager for admiration of their beauty. Their annual triumph was brief, for the wind was plucking away the fall color season only a week after it had begun in earnest.

Beige leaves twirled by the thousands and skittered across the road. Driving through the whirlwinds, Don felt an exquisite ache of joy and dread. He was in love, which also meant he was in trouble.

He reached Bruce's house and sent him a text, the modern version of the driveway beeps of his youth that made perfect sense to teens but that parents had universally deplored. Moments later, Bruce emerged, dressed in tight jeans and the same dark brown corduroy jacket. Don watched his approach, his confident grin, and his thick legs, each step accentuating the fullness at his crotch.

Bruce hopped in the car. They leaned together for a kiss that started as a quick peck but softened into a lingering and sensual caress of lips, gently tugged by teeth and slicked by tongues. Only after they drew back did Don remember this was North Homestead, not San Francisco, where such kisses between men were woven into the tapestry of the city. Realizing Bruce didn't care if his neighbors saw, he felt proud to be driving away with him, and he hoped someone had been watching.

"What time is Hank expecting us?" Bruce asked.

"He said around five. He and Curtis are taking the red-eye to Cancun, so they wanted to eat early. I told him not to bother with dinner, but he insisted on making a fancy meal when I told him I wanted to introduce him to my boyfriend."

Bruce chuckled, and Don gave him a sideways smile. They developed the boyfriend ruse to get inside Hank's place, but it felt inevitable to Don the moment they agreed to it. It thrilled and sickened him at the same time.

"How are you going to get both Hank and Curtis out of the room?" Don asked.

"Leave it to me."

"Why not just tell me?"

"I can't. I don't know yet. Just be ready to jump and take a look at those photos as soon as you're alone."

Don didn't like putting so much trust in a guy he barely knew. It seemed like he'd known Bruce for years, but that feeling made him wary. It was an intoxicating illusion, the very reason his years of dating were smoking and cratered. At this point in a relationship, a man couldn't be anything but a mystery. Only a fool thought otherwise, and Don wanted to try a new role.

At the door to Hank's unit, Bruce took his hand, grinned, and said, "Boyfriends, remember?" Entwining their fingers felt more intimate than sex because it was more consciously engaged, and Don liked the feeling.

Hank and Curtis welcomed them, smiles and introductions all around. They crowded into the entrance hall, just outside of the kitchen, and Hank brushed up against a large crystal swan on a marble pedestal.

"Careful," Curtis said to his husband. "This is a one of a kind. It's Waterford." He nudged it back into place.

The dining area was down the short hall, next to the living room. The table glittered with an arrangement of utensils, plates, and wine goblets. Slender candles cast a steady glow, spiked inside a seasonal pumpkin centerpiece overflowing with silk autumn leaves.

"You didn't have to go to all this trouble," Don said. "I know you guys are getting ready to leave tonight."

"I had us packed two days ago," Curtis said, waving away his concern. He motioned for everyone to sit before he returned to the kitchen.

"Curtis likes to fold everything just so," Hank said. "He's somewhat obsessive about neat clothing."

"Clothes say a lot about you," Curtis shouted from the kitchen.

The hosts wore slacks, button-down shirts, and sweaters. "What are you trying to say, Hank?" Don asked.

Hank smiled. "My clothes are saying that I have a fussy husband. I'm happy to dress like you two, jeans and a shirt."

"No matter what anyone says," Curtis said, returning with two bottles of wine dangling from the fingers of one hand, carrying a tray of puffy baked things in the other, "people make a million instant assumptions about you by the way you're dressed." He passed the hors d'oeuvres around while Hank uncorked the wine. "We're flying first class to Mexico, and a casual sweater says we're used to good service, but we're not overbearing. Treat us well, and nobody gets hurt."

They toasted to old and new friends, to good food and fine wine, and Curtis insisted they clink their goblets to Brad Pitt.

"This wine is excellent," Bruce said. "I'm not used to drinking, but this is really outstanding." Curtis instantly refilled his glass.

The meal was delicious and presented with flair: saffron rice with poached lobster, chicken breast in a creamy truffle sauce, and a surprisingly delicious wilted kale with caramelized onions and peas. After two weeks of his mother's home cooking, it was good to remember how he usually ate. The conversation flowed easily, and Don kept the focus on Hank and Curtis, not wanting to invent an elaborate story about his relationship with Bruce. They seemed happy to discuss their lives. People usually are.

Every now and again, Don glanced at the drawer in the far wall of the living room where Hank stored his box of unpleasant North Homestead memories. It wouldn't take more than a few seconds to get across the room, but the more he watched Hank and Curtis and their easy-going, affectionate natures, the more certain he was the photos would prove meaningless.

After Bruce finished his third glass of wine, they moved on to the other bottle. Bruce poured his own, and his glass was notably fuller than the others. "Iss really good!" he enthused, his words sanded in one continuous sound, drawing glances from both hosts. He looked flushed.

For dessert, Curtis set out a selection of cheeses with fig compote, sliced pears, and port wine in small glasses. Bruce said that as long as nobody else was drinking the dinner wine, he'd prefer to have that, and he polished off the bottle.

As Bruce got drunker, Don wondered if it was part of his plan. Heavy drinkers are trouble, so maybe this was a major flaw, starkly revealed. Polite fictional roles at the start of dating only led to unpleasant discoveries. Every time.

Curtis asked, "Who wants coffee?" looking directly at Bruce.

Bruce pushed back his chair, rising, grabbing his wine goblet. "I need some water," he said. He stumbled his way to the kitchen, ignoring Curtis, who asked, "Still or sparkling?"

Hank and Curtis handled the situation graciously, smiling, until a great crash of shattering glass came from beyond the wall, bringing them all to their feet. Don knew the crystal swan was on their minds as Hank and Curtis hurried to the kitchen. He started to follow, but suddenly realized he was alone.

As Bruce apologized in a loud, slurred voice, Don was at the drawer in seconds. It slid open with the ease of skillfully crafted furniture. The cardboard lids of the box, tucked into each other, lifted with one pull. The envelope was on top.

Quickly, Don removed the photos in a bunch, grimacing at the crinkle of old paper that anyone in the kitchen could hear. He drew in a deep, silent breath of shock at the first picture. It stopped him cold, amazed. He recognized details like the black refrigerator and the sliding glass doors. His pulse raced. "Holy shit," he muttered.

"I swear to God," Bruce said with the annoying and overly dramatic penitence of a drunk, "I'll pay for everything."

His heart beating, Don flipped through the photos, pausing now and again at yet another image that astounded him. The pictures would have blown North Homestead wide open forty years ago.

"Here, I have some cash," Bruce insisted, and Hank and Curtis tersely responded they didn't want his money.

Just a minute or two later, Don slipped one of the photos into his back pocket, replaced the envelope, and closed the box, not bothering to fold the flaps.

He was halfway to the table when Hank reappeared, looking confused and suspicious to see Don in his living room instead of at the table. In another few steps, Don reached his chair and said, "I'm sorry about that. Obviously, we'll pay for any damage."

"What were you doing in my living room?" Hank asked.

"I needed to get my bearings." He gestured to the kitchen. "This kind of thing has happened before."

Hank nodded. "Don, it's been nice to see you again, and I wish you the best, but I think you should take Bruce home now. He can barely walk."

Don looked deep into his eyes, searching for visual evidence of what the photos revealed about him. "I'm sorry."

Hank spoke with finality. "Sometimes old friendships are best left in memories, Don."

Despite everything, Hank's words saddened him. This was the second time the handsome telescope man drove him away. Don went to the kitchen, surprised and relieved to see the swan still perched on its pedestal, shining with crystalline perfection. Bruce leaned against the kitchen counter, watching as Curtis swept up shards of the wine goblets. Curtis mashed the broom to the floor, fanning the bristles against the tiles, his face enraged.

Mumbled good-byes preceded a hasty exit, Don holding Bruce's arm to keep him steady. The door shut firmly behind them.

In the hallway, Bruce straightened, his face sharpening with awareness. He pulled away, walking steadily. "Did you get a look at the photos?"

"You aren't drunk?"

"A little, but it takes more than five glasses of wine to knock me on my ass like that. When I was younger, I'd hit the bars every night, all night."

So had he. "Let's get down to my car. I don't want to discuss it here."

Don slid into the driver's seat, removed the photo from his pocket, and handed it to Bruce. He gripped the steering wheel, leaning back against the headrest.

Bruce chuckled. "Are all the photos like this one?"

Don nodded, and Bruce said, "Why are you upset about this? It's just a photo of a naked man. You can't even see his face."

"You can see his mouth and chin," Don said. "It's enough to recognize him. It's our old parish priest, Father O'Shay."

"No shit?" Bruce said, chuckling again.

"There were a ton of other photos just like it. I recognized some of the others, too. I'm almost certain one of them was a teacher at St. Anne's."

"What's the big deal? So Hank took dirty pictures of his tricks, so what?"

"I'm not sure I can explain it. I just can't believe all of that was going on at the same time I thought there wasn't another gay person in a hundred miles."

"That wasn't their fault."

"I know, but it pisses me off. But at the same time, it also made me realize how much I admire Hank. When they arrested him, he could have brought the town to its knees with those photos. He doesn't want to see me again."

"Because I was a drunken slob who broke the goblets?"

"Well, yeah, but it's more than that. I remind him about too many things he wants to forget." Don pushed the button to start the car. "I'm happy at least to confirm Hank didn't have the murder photos, although I never thought he did."

"You should be happy about something else," Bruce said. He handed him the photo. "Father O'Shay was packing."

Don studied the picture. "He sure was, wasn't he?"

After a beat, they broke up laughing.

The next morning, his mom asked, "Did you have a good time last night with your friend?"

"Yeah, I did. His name is Bruce." He'd reminded her three or four times already.

"Bruce," she repeated, as she always did. "When are you going to invite him over for dinner so we can meet him? We can have Tim and Sally and Randy here."

"Really?" he replied, grateful for the offer, but unsure. Was he ready for something as serious as introducing Bruce to his family? No other man had lasted long enough to reach that phase, and thank God for that.

"Of course. What does he like to eat?"

"It seems like a pretty serious step, Mom. I'm not sure I'm ready."

"Oh, for heaven's sake. It's not like I'm the Queen of England and you have to clear it through diplomatic channels. You obviously like him. So let us see him and form our own opinions."

Her insistence surprised him. "Okay," he said. "Let me see what works for him."

His dad was awake, looking at a book. Don was never sure if he was reading or just staring at the pages. Dad kept a stack of novels on his bedside table, and as far as Don could tell, he chose and opened them at random. Now that he was used to the higher dose of fentanyl, his mind was lucid and clear, and Don checked in on him frequently during the day in case he was in the mood to talk.

"How are you feeling, Dad?"

He closed the book and set it aside. "Not bad. It took me a while to adjust to these new patches."

"I think they're really working for you. You haven't asked for any extra morphine since you got used to them."

"Yeah, they're good. I'm lucky to have them. If you're going to die of cancer, you might as well be comfortable. I guess that's all I can ask for. How's your work going?"

"Not bad," he said, remembering the conversation with his client the other day when he told them he was withdrawing from the account. They begged him to reconsider, whipping together a conference call with the CEO and promising a healthy but unspecified bump in his hourly rate, but he said they could find younger, hungrier marketing analysts for a lot less. He'd managed the company's social media for six years, and it was time for fresh blood. After he hung up, he was down to three accounts and seriously considering his options on those.

He looked at the books on his dad's table, and an idea suddenly popped into his head. "Would you be interested in watching some movies or something? I can get you a tablet to play them."

His dad looked intrigued by the offer. "I wouldn't know how to work something like that."

"It's super easy, Dad. I could set it all up for you so you'd only have to touch one icon and type in the title of what you want to watch. I promise you'll have no problem with it."

"Could I watch some documentaries, too?"

"Yeah. Tons of them." He stood, wondering why this hadn't occurred to him before. "I'll head out now to buy one."

"Have your mother give you the money."

"Okay, will do."

Within two hours, his dad held a tablet with two icons on the display that Don labeled "Movies and TV" and "Documentaries." In addition to buying the tablet, Don also paid for six streaming subscriptions and consolidated the search features, so his dad only needed to punch in the title or category once. He left him sitting up in bed, scrolling through the options, amazed by so many choices.

His mother dealt with bills and a checkbook at the kitchen table. "I checked with your brothers. They can both make it tomorrow night for dinner, so ask your friend. Bruce, I mean."

Surprised again at her determination to meet Bruce, he sent off a text. Within in a minute, Bruce replied: *Terrific!*

"Okay, we're on for tomorrow, Mom." He felt a beat of anxiety but pushed it away.

"Great. I'll make a nice pork roast."

Don joined his mom at the table, opening his laptop to type out his thoughts about the murders, now that Hank was in the clear and he'd chased down every other lead. He wrote a short argument naming Tom Malicheski as the killer. He was surprised the case against Tom was stronger than he thought. Short of finding the Polaroid photos or the clothes, he had no way to connect the crimes to anyone, but he liked Tom as the killer.

He suddenly realized he might know a way to get physical evidence implicating Tom. He opened his web browser and typed in Tom's name, getting several links to sites that detailed the crimes of serial killers. He clicked, and a picture of Tom blipped on the screen. Don felt a stab of ancient hatred. The photo was taken just after Tom's sentencing, and he wore the same vacant smile, unconcerned with the anguish and turmoil he'd spread. Don checked some of the other links. Tom's case was apparently routine, and all the web sites seemed to use the same source material.

But maybe, during the investigation after Tom's arrest, the police in South Dakota discovered the clothes of three unknown boys, garments that reeked of sinister things. They didn't find the photos, obviously, but it was plausible they'd arrested Tom, discovered the clothes, and didn't know what to make of them.

Linnette arrived for her afternoon appointment, and Don joined her as she chatted with his dad, who proudly demonstrated the tablet for her.

"Don said it would be easy, and it is!" he enthused. He typed *War Movies* into the search field and scrolled through the choices. "I haven't seen *The Longest Day* in years," he said. "I'm going to watch it just after *Bridge on the River Kwai*. That's a terrific movie, one of the best. Man's ego blinding him to everyone else's concerns, the search for immortality, the disregard for everything when your own accomplishments are on the line. The only problem with this tablet thingy is the volume. I can't seem to adjust it properly."

"I should have gotten you some headphones," Don said. "Why don't I run out to the store and get them right now?"

"Are you going to the mall?" Linnette asked. He nodded and she turned to his dad. "Rob, do you mind if I go with Don? You seem to be doing great today, and I need to pick up my new glasses."

His dad lifted the tablet and said happily, "I don't mind at all. I got a lot of watching to do."

Don drove, and after Linnette finished praising the car interior, she said, "Your dad has really adjusted to the new dosage. I'm glad we started him on it so early. He might be able to go as long as a month or more without an increase."

"He hasn't asked for any morphine beyond the shot I give him after putting on the patch."

"That's good, but remember to give it to him whenever he wants. How have his spirits been?"

"Up and down, as usual."

"Well, like I said, people who are good-natured maintain that up until death, at least that's what I've observed. There's no difference between how saints and sinners feel on the inside. They all get angry and feel like breaking something or spitting in someone's face, but it's how you deal with those emotions that counts, and your dad is a good person."

Don shot her a look of admiration. "That was a very insightful thing to say about saints and sinners."

"Thanks."

The moment dropped into his lap. Now was the time to ask. If she knew about his dad, all would be well. If not, she could ask for another client if she wanted to. "Linnette, did you recognize my dad's name when you first got him as a client?"

Her face went blank. "What do you mean?"

"I mean do you know about the rumors that have been following our family for more than forty years?"

She blinked. "Of course, Don. Everyone who was alive and thinking back then remembers what happened to the Eskers. It was disgusting." She made a delicate high-pitched whine in her throat, like a kitten testing its voice. "Did Bruce tell you Danny was my brother?"

"Yes. He wasn't gossiping. He just wanted me to know."

She nodded. "I knew it would all come out when you started dating. Sometimes when I think about God, I'm not sure I believe, but I'll always be a Christian because of my parents' example. They were the only people in this town who had the right to be irrational about your dad, but they refused to be so unkind. It's just the most beautiful example of Christian charity I can think of." She went quiet for a while. "I relive what happened to Danny every day. I was only inside for a few minutes. He was right there in the front yard, and then he was gone. I tried believing an angel came and took him directly to heaven. I tried so hard to believe that, but I could never escape the fact that they found his body behind McDonald's, and no angel scooped him away. It wouldn't have happened if I'd been there."

"How old were you?"

"Twelve."

"That's a big burden for anyone to carry around, let alone a twelve-year-old girl."

"I've been carrying it my whole life."

"Linnette, this might sound corny, but there came a point in my life when I had to make an active decision to forgive almost everyone for years of insults and put-downs. They didn't know they were doing that to me, but they still did it, and I cleared the slate for all of them and started fresh. It was years before I realized I'd neglected to forgive someone."

"Who?"

"Myself. All the anger and frustration of those years. I could be cruel sometimes, and thoughtless. Self-righteous. All the things other people did to me. And I took responsibility for things that weren't mine. But I had to wipe my own slate clean. It changed a lot of things when I realized I could also forgive myself."

"Did it work?"

"Better than I ever hoped. Give yourself a break, Linnette. You were a child and didn't expect anything to happen to your brother. Nobody ever does, believe me." He paused. "I know what I'm talking about."

"Thanks," she said softly. "I'm glad that worked for you. I can't tell you how many people have said something similar to me, and I appreciate the thought, but I don't even know how to begin wiping my own slate. If you can tell me how to do it, I'd love it."

"I wish I could."

The parchment leaves gathered in drifts outside, and the wind lifted them at the crests. They sailed and swirled, evolution's artistry, before landing to mulch the ground. Every year for tens of millions of seasons, the cycle renewed with the stillness of certainty, oblivious to humans who build, roam, kill, and suffer. Nature's repetition is the universe in meditation, the only tranquility. People don't stand a chance.

He sat up with a thought. "Linnette, maybe it will help you to know I may have discovered who killed your brother and the others."

She took a deep breath. Her expression was disbelieving, but at the same time desperate for it to be true. "You have?"

"Maybe. I still have to check on some things, but it looks good."

"I gave up hope years ago." Her eyes brightened with tears.

He shouldn't have said anything, and he rushed to quell her hopes. At least he knew how to do that. "I'm working on a very thin lead. I've learned some things I never knew about the case, and it's taken me on some interesting paths, but it's more than likely that the best I will come up with is an educated guess. I doubt we can expect more than that after all these years."

"Do you have someone in particular in mind?"

"Yes."

"Who is he?"

"I don't want to say just yet."

She seemed disappointed but was apparently used to it. "I've always felt if they caught him or we knew who he was, I could find some relief. It would never take away my failure to look after Danny that day, but it will settle responsibility on someone else, a person, not a phantom. That's what I've been hoping for all these years. Do you know what kind of a person he was?"

"I don't know if he was the killer," he reminded her. "I actually knew him a little back then but not very well. I have only the roughest outline of his life, so I can't say what made him tick. I can tell you he was as evil a person as I've ever set eyes on."

She looked out the window. "Obviously anyone who could do what he did must be evil, but that's not the main thing to know about him."

"What do you mean?"

"I've thought about this a lot over the years, and the biggest thing is that he was a liar. I don't just mean he had to tell a thousand lies to cover his crimes. I mean he was a fake, through and through. He didn't fool the people closest to him, but a lot of people were taken in.

I always knew if I found someone whose whole life was based on a lie, he'd be the one who did it."

It was a powerful insight, he realized. She was most likely correct, and it almost certainly applied to Tom, acting normal to lure desperate women into the cab of his truck for the final moments of their lives. Linnette was describing that very degree of dishonesty, but it was too soon to share his theory with her.

That night after he cleaned the kitchen, Don carried spaghetti and meatballs to the Tedesco home. As usual, Billy greeted him wordlessly at the door, his eyes pleading for his friendship. Don wondered whether to tell him that he'd met his son but didn't see the point. Don handed him the containers and turned to leave.

"Donnie?" Chief Tedesco called.

Shit. "Yes, Chief Tedesco?"

"Can you come in here for a minute? I need your help with something."

Shit, shit, shit. He stepped inside and a black picture frame, already split at the joints, crunched underfoot. A group of about twenty young men in white Navy uniforms and hats looked out from behind a web of cracked glass, a young Chief Tedesco among them. Don remembered Billy's mom pointing him out in this very picture, but like most photos of groups of men in uniform, they looked identical.

"Watch where you walk," the chief said. "My son, the pride of North Homestead, had a little fit yesterday." As Billy carried the containers to the kitchen, the chief motioned to the living room, strewn with the shattered remains of his Navy SEAL memorabilia. Divots dented the plaster where the mementos had hit the walls.

"What happened?"

"It's the head wound. They said it would make him crazy at times, but he was always that way. If he'd had any sense at all, he'd have used his temper to make a decent living. There are plenty of ways for men to do that. But Billy wasted his anger on bar fights and women. Useless shit." He shrugged. "Well, it's been that way forever. Weak men outnumber the strong twenty to one, but all the heavy lifting falls on our shoulders. I shouldn't be surprised."

Billy's silhouette, just behind his father, listened to every word.

"I'm not interested, Chief," Don snapped. "What is it you want?"

"Over there." He pointed. "In the corner behind that table. I can't reach it. My SEAL insignia medal."

Don stepped around the debris and crouched. He picked up a gold object he recognized as the central object of the SEAL wall display. He'd never really looked at it. It was a heavy pin featuring an American eagle whose wings were braced to land atop an artfully designed gathering of an anchor, a trident, and a musket.

He gave it to the chief, who looked relieved.

Don was leaving when the chief said, "Hang on a minute. I have something important to say." He held up the gold pin. "My son shattered the frame. The rest of this junk," he waved and shrugged, "it's just display stuff, something for guys to put on their walls and impress people, but that never mattered to me." Don remembered awestruck visitors responding to the objects as if they were in church while the chief beamed. "But this is my SEAL insignia medal, the one I got when I graduated from training."

The chief breathed a light dew across its golden surface and rubbed it to a shine with a finger that tented his T-shirt. "I need to have it reframed. It needs to be in the exact center of a red velvet-lined shadow box, a square foot, sticking out an inch or two. The mounts have to be solid gold to match the medal. Polished wood frame, but a hardwood. Cherry. Teak. Ash. Something nice. It's going into the ground with me, in my arm." He held it up to Don. "I hate to let it out of my sight, but I need you to take it to that frame shop on Lorain Road, the one near the furniture store. I don't care what it costs."

"That frame shop closed years ago," Don said, not taking the medal.

The chief looked surprised. "Okay. I'm sure there's another frame shop around." Don didn't move. The chief lowered the pin to his lap. "It's not too much to ask. I'll throw in a hundred bucks on top for your trouble. I know you're loaded, but a hundred bucks is a hundred bucks."

A previously inconceivable idea came to him. "That's not enough. I'll take the hundred bucks because it will be a hassle, but you can make the rest of your payment with information."

The chief looked cautious. "What kind of information?"

"I want to know everything about those murders. I want my dad to die in peace. Right now, he can't because of how badly you mismanaged that case, but you can make it up to him now."

"We cleared your dad. His alibi held up."

Don ticked his tongue, shaking his head. "The suspicion has followed him ever since, and you know it. People remember. I want to find the killer. That's the only way to clear his name."

"You can't find the killer. He's long gone. It's the one thing I regret more than anything else, that he got away from us." His face hardened, and his voice cut through the air. "He killed my son. The smart one. Eddie would have made something of himself. Nobody wanted to find him more than I did."

Don glanced at Billy's shadow again, still listening.

Fuming, Don replied, "You're wrong about that, and I'm going to find him."

"Okay, it's a deal, but I'll need some time to remember. Dust off the cobwebs. It all happened a million years ago. Bring this back framed the way I told you, and I'll tell you anything you want to know."

Don closed his fist around the medal. The points pressed like needles. "You're not getting this back until I get all the information I want."

Billy shuffled into the light. "Don," he said. Don waited for him to finish, but the chief growled, "Go serve our dinner."

Billy stepped past the wheelchair. "I'm sorry," he said.

Don looked into the living room and shrugged. "Don't apologize to me, Billy. I don't care."

"That's right," the chief said. "How about telling me you're sorry?"

Billy ran his eyes over the debris. He shook his head quickly. "No. The recreation center." His features went tight. "I'm sorry."

It's the classy thing to do.

The memory of the bell rang in Don's ears. Images raced: dental surgery, chest casts for a broken rib, a bedside table of white pill bottles. Billy's hair flying, with a trim of white light. The pain, the humiliation, the way Billy flipped him the bird the first time they saw each other afterward.

I'll never say it. Shut up.

Billy took another tentative step. His lower lip trembled and his eyes glinted.

"What the hell are you talking about?" the chief said.

Forgiveness heals, he'd told Linnette just a few hours ago.

Don could only nod, slightly, and Billy's face went wide with hope.

Don left. He felt nothing.

The next day, Bruce arrived an hour before the others were expected. Don was surprised he was so nervous about introducing Bruce to his family. This was a new and important step. He was sure everyone would be perfectly civil, but would they like Bruce? Would Bruce like them? He'd never faced these issues before. He was fifty-three years old, and as nervous as a teenager introducing his prom date.

Mom appraised Bruce even as she smiled pleasantly. "It's nice to meet you, Bruce. Don speaks very highly of you." Bruce responded with similar sentiments.

Dad was watching a documentary about the pyramids, and with the ease of an expert, he paused the video and set the tablet aside for the introduction. Dad smiled, nodded, and said he was happy to meet him and, once again, Bruce responded in kind. They talked for a few minutes, the conversation easy.

"Let me show you the room where I grew up," Don said, ushering him inside the small space. His suitcase spilled open on a wheeled table. He closed the door, and they came together in a tight hug and lingering kiss. They squeezed and rubbed each other at the crotch but kept it brief. As Bruce pulled back, he asked, "Is this the room you shared with your brother Randy?"

"Only until Tim joined the Marines. Since there were only two of us left, we each got our own room."

Bruce spotted the golden SEAL insignia on the dresser. "What's this?"

"Let's not talk about this thing right now."

A little while later, Tim and Sally arrived, eagerly looking about for the stranger. Don introduced Bruce, and Tim shook his hand firmly, with a big grin and a hearty pump. Sally smiled sweetly, and after exchanging pleasantries, gave Don a private flick of her eyebrows, a silent acknowledgment that she found his date attractive.

Randy arrived soon after, his stony expression of marital rage breaking into a smile, and he gave Bruce yet another manly handshake, as if welcoming him to the club.

They sat down to dinner, and Don was sorry their dad couldn't join them. Mom had changed her mind about the menu and served beef stew, as comforting as flannel. Bruce melted at the first bite, and said, "Ma'am, this is the most delicious beef stew I've had since I was on vacation in British Columbia and got stranded in a log cabin during a blizzard. After hiking in the snow all day, I thought nothing would ever taste as good, but I was wrong."

Mom blinked and blushed, and silence enveloped the room until Randy asked, "What were you doing on vacation in a log cabin during a blizzard?"

"I went up to volunteer on a paleontology dig at the Burgess Shale."

"No shit?" Randy said, eyes bugging. "I've always wanted to do that."

"What's the Burgess Shale?" Tim asked.

"It's a fossil bed from the Cambrian explosion," Bruce said. "About half a billion years ago. I'm sure there's a better way to put it, but it's when life on earth started to take on shapes we clearly recognize as animals. A landslide buried part of an inland sea, and the sediment was so fine you can see the soft tissue. The animals are starting to show the features that still dominate. Four limbs. Backbones. Eyes in front, a nose. It's amazing."

Randy piped up. "Yeah, but the thing about the Burgess Shale is that there all kinds of weird forms that didn't survive. Animals with two opposing backbones, eyes in strange places, limbs that can't operate efficiently in our gravity."

Bruce nodded. "It's like life automatically offers a huge variety of forms to every new environment where it takes hold. The ones that make sense for that world, they flourish. The ones that don't," he waved, "sayonara."

"Well, I'm not sure what you're talking about, but thank you," Mom said with a giggle. "I don't think I've ever had such a compliment. Imagine that. A log cabin in a blizzard!"

His family was clearly impressed. Sally popped her eyebrows at Don again, this time for more than Bruce's looks.

It went as well as Don had hoped, and both of his brothers gave him an extra "good job" pat on the arm as they hugged good-bye. Sally turned on her old coquettish charm for Bruce and said she couldn't wait to spend more time getting to know him. After they left, Don felt another piece of his life align with the world, another railway tie set in place, allowing him to advance. Gay people born long before gay rock musicians, movie stars, and senators laid these tracks out of the usual order, sometimes stranding them for years along a lonely stretch. It wasn't fair this one came so late in Don's life, but he was used to it.

After Bruce said good-bye to his parents, Don escorted him to the driveway. Freezing needles in the wind heralded winter's approach. In the backyard, a small herd of deer raised their nervous heads from the grass, eyes aglow with the lights from the family room. Don and Bruce went still to keep them calm and let them forage, but the restive animals turned and hopped into the safety of the trees, silent save for the snap of sticks.

"You never used to see deer around here," Don said. "All the new development around is pushing them in."

"They're beautiful." He took Don's arm. "I think you're beautiful, too." They drew together for a slow kiss, and their breaths trailed away like fingers of fog into the cold.

"Thanks for coming," Don said. "My family really likes you."

"I like them."

"So when will I see you again?"

"Whenever you like," Bruce said with a grin.

Don loosened his grip and stepped back. "I want your opinion about something. There's one thing about the investigation I haven't told you. Like I said, a lot of people think the killer was a teenager or a young adult. The FBI profile even specified that the guy might have joined the military, and that's why the killings stopped." He went silent.

"So?"

"That fits my brother Tim," he said softly, feeling traitorous for even speaking the words.

Bruce shook his head. "No. No way. Not him. Plus, I thought Tim didn't join the Marines until after Rich died. That was, what, a year and a half after the last murder?"

"I know. It doesn't fit, and I don't think Tim is capable of something like that, but I haven't been able to discuss it with anybody, and I wanted another opinion."

"Well, you have another opinion now. It wasn't him. Don't ever worry about that again." Bruce's conviction swept away the last of his concerns about his brother.

"There's something else," Don said. "It happened yesterday. It was really strange." He relayed the scene at the Tedesco home the previous night. "His medal is that gold pin you saw on the dresser."

"And he'll tell you anything you want to know if you get it framed?"

"Yeah, but the more I think about it, the more I think I'm getting the losing end of the deal. What's he going to tell me that I don't already know? He doesn't know who the killer is, so at best I'm going to get a couple of more useless leads to chase down." He told Bruce about his plan to find out if the police in South Dakota discovered a trio of boys' outfits during the Tom Malicheski investigation. "If they have the clothes, case closed. But if they don't, where does that leave me? What am I supposed to ask the chief?"

"Well, you need to be ready with a list of questions."

"But I don't know what to ask."

Bruce blew out a long white funnel and thought for a while. "You need to go back to a reliable source. Wasn't that ex-cop at the retirement home willing to tell you anything?"

"Yeah, but I think he told me everything he knows."

"What about that other guy who was chief of police after Tedesco retired?"

"Ladmore. But he couldn't tell me anything, either."

"What about going back to where you started?"

"What do you mean?"

"Do you think that lady at the police archives will be willing to tell you more?"

Don felt a small burst of excitement that deflated just as quickly. "Dolores might be willing to give me a little tidbit or two, but it won't be much without a form signed by the chief." Don remembered Dolores passing in front of his car in the crosswalk on Halloween, and a possibility bloomed. "Maybe I won't need a form," he said.

CHAPTER TWENTY-TWO

1984–present

Two weeks before Don graduated from St. Peter's High School in June of 1984, summa cum laude and the valedictorian, he felt sick with dread.

"I don't want to give a speech at graduation," Don said, squirming in the chair of his guidance counselor's office. Mr. Mobely was pudgy and bald on top, with a strip of graying hair that looked like Velcro keeping his ears in place. Under his thin blue shirt, the short sleeves of a white T-shirt scrunched in his armpits.

"Don," he said, his voice a soothing rumble, "you've been accepted to Harvard on a full scholarship. That's a first for this school. It's your moment, so take it. Besides, people are going to ask why I couldn't persuade you to speak when I'm your guidance counselor. You're going to make me look bad."

Don shook his head firmly, glaring, but off to the side because he liked Mr. Mobely. He didn't want to cause trouble for him, but he couldn't imagine standing at that podium. "I don't know what to say. I'd probably be dragged off the stage and strung up if I said what I really think."

Mr. Mobely rolled his eyes. "Don, I've been your counselor since you were a freshman, and we've built a solid rapport, am I right?"

"Yeah," Don said. Mr. Mobely was smart, funny, and easy to talk to, but he always spoke to him as an intellectual equal.

"Then I think I've earned the right to use some plain language. Close the door."

Tightening his grip on the books in his lap, Don leaned and gave the door a light push. It sailed into its frame with a thump. The small office went hushed.

For the first time Don could ever recall, Mr. Mobely's smile morphed to anger. "I've tried saying this nicely to you many times, and as smart as you are, you still don't get it, so I'm going to lay it out for you, man-to-man." He raised his voice. "Don't let the shitheads get in your way! Fuck them!"

Don blinked, drawing back.

"After you graduate, you'll only see these knuckleheads again if you're handing them the keys so they can park your fancy new car." He pointed in the direction of the main hallway. "Whatever prestige they have will disappear the moment they leave this school for the last time. I've seen it a million times. These strutting jerkwads will wake up one morning sometime in the next few years and wonder what the fuck happened. They used to be big shots, and now their asses get handed to them in a bucket of their own shit every fucking day."

Don's mouth dropped.

Mr. Mobely lowered his voice, smiling again. "Give the speech. It can be about whatever you want. I'm supposed to approve it, but if you don't want to show me beforehand, that's fine. I trust you. If you want, write something that fucks with them, but do it in a way that sails right over their heads. My ass will be grass if you're too obvious, and I have a wife and two little girls at home. You're smart enough to come up with something."

Don eventually agreed, but he couldn't write a word for days, blocked by a wall of hypocrisy he refused to scale, even for Mr. Mobely's sake. He couldn't use even neutral terms for St. Peter's, so talking about the school was impossible. He felt no pride in the Class of '84. The topic of community was crowded with targets for his rage, and morality and religion drowned in his contempt. The futures of his fellow graduates didn't concern him at all.

His mind wandered and he daydreamed, and without any buildup, an idea burst in his mind. He sat up and smiled at the audacity of his topic, seeing how perfectly it matched Mr. Mobely's challenge. His excitement rose when he realized he could manipulate the adults and confuse the shit out of the graduates.

He wrote. It took an hour or so to finish, and even longer to carefully refine and shape. The true meaning was visible at a squinted angle, but the emotional glare would blind his audience. He timed the speech at about five minutes. He wondered if it was as good as he suspected it was.

At graduation, he sat on the stage between the granite blocks otherwise known as the principal and dean. As the world's most spiritless valedictorian, he spoke to these men only when necessary, and they repaid the favor.

After the class president gave a speech steeped in the strident pomposity also popular with cult leaders, he read Don's introductory paragraph. He gestured and smiled at Don throughout, as if they were old friends. Don refused to play along, keeping his eyes on the audience. In the white haze of the stage lights, they looked like envious spirits mesmerized by the scenes on this side of the scrim of life, desperate for something interesting to see, and they stirred at last with the mention of Harvard. Don walked to the podium to light applause.

He skipped the customary gratitude doled out to faculty and jumped right into sharing his dream of stepping through a time portal to live among the men of the classical, ancient world. He praised their rugged nobility and fiery spirits, stressing how their love for one another created an easy brotherhood of mutual regard. His words soared as he spoke of their commitment to new ideas and their untamed curiosity for both the intellectual and physical worlds, never hiding anything from each other, always ready to lend each other a hand, to pick each other up, have their backs, share their loads. Don described his joy at their welcome, and his eagerness to learn everything they could teach him.

He almost heard the names as they popped into minds all over the room, names not in his speech: Plato, Aristotle, Euclid, Pericles. Even that overrated boor Cicero was probably taking a perfumed stroll in someone's head. Watery eyes glinted in the shadows on the upper level where the parents sat, shining with fevered agreement at this unexpected and stirring defense of traditional Western standards under attack from so many undesirable people. "I intend to learn from and live among them forever," Don concluded. "Thank you."

The top tier leaped to their feet, as did the faculty onstage, forcing the uncertain graduates to do the same. As Don returned to his seat, the applause still hearty, he stopped to shake Mr. Mobely's hand. He leaned in and said, "Right over their heads." His guidance counselor responded with a chuckle and a thumbs-up. Even the granite blocks gave him handshakes of admiration for the marble weight of such a manly topic. He scanned the room to enjoy the acclaim for his fantasy of living in a magical land of naked men. He smiled. His four-year sentence at St. Peter's seemed almost worth this moment.

His parents raved about his speech in the car. Don didn't like making them victims of the joke, but he couldn't do anything about it.

When they reached home, he spotted Billy across the street, running across the porch to a rusted-out car idling like a crackpot scientist's machine in the Tedesco driveway. The car vibrated with bass notes, radiating a metallic buzz. Billy opened the passenger door, his hair flopping like a towel halfway down his back. A shitty beard patched his face, looking as sorry as when it first appeared last year. Don snarled with contempt.

The day he left for Harvard, his parents cried, gasping and choking, setting off Don as well. For his family, grief always sprang from the massive aquifer of pain that formed when Rich died, every tear created then. Don seethed at the injustice. If not for that one night when Chief Tedesco led his dad away, leaving a stain still visible nine years on, the tears would be sweet and sentimental as Don departed for the land of mahogany hallways and ivy-covered bricks.

His feelings confused him as the plane lifted into the sky. He'd anticipated a joyful sense of escape. He never imagined leaving North Homestead would fill him with a sinking regret. But Don thrived at Harvard, feeling an easy bond with students who burned with intellectual fever and expressed opinions that amazed him. At a literature study group, one guy snorted at the mention of Oscar Wilde and called him a fag.

"What did gay people do to you that you should judge them so harshly?" a girl asked.

The guy blinked in surprise when he realized that everyone in the group was waiting for his reply. It shocked Don, too. The guy started to stammer out a reference to the Bible, but the girl shook her head impatiently.

"That's a weak dodge. We've been in this same group for months, and this is the first time you've mentioned your strict devotion to the Bible. I find it hard to credit, frankly, given your infatuation with

Alisoun from *The Miller's Tale*. You weren't concerned with biblical morality then."

The group chuckled, remembering his unabashed enthusiasm for the scene when Alisoun sticks her ass out the window so Absolon can kiss it at the same time she's having sex with Nicholas. He'd been too rapturous in his praise for Alisoun's sexual freedom to deny it, and he blushed.

The confrontation left Don reeling with excitement. An old voice returned: *say my name*. The shadow spoke without a hiss. Don returned to that misty pasture in his mind. Light shredded the fog, shrinking the shadow.

In the spring of 1985, Don felt content. Nobody knew about his dad or Rich, and nobody called him a faggot. He wasn't at the top of his class any longer, but it didn't bother him because too many others were experiencing the same dislocation. High school valedictorians filled Harvard, and almost all struggled to keep up.

In April of 1985, after leaving his last class of the day, he headed for a new study group for his Introduction to Astronomy class. For some reason, the group was proving exceptionally difficult to organize. Nobody could agree on times or places, and only recently did four students manage to set up a meeting in a small lounge tucked away at the end of a sleepy corridor of the Science Center. Twenty minutes late, Don trotted down the hall, his footfalls echoing. He walked in the open door and found a person waiting.

A beat-up sofa and three wooden chairs surrounded a scratched coffee table in the small windowless room. Other than a periodic table tacked at an angle, the walls were empty.

A guy named Jamie looked up from the sofa and smiled, and Don felt a hot rush. He'd been hoping Jamie would make it. His hair was the color of chestnuts, his face soft with a trimmed beard. He wore jeans and a plain polo shirt, his arms sculpted by weights. He lived in California, where his father owned a regional chain of grocery stores.

Jamie always gave him smiles and nods, even when across the room. They seemed deliberately intended and full of meaning, and they confused Don. Jamie made his heart pound, and Don never entertained hopes about such attractive men.

Don sat in a chair opposite, putting his books on the table, next to Jamie's. "Sorry I'm so late."

Jamie shrugged. "We're busy people. Do you think anyone else will show?"

"I hope so." But he didn't.

"Where are you from?"

"Ohio. Just outside of Cleveland."

"What does your dad do?"

"He runs an aerospace engineering firm." Jamie gave an admiring nod, the same look the answer always seemed to elicit at Harvard. Don never clarified that his dad managed the company and wasn't an engineer.

"Are you going back to Ohio for the summer?"

"Yeah. Are you going home to California?"

"Oh, yeah. Everyone thinks California is so glamorous. I just let them think whatever they want. My family lives in Palmdale. It's in the middle of nowhere, almost two hours from L.A. I was born in Santa Monica, but my dad thought Los Angeles was getting too crazy so he moved us to the desert. At least we have a swimming pool."

"Do you ever go to Los Angeles?"

Jamie laughed. "Only every chance I get." He shook his head. "I don't know what my old man was thinking. In Palmdale, you have to check your shoes for scorpions. There's nothing to do, so my dad got me some weights, and that's where I learned to work out."

"You look like you spend a lot of time at the gym." The comment allowed him to scan Jamie's body without worry.

"Thanks." Jamie looked at his watch. "This study group is cursed. It was supposed to start half an hour ago, but it's pretty clear that nobody else is coming."

"We could have our own group. Just the two of us."

Jamie smiled. "Do you feel like talking about astronomy right now? I'm burned out today. Let's talk about something else."

Don hoped his excitement didn't show. "Sure. What do you want to talk about?"

"Have you ever thought about working out?"

The lockers of St. Peter's banged in his head. "I'm not much for the gym."

"It's not as hard as you think it is. I really don't work out that much. If you want to be Mr. Universe, you need to work out three hours every day and jog for two more, but if you just want a nice body it doesn't take nearly as long as everyone thinks. Just three or four times a week." Jamie checked the door before standing, reaching behind, and yanking off his shirt.

Don inhaled with disbelief and flushed as he stared at Jamie's torso. Smooth muscles carved his shoulders and arms. The same chestnut-brown hair fuzzed his chest and trailed away into his jeans.

"See what I mean?" Jamie said, rubbing his shoulders and arms before swirling a hand in his chest hair. "Shoulders and arms are easy. Legs are hard, though, and lots of guys skip them completely." He took two steps, nudged the door shut, and turned. Smiling, he kicked off his shoes while undoing his belt. He held Don's gaze as he pushed his jeans down and tossed them to the side.

"Check it out," Jamie said, flexing and displaying his legs. His striped underwear looked like skimpy swim trunks, and the trail of hair drained into a thicket of even darker hair.

It seemed impossible to believe, but perhaps the long-awaited moment had finally arrived.

The stripes on Jamie's underwear started to stretch and distort, and he rubbed the spot with a grin that made Don dizzy. It seemed unbelievable, but this handsome guy, one he'd lusted after for months, wanted to have sex with him. And just to blow away the last remaining doubt, Jamie pulled his underwear away and bounced into full view. Grinning, he hooked his hands behind his head to reveal the starburst hair in his armpits and said, "I think you're really hot."

Oh, fuck yes, I'll say your name.

He never heard the shadow again.

Don stood, hoping his legs wouldn't give out, and took off his shirt.

As they dressed afterward, Don's mind spiraled with awe and joy, feeling as if he'd been born for the sole purpose of being here this afternoon with Jamie. From their first kiss, hard against each other, feeling his mustache on his lips, to the smells and tastes and the exhilarating thrill of having permission to explore at will, nothing felt awkward or forced.

"Holy shit," Don said. The millions of shouted and whispered "faggots" filled his mind. He giggled. Thank God he was a faggot and got to do these things. He laughed. "That was fucking amazing."

Jamie smiled, as if pleased. "It was your first time, right?"

"Yeah," he said, grinning. "I didn't really know what to expect, but holy fuck, that was awesome."

Jamie said, "I thought you were a newbie. You had that look about you, scared of your own shadow. It's funny how different guys react to their first time. Some can't even look at you. I've even had a few cry. But a lot of them are like you, ready to blow up the closet completely. It's my thing. I look for guys like you."

Don asked what he meant.

"I only get off on having sex with guys who've never had a little homo love before. After that, I'm not usually interested."

Don started. "You mean we can't do that again?"

Jamie shook his head. "Don't worry, we can be friends. I'd like that, actually. In fact, if you want, after term I'm driving down to Fire Island for a couple of weeks before I go home. I'm renting a house with a couple of guys from Boston, and we have an extra room. You're welcome to join us. Your share would be around two hundred and fifty dollars. We have another guy interested, so I'd need your answer soon."

The figure loomed as an obstacle, as did a believable story for his parents, but he'd worry about all of that later. "I'll go. But are you serious when you say we can't have sex again?" He couldn't believe it.

"Don't worry," Jamie said. His mood became breezier and relaxed, as if confident now to show himself for real. "You're going to get a ton of action on Fire Island. You'll be a whore in no time."

They became tight friends, and Don drained the last of his savings account to pay for his share of the bungalow on Fire Island. He told his parents he was going to Long Island.

The dumpy beachside house disappointed Don. Jamie told him to lighten up and have fun. His first night, Don met Buck, a handsome redheaded guy from Kansas who only wanted to exchange hand jobs.

"We can't even kiss?"

Buck shook his head. "There's some ugly stuff going around, in case you haven't heard."

"Like what?"

Are you crazy? You haven't heard about AIDS?"

"But that's only in places like New York and San Francisco. Los Angeles."

"No, it's not. And even if it was, this place is crawling with guys from New York and San Francisco. Isn't your friend Jamie from L.A.?"

Don sat back, the implications hitting him from every direction.

"Welcome to the real world, buddy. Now, do you want to start stroking or what?"

The next morning as they drank coffee on the veranda with a view of the ocean, Jamie blew off Don's concerns. "I'm not going to let fear rule my life. Besides, you know I like newbies, and the only thing I'll catch from a virgin is a cold."

"Yeah, but you don't know if they're really virgins or not. Besides, I've seen you go off with guys who are obviously not virgins. We need to be careful."

"You handle it your way, I'll handle it mine."

Don watched the way Jamie handled it with concern, a constant stream of men from Fire Island bars and parties, none of whom made any pretense at being a blushing newbie.

In the dark of the early morning of their last full day on Fire Island, Don escorted a guy from his bedroom to the veranda. They'd met a few hours before.

"Thanks," the man growled at the top of the stairs. He trotted down to the narrow boardwalk, and Don watched his shadow until he couldn't see him any longer.

Warmth softened the night. The stars shone, brilliant sparks of white against the black sweep of the cosmos. The Milky Way fogged a trail on the canvas behind them. The billions of suns looked like mist, so distant it took some fifteen thousand years for a photon of light from earth to travel across the expanse, but Don didn't want to go anywhere.

A sliver of moon hung low on the horizon, splashing a narrow river of light across the sea that twinkled playfully, as if the waves tickled. The liquid cobalt of the ocean rolled to the shore, where it curled on the sand. The beach glowed, a pristine silvery blue, and the long seaside grasses rustled.

Don heard the voices of two men, distinct in tenor but muted with distance. They walked hand in hand on the sand. They stopped, and one silhouette backed away with a laugh before returning for an embrace and a lingering kiss. Don almost looked away from such a romantic and intimate moment, but he couldn't. He felt a bubbling in his chest, inflating a giddy hope he would soon be part of a scene that so perfectly expressed everything he felt. He felt so distant from the angry boy thrown off-kilter by the topic of his graduation speech. *Was that only last year?*

With a thundering shock, he realized in a matter of hours, the sun would rise on the tenth anniversary of Eddie Tedesco's disappearance, a decade since the dawn that changed everything. Amazingly, the flawless Fire Island morning softened the tumult of those years until he brushed it all away.

Silent tears of happiness traced down his face as he watched the men kiss. The realization came to him at that moment: *I survived.*

Ten years later, in 1995, Don lived in San Francisco. He'd tired of Boston after four years at Harvard and three more at Harvard Business. Ever since his valedictorian speech, the ability to get across different ideas to different people using the same words fascinated him, and he majored in marketing. He accepted a job on the West Coast at a company called Yahoo! that promised to revolutionize the experience of the information superhighway. Half his salary came in stock options. Jamie would have been proud of him, but he'd died years ago, skeletal and coughing in a Los Angeles hospital bed as Don held his hand.

Ten years later, in 2005, Don had accumulated more stock options from Google, an internet search engine that nobody had heard of when he joined. Options from Facebook and Twitter followed.

By 2015, Don could spend the rest of his life staring at the bayside view from his glassy, high-rise condo if he wanted, but he couldn't imagine such a life, so he worked on contracts, mostly for friends who desperately needed his experience for their start-ups.

After his dad was diagnosed with cancer, he started to visit North Homestead more frequently, four or five times a year. His dad ebbed away slowly, his world shrinking along the way. It took a couple of years to reach confinement to one room, before the final phase of a bed.

Mom called. She hated to ask, but could Don afford to pay for twenty-four-hour home care? "I can't handle it myself any longer, Donnie," she said, tearfully. "Your brothers do what they can, but they're so busy. I need someone here to help all the time."

"I'll pay for whatever you need, Mom. But I'll come home and help."

"How long can you stay?"

"I'll stay to the end."

"Are you sure? I'd much rather have you here than strangers. I know your father feels the same way."

"Yeah. I want to."

CHAPTER TWENTY-THREE

Don took Chief Tedecso's Navy SEAL insignia medal to a frame shop in nearby Fairview Park and explained the requirements.

"I don't want to spare any expense," Don said to the shop owner, gleefully remembering the chief's careless declaration that money was no object. Don looked forward to handing him the bill. "Everything has to be first-class."

"I know a custom jeweler in New Mexico. If you want this done properly, I can ship the medal there, and they can make a single, solid gold mount. It might take a while."

"How long?"

The man shrugged. "They'll do a superb job. All the measurements will be perfect. The medal will look like it's just floating in the center of the box. I promise you'll love it."

"Can they get it done in a couple of weeks?"

The man shrugged. "They'll have to make a special lead mold. That's the tricky part. If they don't get the measurements perfect, they'll have to start all over again. It requires a gifted craftsman."

A gifted craftsman's bill might give Tedesco a heart attack, and Don needed time to prepare a list of questions anyway. "Okay, do it." He went on to say that a tip of one hundred dollars awaited a speedy delivery.

"We'll do the best we can."

Don tried to find someone in South Dakota who knew something about the Tom Malicheski investigation, but he got nowhere after making numerous calls over several days. No one remembered the case, and nobody had the slightest interest in looking up details. After his fifth referral to the public information officer, a title that promised a public relations runaround, he finally called.

The officer said, "If what you say is true, that case is closed, mister."

"But there's a possibility he committed similar crimes here in Ohio. I just need to know what they discovered when they searched his truck and residence."

"All of that information should be at the courthouse."

"I tried that already. They have transcripts of the trial, but that won't help. This evidence wouldn't have been used to convict him for killing those women." He listed all the agencies he'd tried. "It's like as soon as he was executed, everyone just wiped their hands of the case."

"Wouldn't you?"

"Yeah, but I can't because I'm trying to see if he's connected to the murders here. There has to be evidence stored somewhere. You know, the stuff they collected but didn't use in court."

"Why would we keep ancillary evidence for someone who was convicted and executed? What you're asking for makes no sense."

Don chuckled that the public relations guy had proved useful after all, saying what he needed to hear. "You're right. It doesn't."

Dad improved on the stronger fentanyl, and it seemed likely he'd live through the holidays. He watched the shows on his tablet incessantly and discussed them with Don, the science documentaries especially.

Tim and Sally made Thanksgiving dinner but brought the ingredients uncooked to the house so that Dad, who couldn't rouse himself for even a few minutes at the table, could at least smell the turkey roasting and feel included. Sally complained their son Robbie and his family couldn't join them because it was his wife's turn to spend Thanksgiving with her family.

"She knows this will be Dad's last year," Sally said, furiously peeling potatoes at the sink like she was whittling a spear. "Why not break a rule, just one time?" Tim tried to soothe her by rubbing her shoulders, but she brushed his hands away.

Randy's daughter Julie also begged off. "That bitch Renee is keeping her from me," Randy said. Mom explained that Julie knew her mother was alone, while he had a family.

Bruce arrived with his first homemade cheesecake. He didn't have a spring form pan and baked it in a glass roasting dish Don recognized as the one he'd used for the lasagna. Bruce apologized for the two fissures on the surface of the cake, but Don said it didn't matter.

Bruce said, "My family understands that I can't join them this year. I told them your dad doesn't have much longer. It would be nice if our families got to know each other. We might be able to do some Christmas things together."

Don nodded. *Mix the families before Christmas?* Worried Bruce was moving too fast, he said, "Yeah, maybe. Let's see."

Bruce picked up on his hesitation. "I'd like to spend as much time with you over the holidays as I can, but I need to see my family for Christmas. It would be easier if we could do things in a big group. I can host something at my place."

"You have a grand total of three chairs in your house."

Bruce smiled. "I guess you have a point. I never needed chairs before."

All through dinner, Sally sulked and Randy fumed. They made an effort to be pleasant for Bruce's sake, but Don knew they were leaning on the assumption that any adult knows what it's like to be angry at family, and Bruce would understand. It seemed like he did.

Soon after dinner, when Don and Bruce assured everyone they would clean up, Tim and Sally left. Randy followed a few minutes later. Dad watched holiday movies on the tablet, and Mom started scooping leftovers into plastic containers.

"No, Mom," Don said. "I'm not taking Thanksgiving dinner across the street. Just forget about it."

"But it's…"

"No. It's not happening. Not tonight. Let it go. Thanksgiving is too personal to share with them."

She looked surprised, as if suddenly understanding his logic. "Okay. I can see your point." She sat at the kitchen table while they cleaned. "You two are sure a big help. Thank you again, Bruce, for making that delicious cheesecake."

"Sorry it was cracked."

She flipped her hand. "A little whipped cream fixes all mistakes."

She looked pleased when they laughed. She gave a big yawn, the inevitable end of the Thanksgiving feast, and pushed herself to her feet. "Thank you again for coming, Bruce. I hope you had a good time."

"Thank you for having me. And I did."

She put a hand on his shoulder and rose on her toes. Startled, he bent and she kissed his cheek. She turned and disappeared down the hallway, as if she'd done it a million times.

Don and Bruce stared after her.

"Does that mean she likes me?"

"I think it's even better than that," Don said. "I think it means she likes *us*."

The next morning while Don and his mom drank coffee at the kitchen table, he said, "Mom, thank you for that nice gesture last night. Giving Bruce a kiss. It meant a lot to both of us."

She smiled. "I'm glad to hear that, Don. He seems like a very nice man. It's as clear as can be you two are crazy about each other. I know you'll have a nice life together."

"Whoa," he said, laughing, holding his palm out, stop in the name of love. "That's going a bit fast, Mom. Let's see if we can make it through the holidays together."

She looked surprised. "He's absolutely in love with you. It's as plain as can be. Are you in love with him?"

He spluttered. "I don't know. I've never been in love before. I've had infatuations, but never anything as serious as love."

She leaned forward. "Do you feel like you've been hit with a brick, like you can't believe you met someone like him, that you'd go crazy if he wasn't in your life?"

"Well, I don't know. I mean, I guess."

"You guess? For heaven's sake, Don. I know you had to learn things differently than the rest of us, but those are pretty basic things. Are they true?"

"Well, yeah…"

"Then you're in love." She looked at the hallway. "I knew I was in love with your father within ten minutes. We've had our challenges, of course, most of the major ones not of our making. In spite of everything, I wouldn't trade any of it away. We had each other for support, and boy, there were times when we really needed it. Of course, it has to be right, and when it isn't, it's just awful. Look at your brothers. But when it is, you shouldn't let it slip away just because you've had so many bad experiences. You're not going to get many chances." She shrugged. "Well, I guess you know that already."

Don leaned back.

His mom sipped coffee for a while before she asked in a near-whisper, "Don, I've been wondering if you ever found out anything that would make your dad feel better."

"What do you mean?"

She leaned in. "You know. How you're looking into the murders." She couldn't hold eye contact for long while discussing the topic, so she stared into her coffee. "I hate it's something we need to think about, but there's no point in pretending. I know it will make all the difference for your father in his final days. He already thinks the world of you. We both do. If you can bring him some peace of mind before he dies, it will be the most valuable thing you can do for him, and for me."

He thought for a moment before shaking his head. "I can't give you false hope, Mom. I won't do that. I've looked into every lead I could find, and the best I've come up with is the name of someone who might have done it, but I've exhausted every potential clue, and I still can't prove it."

"Who is he?" she asked, softly.

He couldn't tell her that Rich's drug dealer may have inflicted far more pain than they'd ever realized. "No. I'm not saying anything until I can prove it."

"Don," she grabbed his wrist and dropped her voice. "Maybe we can tell your father we have proof we don't have."

The idea intrigued him. "I'd be up for that, if we get to that point. Let's talk about that. For his sake. But I have a couple of things to do first." He grinned. "Best you don't ask, Mom."

She looked worried. "Is it illegal?"

He snorted. "Yes. Very."

"Is Bruce going to help you with it?"

"Yeah."

"That's okay, then. You make a good team."

On Monday morning, he pulled his gym bag from his luggage. He still hadn't worked out for more than a month now. He threw it in the backseat and drove to Bruce's house.

Bruce had spent the long holiday weekend with his family in Akron, and they hadn't seen each other in three days. He slid into the car, and they leaned in for a heavy kiss that went on for a long time.

"I missed you," Bruce said.

"Same here." Don stroked Bruce's cheek and chuffed his chin. "Maybe I should have stopped by half an hour earlier so we could take care of each other first."

Bruce grinned. "That wouldn't have been enough time, and we'll get to that. Right now, I have to meet Dolores."

"Do you have something to prop in the door?"

Bruce slid his leg forward and reached into his pocket, pulling out a small twig. "How's this?"

"Should work. Do you have a good story?"

"I'll tell Dolores I was arrested for marijuana possession when I was a teenager, and I'm working with a lawyer to get the record expunged. I need a list of the evidence so the judge can dismiss everything. I'll give her some fake names, and when she can't find anything after a couple of minutes, I'll invite her to McDonald's to thank her for her trouble."

"Thanks for doing this. I hope it works."

"It's worth a shot."

The late November morning was icy. A steady wind ripped the trees clean, and only the heartiest brown leaves fluttered in the stiff breezes, clinging desperately to their branches as the only life they ever knew.

In the parking lot of the North Homestead police department, Don said, "There's no way to coordinate the timing. Dolores will go at her own pace. I'll give you a few minutes after you get inside to get her busy at the computer, but if it goes wrong…"

Bruce grabbed his arm. "The worst that will happen is that she sees you when you come in. That's nothing. The problem will be if she sees you at any point after that."

"I'll do my best. And remember, she doesn't move very fast, so you need to give her a few minutes to get the door. And you have to knock really loudly."

"Got it," Bruce said. Don grabbed his gym bag.

Bruce headed to the door of the archive building, while Don ducked around the corner. Bruce knocked, and when nobody answered he escalated to pounding. Don worried Dolores wasn't there, and just then she shouted, "Hold your horses." He smiled.

Don heard them talking, and then suddenly he didn't. He peeked around the corner. Bruce was inside. Casually, he walked to the door. The twig left a slight gap at the frame.

He tapped at his phone, giving Bruce time, pretending to ignore the uniformed officers leaving and entering the big gray police station to his right. After a minute or two, he pinched the twig and opened the door.

In the far room, Dolores looked irritated as she squinted at the monitor. Bruce spotted Don and took a quick step to block her view.

Don crept to the closet on the far wall. He opened the door, and his heart stopped at a parka on a hanger. Dolores would want to bundle up in the cold.

A broom with a dustpan clipped to the stick rested against the wall, and a roll of paper towels sat on the floor. No place to hide.

"Well, thanks for looking. Let me buy you lunch," Bruce said.

Quickly, he pulled the parka from the hanger and hooked it to the outside handle. He stepped into the closet, but the coat fell. He reached around and hung it more securely just as Bruce stepped out. Their eyes met for one second before he closed the door.

He heard Dolores say, "I get a fifty percent discount, just so you know. It's the uniform." Footsteps on the wooden floor. "What the hell…" Dolores said. "I always hang up my parka."

"I do that all the time," Bruce said. "Take off my coat and just put it wherever."

"I never do that."

The door handle rattled and Don pulled in his legs and squeezed into the corner. Light flooded the closet as Dolores opened the door, but she didn't stick her head inside.

"Huh," Dolores said. "I don't remember leaving it on the handle. Maybe I'm getting senile."

At a soft thump, the closet went dark again. "Okay," she said. "Just so you know, I like to pick up something for dinner when I get lunch, so you'll have to spring for my husband, too."

"Great!" Bruce said, maybe a touch too enthusiastically, but he'd handled everything brilliantly so far.

More footsteps. Cold air rushed in and puffed beneath the door. The front door slammed, and the lock jangled.

He cracked the door. The room was empty.

Don swung the gym bag onto his back and made for the desk. He opened the top right-hand drawer. There they sat, the ring of keys she unhooked from her belt whenever she left for McDonald's.

At least thirty keys jangled on the thick ring. Don decided the largest one probably unlocked the massive storage room, and it did. He slipped inside, looking up, an automatic human response to entering a large building, perhaps an instinct to look for the most obvious threats first. On the ceiling, fluorescent tubes buzzed.

He went right for the cage with the archives from 1975. Now for the hard part.

He tried key after key. His hands shook and he worked rapidly, but none fit the padlock. He took a deep breath. *Just go slowly.* Dolores had opened the lock with one of these keys. *Just be methodical.*

The second time around, about halfway through, a key slid neatly into the slot and turned. The U-shaped bar snapped open. He blew out a breath as he opened the gate, hooking the lock to the outside brace. The door opened with a rattling screech.

He tossed his gym bag on the metal table and pulled the first evidence box from the shelf. Ripping off the lid, he removed the thin binder with the *Summary of Evidence* label. He opened it, took out his phone, and snapped pictures of the first few pages but noticed another binder beneath. And another. Even worse, a huge stack of loose pages sat at the bottom. Photographing each page would take hours.

He paused, stumped.

Reaching into the box, he couldn't even work his fingers to the bottom. Between the binders and these sheets, there must be two thousand pages or more. He noticed a photocopy of a three-ring punch on the left side of every sheet and realized with relief the loose sheets were photocopies of both murder books. He transferred them to his gym bag, careful to keep them in order.

The second evidence box held a stack of manila folders, each one labeled with a series of numbers. He flipped open the top folder and saw he was holding the original crime scene photos. He looked through the first few black-and-white pictures of police officers in the woods. They stooped and pointed at evidence on the ground. The fourth photo stopped him cold.

An officer knelt among the trees, his finger aimed at something on the ground, apparently oblivious to the facedown body of a young boy, shockingly small, his naked buttocks to the sky. The cop pointed at a recorder about a foot away, Dad's artistry painfully familiar.

Danny Miller. Linnette's brother. His tiny feet formed an upside-down "V" and his face looked away, mercifully hiding his last expression.

Don sank to the metal chair. He swallowed, taking deep breaths. He felt a surge of primal rage. Unaware an older person might see his body as a source of excitement, Danny Miller was helpless. Someone slaughtered him for a moment of pleasure before tossing him aside in the woods, a life no more important than hamburger wrappers. No wonder the police stormed the three houses. Who wouldn't crash through every door to find the person who'd valued his lust above this boy's life?

Don shook his head to drive the thoughts away. He understood the rage, but it didn't justify the persecution of innocent men and their families. Official police sanction of suspicion against blameless people could only bring destruction. He couldn't look at any more pictures, so he replaced the box.

He removed the third box, the fourth, and several beyond. They held heavy, clear plastic bags sealed with yellow tape, stuffed with the standard trash found in the woods: McDonald's hamburger wrappers, the distinctive rubber rings of condoms, straws, cups, coins, pull tabs, beer cans, cigarette butts.

He moved on, hurrying, giving each evidence bag a quick scan. He found one that tinkled with glass. Inside, a thin silver spear rested in a pile of shards, the shattered remains of the hypodermic needle, thrown among the rest of the evidence with no attempt to pad the glass. He shoved it into his gym bag, vaguely wondering about potential DNA evidence, shaking his head with disgust at the shoddy preservation methods.

In the second-to-last box, he found the recorder. His father's handiwork rooted him to the spot. If Dad hadn't made this very recorder, how different things might be. He shoved it in the gym bag. In the next-to-last box, a jumble of things were tangled with no attempt to label or separate them. Belts and ties and thin ropes, many of them belonging to his family, no doubt, removed that surreal night when they took Dad away. A Polaroid instant camera clunked at the bottom, probably the one the police told the Hartners they'd lost. He considered returning it to Agnes, but that probably wasn't a good idea, so he returned the box to the shelf.

The last box contained more of the same, but with a child's Cleveland Browns baseball cap among the tangled items. He shook it free and held it up. The crown of the deep brown cap featured the old-fashioned elf-like mascot for the team, long out of use. He dimly remembered Jeffrey Talent had gone outside to retrieve a Cleveland Browns baseball cap and never returned, but this cap was simply smashed among the other things, not even preserved in plastic. Was this Jeffrey Talent's actual cap? He shivered, shoved it into his bag, and replaced the box.

He lifted his bag. Even with all the paper, the heft suggested a paltry haul with the slight weight of a moral victory.

After locking up and returning the keys to Dolores's desk, Don returned to his car and started the engine for the heater. He unzipped his gym bag on the passenger seat. He took a long look at the cap before removing the pages carefully and setting them on his lap.

He flipped through the top sheets, putting them facedown on the passenger seat when finished. They held lists of the victims and their families, the investigative team, the police officers, witnesses, forensics experts, and so on.

Don recognized enough of the names to realize how far he'd come since he'd parked in this lot on a whim and offered to pay for DNA tests. He'd even talked to two of the officers: Eric Ladmore, the rookie who used his connections to his uncle in the Navy to become deputy chief, and Chris O'Donnell, the far superior cop, driven off to run security at the mall, smoking the whole time. For Don, the fates of these men illustrated the incompetence of the investigation, doomed from the start.

The final list contained just three names under the heading "Possible Suspects." Hank Swoboda, Robert Esker, Elmer Hartner. Possible Suspects. Dark implications filled the words, so disturbing the three innocent men would never shake them. The page held nothing but this short list.

Danny Miller's name headed the next section, and the opening pages outlined the discovery of his body, the first photograph showing McDonald's. Typical of a photocopy of a picture, the overpowering whites and unforgiving blacks conspired to crush all the grays. He'd forgotten the benches that used to be in front of McDonald's back then, and he held up the page to compare it to the building across the street.

Dolores and Bruce approached, and both saw him. Dolores seemed sharply inquisitive, and Bruce looked nervous.

They were still a few feet away, so Don plastered a smile while grabbing the pages in the passenger seat to pile on the ones in his lap. One fluttered to the floor, but Dolores had already reached his window, squinting through her glasses, clutching two bags of food. She motioned for him to unroll the glass, using a crank gesture.

Still smiling, he pushed the button and the window sank away. The murder book sat in his lap and the evidence bags in the back. He didn't know the penalties for stealing such things, and didn't want to find out.

Bruce stood behind, looking worried. She noticed when they exchanged a glance and flipped her hand back and forth while asking, "You two know each other?"

Neither replied, which struck Don as so suspicious he blurted, "Yes," while hoping Bruce didn't say, "No," at the same time. Thankfully, Bruce kept silent.

Dolores crinkled her forehead in suspicion. "It's funny you both had business with the police archives so close together. I swear I go weeks at a time without a single civilian at the door." She looked down at the papers in his lap, and her eyes flicked to the stray sheet on the floor. Don hoped it had landed facedown.

Dolores stared at the spot for a moment before she looked back at him. "I was just wondering how your dad is doing."

Don blew out a strong breath of relief but turned it into a grateful sigh and a nod. "Thanks for asking. He's actually doing a little better right now. He'll make it through the holidays."

Again, she looked consumed by something puzzling. Finally, she patted the sill and said, "Okay then. Best of luck. Make the most of the time you have left."

"Thank you, I will."

She turned to Bruce. "Remember, get your lawyer to file the paperwork with the chief's office, and we can take it from there." After one more look back and forth, Dolores shuffled away.

He shared a look of disbelief with Bruce, who headed for the passenger door. He checked the floor. The page had landed face-up.

He reached for it, but Bruce slid into the seat and picked it up instead. He scanned it before handing it to Don. Possible Suspects.

Bruce insisted they take the murder book and evidence bags to his house.

"No," Don said. "What if Dolores starts to get suspicious and looks in the evidence boxes and realizes things are missing? If they find this stuff at your place, you're going to be in a lot of trouble, and I don't want to be responsible for that."

Bruce scoffed. "Dolores is a nice person, but she's a government bureaucrat. She's not going to bother to do anything beyond the guidelines of her job."

"How can you be so sure?"

"Trust me. This stuff is more likely to be discovered at your house. My place has a lot less traffic. Now stop worrying and drive."

At Bruce's kitchen table, Don showed him the heavy plastic bags with the recorder and the shattered needle.

Bruce said, "I can understand taking the recorder. That's just a matter of justice. But why'd you take the needle?"

"I thought of DNA. I'm sure there's some in here, but now that I think about it, I don't know what good it will do." He lifted the baseball cap. When Bruce gave him a wondering look, he said, "Jeffrey Talent was running outside to get his Browns cap. This can't be it, can it? It wasn't even preserved in an evidence bag."

"What else can it be? It has that old mascot, that weird elf thing. It has to be."

"But what does it mean that he didn't even get far enough to get his cap?"

"I have no idea. Maybe there's something in here that can tell us." He flipped through the pages of the murder book, separating a section and handing it to Don. "You read about Danny Miller. I'll read the Jeffrey Talent stuff. We can get to Eddie Tedesco later."

"Okay, but I'm warning you. I saw some of the photos in the evidence boxes. They're rough."

Bruce nodded. "The world can be an ugly place sometimes."

Don read the statements from the teens who found Danny Miller's body, a recitation of facts like, "We entered the woods at the southwest corner of the parking lot at approximately half past twelve." All the sobbing, hair-pulling, and screaming were stripped away. Don only saw the one photo, and from that alone, he knew those kids were in a state of sheer panic for at least several days.

He flipped to a page with printed silhouettes of a man's body, front and back. It struck him as strange to see a fully grown man represent that little boy in the woods. A hand drawn arrow pointing to the neck showed the position of a "ligature mark, ¾ inch." Other arrows noted minor scratches and bruises.

Interviews with Danny's family followed. Because these were transcribed by officers, parenthetical notes relayed the emotions like stage directions (mother unable to speak for several minutes) (father distraught, unable to continue until officer offered whiskey) (sister in a state of near catatonia). Don glanced up at Bruce but decided not to share this about Linnette. It felt like a violation of her privacy.

One sentence caught his attention: "Mother reports that the boy was dressed in an orange and brown striped crew T-shirt, red shorts (faded), white underpants (Hanes), knee-high sports socks, and Keds sneakers."

Brief statements from neighbors followed. Somebody a few doors down thought he saw a blue or black sedan from the corner of his eye, but it was getting dark, and he wasn't paying attention. Another neighbor saw a boy on a bike earlier in the day, and she was suspicious of him because he steered with one hand and carried a book in the other, "not things for sports as boys usually carry." The other neighbors reported seeing and hearing nothing until the family started crying out for help.

Next came a list of evidence gathered in the woods behind McDonald's, along with codes that identified the forensics labs. Big, hand-drawn asterisks singled out three items: adult men's underwear (old, likely in woods for many weeks or months); a recorder (handmade, little used, not weathered); three contact papers from Polaroid instant camera (fresh, new, damp from rain).

He turned the page. The top line read, "Interrogation of suspect, Robert Esker. Transcribed from recordings on file."

Don couldn't bring himself to read it. Instead, he flipped through the pages rapidly, his eyes catching fragments. "I've never seen that boy." "But you do admit that you made this?" "What time did you leave work again?" "My family must be very upset right now." "Let's go over this again." "I won't play favorites with anybody, even a neighbor." "I had nothing to do with any of this." "Tell me again why you decided to start making recorders." "You only gave them to little children?" "You are not to leave the state." "I have four boys. I wouldn't hurt a child."

The photographs followed, and Don couldn't look at them. He set the pages aside. Bruce looked up.

"I can't read any more," Don said.

"Did you learn anything?"

"Yeah, but minor stuff. Nothing useful. I know what Danny was wearing."

Bruce nodded. "Jeffrey Talent was getting ready for bed and he was only wearing *Planet of the Apes* pajamas. No underwear or even socks. He was just running outside for a second to get his baseball cap. And about that cap." It sat on the table and he picked it up. "This isn't the actual cap. They never found the one he ran outside to get. Jeffrey's father bought this one after his son went missing to show the police, in case they found a similar one. So whoever killed Jeffrey grabbed him after he got the cap."

Don remembered the way Mr. Talent shuffled along after his wife attacked him and Dad led him away to have a beer. He leaned back. "My mom wants me to lie to my dad. She wants me tell him that I found evidence that ties Tom Malicheski directly to the murders."

Bruce looked like he thought the idea had merit. "You know, if it brings him some peace before the end, what's the harm?"

Don looked at the hundreds of pages on the table. Maybe he could find the answer in there if he looked hard enough. He picked up the plastic bag with the remains of the needle. "Even if someone's DNA is in here, it wouldn't mean he was the killer. Just that he was using a needle near where the body was found."

Bruce shuffled pages. "Yeah, here it is. They found the needle about ten feet from Jeffrey's body. It looked too clean to have been outside for long."

Don set the bag aside. "We're getting lost in the details. None of this gets us any closer."

"Hey, we're not going to solve anything at this table right now. The idea is to compile information and get the chief to answer some questions, right?"

"Yeah, but then what? Unless we find the clothes or those photos, we have nothing."

Bruce grabbed his hand. "Why don't you take a break? I'll be glad to go through this page by page. I actually find it fascinating. A new set of eyes might see something nobody else has. Go make sure your dad's doing okay, and I'll swing by later."

"You sure? Okay." Bruce squeezed his hand and went back to reading.

Don watched Bruce for a moment as he scanned a page, his mouth slightly open, intense and focused. Bruce was immersing himself in this squalid and frustrating project for his sake, because he wanted to help him.

Don kissed Bruce on the top of his head. Bruce reached back and squeezed his thigh but kept reading.

When Don reached the door, Bruce called out, "Yeah, hey, Don?"

He turned. Bruce walked into the archway, smiling. "I think I have something." He held up a page. "Anyone ever say anything about fingerprints?"

❖

The next week, on December fifth, Don and Bruce helped his mother up the hill at Memorial Park Cemetery. His brothers had already visited. A spray of winter-gray roses fanned the bottom edge of the gravestone, obviously left by Tim and Sally. Randy always brought a single rose and laid it diagonally across the surface.

Mom clucked with frustration. "I don't know why Randy does that. It covers his name. He knows I don't like it. Donnie, fix that, would you?"

Don moved the rose to the top edge and helped his mother to kneel. She nudged the flowers from Tim and Sally to one side and placed her red roses next to them. She crossed herself and dropped her head.

Don motioned for Bruce to follow him back a good twenty feet. "She likes a little privacy for this."

"What's it like for you to come here?"

"It's not as important to me as it is to her, or my brothers." He told Bruce about the boxes in the attic. "That's where I've always felt closest to Rich." Maybe someday he'd explain to Bruce how the cemetery workers had poisoned the grave for him.

"Were you able to talk to the guy at the frame shop this morning?"

Don made a sound of frustration. "They still haven't cast the lead molds in New Mexico."

"What's taking so long?"

He shrugged. "They're busy, and the wax model is taking longer than they expected. I'm worried. My dad's not looking too good. He started asking for more morphine again yesterday. We're going to have to increase the fentanyl dosage soon. Probably in a week or so." He rubbed his forehead. "I was so fucking happy about making Tedesco pay out the ass, and it's backfiring on me."

Bruce reached under Don's coat and rubbed circles on his back. "Don't make yourself crazy. You're doing all you can."

❖

Mid-December, after more than two weeks with the murder book, Don and Bruce separately compiled a list of impressions. They sprawled in Bruce's living room to compare notes. A winter storm had been blowing but was now ebbing away. Bruce cranked up the heater and drew the blinds, and they conferred naked among the scattered papers. They pecked at their respective laptops, rolled about, stood, walked, and shifted positions as they talked.

Don said, "For me, the most significant detail is that the killer took six photos of Jeffrey but only three of Danny. There has to be a reason for that."

"Like what?"

"I'm thinking that maybe the killer knew Jeffrey, and he wanted a more thorough record of the scene. The Talents lived just up the street and around the corner, and that means the psycho was from my immediate neighborhood, probably somebody I knew or at least saw regularly. It's really sinking in."

Bruce rubbed his hand from his chest to his pubic hair. "For me, the biggest detail is that they found those partial fingerprints on the contact paper near Jeffrey's body, but there's never another mention of them. Here they had a major clue, and they just threw it away. Did they take your dad's fingerprints? Or Mr. Hartner's?"

"There was no reason to take my dad's because his alibi checked out before they found the fingerprints."

"Then what about Elmer Hartner? I've looked through that file a million times and didn't see any mention of anyone taking his fingerprints to compare. There's something fishy about that, like they knew he was innocent or something so they didn't even bother."

"Or his fingerprints didn't match, so they didn't keep a record of the report. Or it got lost. Or they couldn't get a solid match with only partials."

"Write it up," Bruce said. "You need to hammer Tedesco hard on those fingerprints."

After typing, Don leaned back and scratched an itch high on his inner thigh. "It's driving me crazy that I can't march into Tedesco's house right now and start peppering the asshole with questions."

Bruce stood just as the sun broke through the depleted storm and beamed through the split in the drapes. It radiated against his skin, creating the luminous perfection of Grecian marble, and he distractedly tugged his balls and chuckled. "I'd like to see you walk in there naked." His easy smile in the crackling light transfixed Don until Bruce asked, "Did you hear anything more about when the medal will be ready?"

"They say we might have the medal back by next week. I've been thinking about ordering a fake one and having it framed so I can talk to him right away. They're easy to buy online."

"He'll see the difference. There's probably something distinctive about the real medals."

"But he won't see it up close if it's in a shadow box and I keep it from him until he's answered all my questions."

"Do you feel ready to confront him?"

Don sighed and looked at the papers on the floor. "No. If I'm honest, I don't feel prepared at all. I feel like I probably know more about the evidence than he does. He's probably forgotten most of it, but it's fresh in my mind, and I can't make heads or tails of it."

"Stop stressing. We're making headway."

"Not fast enough."

Bruce pushed himself to his feet and hugged him. It felt warm and bolstering, just as he imagined a naked embrace would sometimes feel after stepping through a portal in time.

❖

The week before Christmas, Linnette sat with Don and his mom at the kitchen table. "Well, he's gotten used to the highest fentanyl dose, and I can tell he's comfortable." In his bed, Dad was consumed by the exhaustive documentary series *The World at War*. "He probably won't need any more extra morphine for a week or so, but he'll start asking for it again, so just be prepared."

With grieving eyes, Mom asked, "How much longer do you think he has?"

"I never like to predict these things, but I can say with some certainty we're down to a matter of weeks. Maybe a month, but I doubt it."

Mom swallowed and nodded.

Linnette patted her hand. "I'll see you tomorrow." She looked up. "Don, would you mind walking to my car with me? I have a question for you."

As Don left, he glanced at his mother at the end of the kitchen table. She looked a million miles away, a figure of aching loneliness, her instinct to protect crushed by brutal reality, helpless. He knew she'd felt it before. So had Don, and the sensation was one of injustice.

It had snowed. The first dusk of a longer winter night dimmed the clouds, even though it was just four o'clock. A heavy snowstorm would hit in a few hours.

Linnette pulled her heavy, stylish patchwork coat tighter. "I know you'll tell me as soon as you can, but I'm wondering if you know anything more about, you know, my brother and the others?"

"I'm doing my best, but I have to tell you that I'm not optimistic." Her face sagged, and he went on, "I haven't given up, and I have a big thing coming up soon, but I'm running out of time."

"I'm worried that your dad will die and you'll stop looking. Will you keep trying to find him?"

He couldn't answer either way. "I haven't made any plans past that point. But I promise to share everything with you at the right time."

"Are you any more certain about his identity than you were the last time we talked about it?"

He couldn't lie. He shook his head.

She pursed her lips. "Please keep trying," she said softly. As she walked to her car, he looked up at the bare branches. Underneath all the leaves, trees are just sticks. They're pointy and crooked and sharp, like broken bones in the sky.

Inside, Mom sat in the same spot. She gave him an expectant look and he asked, "What is it, Mom?"

"Donnie, I know you'd tell me anything if you could, but do you have any hope of finding that man in the next few weeks?" Her eyes glistened.

He closed his eyes and dropped his head.

"I'm sorry," she said, crying. "I don't mean to put you on the spot."

"Don't apologize, Mom," he said, kneeling and taking her hand. Her face crinkled with grief and guilt. "It's okay for you to ask, but I'm just not ready to say anything yet. I promise you that the second I can tell you something, I will."

"I know," she said, her voice thick from a plugged nose. "What about the other possibility that we discussed? Telling your father we have the answer even if we don't."

"If we decide to do that, it won't take long to figure out a story. Let's not worry about that right now."

She grabbed a paper napkin from the holder and pressed it to her eyes.

Don let her cry and plopped on the sofa in the family room. He texted Bruce: *Want to take a short drive? I have a really cool place to show you.*

A minute later, Bruce texted back: *Big snow coming.*

Best time to see it.

Cool. Come over.

Don was at Bruce's house in fifteen minutes. The snow fell heavier. After they kissed, Bruce asked, "Where are we going?"

"A really cool spot. I haven't been there in years. It's so beautiful in the snow you can't even believe it. It's been coming down for hours now, so there's plenty already."

The traffic was sparse. Midwesterners need no encouragement to stay indoors when a snowstorm looms. Get some hot chocolate or apple cider, curl up inside a warm house, and you can handle Antarctica like a champ.

Don drove carefully, keeping his wheels on the black asphalt strips, the melted tracks of earlier cars. A bright snowy line ran down the center. In a few hours, the snow would outlast the tires, and cars would creep along in slick, white grooves.

In only a few minutes, Don turned left onto a road that sloped into the Cuyahoga River Valley, a lush parkland encircling the entire region. At the bottom, Don turned and the land rose on a gentle slope. The street curved here and there. At one point, the car slid and wiggled out a fishtail. "Oh, boy," Don said. "It's going to be even more fun driving back."

Bruce grinned.

After another mile or so, Don slowed. The spot came into view on his left. "Here it is." Except for a maintenance truck that looked as if someone had parked and forgotten it months ago, the lot was empty.

"Come on," Don said. "You have to be in the middle of the field to get the full effect."

They got out and walked through a leafless wood, emerging into a vast field of white. The snow covered the ground evenly, perfectly balanced, a clean and inviting carpet.

"Whoa," Bruce said, looking at the pines on the far end.

"The view is even better from the middle."

The snow swirled, noticeably heavier, and they walked into a world of white. The light from a nighttime snowstorm is a like a panoramic trick of the eye. The sun has set, yet the whiteness everywhere reflects onto other white surfaces, and a glow bright enough to light the underside of clouds fills the land.

The flakes accumulated on Bruce's head and small drifts formed on his shoulders. "Hey." Don laughed, ruffling Bruce's hair clean of snow. New flakes immediately landed and stuck. "You're the abominable snowman."

Bruce looked at Don and laughed, slapping his thighs. "You look like a kid whose backyard igloo just collapsed." He cleaned Don's head, but he misjudged the direction and the snow tumbled down Don's face, inside his coat, and slipped past his shirt collar. A bracing cold stung his neck and chest, and Don gasped and stepped back, his head low. He cried with outrage undermined by laughter and a wide smile.

"Oh, that's it!" Don said, scooping up a pile of snow.

"No!" Bruce bent to gather his own arsenal.

One step ahead, Don lifted the collar of Bruce's coat and shoved the snow down his neck.

Bruce rose, roaring. The falling snow padded the air and kept the sound close, audible only to the men who laughed alone in their world of white.

Bruce lunged, but Don stepped back. He slipped and went down on his ass, and Bruce, thrown off balance by the sudden change in aim, fell on top of him.

Don threw his arms across Bruce's back. They laughed and rocked. Bruce braced himself against the ground and lifted, until their laughter tapered, and he lowered his head to give him a quick kiss, lifting with a smile. His face gleamed in the snow's light, glazed by crystal.

Don pushed up to return the kiss, then scooted away and stood, helping Bruce to his feet. "Look," he said.

On three sides of the field, the snow trimmed the empty branches, arranged with elegant precision on every crook, spike, and dip. On the fourth, it frosted a forest of towering pines with the same delicate care, every flake placed to highlight the deep green needles.

They held each other at their waists. The thickening snow cloaked them from shoulder to shoulder.

"It's amazing," Bruce said, hushed. "Thanks for showing this to me."

"I'm glad I can share it with you."

Bruce looked up. "It's really coming down. If we don't leave soon, you might get stuck in the parking lot."

"Yeah, I guess so." He didn't move.

"What's up?" Bruce said, slipping his arm free. "Did something happen?"

He nodded and told Bruce what Linnette said about Dad having only a matter of weeks.

"I'm sorry."

"But that's not all." Don told him about Mom and Linnette asking about the investigation. "Tim hasn't asked me directly, but I can see he's thinking about it, especially as the end gets closer. It's only a matter of time before he does."

"So you're feeling pressure from all these people who are counting on you to succeed?"

"Story of my life."

Bruce put his hands on his hips, breathing deeply. "Don, I think it's time for you to face something you don't want to face. I've been holding off on saying anything, but you don't have the luxury of denial any longer."

"I'm in denial?"

"You know what I mean. Deep down."

"About the killer?"

Bruce nodded.

"What about him?"

"Come on, Don. Aren't you just a little suspicious?"

"About what?"

"Don, it was obvious to me from the start that you were ignoring the one person who fits every detail."

"What are you talking about?"

Bruce gestured on each point. "A teenager. From the neighborhood. Someone everyone knew. Someone *you* knew. Someone who disappeared from the scene. Someone with secrets." He dropped his voice. "Someone who used a hypodermic needle."

"Rich?"

"Do you think Tim really lost that Polaroid camera? Isn't it possible somebody stole it, like somebody he shared a bedroom with? You tell me why it wasn't him."

"What are you saying?"

"I'm saying this search has taken you to a place you don't want to go, but you need to face it anyway." He offered his hand, palm up, but Don looked at it with loathing. Bruce noticed and seemed hurt, but said, "I'll be there to help you face it, Don, but I can't force you."

"Holy shit," Don said, shaking his head. "Who the fuck are you to accuse my brother?"

Bruce raised his voice. "You accused your brother. But one who's still alive, who has the everyday flaws that all of us have, who has a rocky marriage and who's put on too much weight. He's not the perfect brother, is he? He's not the one who died more than forty years ago, and all that time you've carried the guilt of not speaking up soon enough to prevent his overdose. And you've punished yourself for that by turning him into a saint."

Don took another step back.

"You need to look in those boxes, Don. The ones in the attic. The ones you're too afraid to open, so you've convinced yourself that they're these holy relics you can't disturb."

"What do you expect me to find in those boxes?"

"You still can't admit it, even when I've explained it?"

"Tell me," Don growled. "Tell me what I'm going to find in those boxes."

The flakes plunged between them like a rain of tiny softballs.

"Oh, let's see, maybe a brown and orange striped T-shirt. A pair of Keds. *Planet of the Apes* pajamas. An old Cleveland Browns cap. I don't think you'll find any Polaroid instant photos, though. I'm sure he realized the danger and destroyed them."

His voice nearly a whisper, Don said, "My mom packed those boxes."

"Yeah, you told me. I'm not sure she was in the right frame of mind to comprehend what she was seeing."

Furious, Don stalked across the frozen field. Bruce kept pace for a while. "Go, Don, but call me when you're ready to face the truth. I'll be here. And don't worry about me. It won't take more than twenty minutes to walk home, even in this weather, so I'll be fine. I survived a blizzard in British Columbia, remember?"

Don didn't care if he survived this one.

❖

On the night before Christmas Eve, while they drank mulled wine at the kitchen table, Mom asked, "Where is Bruce? I've gotten so used to having him around."

"We're having a little disagreement," Don said.

"Oh. I hope it's nothing serious."

"I don't know, Mom. I don't think I'm ever going to find someone. Not the way you and Dad found each other."

"You love him."

"Maybe. I used to."

"I'm sorry, Donnie." Her eyes melted with sympathy. "Just be sure it's important. Little things, they're nothing. The key is to have the wisdom to know the difference." She paused. "You've always been so intelligent, so I hate to question your judgment, but do you have a clear perspective on the little things?"

Don rubbed his face, his elbows on the table. "Mom, I don't have any perspective on relationships. I've never had a real one. But this isn't a little thing."

"Was it something he said, or something he did?"

"Both, in a way. He said something, but it revealed that he thought something really awful. Thinking is something you do, right? So he did something, too."

Hesitation slowed her voice. "I just want you to consider something, Donnie. Bruce met you at a very difficult time in your life. Your father is dying, and we're all going through so much. All of us are thinking about your dad's life, the injustice, those terrible times. Rich."

Don closed his eyes.

"I'm sure you shared some of it with Bruce, maybe all of it. We've had years to find the coping skills, but he's only had about two months. It would be a lot for anyone to absorb."

He took a sip of wine, strong with cloves and spices. "I already thought about that. But he crossed a line."

"Well, again, I don't want to question your judgment, but can I give you a little bit of advice?"

"Sure. I'd like to hear what you think."

"Then remember you have a tendency to think about things too much. You always have, so it might seem natural to you, but the rest of the world doesn't work that way. People say things for different reasons. Sometimes they have bad intentions, but I'm certain Bruce doesn't have an ulterior motive. You say he crossed a line. But, Donnie, is it possible you set the line too far away because you're afraid of anyone getting too close?"

He sat back. Did she just nail his whole life?

"Think about it. Bruce is a special man, and that's exactly what you deserve." She took a sip. "This is really delicious, Donnie. Thank you for making it. What a treat."

Don cleaned the kitchen and checked on his dad, who was staring at the wall, the tablet and earphones beside him.

"Did you watch every movie and documentary ever made already?"

Dad chuckled. "I started on the BBC documentaries today. That should get me through half the century. But they did some really great stuff."

"Then why are you staring off into space?"

Dad shrugged. "I'm just thinking about stuff."

"Like what?"

"My life. The things I did wrong. The things that went wrong, but weren't my fault." He paused, moving his lips in and out. "It's funny, Donnie, but it took me all these years to realize something about myself."

"What's that?"

"Well, I've hinted at this over the years but I never came right out and said it, but my dad was an SOB when he drank." His eyes, pale and dim, looked back on his boyhood. "He'd get that look on his face, and you wanted to run all the way to China. He'd beat my mother when he got like that, did I ever tell you that?"

"No."

"I don't know if you can imagine what it's like for a kid, a boy, to watch your mom get hurt like that. You were supposed to protect her. You wanted to take that pain on yourself so she wouldn't feel it. And the guy doing it was the only guy in the world you couldn't raise a hand to." He shook his head. "All of my anger came from that, for my whole life." Dad looked over at Don, his eyes swimming. "Parents can really mess you up. I hope I didn't do that to you."

"Dad, no, not in the least."

"Where does your anger come from, Don? You were so angry when you were a teenager. You hated St. Peter's. You were the valedictorian, but you only went to graduation. They had all kinds of dinners and ceremonies for the best graduates in the school, but you didn't go to any of them."

Billy leaping. "Leave this one to me." "There's only one thing to do to faggots."

"Being gay made me angry. Not specifically that, but the way people reacted to it. The things they said and did."

"Did I ever say anything?"

"Funny enough, Dad, I don't ever remember you saying anything. Everyone else did. Even Mom. But not you."

"I tried to watch myself. I knew you were gay when you were

little, Donnie. I never said anything to you, not directly, but I should have."

"Jesus."

"There was a kid in my high school. He had all the mannerisms, you know, the voice and everything. He was a nice guy, but we were so stupid and we teased him all the time. It never crossed my mind he took us seriously, but he shot himself." He shook his head. "Life can be brutal." Dad cleared his throat. "I need to ask you something. That time you said you fell down the stairs? Was that what it was? Being gay?"

Don took a deep breath. "Yes."

"Who was it?"

"Billy Tedesco."

Dad sat up a bit, his eyes wide. "No kidding? Well, I can't say I'm surprised. He was messed up, especially as he got older. But I was happy about that because he made his dad's life hell."

They chuckled.

"Do you want to talk about it?" Dad asked.

"Not really."

He nodded, picking up the tablet and earphones. "Enough of the happy memories. Time for some stick-up-the-ass British snobbery. They do it better than anyone."

Don went to the family room but didn't turn on the lights. His phone buzzed, and he sat up when he recognized the number as belonging to the frame shop. "Did the medal come in today?"

"It did. Just finished framing it. It's ready for pickup."

"I can come right now. I'll be there in thirty minutes."

"Tomorrow. My wife does this big dinner the night before Christmas Eve, so I'm closing up."

"Come on. You've kept me waiting way longer than I ever expected."

"You'll have it in time for Christmas, so just relax. I know you've been waiting, but I'm not going to be late for my wife's dinner on anyone's account. I'll open early if you want, say nine thirty?"

"Okay."

He leaned back on the sofa, his phone clutched at his stomach. He thought about the questions he'd typed up for Chief Tedesco, but he knew them all. He also knew they wouldn't solve anything. Maybe the chief could satisfy Don's curiosity about a few things, but that wouldn't provide the justice that everyone needed.

The door to the attic stairs was just off the kitchen. Don couldn't see it from the sofa.

Don ran the list in his mind: a teenager; from the neighborhood; everyone knew him; a hypodermic needle; the clothes were missing; sealed boxes in the attic untouched since 1976.

If Rich was the killer, he'd been shooting dope far longer than Don ever suspected, but maybe that's what set off the murders in the first place. Maybe Rich found dark, unspeakable thoughts in his head and chained them tightly, but heroin set them free.

"Fuck their son!" Rich had screamed, shocking everyone the night the parents of Jeffrey Talent came to the door. Don always assumed Rich had directed his rage at the young couple because they symbolized the injustice suffered by the Eskers, but was there a different reason all this time?

Don looked at his phone, but the screen was blank. No call or text from Bruce in a week.

Rich's addiction grew until it consumed him, all the time, every day. Did Rich escalate his drug use to silence those thoughts? Grisly fantasies consumed the teenage Jeffrey Dahmer, the cannibal who grew up down by Akron, who used alcohol to numb them away.

Don sat alone for a long time, thinking.

The next morning, Don pulled into Bruce's driveway. A light shower overnight had washed away the remaining snow. He walked to the door slowly, his shoes squeaking on the wet cement. He pushed the doorbell.

A minute later, Bruce opened the door, wearing underwear. Don knew he'd just slipped it on because Bruce stayed naked whenever possible, just like the men on the other side of the time portal.

Bruce looked uncertain, but he opened the storm door and stood back as Don entered.

After a moment, Don asked, "Will you look in the boxes for me?"

Bruce's eyes and mouth opened slightly with appreciation for the difficulty of the request. "Sure."

"I don't know what I'm going to do if you find the clothes, but I'm not telling my family. I'm definitely not going to say anything to my dad in his final days. I know I'm asking a lot, but can you promise you won't say anything to anybody else if you find them?"

"Yeah, absolutely."

"I might have a moral obligation to be honest with Linnette, but it would kill my mom and destroy my brothers. They've been through enough for one life." He stopped, breathed. "You won't say anything to Linnette until I figure out how to handle it?"

"I'll go along with whatever you decide. I promise. When do you want me to do this?"

"As soon as you can. My mom has a Christmas thing at the community center this morning. I know it's last minute, but if you're free you can come with me. If you can't get away right now, we can arrange another time."

"Are you sure you're ready to find out?"

Don shrugged. "I'm never going to be ready for you to find those clothes in Rich's stuff, so it doesn't matter."

"Okay. I have a holiday lunch thing in a couple of hours, but if I miss it, it's no big deal."

"It won't take that long. There are only four boxes. Shouldn't take more than a few minutes."

"I meant that I'm going to have to, you know, hold your hand, be there for you, give you a shoulder to lean on…if I find what I think I'm going to find."

"Thanks."

Bruce hadn't showered, and Don caught the scent that filled him with desire. Sleep smashed and spiked his hair.

"I'm sorry I left you in the snow last week."

"It's okay. It was a tough thing to hear. Hell, it was a tough thing to say."

"The medal finally came in. I'm on my way to the frame shop. I still want to clear up a few things with Tedesco, so I'll wrap that up this morning."

"Do you want me to come with you to his house?"

"No. He doesn't know anything. My mom is waiting for me to come home so she can leave. My dad can't be alone. If we're going to do this now, we should get going."

"Okay. I have to take a shower and get dressed, but it won't take more than a few minutes."

They didn't move.

"You just have to understand how much I loved him," Don said. "I didn't even know how much until after he was gone. Rich and I understood each other better than anyone else in the family. We would have been really close friends our whole lives. I don't think a day has gone by in forty years when I didn't wish I could see or talk to him. If you find those clothes, it's going to be like his death all over again."

Bruce kissed his cheek before embracing him. Don breathed in his scent, savoring the happiness and comfort it gave him at times, the rocketing lust at others. How could one man be so many things?

Bruce was ready in minutes. They spoke little as they drove to the frame shop and went inside to pick up the medal. Don paid the hefty price with his credit card.

When they pulled into his parents' driveway, Bruce squeezed Don's leg. He left the medal in the car so his mom wouldn't see it and ask questions.

Mom looked pleased and surprised when Bruce followed Don inside. Her smile broke Don's heart. He couldn't imagine her pain if she knew why Bruce was here this morning.

"Will you be here when I get back, Bruce? I'll only be a few hours."

"I'm not sure."

"I'd like to spend a little time with you, so if you can manage it, please stay."

She left, and Don opened the door to the attic stairs.

"You'll see the boxes in the corner."

"Will I be able to tell them apart from the others?"

"You'll have no trouble." Don grimaced and looked down. "I'm tempted to ask you not to tell me in words. Maybe just give me some sort of visual clue."

Bruce gave him a hug. "We'll handle it together. I promise."

"I'll take the medal across the street while you're up there. I just have a few questions for the chief."

"Okay," Bruce said as he climbed the stairs. When Bruce reached the trapdoor, Don left, retrieved the medal from his car, and started across the street. He paused and looked back at the roof. Bruce was probably already searching through Rich's boxes. Maybe he'd already discovered the clothes. It hit Don this might turn out to be the worst day of his life.

Billy answered the door, his head wound still painful to see. He wore a T-shirt and shorts and looked at the bag, curious.

"It's for your dad," he said, stepping inside.

In the kitchen, a TV went silent and the wheelchair whirred into view. Chief Tedesco looked at the bag and smiled.

"Let me see it," he said, raising his hands.

"I told you you're not getting it until you answer a few questions."

His head hanging, Billy disappeared down the hall.

The chief nodded. "Go ahead. Ask anything you like. I don't know what I can remember."

Don asked about the fingerprints.

"How did you find out about that?"

"Just answer."

"They were partials," the chief grudgingly replied. "We never could get a clean image, and they were badly smudged."

"Did you take the fingerprints of Elmer Hartner?"

"No. There was no point. A few little fingerprint ridges wouldn't prove anything."

"So you never compared them with anyone?"

"How many times are you gonna make me say it? The fingerprints were useless."

"Did you ever develop a theory about why he took six photos of Jeffrey, but only three of Danny?"

"Where did you learn that?" he barked.

"Just answer the question."

He scowled. "We developed a lot of theories about that. Without hearing the story from his own lips, I can't tell you what the killer was thinking. There was some drug paraphernalia near the second body."

"The needle."

The chief looked ready to explode but gritted his teeth and said, "The killer was a junkie, okay? Not everyone agreed with me, but it was as plain as day as soon as we found the needle. He took more photos of the second body because he shot up right then and there. Maybe he was celebrating. Maybe he was trying to turn off the voices in his head, I don't know. But the drugs made him feel good, so he spent more time with the body and took more photos."

Don took a deep breath and looked away. Bruce was probably finished looking through the boxes.

In the Tedesco living room, all that remained of the SEAL display was the photo that Don had stepped on that night about a month ago. Frameless, it hung at an odd angle above a waiting nail.

"Do you have any more questions?" the chief asked.

Don paused before shaking his head. He let it sink in that he was now fully defeated. All of that effort, and the answer was probably above his head in the attic all the time, patiently waiting to be discovered.

He handed the bag to the chief. "Here. The receipt's in the bag. The total came to twelve hundred and fifty dollars. With the extra hundred, I need a check for thirteen-fifty."

"What?"

His reaction was worth the wait. "You said to spare no expense."

"I think I spent a hundred bucks the last time, and I thought I was getting shafted then." He removed the frame and his face went soft. "Oh, they did a hell of a job, though. It's a beauty. It's exactly what I wanted." He nodded, gazing with worship at the visible sign of his life's triumph. He set it in his lap, reversed the wheelchair, and grabbed a checkbook from the dining room table.

As he rolled forward, he asked, "Can you do me a favor while I write the check?"

"No."

"Come on. I just need you to hang it on the wall under my graduation photo. I don't trust Billy to get anything right, and I can't reach it from my wheelchair. I had Roxanne get everything ready. It will only take a second."

Don didn't move.

"Jesus Christ," the chief muttered. "Look, Don, I'm not stupid. I know you hate my guts and it ate you up to do this, but it's almost over, okay? Do this one last thing, and you'll never have to see my ugly mug again. Deal?"

Don sighed, wondering if Bruce was already waiting to deliver the worst news of his life. Almost without thinking, he took the shadowbox. The chief said, "They pinned the gold on me the day that picture was taken, and it's been with me ever since."

Don balanced the shadowbox wire on the nail. He glanced at the unframed photo and smiled. Roxanne could have used a tack to hang it, but she drove a big nail through the top, two inches into the picture itself, in the middle of a sign that read, "Naval Special Warfare Center." The photo was askew. He could almost hear Roxanne thinking, "Fuck you, Chief."

The men in the photo grinned joyfully. Even though Tedesco was among them, Don understood why they were so proud. After the grueling training that defeats so many and even kills some, they'd joined the ranks of the most revered warriors in the land, and a lifetime of action, acclaim and glory awaited. They looked dashing in their crisp white uniforms and peaked military caps, white at the crown with brims of gleaming black. The men looked identical save for height and skin tones, and their varying ribbons. Their new SEAL insignias topped all others, high on their chests, the award they would cherish until they ended housebound in a wheelchair.

A small detail caught Don's eye. He blinked, curious.

He glanced down at the newly framed gold medal, before doing a methodical examination of the graduates, one by one, man by man, chest by chest. Medal by medal.

Silver medals.

"Holy shit," Don cried, taking a step back.

Just moments ago: *They pinned the gold on me the day that picture was taken, and it's been with me ever since.*

"What's wrong?" the chief asked. Don turned, and the chief grew wary at his expression, raising his hands from the checkbook. Don looked back at the wall. Now that he saw it, it was obvious. He faced the chief.

"You were never a Navy SEAL."

His mind flashed to the Bicentennial celebration where the chief helped preside as a military hero. While the mayor had showered him with tributes, the chief made a show of bashfully turning his head, giving little dismissive waves. Don remembered thinking, *If you don't want to hear these things, why did you agree to come?*

Don felt an urge to laugh.

The chief's mistake was classic bonehead. Buy a photograph where uniforms and caps hide unique features, buy a medal, and presto! Instant valor the easy way, except that officer gold and enlisted man silver are not the same. The chief never bothered to make sure the details matched, probably never thought about it, the insignias being so small in the photo. Most frauds are incompetents, and all the evidence proved the chief was incompetent.

Nobody noticed the discrepancy over the years, but why would they, dazzled by the gold of such a distinguished medal? The assumptions unconsciously deflected doubt. Nobody would lie about such a thing. The city carefully corroborated his story. Fraud would be uncovered by someone.

"Oh, my God. Your whole life. Your whole career. It was all a lie."

Don saw Billy's shadow in the hallway as the chief scanned the wall, desperate to know what had exposed him. "What did you see?" he asked, his voice trembling as his bravado shattered.

Don shook his head, refusing to give him a chance to sputter lies about mixed-up photos, different medals, gee thanks for pointing that out, anything to worm his way free.

Billy came into the room behind his father.

"Your lies are right on your wall for anyone to see," Don said.

The chief stuttered and grasped for a reply. "How…what's the…I mean…" His face twitched, as if trying on various expressions and throwing them aside just as quickly, frantic to find one that would help him escape. He retreated to his old standby.

"What are you talking about?" he raged. Blood filled his face. "How dare you question my accomplishments, you homo." He went on with more words all meant to do the same thing, words that had stopped working on Don one afternoon in a sleepy lounge in the Science Center at Harvard.

Billy bit his fist, ignoring his father to fix on Don.

The chief jerked about, scarlet-faced, spit flying, words shooting from his mouth scattershot, almost unintelligible, like a screaming baby. That's all he was this whole time. A ridiculous man-baby.

Don laughed.

Stunned, the chief stopped. He panted, eyes wide.

"I haven't seen anyone look as frightened as you do right now since my brother needed a heroin fix."

The chief seemed ready for another round of rage, but instead he dropped his head.

"I'm sorry, Don," Billy said, reaching behind to remove something he'd tucked into the waist of his shorts. "I'm sorry for everything."

Don inhaled at the first sight of deep brown fabric in Billy's hand. As Billy brought the object around, Don realized it was a small baseball cap that Billy put on. The child's cap balanced on his crown, the strange little elf cavorting with a manic smile.

Suddenly, Linnette's voice: *I always knew that if I found someone whose whole life was based on a lie, that he'd be the one who did it.*

Don felt a pump of awareness for the enormity of the insight and the sight of the cap perched on Billy's head. He was certain the chief wasn't a sexual psychopath. The murders were too few, too contained, but a man who defrauded an entire community was a sociopath and capable of murder. The chief was the killer. *But why?*

The chief's face was still down, and he didn't know that his son was wearing Jeffrey Talent's cap.

Filling with icy hatred for the pathetic man in the wheelchair, and a searing sense of horror at the ill-placed cap atop Billy, he asked, "Why did you kill those boys?"

The chief reared up. "I wouldn't kill my own son," he roared, but with clarity and honesty. "Eddie would have made something of his life! He'd have done things to make me and his mother proud! He was the good one! I wouldn't have harmed him for anything!"

Billy rushed forward, grabbing the handles of the wheelchair. The cap flew from his head. His father looked back. "Stop it!" he shouted.

Billy pushed the chair in a wide circle to bring it around while his father uselessly worked the controls. The engine screeched as human force overpowered it. Billy aimed into the hallway.

"Don," Billy said, in an almost friendly voice. "Come on. Let me show you something."

He pushed down the hallway while his father ranted. Don raced to follow. The short hallway opened to a square with three doors. Don remembered that Billy and Eddie's room was to the left, the chief and his wife slept to the right, the bathroom just ahead.

Don hadn't been this deep inside the home since just before Eddie vanished. It looked decrepit. The paint was faded in uneven blotches, and the wheelchair had chewed up the carpet.

Billy pushed the chief to the bathroom. The chief screamed in fury as Billy gave the chair a hard shove, and it sailed inside. Don heard a crash, followed by the chief's rage.

Billy yanked the door closed as the wheelchair engine whined in a desperate attempt to escape, like a wasp in a jar. Billy pulled a padlock from his pocket and held it up. "He hides it, but I know where."

Billy flipped a metal flap, low on the door, over a bar on the wall. The door rattled and banged, but Billy held tight until he slipped the lock in place and snapped it shut.

He turned, smiling. Don looked at the clumsy, sinister lock in disbelief.

"He sometimes locks me up."

The door shook with kicks, pounds and shouts.

Billy said, "Come on," as he went to his room.

Don followed, but only as far as the door. A meaningless jumble cluttered the top of the dresser and the drawers hung open, as if puking things to the floor. Where Don could see the carpet, it was grimy with years of neglect.

Against the far wall, Eddie's bed shone like a shrine under the window. Don recognized the blue polyester bedspread printed with cowboys doing cowboy things, quilted like a gentle sea floor. The bed sat tidy, neatly made, coated by a thick layer of undisturbed dust.

"Watch," Billy said. He leaped on his chaotic bed, and the old mattress squeaked with every move. He shoved aside a modern, airy black comforter streaked with dried fluids, searched about and found his pillow, throwing it to the top. The twisted and torn sheets were so rank that Don smelled them from the door.

Billy rested on his back, placing his hands on his chest, smiling in a pantomime of pleasant sleep.

Suddenly, his face went hard. He opened his eyes, and his mouth twisted with a snarl. Slowly, he turned his head and glared at Eddie's bed. He sat up, swinging his legs to the floor. He reached back for his pillow and clutched it to his chest.

Don drew in a long, deep breath.

He rose from his bed and crept across the room. He knelt on his brother's mattress and swung a leg wide, straddling Eddie's imaginary body, gone for more than forty years. He held the pillow high with both hands. Clouds of disturbed dust billowed about his knees.

With a brief roar, he slammed the pillow down. At the same time, he crashed his legs into his brother's chest. He grunted with rage as he twisted and turned, hammering Eddie with knees to control his struggles, make him obey and accept his fate. The dust roiled and swirled in the light coming through the window, tiny clouds buffeted by winds of rage.

The battering against the bathroom door grew weaker.

Billy squirmed and kicked, burning with hatred and jealousy for the brother their parents preferred, who would make them proud. He jiggled with middle-aged flab, but he reenacted his ten-year-old self's moves in detail, like a brief moment when he held the pillow with one hand directly in the center to grab a flailing, invisible arm and trap it with his leg.

Billy's efforts faded as his brother weakened and finally went still. Dispirited thumps came from the bathroom door.

Don let out a long breath. "Billy," he said.

With the languid movements of a sloth, Billy turned and sat on the edge of Eddie's bed, his face impassive, holding the pillow in his lap. The dust settled into floating layers.

"Where is Eddie?" Don asked softly.

"In the basement."

All this time.

"Did you kill the others?"

Billy shook his head.

"Did your dad?"

He nodded and pointed to the floor on the other side of the dresser. "I hid them so he couldn't throw them away."

Don stepped carefully into the room. Billy had cleared a space in front of his closet where it looked like two little boys had suddenly vanished while they slept, leaving their clothes behind: a brown and orange T-shirt above a pair of faded red shorts, socks and Keds; a set of flimsy beige pajamas with a collection of humanoid ape faces.

Don took a deep breath and closed his eyes, but forced them open. Grief, shock and reflection could wait. "Do you have the photos?"

"In my secret compartment. Remember?"

With a start, Don knelt in front of the dresser and pushed the upper drawers out of his way. He removed the bottom drawer and set it atop a pile of junk, where it slipped into an off-balanced tilt.

The top picture sat face-up in the shallow recession. Don recognized Danny Miller's body.

The ten year-old Billy, Don's best friend, stood beside the dead boy, his arms crossed upward with his hands clenching his shoulders, his face grim, angry, and terrorized. A flashbulb illuminated the chilling nighttime scene. The light brightened the tree trunks and deepened the spaces in between, trapping Billy in this dark, horrific secret, with the recorder at his feet. The camera pointed down from the height of a grown man.

Don gathered the small stack of photos and slid them into his back pocket. He didn't want to see the rest.

Don sat on his knees, thinking. The pieces of the story swirled in his head, and he plucked bits and fitted them together, enough to see a rough outline. It didn't explain everything yet, but the basic story became visible.

Don stood. "Stay right here, Billy, okay?"

Billy nodded.

The exhausted chief could only manage defeated thumps against the wood.

Don raised his voice at the door. "I'm going to keep you locked in there until the police come." All movement stopped. "I have quite a story to tell them, about how you panicked when one of your sons killed the other, because you were afraid the county sheriff's department would look into your background and discover that you were a fraud. That you were never a Navy SEAL and you fooled the whole community. Did the sheriff say they had to investigate Eddie's disappearance because you always have to start with the family? Is that what happened?"

He took the chief's silence as meaningful. "So you killed two other boys and kept their clothes to make it look like a sexual psychopath was at work. All of a sudden, you had the power to tell the sheriff to get lost because it wasn't a family matter any longer. It explains a lot. Like why those boys went off with someone when they knew there was a killer around, because nobody told them to be suspicious of the chief of police. It explains why you ran that investigation like a carnival, making decisions that nobody else could understand."

Don felt his anger escalate with spiraling momentum. He clenched his teeth, gripped his fists and cried out, beating the anger down. He couldn't lose control now.

"You punished the son you scorned by making him part of the murders, so he'd always be at the end of your leash. You took pictures..." He inhaled a shuddering, enraged breath. "You took pictures like a kiddie pornographer, and you left the contact sheets to make it look like the killer wanted souvenirs, with smudged fingerprints to give a single physical clue, but not enough to make a difference. You posed your son next to the bodies so that he'd never say anything. Well, he has now," he shouted the final word full-throttle, "Chief!"

He lifted his phone from his pocket and dialed. "I'd like to report a murder."

Chapter Twenty-four

The next morning, Christmas day, Bruce arrived and pulled Don aside. He looked nervous.

"I wanted to say I've never been so happy to be as wrong about something as I was about Rich. I tried telling you yesterday, but things were a little crazy."

"A little?" Don chuckled. "Thanks for apologizing. I don't blame you. You were right about my guilt, and I started to suspect Rich, too, but it's all over now, so let's move on. Is your family upset that you're not with them today?"

"Yeah, but they're really distracted." He hooked a thumb to the street. "They've been watching the coverage obsessively. They want to know if I know anyone involved." They shared a soft laugh. "I told them I might be able to tell them something interesting someday."

"Thanks for not blowing my cover," Don said. "The police are going to keep my name quiet for as long as they can."

The Esker family had gathered in the living room. Everyone came, even Tim and Sally's son with his wife and three kids, along with Randy's daughter Julie and her semi-official boyfriend. Linnette looked out the window, crying silent tears.

"Look," Don said, raising his voice so that everyone could hear, "We've decided it's just going to be…"

A helicopter flew over, forcing him to wait. As it thumped away, he continued, "It's just going to be Mom and us brothers. We went through it together, and we want to tell him ourselves."

"Let's go," Tim said, wrapping his arm around Mom's shoulders. She cried softly as they shuffled down the hallway. Randy followed.

"Dad?" Don said, knocking lightly and opening the door at the same time.

Dad sat up, holding the tablet. He looked alert, and as they entered, he removed his headphones. "What's all that racket about? I keep hearing sirens and helicopters, even with the headphones."

They gathered around. Dad went serious. "What is it?"

"You tell him, Don," Mom said. "I don't think I can get it out."

Dad's alarm grew. "What happened?"

Don took a deep breath. "Dad, they found out who killed those boys." He told him who, and why.

Dad seemed to absorb the news slowly. As it filled him, he grew visibly numb and dazed. Slowly, his mouth dropped.

"That's what all the racket is about, Dad. There are about a million cops and reporters across the street. They arrested Billy and Chief Tedesco yesterday, but we waited to tell you because we wanted to be together."

Dad drew back and stared into the distance.

"We're all happy you lived to see this day, Dad," Tim said.

"Yeah, we are," Randy added. "Even Renee called me last night…" Everyone looked. "She wanted to say she loves you and thinks you're as much of a victim in this as anyone else."

After a long silence, Dad slowly shook his head. "No. Those boys were the victims. Rich was a victim. Not me. Not us. Not anymore." He sighed. "It's funny. I don't feel happy. I always wondered how I'd feel if this day ever came, and I never expected to be just…content. I know I'm dying, but I feel like…a survivor. I survived."

With watery eyes, he raised both arms and everyone clung to them and huddled close.

"All of you survived, too," Dad said, crying.

❖

Two hours later, a rumor circulated that the police would soon remove Eddie's remains. They got Dad's wheelchair and rolled him to the porch. The day was cool but comfortable. Randy raced to the foot of the stairs, with Tim above holding the handles. Dad looked nervous as the brothers argued.

"Tim, goddamn it, just push the wheels a little off the edge and I'll grab them."

"No," Tim replied. "They're wheels, you bonehead. They're going to start spinning the second they aren't grounded and you'll lose control and knock us all on our asses. Grab it by the support bars."

Don slapped Bruce's shoulder and motioned for him to follow. "Hey, guys, stand back, okay? Bruce and I can handle this."

Tim and Randy stepped aside. Don grabbed the handles and turned the chair about, lowering it down the steps backward. Bruce stooped and held the supports above. Gently, they lowered Dad to the driveway.

"Thank God for you guys," Dad said softly. "Those two were gonna break their necks and kill me in the bargain."

Don pushed, with Bruce and Linnette at his side. Mom rested a hand on Dad's shoulder. The rest of the family followed.

Police cars flashed and white evidence vans idled. Neighbors stood by the hundreds, this time looking away from the Esker home. Up and down the street, massive news vans lined the road between the driveways. The story captured national attention as soon as the details spread online yesterday: a forty-year-old cold case, a chief of police, his son one of the victims, a former Navy SEAL. They didn't have the details right, but it was sensational enough to warrant Christmas Day coverage.

As they reached the apron, an officer stepped from the Tedesco door and shouted, "May we have some silence out of respect for the victim?"

A hushed anticipation fell, but nothing happened for a minute.

Mom whispered to Don, "I didn't know Patty Tedesco well at all, but I thought she was a nice lady. Do you think she had any idea of what went on in her home?"

"I don't see how she couldn't have known. Maybe she didn't know about the other boys, but she knew Billy killed Eddie and her husband buried him in the basement."

Mom pursed her lips. "I can't imagine a mother not saying anything."

The Tedesco door opened, and news photographers clicked at a manic pace. Two police officers wearing white gloves emerged, carrying a small box shrouded with white fabric. Bulbs flashed a relentless, unnatural, pulsating light.

The small box could only hold bones. Linnette wept, and Bruce put his arm about her shoulder.

Don looked about at the people rooted by the scene. Down the street a bit, he spotted Agnes with her purple-tipped hair. The greasy guy from the bar held her protectively from behind while she covered her mouth with both hands, her eyes glistening with tears. She broke down in sobs, and the man led her away. He wondered if he should catch up to her, but he wouldn't know what to say.

Don remembered Billy breaking the refrigerator handle, rescuing Eddie. One week later, Billy killed him.

Mesmerized, the crowd watched as the officers solemnly walked to the street and placed the bones in the back of a white van. As it drove away, the crowd seemed to relax as one.

A gorgeous television reporter approached, carrying a microphone, followed by a tall woman balancing a camera on her shoulder. Don recognized the reporter. She was famous, a celebrity journalist, although the term always made Don shake his head.

"Did any of you know Chief Tedesco?" she asked.

"No," Dad said firmly. "We never knew the man. We never knew him at all."

The reporter frowned and moved along.

❖

They crowded into Dad's room on New Year's Eve. Glittering hats, horns, and noisemakers were piled on the dresser.

Don and Bruce sat next to each other, holding hands. Tim and Sally did the same, a nice thing to see. Randy leaned on the doorframe, holding a flute of bubbly. Mom sat next to Dad's bed.

Randy checked his phone. "It's getting close to midnight," he said.

Dad groaned. He struggled to breathe. His head hadn't moved for half an hour. His mouth hung open, so wide his cheeks sank inside. His eyelids were half-closed.

A sweet ripeness scented the air. Fruit baskets and flowers filled the kitchen, overflowing into the living room, a steady stream of deliveries since the people of North Homestead learned the truth. Almost none arrived signed.

The deliveries cheered Dad. Mom seemed to like them, too. Don and his brothers didn't tell their parents of their scorn for these tokens of regret and apology, although the number of people who remembered shocked them.

"Here we go," Randy said. "Ready? Ten, nine…"

The room took up the countdown in hushed voices and ended with soft cries of "Happy New Year, Dad." Tim and Sally smacked out a quick, obligatory kiss. Don and Bruce gave theirs more enthusiasm but kept it short.

Mom kissed Dad. "Happy New Year, Rob," she said, stroking his forehead.

Randy handed out champagne flutes, but nobody took more than an occasional sip.

Another twenty minutes passed.

Dad stared at the ceiling. "I'm going to see Rich," he said weakly, and Tim said, "Tell him I said hi." Crying, Mom added, "Tell him I love him so much, and I miss him with all my heart."

About half an hour into the New Year, Dad took a deep breath. As his chest deflated, he groaned with a timbre and tone that captured the essence of his voice, a sound only he could make, and Robert Esker died, a survivor, an innocent man.

❖

Tim and Sally drove off, winding slowly through the lanes of Memorial Park Cemetery, followed by their son and his family.

Randy helped Mom into his car, Julie and her boyfriend in the backseat. Even Renee came to the funeral and graveside service, but she drove herself and had already left.

Don turned. Bruce stood uphill, incredibly handsome in a suit. Don held out his hand as he approached, and Bruce took it with a smile. They walked up the slope, stopping at Rich's grave. Cemetery workers, busy at the next spot burying Dad, saw their clasped hands. Maybe the workers would talk about it later, maybe not. It didn't matter.

"It was the same way with Rich," Don said. "Mom insisted

someone stay behind to make sure he was buried. Back then, it was Dad who stayed."

"Why does she worry about something like that?"

Don shrugged. "I'm not really sure. Just a thing she has. She wants to make sure that people are safe, even in their graves."

Shovels sliced into the wet clay on the tarp. The clumps fell into the grave with hushed thumps.

"I have to tell you something," Bruce said in a confessional tone. "I paid a little visit to Chief Ladmore yesterday."

"Why did you do that?"

"To chew his head off. I told him that I figured it out. Tedesco didn't give Ladmore a promotion because he owed his uncle in the Navy a favor. Ladmore's uncle told him that Tedesco was never a SEAL. Ladmore was greedy and used the information to blackmail Tedesco for the promotion. If he'd exposed the sicko instead, they might have found Eddie years ago. The clothes and photos. People would have known the truth about your dad way back then."

"I should have put that together. Good job."

"I asked him if Tedesco covered up something for him to keep his mouth shut, too. He didn't answer, but I could see it in his eyes. Tedesco had something on Ladmore. A sex thing or something. They were blackmailing each other." He snorted. "What a pair." He raised a finger. "I told him... '

"Hey, Bruce," Don said, taking and lowering his hand. "My dad's been exonerated. That's all he ever wanted, all any of us ever wanted. I don't care anymore what happens to any of them. I want to start enjoying life without all of that in the background."

Bruce looked pained, breathing hard. "Where, Don? Where are you going to enjoy your life? Back in San Francisco?"

"Wherever you are, okay?"

Bruce looked hopeful, but still guarded. He shot a breath from his nostrils. "Really? You want to give it a try?"

"The thing is," Don said, taking his hands and squeezing, "there's something I need to tell you. About a portal in time."

About the Author

Bud Gundy has won two Emmy Awards as a producer, director, writer, and on-air host for KQED, San Francisco's PBS and NPR affiliate. He's worked as a television and print journalist and is one-half of a popular on-air fundraising duo. He was raised in North Olmsted, Ohio, as the youngest of ten children. He lives with his boyfriend, Chris, in much-needed peace and harmony in San Francisco.

Books Available From Bold Strokes Books

Sinister Justice by Steve Pickens. When a vigilante targets citizens of Jake Finnigan's hometown, Jake and his partner Sam fall under suspicion themselves as they investigate the murders. (978-1-63555-094-8)

Club Arcana: Operation Janus by Jon Wilson. Wizards, demons, Elder Gods: Who knew the universe was so crowded, and that they'd all be out to get Angus McAslan? (978-1-62639-969-3)

The Lurid Sea by Tom Cardamone. Cursed to spend eternity on his knees, Nerites is having the time of his life. (978-1-62639-911-2)

Triad Soul by 'Nathan Burgoine. Luc, Anders, and Curtis—vampire, demon, and wizard—must use their powers of blood, soul, and magic to defeat a murderer determined to turn their city into a battlefield. (978-1-62639-863-4)

Gatecrasher by Stephen Graham King. Aided by a high-tech thief, the Maverick Heart crew race against time to prevent a cadre of savage corporate mercenaries from seizing control of a revolutionary wormhole technology. (978-1-62639-936-5)

Wicked Frat Boy Ways by Todd Gregory. Beta Kappa brothers Brandon Benson and Phil Connor play an increasingly dangerous game of love, seduction, and emotional manipulation. (978-1-62639-671-5)

Death Goes Overboard by David S. Pederson. Heath Barrington and Alan Keyes are two sides of a steamy love triangle as they encounter gangsters, con men, murder, and more aboard an old lake steamer. (978-1-62639-907-5)

A Careful Heart by Ralph Josiah Bardsley. Be careful what you wish for…love changes everything. (978-1-62639-887-0)

Worms of Sin by Lyle Blake Smythers. A haunted mental asylum turned drug treatment facility exposes supernatural detective Finn M'Coul to an outbreak of murderous insanity, a strange parasite, and ghosts that seek sex with the living. (978-1-62639-823-8)

Tartarus by Eric Andrews-Katz. When Echidna, Mother of all Monsters, escapes from Tartarus and into the modern world, only an Olympian has the power to oppose her. (978-1-62639-746-0)

Rank by Richard Compson Sater. Rank means nothing to the heart, but the Air Force isn't as impartial. Every airman learns that rank has its privileges. What about love? (978-1-62639-845-0)

The Grim Reaper's Calling Card by Donald Webb. When Katsuro Tanaka begins investigating the disappearance of a young nurse, he discovers more missing persons, and they all have one thing in common: The Grim Reaper Tarot Card. (978-1-62639-748-4)

Smoldering Desires by C.E. Knipes. Evan McGarrity has found the man of his dreams in Sebastian Tantalos. When an old boyfriend from Sebastian's past enters the picture, Evan must fight for the man he loves. (978-1-62639-714-9)

Tallulah Bankhead Slept Here by Sam Lollar. A coming of age/ coming out story, set in El Paso of 1967, that tells of Aaron's adventures with movie stars, cool cars, and topless bars. (978-1-62639-710-1)

Death Came Calling by Donald Webb. When private investigator Katsuro Tanaka is hired to look into the death of a high-profile lawyer, he becomes embroiled in a case of murder and mayhem. (978-1-60282-979-4)

The City of Seven Gods by Andrew J. Peters. In an ancient city of aerie temples, a young priest and a barbarian mercenary struggle to refashion their lives after their worlds are torn apart by betrayal. (978-1-62639-775-0)

Lysistrata Cove by Dena Hankins. Jack and Eve navigate the maelstrom of their darkest desires and find love by transgressing gender, dominance, submission, and the law on the crystal blue Caribbean Sea. (978-1-62639-821-4)

Garden District Gothic by Greg Herren. Scotty Bradley has to solve a notorious thirty-year-old unsolved murder that has terrible repercussions in the present. (978-1-62639-667-8)

The Man on Top of the World by Vanessa Clark. Jonathan Maxwell falling in love with Izzy Rich, the world's hottest glam rock superstar, is not only unpredictable but complicated when a bold teenage fan-girl changes everything. (978-1-62639-699-9)

The Orchard of Flesh by Christian Baines. With two hotheaded men under his roof including his werewolf lover, a vampire tries to solve an increasingly lethal mystery while keeping Sydney's supernatural factions from the brink of war. (978-1-62639-649-4)

Funny Bone by Daniel W. Kelly. Sometimes sex feels so good you just gotta giggle! (978-1-62639-683-8)

The Thassos Confabulation by Sam Sommer. With the inheritance of a great deal of money, David and Chris also inherit a nondescript brown paper parcel and a strange and perplexing letter that sends David on a quest to understand its meaning. (978-1-62639-665-4)

The Photographer's Truth by Ralph Josiah Bardsley. Silicon Valley tech geek Ian Baines gets more than he bargained for on an unexpected journey of self-discovery through the lustrous nightlife of Paris. (978-1-62639-637-1)

Crimson Souls by William Holden. A scorned shadow demon brings a centuries-old vendetta to a bloody end as he assembles the last of the descendants of Harvard's Secret Court. (978-1-62639-628-9)

The Long Season by Michael Vance Gurley. When Brett Bennett enters the professional hockey world of 1926 Chicago, will he meet his match in either handsome goalie Jean-Paul or in the man who may destroy everything? (978-1-62639-655-5)

Triad Blood by 'Nathan Burgoine. Cheating tradition, Luc, Anders, and Curtis—vampire, demon, and wizard—form a bond to gain their freedom, but will surviving those they cheated be beyond their combined power? (978-1-62639-587-9)

Death Comes Darkly by David S. Pederson. Can dashing detective Heath Barrington solve the murder of an eccentric millionaire and find love with policeman Alan Keyes, who, despite his lust, harbors feelings of guilt and shame? (978-1-62639-625-8)

Slaves of Greenworld by David Holly. On the planet Greenworld, the amnesiac Dove must cope with intrigues, alien monsters, and a growing slave revolt, while reveling in homoerotic sexual intimacy with his own slave Raret. (978-1-62639-623-4)

Men in Love: M/M Romance, edited by Jerry L. Wheeler. Love stories between men, from first blush to wedding bells and beyond. (978-1-62639-7361)

Love on the Jersey Shore by Richard Natale. Two working-class cousins help one another navigate the choppy waters of sexual chemistry and true love. (978-1-62639-550-3)

Final Departure by Steve Pickens. What do you do when an unexpected body interrupts the worst day of your life? (978-1-62639-536-7)

Night Sweats by Tom Cardamone. These stories are as gripping as the hand on your throat. (978-1-62639-572-5)

Soul's Blood by Stephen Graham King. After receiving a summons from a love long past, Keene and his associates, Lexa-Blue and the sentient ship Maverick Heart, are plunged into turmoil on a planet poised for war. (978-1-62639-508-4)

Corpus Calvin by David Swatling. Cloverkist Inn may be haunted, but a ghost materializes from Jason Dekker's past and Calvin's canine instinct kicks in to protect a young boy from mortal danger. (978-1-62639-428-5)

Brothers by Ralph Josiah Bardsley. Blood is thicker than water, but you can drown in either. Jamus Cork and Sean Malloy struggle against tradition to find love in the Irish enclave of South Boston. (978-1-62639-538-1)

Every Unworthy Thing by Jon Wilson. Gang wars, racial tensions, a kidnapped girl, and a lone PI! What could go wrong? (978-1-62639-514-5)